Dear Reader,

FalconClaw – Fraternal is a psychological and paranormal crime drama that will keep you up at night and have you guessing what will happen next.

With the rugged North Philadelphia area as the backdrop, you get to walk in the footsteps of Philadelphia Police Detectives Frank Collazo and Penelope Bristow as they attempt to apprehend someone killing cops. The killer or killers begin to seem familiar to Frank as he struggles with his past demons and current hell.

This story incorporates real-life and fictional situations and people whose stories must be told. While the ending to some real-life characters and situations has been fictionalized for dramatic effect, the book is designed for entertainment purposes and not to change history.

I hope you come to know and love these characters and are thrilled with all the twists and turns this fast-paced drama brings you. My wish is that this story will keep you turning the pages and questioning everything. Enjoy!

Happy Reading,

Acknowledgments:

Thank you for letting me share this work of fiction that ties in some actual historical events and places. The story of FalconClaw – Fraternal is book four in the FalconClaw Detective Series but is also great as a stand-alone.

I want to thank my wife and children: Kristin, Aubrey Carin, Lola Kristine, Maggie Mae, and Carrick Michael, for helping me to breathe life into the characters that you're about to meet. I would also like to thank my beta-readers and editors, Maribeth Pickens, Vern Preston, Karen Cook, Bob Nielsen, and my Editor, Andy Kastelik. These wonderful friends and family members supported my journey; this book wouldn't have been written without them.

To my best friend and business partner, Piyush Bhula, thanks for always being there at every turn. And finally, to Jeremy Ledbetter, for always being there and for his wonderful cover design work.

I would also like to make a special shout-out to my new friend, Bonnie Ross. Bonnie was there from the literal beginning of the Old Man Winter series as she hung out with the woman who inspired the powerful female lead in book one, Penelope Brace. Thanks for showing me around the mean streets of Philly, and thanks for always making women's rights top of mind and fighting the good fight.

Fine Print:

This book is a work of fiction and is drawn completely from my imagination. The actual historical figures and places characterized in this book are intended to be portrayed positively. Any references to past historical events are for entertainment purposes only and are not meant to be taken literally. Any actual organizations or federal entities portrayed in this book serve only to enhance the story and are not meant to defame, devalue, or besmirch those institutions in any way. Actual living people portrayed in this book were contacted and provided their permission. See the back of the book.

FalconClaw Media owns all copyrights. All rights reserved. No part of this book shall be used or reproduced without the express written consent of FalconClaw Media, LLC. or Michael Cook. All Inquiries should be mailed to FalconClaw Media, LLC. 1111 Alderman Drive, Suite 210, Alpharetta, GA. 30005.

www.FalconClawSeries.com

"Walls covered with tear-filled cracks
What stories could they tell?
The pain that lies within this room
Could make sick a man who's well"

Michael Cook is a published poet, author, and accomplished business professional and entrepreneur. Most notably, Michael is the author of the acclaimed Black Earth Saga.

A resident of Suwanee, GA. Michael is a father of four children, a husband, a brother, and a friend.

Michael Cook

A novel by Michael Cook
© 2023

Prologue – Someone Always Dies First

A good friend once told me that every relationship has an expiration date. And he was right. That friend was Frank Collazo.

With the loss of his father, Salvatore, at the age of only fourteen, Frank learned far too young that sometimes death ended relationships with a finality that slowly drained one's soul of any desire or willingness to carry on. He used to say that the notion of 'til death do us part' was a tragedy because someone always dies first. The living half of the relationship must go on surviving. To go on drifting and wandering through life, its maze of uncertainty, and its caldron of loneliness and despair.

Frank would learn at a young age that the survivor who lost a loved one would sometimes wallow in hopelessness and misery, almost wishing for death. Frank knew he wouldn't live forever, and that thought was the only thing that kept him going, marching through his agonizing pain and impossible sadness.

In the end, I imagine Frank looking down at his feet and then back up at Penny and smiling. Reaching for her hand, he looked at his little Bonnie, safe in her mother's arms, and then back to Penny. I bet little Bonnie looked at her father, returned his smile, and ran for him. Yeah, I can see it now. That little girl ran. She ran for her father.

I'm sure on that day, many of Frank's friends were there to meet him. All, ready to comfort him and help him continue his story. I wasn't there, though, and that brings me great sadness. Oh, how I wish I were there.

I wasn't there that day, but I can only hope that my friend got confirmation of what he already knew; he and Penny would be together forever. While confused during troubled times, I'm sure everything made sense to him for the first time since he was fourteen. Any hint of sadness, confusion, or emptiness would've been gone.

You see, my friend Frank Collazo wandered through most of his life, never really knowing how things would end up. Sometimes, he felt he would push through and fill the void left by his father. Other times, he felt that his pain and loss were insurmountable and a mountain far too big to climb. But, oh, he did climb that mountain. He knew he would become whole again when he reached the top.

Time after time, we'd sit and talk about life; his and mine, and he'd tell me that he would sometimes stare out at the picket fence and hope one day it would finally be mended.

I haven't seen him for a while now, and I miss him. Frank Collazo wasn't just my friend, you see; he was like a son to me. I'm not sure where he, Penny, and Bonnie went, but I can't leave until he visits me so that we can catch up and talk about the old times. Hearing his voice echoing in the wind again would bring me great joy and maybe even a laugh.

Don't forget about your friends, Frank. Come back and see us again, would you?

Chapter 1 – Take Me to Church

As the gentrification of poor black neighborhoods in Central, West, and South Philly continued, parishioners of Historic Black Churches fled in droves. For three decades, former parishioners of St. Peter Claver Roman Church, on the corner of 12th & Lombard Street in the heart of South-Central Philadelphia, prayed for a miracle. They had hoped to stave off the demolition of the one-hundred-seventy-six-year-old church, which was officially closed by Philadelphia's Archdiocese in 2014 in a potential revenue-generating move.

Like the church's fabled history, a nine-foot, tarped chain-link fence concealed a blue, iron historical landmark placard sign just outside the boarded-up double doors of the dormant house of worship. The sign read: *St. Peter Claver Catholic Church – Dedicated in 1892 and named for the 16th-century saint who fought the slave trade. This was the first Roman Catholic church for Blacks in the city. It has served as a Black community Cultural Center since the 1920s.*

Serving as the mother church for practicing Black Catholics in South-Central Philadelphia, just a half mile south of City Hall, locals, parishioners, and non-religious historians all lobbied against the church's imminent demise, even appealing to Pope Francis in the Vatican. Perhaps, if those seeking to save the church knew of the evil residing in its subterranean underbelly, they, too, would flee.

Sitting dormant, waiting for its sale or demolition, homeless people and drug addicts sought its shelter from the city's harsh northeast winters and cruel summer heat. Though fenced in, like rats, the depraved, nefarious, and unprincipled sought and gained refuge from a world that saw them as castoffs. No fence would keep out the most desperate and forlorn.

In the early morning hours of May 15, 2021, two of those very miscreants entered into a celebration of flesh in the bowels of the now unholy place. The two consummated their evil bond after two of what would become many kills. Their bloodlust continued and would only end after they or their muse was silenced forever.

The lyrics of Hozier's *Take Me to Church* echoed through the belly of St. Peter Claver's once-hallowed halls from the tiny speakers of a cell phone that sat on a makeshift cardboard table. Dirty blankets, hay, and balled-up newspaper cushioned the union of unholy souls.

The room was dark, musty, and littered with rat feces, candy bar wrappers, used syringes and condoms, and empty beer cans. The single candle, which bore witness to the lewd encounter, was nearly consumed by its flame just as the malevolent two were consumed by their thirst.

The music sounded like a baptism of wretched evil that revealed itself through sweat and debauchery.

Every day was *more bleak*.... for the two.

Their *fresh poison* would be someone shrouded in a blue uniform donning a shiny badge. Deemed as good by society, the men and women who swore to serve and protect would be sentenced to hell by the pair's evil union. One Philadelphia Police Detective, in particular, would serve to crown their affair. Their muse, however, would prove himself hard to kill. After all, is it possible to kill someone who's not really alive?

Listening to the screaming lyrics, the two felt they were born sick, and they lived the words when singing along. It was their song, and it best captured their maleficence.

The church above them would offer no absolution, and they sought none as they groaned in their perverse communion.

Talon Grayson sang loudly as his goddess moaned. The two ravenous lovers reached climax simultaneously as the chorus rang out from the tiny speakers.

When the two finished, they laid on their backs, side by side, covered in sweat and an unquenchable desire to kill. Both stared at the decaying ceiling above them and ignored the curious rats at their feet, aroused by the scent of sweat, mold, and human lechery.

Later, before falling asleep, the two carved ritualistic tally marks onto the other's back, celebrating the start of their demonic mission. The mission would end after taking their own lives, but not before killing their muse.

On the dawn of what would become Frank Collazo's new living hell, the unholy pair looked at each other with disgust....

"I hate you." Talon's disdain for himself and his lover seeped from his gaze.

"I hate you more." Genesis looked at her only reason for living and shared his vile repulsion, spitting in his direction.

Earlier the previous afternoon, Frank cut the grass while Penny and little Bonnie ran errands. Crisscrossing lawn mower lines in the backyard, Frank kept staring at the scarred fence, hoping to see his father. Back to the present, a cold rain got his attention as the North Philly skies opened. Frank groaned, knowing he wouldn't finish the lawn until the next day.

After stowing the lawn mower back into the detached garage, he sprinted for the back door. In his haste, Frank thought he spotted Old Man Winter at the scarred fence talking with his father, Salvatore. The strange scene caught him off guard, and he couldn't process the unexpected appearance of the two chatting in the pouring rain.

Garrison Winter methodically turned toward Frank and slowly nodded. His father then turned to his son and lowered his head in a show of empathy. Still processing the moment, Frank's heart sank, and he immediately knew something was wrong. His mind raced, and he thought of Penny and Bonnie. Looking toward the fence again, the ghosts that had guided him for the previous four years had gone.

Soaking from the rain, Frank dragged grass clippings from his boots through the back door and into the kitchen. Locating his phone on the table, he frantically dialed Penny's cell, but it went to voicemail after five rings. Still unsure if he was imagining things, he looked out the back door, hoping to see Winter again; instead, seeing a deluge.

"Come on! Come on!" Frank groaned aloud in frustration, trying Penny's cell again. Again, getting her voicemail.

Penny was returning from Walmart twenty minutes earlier when the rain began to fall heavily. Driving southeast on Cheltenham Avenue, she gripped the steering wheel tightly at ten and two and looked back to see Bonnie strapped into her car seat in the middle of the Accord's back seat. Bonnie stared out at the rain contently when Penny caught her eye in the rearview mirror, causing Bonnie to smile. Penny momentarily felt relieved until her eyes went over Bonnie's head to see a white Ford van following too closely for conditions.

As Penny looked back to the road in front of her, she saw what appeared to be a large truck approaching from the distance in the westbound lane. With visibility low, she moved from the passing lane to the right lane, preparing to turn south onto Limekiln Road. Looking in the rearview mirror again, she saw the white van barreling down on her, and she braced herself, accelerating to lessen the impact.

Now in front of Enon Baptist Church, the van trailing Penny struck the back of the Accord, causing it to lose control. Penny swerved from right to left, trying to regain control of the car when it crossed the double yellow lines. With no center median to obstruct her path, Penny's heart froze in a panic as the car crossed the double yellow lines and into oncoming traffic. Unable to avoid the Accord, a large white cement truck collided head-on with Penny. In a haze and bleeding from her forehead, she gasped, struggling for the rearview mirror; she positioned it so she could make eye contact with little Bonnie again. To her surprise, Bonnie smiled back at her as if the accident had never happened. Relieved, Penny took a deep breath and closed her eyes.

Without pain, she opened her eyes again and heard nothing. Vague shadows circled the car frantically as the rain intensified. She and Bonnie stared at each other in the mirror. Unable to move, she just stared and smiled at her little girl.

Muffled voices and distant sirens could now be heard as the inevitable darkness came, but Penny didn't panic. She knew help was on the way. She knew Frank was coming for her and Bonnie.

Frank's panic worsened, and he raced out the back door and jumped in his Dodge Charger, hoping to trace the path Penny would be driving home. Activating his blue police flashers, he backed out onto East Locust Avenue and gunned it north to Musgrave.

Cracking thunder and pouring rain muted the sound of spinning tires and the revving engine as the Dodge Charger raced north to Magnolia.

Chapter 2 – Can you see them, Penny?

Five months after the accident, Frank apprehensively pulled into 454 East Locust Avenue, the place he used to share with Penny and his daughter, Bonnie. It was a cold, gray Saturday in East Germantown, October 21, 2021, and he hadn't been back to the house since early August when he'd collected the last of his things and taken them to his tiny apartment up in Manayunk.

Frank was melancholy about his return and wasn't sure how it would go. Would he see Penny and Bonnie this time? He wasn't sure but was hopeful. Sitting in the driveway, Frank remotely opened the garage door and stared in at the repaired Honda Accord, which looked as if it hadn't been moved since it was returned home. Suddenly losing his will to exit his vehicle, Frank looked to his right and saw Frank Bruno sitting in the front seat next to him. Bruno, a man of few words, didn't speak; he just looked out his window to the backyard of the house. In the back seat, however, Old Man Winter smiled at Frank in the rearview mirror and lifted his chin, encouraging him to get out.

Frank squeezed his lips resolutely and summoned the courage to open the door and step out. The wind howled as the gray skies signaled another drop in temperature. Frank could barely feel the 42-degree October evening as it ran up the back of his windblown, unzipped Philly P.D. jacket. Looking again at the Accord, his head grew heavy, and tears began to well in his eyes. His legs, too, felt a little heavy, but he trudged forward around the car onto the sidewalk leading to the house's back steps.

His damaged right leg was all but fully healed when the cold reminded him of the fateful night in the attic of the William Sharpless House back in July 2019. It reminded him of Isak. He managed a slight smile and a tear when he thought of him and his old man sitting on the back steps of his childhood home. Frank's father, Salvatore, was murdered on Halloween 1992 by a serial killer named Vincent Charmaine Walker, and those steps were the last place he saw his father alive before he'd stormed off and gone to his baseball game without his dad.

Salvatore had missed more games than Frank could count, sacrificing time with his only son so that he could chase the bad guys. Frank once again realized that he was just like his old man. He'd always put being a cop first, making the excuse that ridding society of the filth and scum that plagued the mean streets of Philadelphia made his family safer. In reality, though, Frank knew if he spent more time with Penny and Bonnie, maybe, just maybe, they would all still be together.

Walking toward the back steps, Frank looked back at the scarred fence and smiled, almost laughing when he saw his father playing catch with an eleven-year-old Isak Cameron. Frank was glad to see both of them enjoying a game of catch in his childhood home's backyard. Behind him, he heard two car doors shut. Turning, he saw Frank Bruno and Garrison Old Man Winter chatting near the front of his Dodge Charger.

Looking back at the empty steps, Frank felt uneasy again. He knew he couldn't go inside the house he used to share with his family and that he'd instead settle for sitting on the steps watching his old man and little Isak playing catch. Sitting there for several minutes, terrified to look back, afraid Penny wouldn't come out, he just looked at his father and Isak and then over to his left, where Old Man Winter nodded at him and flashed a reassuring smile.

Another minute passed, and Frank had lost hope that he'd see his family. About to stand, he heard the familiar screen door squeal as it opened. Afraid to smile in anticipation, Frank held his breath instead. Afraid to look back, he closed his eyes and waited for the touch he'd longed for since mid-May, the last time he'd held Penny and little Bonnie in his arms. And there it was. Penny's hand gently fell upon his left shoulder just as the wind picked up and chased away the spirits of his father and little Isak. Looking over to Penny, he smiled and cried all at once. The bittersweet moment was both a blessing and a curse. Frank was tortured by the woman he knew he could never have again but was thankful to feel the touch he'd longed for.

Sitting on the steps to his left, Penny said, "How've you been, Frankie?" She smiled at the only man she'd ever truly loved. "Bonnie and I missed you. We weren't sure you would ever come back."

Frank began to sob. "Penny, I miss you so much." Reaching for her, he cried, "I need you, Penny! I need you and Bonnie back in my life."

Penny held Frank and said, "I know. I know. Bonnie misses her papa, and I miss my man."

"Where's your jacket? It's chilly out here."

"I'm good." Penny seemed unfazed by the late October chill.

Frank studied Penny from head to toe and noticed she was wearing the same jeans and T-shirt as the day of the accident. The memory of that day tugged on his heart. He couldn't understand why Penny would wear those clothes ever again.

Frank wailed, "Is she here? Is Bonnie here?" His tears were relentless and blurred his vision. Wiping them away, he saw Penny smile and look just past him, to his right.

Frank, almost afraid to turn away from Penny and fearing she'd leave, reluctantly turned to see his little Bonnie standing on the top steps, arms extended, reaching for her father. Seeing her, Frank cried again, reaching for his little girl, who timidly smiled.

"How's my Bon-Bon?" Frank smiled through tears, hugging his little girl tightly. "I missed you, Baby Girl!"

Bonnie didn't speak; she just held on to her father as he quietly wept. Still holding his daughter, Frank looked over at Penny with a heart-wrenched question in his eyes.

Penny knew what Frank was thinking. Pursing her lips, she nodded with a consolatory look and said, "She hasn't spoken since that day. Bonnie's okay, though," Penny was reassuring. "She's still trying to process what happened. That's all."

"Can I come home, Penny?" Frank cried as he released Bonnie and turned back toward the only woman he'd ever loved. "Please, Penny. I'll do anything to be with you guys again."

Penny again pursed her lips and shook her head. "I'm sorry, Frankie. Now's not the right time."

Frank cried, and Penny held him again. "Come back soon, okay?" Penny stood and helped Frank to his feet. Holding his hand tightly, she added, "You're the only one for me, Frankie. I'll never love another, but we can't be together right now. Not yet."

Frank sobbed as Penny released his hand. "I know. But I'm coming home soon. I have to!" he cried.

Frank hugged Penny goodbye, and as they released, he studied the hairline above her left eye, looking for a scar. "Does it still hurt?"

Penny shook her head. "No, it doesn't. Not anymore. It's fine, Frankie. Bonnie and I are fine now."

Frank nodded his head and cried, riddled with guilt. "That's good, Pen. That's real good." He tried hard to stay strong in the moment, but his heart was shattered, and it always would be.

"Why don't you ever answer your phone," he pleaded. "I call every day, and you never answer."

"I know, Frankie." Penny looked sad. She felt so much empathy for Frank. "It would be impossible to explain it. I will in due time. I promise you."

"I call it sometimes just to hear your voice. To feel close to you." Frank slumped over in agony. He was lost and couldn't make sense of anything anymore.

"I know, Baby." Penny stroked his hair the way she had done hundreds of times before.

Looking up and over Penny's left shoulder, Frank saw Bruno and Winter get back into the car, and he knew it was time to leave. Looking to his right, he'd hoped to see his father and Isak again, but they hadn't reappeared.

"Can you see them, Penny?" Frank wiped away his tears. "Can you see them, sometimes?"

Penny smiled and nodded. "They're always out there throwing the ball. I see them every day." She rubbed Frank's arm to console him. "I think they need each other. Yeah, they each fill the other's void. Isak needs a father, and Sal needs a son."

Frank nodded, staring at the wooden fence. "I think you might be right." Comforted by the notion that they'd had each other, Frank turned back to Penny, but she and Bonnie had gone. His face pale, Frank heard the screen door close and cried again.

Looking back at the scarred fence, Frank could feel his crippled heart slow, and stood frozen in his tracks. His attention went to the back door and then over toward Old Man Winter and Frank Bruno. Winter smiled and motioned Frank back to the car with a slight turn of his head. Frank took one more desirous look at the back door before reluctantly rejoining his friends back at the car.

Chapter 3 – The Dickinson Narrows

As Frank drove back to his apartment in Manayunk, a call came in from his partner, Jon Sullivan, known to his friends and co-workers simply as 'Bones.' The name didn't seem to fit, though, because Sullivan was a former Golden Gloves, light-heavyweight fighter in his teens and twenties and was now easily twenty-five to thirty pounds over his fighting weight. Now training as an MMA fighter made him even more intimidating to the bad guys and his fellow cops.

"Hey, Bonesie, what's up?"

"Well, did you go to the house?"

"Yeah, I went." Frank didn't feel much like talking about it.

"And? How'd it go?" Bones seemed to nudge Frank into telling him how he felt.

"And nothing. I don't want to talk about it."

"Frank, it might help to just let it out. You've been through a lot."

Frank reluctantly told his partner that he'd seen Penny. "I saw her."

"Saw who?" Bones was confused.

Frank was agitated. "You asked me how it went, and I'm telling you.... I saw Penny. We talked"

"You saw her? Talked?" Eyes wide with confusion, Bones became uncomfortable and immediately tried to change the subject.

Bones had been his partner since Frank returned to the force after making his trek to Sweden in July 2020. The two had become close since Bones transferred in from the nearby 24th District after the 39th lost Kyle Wade during the Isak Cameron bloodbath that had consumed eight lives, including four cops, three from the 39th. After Penny's accident, the 39th was down yet another detective.

"Ah!" Frank groaned. "Just drop it, would ya?" It was rare that Frank would tell anyone about his personal life or how he was feeling, and he quickly regretted saying anything about his visit with Penny. "It's Saturday. You called me, so what's up, man?"

"Two more of our brothers are dead. That makes five since June. I was wondering if you wanted to take a ride?"

"Goddammit! Where did it happen this time?"

"The Dickinson Narrows." Bones was a matter of fact, expressing little emotion.

"Same M.O.?"

"Yep. 911 call early this morning. Domestic dispute. Those guys drove into an ambush. Never even made it out of their car."

"Fuck," Frank grumbled and cursed under his breath. "That prick better not show his face up in East Falls."

Just a matter of time. Bones thought to himself.

"So, whattaya say.... you wanna meet me down there?" Bones was gentle in his nudge. He knew Frank was in the dumps and wanted to keep him busy, even on the weekends. "We need to get you out of that pit you're living in."

"Fine. What's the address?" Frank wasn't fooling his friend and partner. He, too, wanted to stay busy. Anything to take his mind off Penny, Bonnie, and what happened back in May.

"1815 6th Street. The corner of McClellan and 6th. Just look for all the flashing lights."

"Yeah, I know where it is." Frank was almost dismissive. "That's a real shit hole down there."

"Used to be," said Bones. "It's getting better ever since the sale of the riverfront property went through. The south part of the Narrows is still pretty shitty, though," he added. "Two dead cops in the street.... I say we go hunting for this prick. Why wait until he turns up in the 39th District?" Bones only half-joked. He was a Philly Boy through and through and idolized guys like Smokin' Joe Frazier and Rocky Balboa. Bones often referred to the fictional *Rocky* character as if he were a real person. "Whatta ya say, Frank? Wanna go hunting?"

"Easy, Killer!" Frank half laughed. "We don't even know if it's the same guy yet."

"Same M.O., brother! Of course, it's the same prick. He's up to five of our brothers in blue. Laurel Hill's gonna run out of plots before we know it."

Bones' words struck a chord with Frank. He had friends and loved ones buried in Laurel Hill Cemetery, and the last time he was there was with Penny for Ali Ashfaq's burial. His mind went back to that day, and he remembered that, along with Ali, they buried some poor sap whose cremated remains were mistaken for Kyle Wade, the disgraced, former Philly P.D. Detective and accomplice of Isak Cameron.

"I'll see you there." Frank needed to get off the phone and wallow in his depression a little longer, although his trip downtown was a welcome distraction from the hell he was living in.

Officially called Dickinson Square West since 2013, the rundown neighborhood was hardly a square. Running from the north, Washington Avenue, eight blocks south down to Mifflin Street, the neighborhood was eight blocks long and just two blocks wide, earning part of its name.

Just five blocks west of the Delaware River and just across from the rough and tumble South Jersey city of Camden, the area was experiencing a renaissance of sorts. East of the Narrows to the river, real estate investors were buying up land and building parks, restaurants, nightclubs, and high-rent condominiums, luring young professionals in an effort to revitalize Philly's Lower Eastside.

The developers had somehow forgotten about the Narrows, though. While the Narrows weren't bad north of Tasker, south down to Mifflin, the doors and windows of shops and duplexes were barred and looked more like Rocky Balboa's old neighborhood from the nineteen seventies.

As he drove, Frank could see punks on the corners bouncing handballs, thugs hanging outside the Jade Palace Chinese take-out on Watkins, and the burned-out remains of the Fuji Food Market on the corner of 5th & Moore. The Dickinson Narrows were just as Frank remembered from his brief stint in the 3rd District in 2011 before being transferred to the 39th in East Falls, where he would eventually be partnered with Penny in 2014.

The sights and the smells pervading the cabin of Frank's Dodge Charger and his psyche were only foreshadowing what he would find behind the yellow police tape and flashers that were now in his sight. The tiny one-way street separating a three-story, rat-invested townhouse and a fenced-off lot across the street was now a killing field. A gray concrete jungle served as a backdrop to the blue flashing lights that blinded Frank through his windshield as the Philly skies spat on the Dodge. Pulling to a stop, he exited his vehicle just as the rain began to fall.

Two ambulances sat benignly, void of life, and haphazardly parked, half on the street and half on the broken sidewalk. Their red lights off signaled to Frank and those gathered at the scene that medical care was no longer needed. As the rats scurried, avoiding Frank's three-quarter-high Horex boots and the rain, two of Philly's finest lay dead just ahead. Slumped in their cruiser, cameras clicked while their flashes flickered, making everything seem as if it were in slow motion to Frank, causing him to wince as he approached. For months, Frank had heard a clicking in his head that brought with it pain, bad memories, and a blinding white snow that chilled his broken heart.

From his viewpoint, looking beyond the gathering public, press, uniformed Police, and detectives, Frank could see a Philly P.D. patrol car cordoned off from the public. The car and surrounding street was a crime scene. Getting closer, Frank saw Bones talking to the detectives from the 3rd District, located just five blocks west of the Narrows, one of whom he'd worked with years prior.

Turning again to the crime scene, Frank saw nearly a dozen yellow evidence marker tents; the highest number marker Frank could see was eight. Now, just feet away, he saw the numbered tents marking shell casings. Despite the rain, Frank's keen eye told him that the shells were .40 caliber. Shaking his head, he knew what a .40 cal. could do to a human body.

Walking past ambulances and coroner vans, Frank could now see the bodies of his brethren. As the rain fell harder, umbrellas started popping up, and the curiosity-seekers quickly dispersed.

Frank winced from his vantage point when seeing the driver slumped over the steering wheel and the passenger leaning back with his head half hung out the shattered lowered window.

"Son of a bitch!" Frank clenched his teeth. His first impulse was revenge.

Forensics began erecting a bright blue tent over the patrol car in an effort to preserve evidence from being washed away. Seeing broken glass and a bullet-riddled windshield, Frank surmised that the fallen officers must have just rolled up on the scene when the assailant or assailants struck from the car's driver's side.

As the locals peeked through their blinds and over the top of their window-mounted air conditioning units, Frank yelled out to Bones.

"Yo, Frankie!" Bones turned to see his partner approaching.

Frank lifted his chin, acknowledging his partner, then said, "Hey Jimmy," to Detective Jimmy Wagner, standing, talking to Bones.

"Frank. It's been a long time. I heard about Penny's accident a while back. Didn't know if I should call or not. How you holdin' up, man?"

"I'm okay, Jimmy. Good to see you again, Brother." Frank consciously tried not to sound dismissive of Wagner's well wishes. The last thing he wanted to do was to relive that day all over again.

"This shit's something else, ain't it?" Wagner shook his head while looking over at the scene. Talking louder now over the rain and police radio chatter, Wagner said, "That's four uniformed officers and one detective killed across three Districts since June."

"So, whatta we lookin' at here?" Frank turned toward the massacre.

"Sergeant Timmy Falcone and a rookie named Mark Ritchie. He was only twenty-three." Wagner lowered his head. "Falcone had a wife and three kids, all girls. He's gonna be missed."

"That's rough." Frank winced and looked away momentarily. He knew what Wagner's widow and kids would have to suffer through.

"Whatta bout the kid?" Bones wondered if the rookie had a family.

"Still lived at home with his parents and kid sister. His dad used to be a cop over in Cherry Hill." Wagner clenched his teeth in anger. "Somebody's gotta get this motherfucker off the street!"

"Youse guys were pretty tight, then?" Bones saw the anguish on Wagner's face.

"I knew Falcone pretty well but only saw the kid around the district house occasionally."

"Jimmy, how do we know it's related to the other cases?" Frank still wasn't convinced. "I mean.... it's still early."

"Frank, the call that came in was from a cellphone, and they gave the address of that duplex." Wagner lifted his chin, pointing to the three-story dilapidated townhouse on the south side of McClellan & 6th Street. "It was a 10-16 like all the others. The shells are from a .40, and witnesses say they saw a white male, 20-40 years old with some facial hair, blue bandana under a black hoodie running from the scene after the shots rang out."

"That fits, Frank." Bones nodded in agreement with Wagner.

Frank also seemed to agree. "So, what about the occupants of the apartment?"

As the three men stood across the intersection from the crime scene, Wagner looked over to his right, again using his chin to point at the townhouse, and said, "The place is condemned. It's been vacant since the summer of last year."

Frank and Bones looked across the street and saw the yellow police tape on the steel screened door flapping in the wind, which had quickly turned violent.

Frank's brows shot up. "Definitely sounds like the same guy."

"And...." Jimmy Wagner paused.

"And what?" Frank looked at Wagner, then at Bones, and back to Wagner.

"There's another piece." Wagner's brow went up as he nodded.

"Piece? Piece of what?" Bones, like Frank, looked confused.

"Youse guys don't know?" Wagner looked surprised.

"Know what?" Frank had a 'what gives?' look on his face.

"A Scrabble tile. They didn't pull it out yet, but we spotted it on the passenger side floorboard."

"Scrabble?" Frank looked visibly ill and excused himself by holding up a finger. Walking out from under Bones' umbrella, he leaned over the rear of a nearby parked car and vomited. His mind raced and went back to Penny and the day of the accident. She had run to Walmart to pick up a few things for the company they were expecting. Douglas Cantrell and his wife Gaye were due in for a weekend visit, and Penny was to pick up a Scrabble board that day. She had played the game with Gaye and Doug many times while hiding out with the Cantrells during the Isak Cameron murder spree sixteen months earlier. She thought it would be fun for the four of them to play while in town.

Bones, concerned, looked to Wagner and said, "Gimme a second, Jimmy." Walking over to Frank, he touched his partner's back and said, "You okay, Buddy?"

"Yeah. I'm good." Frank rose and wiped his chin. "It must've been the cheese omelet I had this morning." Frank was relieved that the pouring rain quickly washed away his ill-timed retch.

Bones looked down at the yellow chunks and stomach bile and thought. *That was some omelet,* nodding his head, wide-eyed and wincing.

Rejoining Wagner under his umbrella, Bones and Frank questioned the revelation. Though familiar with the recent homicides, the Scrabble piece detail had not been shared in police circles or in the press.

"So, what exactly you sayin, Jimmy?" Frank's curiosity peaked. "They found more Scrabble pieces with the other victims, too?"

"Yeah," said Bones. "What gives?"

"Well, before today, they found one Scrabble letter tablet at each of the previous three scenes," said Wagner.

"No shit!" Frank shook his head. "How do you know that, Jimmy? I didn't hear anything about it." Frank looked at Bones, who also looked puzzled.

"I got a friend up in the 9th working the Lane case."

"Shouldn't the 23rd be handling that one?" Frank asked Wagner, again looking over at Bones.

"Yeah, but.... Detective Bobby Lane was out of the 9th when he was murdered by this prick back in June, so both districts are working it."

Bones shook his head. "I went to the academy with Lane. I didn't know him well, but that's a shame what happened to him. That guy had a family."

"That poor bastard took three in the back...." Frank's memory went to his father and the man who shot him in the back three times on Halloween 1992, Vincent Charmaine Walker.

Bones knew the story of how Frank's father died and realized his partner was hurting at the moment.

"This guy needs to be stopped." Wagner looked out at the rain. "He's picking us off one at a time."

"He's sending a message, huh?" Frank worked hard not to show his fragile psychological state. To him, it seemed he was reminded of his father, Penny, and Bonnie at every turn. He just wanted to be home with his family and couldn't understand why Penny wasn't ready for him to return.

"What letters they got so far?" Bones was now in full detective mode.

"Not sure." Wagner shook his head. "It's a multi-district investigation. They got Captain Justin Smith heading up the case." Wagner paused and added, "Rumor has it that the letters correlate with the street name of the crime scenes." Wagner looked up at the corner street sign, saw McClellan, and added, "I bet the Scrabble piece in the squad car over there is an 'M.' I'd put money on it."

"Jesus Christ. This guy's playing games, too." Frank's eyes narrowed. He figured he could come up with what letters they had so far by making a few calls. "They're running this thing out of Race Street, huh?"

"Yep," Wagner nodded.

"Well," Frank paused. "They got the right guy on it," he said, speaking of Justin Smith. "He's a hardass, but from what I hear, a pretty good cop."

"Makes sense," said Bones, nodding his head. "The three other dead cops are from three other districts." Looking across the street, he added, "Today makes four scenes. Four different districts." Bones then looked over at Frank and said, "Well, if they had you running the investigation, they have the guy by now."

"Yeah, or he'd be dead by now," Wagner laughed out loud.

Frank and Bones stood expressionless. Their gaze told Jimmy Wagner that his joke wasn't funny.

A stoic Frank extended his dripping wet hand to shake Wagner's as the rain refused to yield. "Listen, Jimmy. If there's anything the 39th can do to assist, just give us a call." Frank reached into the pocket of his Philly P.D. raincoat. Here's my card. My cell's on the back. Call me anytime."

"Thanks, man! It's good to see you again. Again, I'm sorry about what you're going through. We all are." Wagner squeezed Frank's hand tightly and held on just long enough to convey his sympathy, and then he turned back toward the scene just as the skies opened further. "And I didn't mean nothin' by what I said a minute ago."

"Don't sweat it, Jimmy."

As Wagner walked away, Bones turned to Frank and said, "You see those shells on the ground on the passenger side of the car?"

"Yeah, I noticed that, too. And there's not much glass on the ground on that side, either. What's that tell you, Bonesie?"

"The shots went in through the passenger side window, not out."

"Two shooters," the two chorused.

"Shells on both sides of the car and the Scrabble tile was found on the passenger side floorboard."

"Yeah.... Might be two guys then."

With the rain now coming down sideways, Bones yelled, "So, Frankie Boy, whattaya say we catch some lunch up at Billy Murphy's before you head back to the Yunk?"

"Nah. I'm not feeling it. You go ahead, though. Tell Dane I said what's up if you go." Frank stepped from beneath the awning the two were standing under and turned toward the direction of his car.

"That's okay, Frankie!" yelled Bones as Frank walked away. "Some other time, then! See you on Monday!"

Frank threw up a listless wave without turning to look at his partner and kept walking.

As the skies unleashed their fury on the Narrows, Frank sat in the Dodge and started thinking. In June, an off-duty detective named Bobby Lane was killed after pursuing two perps he'd had a scuffle with at Stone's Beer & Brewery in Brewerytown. Then he'd recalled a uniformed officer was killed in an ambush responding to a robbery in progress at Jimenez Grocery on Alleghany West & 35th in July. Then another uniformed cop out of the 18th District was shot and killed with a .40 cal. in another fake domestic dispute call in August over in Cobbs Creek. And now, Frank thought, two more cops dead in the Dickinson Narrows. Frank threw on the Dodge's wiper blades as fast as they could go and squinted to see the street signs. He couldn't make out the names of the streets but knew that it was 6th & McClellan.

As Frank hastily scratched the address into his notepad, his eyes went back to the intersection, and he was stunned by what he saw. Not there a moment ago, Frank saw Old Man Winter and Frank Bruno standing beneath the street signs looking back at him. Like a waterfall, rain fell from the brims of their fedoras, but their trench coats almost looked dry. Frank nodded and knew that the appearance of his friends likely meant that he'd be joining the case soon. To signal the two, he flashed his high beams in their direction. When he did, they disappeared.

Minutes later, Frank mumbled under his breath while driving, "This fucker gets around." He looked over his shoulder at the next stop sign and made sure he wouldn't get ambushed like the others.

As Frank headed back up north, he grabbed his cell off the passenger seat and saw missed calls from Douglas Cantrell and Candace Weatherby but nothing from Penny. He tried calling her again, hoping she would answer, but the call had gone straight to voicemail, just as it had since their relationship ended. Frank needed her thoughts on the cop killings, which except for the Scrabble pieces and the murder weapon, would otherwise seem unrelated. After all, it was always cop-hunting season in the City of Brotherly Love. Frank needed to know what letters had been collected so far. He hoped that they would spell out who the killer was.

This prick's coming to the 39th District; when he does, Bones and I will head up the case. "I'll make sure of it," he said under his breath.

Frank hadn't been on a meaningful case since the accident. After taking a month off to deal with his personal life, Frank knew his Captain, Beatrice Jackson, was taking pity on him and keeping his caseload light until he got his head right. But he was ready to get back to work. While Penny was no longer with the department, Frank would ensure he kept her involved. He knew her instincts were good, and he'd lean on them.

Now back up in Manayunk, just like the old days, Frank drove around for a while before parking his car down the street from his third-floor, one-bedroom flat above The Mad River Bar & Grill on the intersection of Main Street & Shurs Lane. It was the same apartment he lived in before he and Penny moved in together. Frank hated it there, but its familiarity gave him comfort. He thought he could repeat history and live there until Penny, for the second time in three years, invited him to live with her in his childhood home on East Locust Ave in Germantown.

After finally finding a parking spot, Frank reclined his seat and turned on the radio to 98.1, looking for the right Oldie to ease his mind. When his cell phone rang out, he foolishly looked and hoped it was Penny. Seeing it was Candace Weatherby again, he swiped right and closed his eyes. Just then, the sound of Player's 'Baby Come Back' filled the car's cabin and, if only for a moment, made Frank feel un-alone in the world. A world that was dark and rainy. A world that was as empty as it had been since Halloween 1992.

....*All day long, wearin' a mask of false bravado*....

No smile could possibly hide his tears when he succumbed to the deluge of memories and false hope.

Chapter 4 – Bones

Later that night, after eating dinner alone at Billy Murphy's again, Bones sat in his black, unmarked Ford Interceptor and, from the garage, stared at the side door of his house in Wissahickon. Like Frank and many other North Philadelphians, Bones lived in the same house as his parents did before they passed on. He thought that his troubled childhood bonded him to Frank and that it helped their partnership to be connected beyond being cops in North Philly. While Bones couldn't understand why Frank left the house that gave him peace, he knew full well why he had trouble walking into his childhood home every night.

You see, while Frank suffered great losses in his life, his house at least was the center of his greatest memories. For Bones, however, his house, his childhood home, was simply a place where he suffered. In fact, Bones could think of almost no good memories of his childhood coming from the home he stared at through the rain from its detached garage.

Bones always left the side door light on to fool himself into thinking he was actually welcomed there. His mom always left it on for him, but his father would always turn it off right before he punished her for the gesture.

Jonathan Bones Sullivan had turned thirty-six years old in July and moved back into his old house again in August after another failed relationship. His rugged chin and chiseled jawline made it easy for him to attract the ladies, but his fragile confidence and tattered psyche made it hard to keep them around.

He never sold the house left to him by his mother because it would serve as his fallback when relationship after relationship ended because of his inability to look forward and not dwell on the past. The house was merely a place to live when Bones wasn't living with a girlfriend who desperately wanted his love but never got it. He got the house instead of one of his other seven siblings because his dad died before his mother did. Bones knew he would have received nothing if his dad had outlived his mother.

Bones was the youngest of his brothers and sisters by far. In fact, he had little memory of ever living in the house with any of his siblings. The next youngest was thirteen years older than him. They were all gone by the time he started kindergarten.

Looking up through the windshield and out of his garage, Bones saw a night sky that was as dark as the memories of his father. Standing six foot three and weighing two hundred and twenty pounds, Bones was always smaller than his father, who'd weighed nearly three hundred pounds and stood six foot six. *If only Mom's side of the family were taller....* "Then maybe I would have stood a chance against that son of a bitch!"

Bones ground his teeth and punched himself in the face with both hands until his mouth bled. Stopping only after the tears came, he sat there and cried as he spewed saliva.

Bones understood Frank's childhood was cut short by a murdered father, and he wished every second of every day since he met Frank that his father had died too when he was fourteen, but he wasn't that lucky.

Bones regained his composure after the skies overhead cleared and washed his house with daylight. Suddenly, he got scared, dropped the basketball in his hand, and hid in the back of the garage when he saw his father's brand new 1992 Buick Roadmaster pull into the driveway off Markle Street. It was 5 o'clock, and seven-year-old Jon had lost track of time. Hiding in fear of his father, little Jon watched as his father, George, parked the car in the driveway. The fifty-seven-year-old was proud of his new car and made sure the neighbors knew all about the big purchase.

As George admired his new car, looking it up and down, inspecting every square inch, he noticed a nearly imperceptible scratch on the front quarter panel and flew into a rage.

"Bones!" George Sullivan screamed at the top of his lungs. So loud that neighbors up and down the street looked up to see what the commotion was all about. They'd all heard the screams before, but when they heard the little boy's name, they worried for him.

Jon got his nickname, Bones, from his father. He was a scrawny, lanky kid, and his father reminded him of that every day.

Bones was always to blame for anything and everything that went wrong or got broken around the house. Never actually to blame for anything, he paid a hefty toll for being an 'unhappy accident,' his father's words. George and Judy didn't plan on having another child after raising seven other children to their teen and adult years but along came Jon, and his father was having none of it. Judy Sullivan, too, ten years younger than her husband, paid a hefty price for the unforgivable sin of bearing one more child.

George was former military, serving one tour in the Korean War at the age of only eighteen and another three in Vietnam. A hard-nosed catholic, he lived by the sword and would kill by the sword those who crossed him. For little Jon, that was every day in the hallway, kitchen, bathroom, and on this day, the driveway.

After retiring from the military in 1969, George Sullivan tried being a Philadelphia police officer but was kicked out of the academy for what his training officers called 'uncontrolled aggression.' He would begrudgingly settle for a factory job instead.

The screen door on the side of the house meekly opened as George again screamed his son's name. "Jon! Get your ass out here!" Afraid to come out, Judy stood by and nervously waited.

With a fearful reluctance, the trembling seven-year-old boy stepped from behind a box in the garage. His head lowered; his steps were tepid, and his strides were short.

"Yes, sir." Jon's gaze went to his towering father standing on the passenger side of the Buick.

"What's my name, Boy?!"

Standing at attention, a frightened Jon replied, "Sir."

"You look up at me and speak up when you talk to me, Boy!"

Grabbing Jon by the shoulder and then the back of his neck, George pulled him closer and shouted, "What's this?!" pointing at the scratch as Judy looked on from the door, terrified for her baby.

"Dad...." Jon cried. "I didn't do it!" The little boy shrieked in fear.

Throwing him down to the ground, George picked Jon up and backhanded him across the face, sending him reeling to the ground and bleeding.

Judy rushed to intervene, and when she did, she, too, met the back of George's open hand.

The two, mother and child, sheltered in each other's arms and pleaded for mercy. Only after the monster could no longer muster the strength to land another blow did the miserable tyrant get into his now blemished Buick and speed away. Backing down his driveway, he nearly hit several worried neighbors who had assembled on the street at the end of his driveway.

Judy wailed in anguish. "I'm so sorry, Jon. I won't let him hurt you ever again." It was a promise his mom had made and broken hundreds of times before.

Jon Bones Sullivan knew from a young age that he would grow up and become a cop. He would do it because his father didn't have what it took to become one. He would serve and protect all those who were too small, too weak, and too fragile to protect themselves.

A loud thunderclap brought Bones back to the present day and to the darkness that had always hung over him. Looking out the windshield, he just stared at the side door of the house. Crying, he saw the light flicker three times. Was it his mother saying, 'I love you?' he wondered. Or was it his father saying, 'I hate you?' Either way, Bones didn't want to go into the house.

Just two miles west of Markle Street, Frank Collazo also sat in his troubled silence. A silence that was louder than his cries. Staring blankly out at the rain, he, too, debated going into his third-floor, claustrophobic hell. On that rainy, cold October Saturday night, Jonathan 'Bones' Sullivan and Francis 'Frank' Collazo would both sleep in their cars.

Chapter 5 – Trick or Treat

The Francis Cope House got its beginnings in 1852 when a Philadelphia ship owner, Henry Cope, purchased forty acres of land in East Germantown near the home of his daughter, Mary. There, he set out to build a grand estate and summer home for himself, his wife Rachel, his two married sons, their wives and children, and another unmarried daughter named Ruth Anna.

Named after a village in Wiltshire, England called Avebury, where the family had emigrated from, the estate would be called Awbury.

By 1861 the estate grew to include other houses for the growing families. That same year, Henry's eldest son, Francis, would build a permanent residence on the estate and live out his remaining days there. Since the early 1900s, it's been known as The Francis Cope House – Awbury Arboretum.

Today, the historic home serves as the headquarters for the Awbury Arboretum Association, which was set up to preserve Awbury's historic house and landscape. While the house is not a museum, it welcomes visitors to view the first floor of the Francis Cope House. Additionally, the home hosted over a dozen weddings a year and had a long waiting list.

On Monday, November 1, 2021, a detective from the Philadelphia Police Department was scheduled to drop off a deposit check for a spring wedding he was planning with his fiancé, Kate. The morning before, Detective Calvin Murphy received a call from the estate's Planning Director, Vanessa Middleton, asking him to arrive the night before, Halloween Sunday, at 6 pm. Thinking it was an unusual request, Murphy, who worked out of the 14th District, located just 1.3 miles south of the estate on 1 Awbury Road, had some things to add to an open case file that Sunday and easily worked it into his schedule.

Upon his arrival, at 5:50 pm on Halloween night, the thirty-seven-year-old didn't see any cars parked behind the estate. Knowing he was a bit early, he waited patiently in his car for the planning director to arrive.

Admiring the three-story cottage from his car, built from Wissahickon Schist stone, and its surrounding landscape, Murphy looked down at the five-thousand-dollar check in his hand and smiled. Having never been married before, he and his bride-to-be Kate would have a grand wedding in historic fashion.

Looking up, he noticed movement at the rear of the home and thought Middleton must have parked in the front of the house and made her way out the back to see if he'd arrived. Not wanting to alarm the woman, he left his service weapon on the front seat before exiting the car. In their previous meetings, he wasn't sure if he'd introduced himself as a Philly Detective or not.

As Murphy exited the car, he thought he saw the woman walking from the back of the home into the large white tent in the rear of the estate, which was permanently erected for wedding receptions. He'd gathered that there had been a wedding the day before, and perhaps the woman was inspecting the area for cleanliness.

Approaching the narrow sidewalk between the mansion's rear entrance and the overgrown foliage from the east, Murphy was momentarily blinded by the setting sun over the house and saw the young woman disappear into the shadows that now enveloped the tent.

"Hello!" Murphy yelled.

After a few seconds of silence and tentative footsteps, Murphy heard a welcoming voice coming from the tent.

"I'm back here, Detective!" said a muffled female voice.

Murphy felt a fleeting sense of foreboding but continued down the narrow sidewalk anyway.

"Detective Murphy? Is that you?"

"Mrs. Middleton?"

As Murphy entered the tent, his eyes took a moment to adjust, and when they did, he saw a slight woman standing in the far west corner of the tent facing away from him. Surveying his surroundings, Murphy noticed a dozen or so folded tables and several dozen chairs. He also noticed that some trash and debris from the reception the night before had not been picked up.

When Murphy's eyes fully adjusted to the fading light, he noticed the woman didn't appear to be the estate's Planning Director. He felt apprehensive because it didn't appear the young woman had anything to do with the Awbury Autumn Estate by how she was dressed. In Murphy's opinion, the clothes the disheveled female wore didn't even appear to be hers, as they seemed too big for her. Her hair seemed shaggy to Murphy, and her makeup appeared haphazardly applied.

Seeing the woman's right hand concealed behind her back, without reaching for it, Murphy thought of his 9mm Glock left back in the car and regretted not bringing it. While the woman was small in stature, Murphy, standing five feet ten inches tall and weighing two-hundred pounds, still felt vulnerable.

"Can I help you?" asked the woman.

"Yes," said Murphy. "I have an appointment with Mrs. Middleton. Is she here?"

"Detective.... Can I ask you a question?"

"Um...." Murphy's eyes narrowed. "Are you a custodian here?"

"Detective, do you know of someone named Frank Collazo? He's very famous."

Confused, Detective Calvin Murphy immediately sensed danger and began to back-peddle slowly. With his right hand on his empty holster, he turned his body sideways, trying to be a smaller target, and then extended his left hand in the woman's direction to keep her at bay.

"I don't know who you are, but you need to back up immediately." Murphy's heart raced as he continued to back up slowly. "I'm with the Philadelphia Police Department, and I'm here to see Mrs. Middleton."

The woman, wearing a stolen, floral print sun dress from a local Goodwill store and a filthy jean jacket, slyly grinned and said, "She's right behind you, Detective."

Murphy experienced only a moment of relief until he saw the woman slowly reveal a steely metal object in her right hand. Turning to run, Murphy witnessed a sinister smile hidden by a light brown, unkept goatee in the instant before an eight-inch blade was plunged into his belly.

Eyes bulging in shock and terror, Murphy fell forward into his assailant's arms before dropping to his knees. Looking up at his killer, he saw the devil before inspecting his hand, which was covered in dark red blood. Gasping for air, Calvin thought of Kate and knew he'd never see their wedding day. At that moment, he felt blade after blade plunge into his back, sides, head, neck, and face. Forty-seven stab wounds later, the soon-to-be-wed, sixteen-year veteran of the Philadelphia P.D. lay dead in a pool of crimson; in his left hand, a Scrabble piece embossed with the letter 'A.' Clutched tightly in his other hand, a bloodstained check made out to the Autumn Awbury Arboretum. On the ground next to his body, in letters one foot tall, three words and one name were scribbled in the victim's blood. Soon the entire city would be shocked, and before long, the nation.

Later, as night fell, killers Talon and Genesis drove off in a stolen 2006 Volvo. Just after midnight, the two carved more tally marks in each other's back. There were now a total of eight wounds on each of their backs.

The following morning, every resident on the Devin Place cul-de-sac, that sat due east of the estate, heard a blood-curdling scream coming from Vanessa Middleton, who, upon arrival, inspected the tent area and found the horrifying display.

Within an hour, every detective from the 14th District would be on scene, along with two from the 39th, who'd be escorted by their Captain.

Forty-five minutes earlier, Frank was awakened by another nightmare, shivering in a pool of sweat as a cold, late October breeze blew in through the back window of his apartment. With it, the sound of a northbound train crossing the Schuylkill seemed to split his head down the middle as he clutched each side with both hands, desperately trying to hold it together.

Too sad to cry, too lonely to scream, he wallowed in his madness and prayed for someone or something to bring him up from his hell. Just then, the phone rang. Grabbing it from the bedside table, he saw the caller ID; it was his Captain.

"Hello," Frank tried to sound sane and collected.

"Frank, I need you to listen to me carefully," said Jackson. "Get up to Awbury Arboretum as fast as you can."

"What's going on, Captain?" Frank was still trying to gather his wits.

"I'll fill you in when you get here," she said. "Oh, and Frank...."

"Yeah, Cap?"

"Watch your back leaving your place, at every intersection you stop at, and every person that crosses your path."

"Captain, what in the hell is going on?"

"I'm hanging up now to call Bones. You just get here fast."

Frank pulled himself from his shallow grave and donned jeans, a T-shirt, boots, and his Philly P.D. windbreaker. Looking in the mirror that hung near the door, he didn't recognize himself anymore. Frank was a shell, a broken one. But like every other day since mid-May, he trudged forward, trying to make sense of it all. Grabbing his keys from the key hook next to the door, he knew whatever it was, was bad.

Now in the Dodge, his cell phone rang; it was Bones.

"Frank, what's goin' on?"

"You tell me. Jackson didn't say much."

"To me, either."

"You on the road yet?" Frank asked as he turned left off of Main and onto Shurs.

"Just walking out now."

"Stay there. I'm swinging by to pick you up."

Four minutes later, Frank's Dodge roared around the corner onto Markle and skidded in front of Bones' house. The driver's side window came down, and Frank yelled, "Get in!"

"So whatta we know?"

"Frank, it's bad," said Bones. "Before you pulled up, Stan Bradshaw called me and told me it's one of his detectives."

Stan Bradshaw was the Detective Sergeant at the 14th District and had been there since 2016. He had worked under Captain Beatrice Jackson before she moved over to the 39th District after Isak Cameron murdered Captain Rosalyn Sumner in May 2019.

"What else did he say?" Frank clutched the wheel, knowing that whatever Bones said next would somehow involve him.

Bones looked over at Frank and paused hesitantly before saying, "Frank, he said to get Collazo here and make it fast."

Frank pushed the accelerator to the floor as the Dodge Charger flew across the Walnut Lane Bridge and over Wissahickon Creek en route to High Street and 1 Awbury Road.

The two men saw news helicopters flying overhead as the Dodge approached the narrow road. Both men looked at each other and knew this wasn't just another dead cop. Without words, their faces conveyed to each other that the remainder of the Cop Killer investigation would include them.

Chapter 6 – Cop Killers

In the late-morning hours of Monday, November 1, 2021, Frank and Bones navigated the narrow, tree-lined road and had to contend with emergency, press, and police vehicles that lined both sides of Awbury Road, obstructing their path. The road was more like a trail running through a park than an actual street. As members of the press abandoned their cars and vans to get a closer look, they looked into Frank's window and recognized his face. Immediately, reporters yelled his name, and cameras began clicking and flashing in rapid succession.

After the Schuylkiller and Isak Cameron cases, Frank's fame rose to something more tabloid-worthy than just a hero cop story. The partnership between him and Penny became that of legend. Frank was a celebrity in Philly and up and down the eastern US, and everyone who knew anything about the two high-profile cases he had helped solve was waiting for the next big one. The string of cop killings around the city, culminating in the murder of Detective Calvin Murphy at Awbury Autumn, appeared to be just that case.

As reporters scratched and clawed at the slow-moving Dodge, some yelled out questions about Penny. Bones knew that Frank's private life was something he desperately wanted to keep private, but he understood his partner's somewhat quiet life was about to become very public.

Frank growled at the mob, armed with cameras and microphones, and was relieved when the historic home was finally in view, and police were there to raise the yellow tape to let him and Bones in and keep the press out.

"That was a fucking circus back there," said Bones, looking into the passenger side mirror and then over at Frank, nervous of his reaction. "This is like 2019 all over again."

Frank was stoic and said nothing. Pulling off the road and into a field in front of the house, at the direction of a uniformed cop, Frank saw his Captain, Beatrice Jackson, and stopped at her feet.

Jackson, being a Captain at a crime scene in the jurisdiction of her former police district, was not that unusual, but Frank and Bones questioned why two detectives from the 39th were called to the scene. No matter the reason, they both understood the gravity of the situation and were ready to get to work.

The Dodge went quiet, and Frank stepped out. He met his Captain at the front of the car, followed by Bones. "Captain, whatever happened inside that house, we're here to help."

Jackson looked over at Bones and, lifting her chin, told him to hang back. She needed to speak to Frank alone.

Again, without words, Jackson motioned for Frank to follow her some ten feet away from the Dodge and the curious ears of Bones and the other uniformed officers and detectives milling around.

"Frank," Jackson was stone-faced. "Remember what happened here in 2019 with the dismembered body buried around back?"

"Of course, they just identified the kid last year," said Frank. "A twenty-year-old kid, Rashid Young, was killed by his boyfriend in August 2019. He was buried just outside the southwest corner of the reception tent behind the house. I think the killer's name was Sheffield."

"Yeah. That's it. Keshaun Sheffield," said Jackson. "Gay lovers. It was a domestic dispute. Stabbed him to death, dismembered his body, and buried him around back."

"Yeah, I followed the case back in the day." Frank nodded. "So, whatta we got? Another body?"

"Yes, and the body is in nearly the same exact spot as the kid from back then."

"You think they're connected?" asked Frank.

"No, I don't." Jackson was quick to dismiss it only as coincidence. Looking around, she said, "Well, as you know, I was the Captain in the 14th before being transferred to the 39th after Roz's murder...."

"I'm aware...." Frank was impatient to know who the victim was.

"Well," Jackson looked side to side and over Frank's shoulder before continuing. "Well, I know the history and backstory of every cop ever killed while serving the 14th District...."

Frank shook his head almost dismissively. He hated pity and felt he was about to receive some from his captain regarding his father, Salvatore, who served his entire career in the 14th District.

"Captain...." Frank pursed his lips. "You don't have to...."

"Frank, let me finish, please." Jackson was stern.

Frank reluctantly conceded with an insincere nod of his head.

"Frank, I know what happened in the belly of FalconClaw on Halloween 1992. I've studied the case closely...."

"You never mentioned that to me before."

"Well, to be honest with you, Frank. I don't like opening up old wounds."

"So, why are you now, then?" Frank was both curious and condescending.

"Because somebody beat me to it last night." Jackson looked over Frank's shoulder again at the house, which was not quite a mansion. "I'm not sure that anyone will ever get married on this estate ever again after what happened here last night."

"Lay it out for me, Captain. What happened in that house, and how does it connect in any way to my father?"

"Frank, what happened last night happened back behind the house in the reception tent. And I won't pretend I know how best to explain it. You're just gonna have to see it for yourself."

"Well then, by all means...." Frank turned and motioned with his hand for his captain to lead the way.

"Bones!" Jackson yelled. "Follow me!"

As Bones joined the two, Jackson began laying out the details of the crime.

"We're gonna walk around the house as Denny, and his team from Manayunk are in there collecting evidence."

"I thought you said the crime took place behind the residence?"

"Well, it looks like there was a break-in on Saturday that's likely connected to the murder," explained Jackson.

Bones studied the house as the three walked around the east side of the home and said, "This place is creepy."

"Who's our victim, Captain?" Frank was all business, knowing it was a detective. Whatever nightmare tormented him the night before, he was now in full detective mode and was ready to get another bad guy off the streets. What he was about to see would torment him even further and rip the still-healing scab off his memory of Halloween 1992.

"Police Detective Calvin Murphy was murdered here last night, fellas. On Halloween night. He was a sixteen-year veteran of the department, all of them out of the 14th, but more than that.... he was a good man." Jackson paused and shook her head, remembering the man and his contributions. And as for his killer or killers, they left a message...." she paused dramatically, "....for Frank."

Frank Collazo's vision immediately went dark. A loud squeal in his head caused him to wince, and the ticking started up again. His psychological episode went unnoticed by his partner and boss as the three walked, but Frank was sure the world could see his momentary breakdown.

"For Frank?" Bones looked puzzled.

Frank's vision returned, and the paralyzing screech in his head ceased. "Killers?" His thoughts went back to the crime scene down in the Dickenson Narrows. *Two Killers,* he thought.

"We're ruling nothing out," said Jackson. "Some evidence at the scene suggests there may have been more than one assailant."

"A detective from the 14th murdered on Halloween night. It's like 1992 all over again, huh?" Frank mumbled under his breath.

"Not quite." Jackson lifted the inner ring of police tape and held it up, allowing her two detectives to pass under it.

In the short distance between the parking lot and the white reception tent, detectives and uniformed officers stared at Frank as if he was the reason their brothers in blue were all being picked off one by one.

At the entrance to the tent stood Captain Cassidy Walker-Jones of the 14th. Jones had served as Jackson's First Lieutenant at the 14th and took over for her after her move to the 39th. Waiting to greet the three from her neighboring district, she had already walked the scene with Jackson before Frank and Bones arrived.

"Hello again, Captain." Walker-Jones kept it professional. "Detectives," she nodded in respect.

Frank barely made eye contact with the 14th's captain when trying to look beyond what he thought was far too many people trampling on the crime scene.

"Don't worry, Frank. The scene has already been processed," said Jones.

"Well, my guess is that you brought me and my partner here to offer our opinions. Kinda hard to do that without seeing the scene as it was before all of this." Frank looked at all the personnel again, counting at least a dozen, and tried hard not to roll his eyes.

Walker-Jones scoffed. "We got pretty good detectives up here in the 14th. That's not why you're here, Detective." Walker-Jones looked at Jackson and said, "You didn't tell him, did you?"

Jackson shook her head in the negative. "No. I thought he should see it first."

"Well, I'm here now.... Let's get on with it." Frank kept looking around and beyond the thinning group of police personnel.

Jones turned and yelled for everyone to clear the scene. When she did, Frank and Bones donned their blue latex gloves and mentally prepared themselves to see a fellow cop who was murdered in cold blood.

Frank couldn't imagine it being worse than seeing his former friend and fellow Detective, Kyle Wade, dismembered by Isak Cameron, using only his bare hands.

As the crowd dispersed, Bones audibly gasped at the scene, and Frank dropped his head in disbelief.

Frank's eyes stood fixed on the bloody letters that spelled out the words COLLAZO and TRICK OR TREAT.

Their fellow detective lay in a pool of blood that appeared to be five feet in diameter. The deep red color of Murphy's coagulating blood seemed to wed the long shadows and meek rays of sunlight permeating the tent's near-total darkness. For Frank and Bones, the scene became even more frightening.

"Jesus Christ!" Bones had to turn away. After a cursory inspection of the victim, he had noticed that it appeared as if the right ear of Murphy had been torn away by the barbarity and recklessness of the knife's raining blows. Looking to the body's right side, several feet away, the solitary ear lay torn and tattered on the outer edge of the five-foot bloody pool.

"1992." That was all Frank said, shaking his head in disbelief.

"Trick or Treat? Huh, Frank?" Jackson looked at her guy.

"Frank, Captain Jackson has briefed me on the relevance of those words, but I'd like you to tell me what they mean to you. And before you do, I would like to extend my condolences to you and your late mother for your family's loss all those years ago," said Walker-Jones. "Your father gave his life defending his family and the people of Philadelphia. For that, I am both grateful and sorry."

Frank still wrestled with his emotions. At any given moment, in a fit of rage, he might blame his father for trying to be a hero and going it alone. While other times, he wept for the man who died a hero and who likely saved others from the killer's wrath that ended his childhood at the young age of only fourteen. Vincent Charmaine Walker was never far from his mind. His only regret was that the madman was executed for his crimes. Frank knew that if Walker were still alive, he would gladly be his executioner.

"Thank you, Captain." Frank took a deep breath before continuing. He wanted to make sure he missed no detail when describing what happened to his father twenty-nine years and one day ago.

"My father, Salvatore Collazo, the lead detective at the 14th, was the eleventh and final victim of Vincent Charmaine Walker." Frank's nerves were steely as he spoke.

"It was a Saturday night, Halloween, 1992, when my father and his partner, Diego Ramirez, followed a lead to FalconClaw. They'd heard from a source that the man they were looking for once worked at FalconClaw as a night-time janitor from 1988 until 1991. Their source suggested that the former employee still had keys to the exterior basement door at the back of the mansion. The week before, they'd received a letter from Walker saying, 'another soul be damned,' at midnight on Halloween. The note was anonymous but addressed to my father and titled, 'Trick or Treat?'"

Bones' jaw sagged as he looked at the bloody words written in the victim's blood. "My god." He shook his head in disbelief.

Frank continued. "The identity of Walker wasn't known yet. But law enforcement knew who it was from. The letter ended with the phrase, 'Go Falcons!' That was the name of my baseball team, but my dad thought Walker was trying to divert him away from FalconClaw that night, thinking that I could be a potential target of the killer. His partner thought the opposite. Ramirez thought it was a trap and that Walker was trying to lure them to the mansion instead. A total of eight districts were on the hunt for Walker, but back then, FalconClaw resided in the 14th District where my father worked."

Frank took another deep breath and said, "Ramirez thought they should go up there with backup, but my father didn't want to spook Walker with a big police presence if he was, in fact, there."

"Anyway, my father had Ramirez ring the bell in the front while he went around to the back of the building to snoop around. He wanted Ramirez to divert any Saturday night staff resources to the front of FalconClaw while he looked for access to the basement in the back," explained Frank while the others stood mesmerized.

"They didn't have a search warrant and didn't want to make a big fuss at the front door. My father just needed a little time to investigate around back."

"My father found the door to the basement unlocked. It was on the southwest corner of the estate and was like one of those old-fashioned farmhouse basement doors. The padlock was off, just sitting on the ground. It must've seemed like an invitation to him, and he accepted it." Frank paused at a moment when those around him thought he would become emotional, but he didn't. "With their radios turned off, Ramirez didn't immediately know that my father was entering the basement."

"He'd told him to wait, but my dad was a hero, and he liked being the hero." Frank was stone cold. "But that was a long time ago."

"Trick or Treat? All these years later." Jackson knew what Frank and the others did too. There was an undeniable connection between what happened in 1992 and Murphy's killing.

"Three shots to the back," Frank shook his head. "This was a knife attack." He was trying to be pragmatic, but he knew better. Frank knew the assailant or assailants knew what happened back in '92, and was trying to send him a message.

"You ain't fooling anyone, Detective," Jackson called Frank's bluff. "It's written all over your face."

"No, no.... you're right," Frank agreed with a nod. "Someone wants me back in the game. And they're calling me out in a gruesome and very personal way." Frank stared at a man he didn't know but was now connected to Calvin Murphy until the end of days.

"Okay, so that's what then....?" Bones did the quick math.

"Twenty-nine years ago," said Jones.

"Do we all agree that this is the work of the son of a bitch who's been killing our guys?" wondered Walker-Jones aloud.

"The others were killed with a .40. This, however, was done with a knife." Bones was skeptical.

"Two knives, we think," said Walker-Jones.

"Two?" Frank was curious about their conclusion before an autopsy could be performed.

"They recovered the tips of two different blades near the body. The blows delivered were done with such force that the blades broke apart when hitting bones," she explained.

"Skull, too." Bones winced as he looked again at Calvin Murphy and to the right side of his bloodied, battered, and bludgeoned head, and to his chagrin, his ear was still missing.

"The letters appear to have been made by two different people, too." Frank noticed that the letters in his name appeared to have been made using two fingers, while the words trick or treat were made with one and were smaller in size compared to his name.

"Yes, that's what we believe," nodded Walker-Jones. "Oh, and there's one more thing...." She purposely paused for effect. "I haven't shared this with your Captain yet." Jones looked over to her old friend.

After another second of intense eye contact with those from the 39th, the Captain of the 14th pulled a tiny evidence bag from her pocket and handed it to Jackson.

"What's this?" Feeling around and peering through the back of the clear bag, Jackson could feel and now see, though covered in blood, the unmistakable letter 'A' on a Scrabble tablet.

Frank and Bones saw what Jackson saw, and any skepticism of whether the other cop killings were connected to Murphy was gone.

Bones' brows found the top of his forehead while Frank exhaled in guilt and frustration.

"So whatta you thinking, Frank?" Jackson looked to her most experienced detective hoping his gut was talking to him.

His gut was screaming out to him, but Frank didn't plan on showing his cards yet.

"We're gonna need your help, Frank," said Captain Cassidy Walker-Jones.

"Yours, too, Bones," Jackson chimed in.

Both men nodded in support of the request.

"They're expecting all five of us down on Race Street tomorrow at 9 am." Jones' eyes narrowed. "We're meeting with Captain Justin Smith, Inspector Jonathan Caffey, and Police Commissioner William Holden."

Frank knew in his heart that another madman or madmen had targeted him in some sick, twisted game that made him the grand prize or at least an inspiration. He knew that, like the Cameron brothers that the killer or killers would only stop their murderous spree after he was dead. Frank now had to live with the burden that he was the reason at least six cops were dead. *But were there more?* He wondered.

Before meeting the others downtown the next morning, Frank would need to consult his former partner, Penny Bristow.

Chapter 7 – Penny

Ever since Penny put a bullet between the eyes of Cameron St. John in the basement of FalconClaw in the early morning hours of August 8, 2017, she hadn't spent much time being a cop. After putting an end to The Schuylkiller with a single round, Penny and Frank retired from the Philadelphia Police Department and settled into a relationship that would soon include a daughter.

Starting their own Detective Agency, Penny soon grew bored of managing the administrative side of the business and chose instead to focus her attention on raising her little Bonnie.

Bonnie Ross Collazo shared a birthday with her father. She was born on June 11, 2018. Little Bonnie was named after her grandmother on her mother's side, Penny's mother, Bonnie Ross.

Bonnie Ross was a retired American Red Cross Nurse who fought hard to advance the women's movement in the 1970s, working closely with the legendary Philly Detective Penny Bryce and even meeting the then-President Jimmy Carter in the White House.

Penelope Denise Bryce sued the City of Philadelphia in Federal Court and finally won her detective badge in 1974 after a protracted legal battle claiming that she was discriminated against for being a woman. Bryce became the first female detective in the history of the Philadelphia Police Department and inspired women and girls of all ages to stand and fight for women's rights. Bonnie Ross was one of those women.

Penny Bryce disappeared at FalconClaw early Christmas morning in 1974, and her body was never found. Her first case ended up being her last. Because of her inspiration, Penny Bryce Bristow was named in her honor, along with hundreds of other little girls in and around Philadelphia in the decades that followed her death. Penny's mother, Bonnie, was also an inspiration. Penny and Frank would name their first and only child after her.

Sadly, the tragedy of Bonnie Ross's death will live in infamy after she was murdered on Easter Sunday, 2017, in the Fabric's Linen Store blaze that also claimed four other innocent victims. Cameron St.

John, The Schuylkiller, set the fire. While avenging her mother's death, Bonnie's daughter, Penny, could never replace her. The closest she would come would be to name her only child after her mother.

After Cameron St. John's twin brother, Isak Cameron, emerged in the spring of 2019, Penny and Frank rejoined the force and attempted to apprehend the maniacal twin. However, Penny, realizing the imminent danger she and her daughter were in, purposely fell off the grid until the threat could be eliminated.

After that, Penny decided to stay home and raise and protect her only child from the evils that seemingly lurked around every corner.

Then, after the car accident involving a hit-and-run, rear-end collision on May 14, 2021, Penny would never return to the police department due to her injuries. She would, however, do whatever she could to help the only man she'd ever truly loved determine the identity of the Cop Killers.

Whether during their time together as detectives or living together and raising a daughter, Frank Collazo came to love, admire, and respect Penny, but mostly he would count on her as a crutch. Frank was damaged goods since the age of fourteen and needed Penny far more than she needed him. Penny knew it and would continue to be there for Frank, no matter the situation.

Chapter 8 – The Throes of November

Later that night, Frank visited his old home in East Germantown. This time, Old Man Winter and Frank Bruno would not join him.

As his headlights led the way of his long journey down the short driveway of 454 E. Locust Avenue, Frank again dreaded getting out of the car. Like before, he was afraid he wouldn't see Penny.

After several minutes, Frank tentatively climbed out of the Dodge, peeked through the garage windows, and saw that the Accord was there. *She's home*, he thought. Somehow he wasn't relieved, though. "She might be home," he whispered. "But will she come out and talk to me."

Frank struggled every second of every day with why Penny wouldn't welcome him back home. That fact tortured him, but he also felt undeserving of being back together with his wife and daughter. The inner conflict coincided with the change in seasons, and Frank knew that the throes of November would be brutal. Looking at the rear of the dark house, he shivered. Would Penny be there? Was she inside? Would she come out? He feared the answer to all of his questions would be no. Closing his eyes and taking the first step, he overcame his fear and made his way back home.

Standing at the steps, Frank was sad. The house was dark and almost looked abandoned. *Maybe they're asleep.* He reasoned to himself. *Maybe they're not home.* He dismissed the thought after seeing the car was in the garage.

Sitting down on the top step, he'd wait. Looking over his shoulder from time to time, he began to lose hope. Sad, standing to leave, he looked into the darkness again and at the scarred fence. Maybe he'd see his father standing there. Instead, he saw Penny at the fence, strangely running her fingers along the scars left by a childhood that never was. *What is she doing there?* Frank was confused. Getting up to investigate, he nervously approached her.

"Penny? What are you doing out here? It's cold, Babe."

"Hey, Frankie. Were you going to come over to talk to me? I was starting to wonder about you."

"What are you talking about?" Frank was confused. "Why didn't you say something when you saw me? Were you there the whole time?"

"Yes. I saw you." Penny looked at Frank with an expression that conveyed both sadness and joy. "I didn't want to talk until you were ready to."

Frank was going mad. "This is crazy! The reason I came here was to see you and to talk to you about something."

"Is it about what's happening?" she paused. "The murdered cops? The detective today?"

"Yes, something's going on." Frank was troubled. "Penny, it's bad. I think we're all in danger again."

"Why, Frankie?" Penny reached out and touched his arm.

"It's like 1992 all over again." Frank was in agony. "My father...." He had trouble articulating his fears. "They're coming to get me, Penny."

"Then get them first, Frankie." Penny rubbed his left shoulder. "Don't let them get you."

Frank was baffled and afraid. "I don't know who *THEY* are!" he paused. I'm scared. I'm scared for you and Bonnie. You're not safe here."

"We'll be fine here," Penny was reassuring. "We're very safe."

"Penny, where's your jacket?! It's freezing out here!" Frank's face was drenched with concern and confusion. Penny was acting strange. He felt like he didn't even know her anymore. She treated him more like a friend.

"I'm good, Frank." She squeezed his arm. "Bonnie and I are good. She's inside resting."

"Can I go and see her? I want to watch her sleep." Frank was downtrodden.

"No, Frankie. Now's not the time. Maybe later." Penny grimaced. She felt bad for her love. She knew he was hurting.

"Why don't you ever call me? Why don't you answer your phone?" Frank was deeply troubled. "What's the matter? Was it something I did?"

"No. No, it wasn't you." Penny's head swayed softly, and she half smiled.

"I want to come home, Penny! I want to come home tonight!"

"Frankie, you can come home whenever you like. But if you do, Bonnie and I won't be here, I'm afraid. Wait a little longer. Everything will work out. You'll see," she smiled again, hoping to ease his pain.

"What are you talking about?" Frank was exasperated. Grabbing Penny's shoulders, he pleaded with her. "What in the hell is going on?! What did I do? What's wrong with you?!"

"You didn't do anything, Baby. You just can't come home yet. Soon though. I promise."

"Yet?! You keep saying 'yet.' What does that even mean?"

"You need to solve this case first. Maybe then...." Penny's voice was calming. "Call Doug. I'm sure he wants to talk to you. He can help."

"He calls me all the time. I don't answer anymore because he only wants to talk about you and the accident."

"Just call him. He can help you with the case.... I'm sure of it."

"Can you help me, Pen?" Frank had lost all confidence in his abilities. "I'm supposed to be downtown tomorrow to meet the brass, but I'm scared I'll make a fool of myself. I don't know much about the other killings. I'm so lost without you."

"I'll help you." Penny's tone was empathetic and supportive. "I'm here for you. You can't be here, though. You can't come home. Not yet."

"Penny, can I hold you?" Frank teared up. "I need a hug, or I'm going to lose my mind."

"Sure, Frankie." Penny moved closer. "I need a hug, too."

"I love you so much." Frank sobbed in her arms.

"I love you, too, Frankie." Penny flashed a reassuring smile but didn't cry. "You can come home soon. Goodbye, Baby."

"I love you, Penny!" Frank hit his knees and cried. His anguish boiled over into a deluge of tears. After picking himself up off the ground, he turned to find that Penny had gone as if picked up by the wind and swept away.

Ten minutes later, Frank took Penny's advice and called Douglas Cantrell from the car. Doug answered on the second ring.

"Frank! My god, are you all right?" Cantrell was beside himself. Gaye and I have been worried sick. I drove down last week to see you, but no one was at the house. I waited in the driveway for hours and tried to call you, but you didn't answer or return my calls!"

"Doug, listen. I'm having a really hard time.... But I don't want to talk about Penny or Bonnie right now. Can you understand that?"

"No, Frank. I can't." Cantrell was baffled. "They're your family, for God's sake."

"Doug. If we're going to talk, then you need to promise me that you won't mention them. Not yet. I'm going through some stuff right now, and I can't talk to you about them. Okay?"

Douglas Cantrell begrudgingly agreed. "Okay, Frank. I'll agree to it if you answer just one question."

"Fine. What is it?"

"Have you seen them? Have you seen Penny and Bonnie since May?"

"Yes. I just saw Penny tonight. We spoke."

"Oh, my goodness," Cantrell choked back tears. "Gaye and I were worried about them. Are they okay?"

"They're fine, but I don't want to get into it right now." Frank was standoffish.

"Okay, I agree. But one more thing, Frank...."

"What is it?"

"Would you tell her that Gaye and I love her so much, and we miss her and Bonnie dearly?" Cantrell again fought his tears.

"I will, Doug."

"Tell her we hope to see her and Bonnie again someday," implored Cantrell. "Please, Frank, I need you to swear."

"I swear to God, Doug. I'll tell her."

"Okay, tell me about the case. I've been going nuts up here. Whatta they got so far?"

"Doug, you're not going to believe it...." Frank didn't know where to begin. "They're all connected. All the killings. All the cops. It's one guy.... maybe two."

"Two? How? What makes them think it's two people?"

"Today, I saw something horrible, Doug."

Frank was emotional, almost trembling. Cantrell could hear and feel his terror.

"Go ahead, Son. You can tell me."

"A detective from the 14th was murdered on Halloween night. Stabbed to death," Frank paused to collect himself. "Too many stab wounds for just one guy...." he mumbled.

"Go ahead...."

"They believe it was more than one assailant because it looked to them, from what they could tell, more than one knife was involved." Frank slowed at an intersection near his apartment as the light turned yellow up ahead. "And...." he grimaced.

"And what, Frank?"

"Hang on a second.... there's a homeless guy with a paper cup in his hand approaching my car." Frank reached for his gun, trusting no one.

"Be careful, Frank."

"Yeah, gimme a second."

Cantrell listened closely, worried for his friend.

"Hey, mister, you got a couple of bucks you can give me? I'm down on my luck, ya know?"

"Not tonight, buddy."

"C'mon, mister. Whatta ya say? Help a brother out."

In full detective mode, Frank took a mental note of the man's description. Late twenties, or early thirties. White male, small build, black hoodie, unshaven face with a goatee, and bad teeth.

"Again, not tonight, friend. Now please get away from my car." Using his left hand, Frank revealed the badge hanging on a ball chain around his neck, pulling it from beneath his jacket and holding it up. All the while, his right hand clutched his Smith & Wesson M&P.

"Whoa! My bad! I didn't know you was Five-o!"

"Yeah, well, you have a good night," said Frank as he rolled his window up and passed through the intersection.

"Everything okay, Frank!" Frank heard Cantrell from his phone, sitting in the passenger seat.

"Sorry about that, Doug. Just some homeless guy down the block from my place."

"Whatta you mean, your place?" Cantrell was confused. "In all the time I spent with you, I never saw homeless people around your house."

"Oh, yeah. I'm not staying there right now. Penny and I are taking a little break." Frank was wishy-washy. "Like I said, I don't want to get into it."

"Gaye and I are worried sick about you. Where in God's name are you staying?"

Frank exhaled heavily, feeling like his father was questioning him. "You're not going to be happy, Doug. I'm down at my old place in Manayunk."

"You're old place? Above the bar?" Cantrell groaned. "Jesus, Frank. You told me that place was awful. You hated it there."

"I do, and it is, but for some reason, it reminds me of Penny, and for now, it's all I've got."

"Frank, do you need money?" Cantrell was concerned. He knew Frank made a good salary and couldn't wrap his head around his decision to live in a place he hated. He remembered that The Schuylkiller had been inside the old apartment, which terrified him.

"Doug, my partner lives just a half a mile from here, and the place is familiar to me. I'm good."

"But Frank...." Cantrell was skeptical. After a moment of hesitancy, he decided not to push his friend. "Okay, I trust you, Son..... So what else can you tell me about the detective who was killed last night? You mentioned something about multiple murder weapons. So, a knife was used, huh?"

Now sitting in his car in the rear parking lot of the Mad River Bar & Grille, Frank kept the motor running because the temperature had dropped into the low thirties. Frank also kept a keen eye on the narrow parking lot entrance coming off of Main & Shurs. He was looking out for the homeless guy who had asked him for money minutes earlier. His M&P was still clutched tightly in his right hand. He was ready for anything.

"Yeah," said Frank. "Looks like two knives. But it's too soon to tell what kind they were."

"Is there something else, Frank?"

"Yeah," he took a deep breath. "It's bad, Doug."

"What is it, Son?"

"It's about my father. It's about what happened back in '92."

"Jesus Christ!" Cantrell sounded like he was going to be sick. "Don't tell me we've got a copycat?"

"Why, Doug?! Why do they keep coming after me? Why?!"

"You're their guy now, Frank," Cantrell reasoned with his friend. "They need you."

"Who is 'they'?!" Frank couldn't make sense of anything. He was tired of fighting and on the verge of giving up.

"Every sick son of a bitch that wishes death upon others and who has a death wish." Cantrell knew that Frank was branded. Branded a target and labeled a source of inspiration for the depraved and the murderous.

"What should I do, Dad?" Frank didn't realize he'd made a Freudian slip when he called Cantrell 'Dad.'

Cantrell heard it loud and clear, though. Swallowing hard before answering the question, he decided to let it pass. Doug knew Frank was hurting. His whole world had fallen apart in just the last six months, and he desperately needed a friend.

"You take it one day at a time, Son. You hear me?"

"My days are long, Dad." Frank teared up as he again addressed his friend as his father. "It's hard, and I don't know if...."

"What happened today, Frank?" Cantrell was beside himself. He was now worried about Frank's mental health. While he never thought Frank could be suicidal, Cantrell knew how much he'd been through in his life and in just the past three years, not to mention the lifelong heartache he'd suffered by losing his father as a young teen.

"In the victim's blood, three words were written on the ground next to the body...."

"What did it say, Frank? Tell me."

"It said, Trick or Treat...." Frank paused, almost trembling.

"I'm confused," Cantrell didn't get it. "Frank, it was Halloween...."

"Doug, do you remember the letter my father got in the days before he was murdered? My dad received a letter from Vincent Charmaine Walker. It was titled, *Trick or Treat.*"

"My God!" Cantrell again sounded sick. "But do you really believe that somehow connects the deaths?"

"Doug, wait. There's more."

"What? What is it?"

"There was another word written on the ground...."

"What is it, Frank? Tell me, Son."

"Collazo." Frank's eyes went wide. "My name was written in another man's blood. How am I supposed to live with that?"

Cantrell was mortified; he knew they were coming for his friend but didn't know who *they* were. "One day at a time, Frank. One day at a time. And you watch your back."

"It's gonna be a long November." Frank could hear the train crossing over the Schuylkill just behind him. The sound both soothed and tortured him. On the one hand, the sound drowned away the voices in his head. On the other, he thought of Kyle Bender and Cindy Stafford hanging from another train trestle just a mile downriver beneath the Twin Bridges.

"Listen, Frank. Will you do me a favor?"

After a moment of silence, Frank relented. "Of course. Anything."

"Will you call me every night for the rest of November? We could just talk. Talk about us, talk about the case, or talk about...." Cantrell caught himself. He almost said, talk about Penny and Bonnie. "We can chat about whatever. Maybe I can help you with the case if you were to need me."

"Sure, Doug. I can do that."

"Oh, and Frank...."

"Yeah?"

"Don't sleep in your car again. I know you did that occasionally when you lived over there. Not until this thing is over with. Okay?"

Frank surrendered a reluctant chuckle. "No problem."

"Goodnight, Frank. I'll talk to you tomorrow."

"Sure, Doug. Goodnight."

Frank raised his seat from the reclined position and changed his mind about sleeping in the car because of Doug. A minute later, he walked back out to the corner and looked up and down Main Street, looking for the homeless guy. He saw no one. After Frank entered the street-level door that led up to his apartment, the homeless man stepped out of the shadows a block away and stared in the direction of the Mad River and the entrance to Frank's place. Wearing a black hoodie, the man was joined by a woman who wore a grey jacket, its hood up, hiding her face in its shadow.

The two stared down the empty street, their now frozen breath evaporating in the air with their every repugnant pant. As the wind picked up and dragged the cold air off the river, another train passed over the Schuylkill, and again, both soothed and tortured the now weary detective who reluctantly called the Mad River home.

Cantrell knew that the Throes of November were calling Frank's name. Now lying in his bed, staring at the ceiling, Douglas Cantrell prayed to God that Frank didn't answer their call.

Frank, also lying in his bed, listened to the rats in the walls and the ones clawing at his sanity. Detective Frank Collazo gripped his 9mm gun tightly. He prayed to Old Man Winter that one of the vermin didn't break through the evident cracks in his psyche. He prayed that Penny would ask him to come home soon. Frank Collazo prayed.

Chapter 9 – The Prodigal Son

"Frank!" Bones shouted to his partner, who was exiting a parking garage at the corner of Race & 17th Street, just east of Police Headquarters. It was 9:55 am. "Let's go, man!" Bones was stressed, knowing they'd never make it to the ten o'clock meeting on time.

Frank seemed to almost meander up the street as if not in a hurry.

"Frankie! Come on, Brother! We're gonna be late!"

"Calm down, Bonesie," Frank said as he approached his partner.

"You should've let me drive today. I could've picked you up, you know?"

"I had an errand to run." Frank looked disinterested, almost as if he didn't want to be there. "And besides....." he paused, shaking his head. "Forget it."

Bones, dismayed by Frank's attitude, shook his head as he pushed in on the revolving glass doors of the high-security building, closely followed by his partner. Once inside, the two men were scolded by their Captain, Beatrice Jackson, for being late. She, too, was stressed by the notion of being late for their big meeting.

Bones threw up his hands in a show of surrender. "I was here twenty minutes ago, Cap. Talk to your boy over here."

"Sorry, Cap. I had an important errand to run this morning."

"More important than dead cops all over Philly?" Jackson was more than annoyed.

Frank didn't actually have an appointment that morning. He had awakened early to hit the streets and visit every crime scene where his fellow cops were shot or stabbed to death. He wanted to ensure he was prepared for whatever his superiors had in mind for him.

In attendance would be Police Commissioner William Holden, Chief Inspector Jonathan Caffey, Special Investigator Captain Justin Smith, 14th District Captain Cassidy Walker-Jones, 39th District Captain Beatrice Jackson, Bones, and Frank.

Before going in, Jackson cautioned her boys to take a back seat. She told them Captain Justin Smith was hard-nosed and in line to become the next Chief Inspector after Jonathan Caffey eventually retired. She warned them not to challenge him in any way.

"Listen, you two. Don't try to stand out in there. It's a big audience, and you need to make sure you don't speak unless spoken to." Jackson's nerves were on full display. "Justin Smith is a hardass and won't react kindly to being shown up by some celebrity cop from the 39th." Jackson stared directly into Frank's eyes, ensuring he knew she was referring to him.

"Roger that, Cap." Bones was equally nervous but also excited. He had never attended such a high-profile meeting in his career and was curious about how it would go.

For Frank, on the other hand, it seemed business as usual. He had met with the brass multiple times while heading up The Schuylkiller and Isak Cameron cases. He was ready for whatever came next.

As the three walked into a large conference room, they immediately felt relieved because the brass from Police Headquarters weren't in the room yet. Walker-Jones sat alone at a large conference table, scrolling through emails and returning text messages on her phone.

"What's going on?" Jackson asked her counterpart from the 14th District.

"They've been going in and out of that room over there." Walker-Jones motioned with her head to a door just off the conference room, and near the door the three had just entered. "They're in there talking about something."

"Did they ask where we were?" Jackson was again nervous.

"No, they haven't been out here since you went out to look for your guys. They probably aren't even aware your boys were late." Walker-Jones lightly jabbed her former boss.

The door opened moments later, and Holden, Caffey, and Captain Justin Smith walked out.

"Welcome, ladies and gentlemen," Police Commissioner William Holden greeted the group. His demeanor told the group he was in a good mood despite the tragic circumstances. "I want to thank all of you for arriving on time today. The traffic around this city is getting worse and worse by the week, it seems."

"If I may, please let me introduce those of you who have never met before," said Holden. "Inspector, you know both of our diligent Captains, and of course, we all know North Philly's own Prodigal Son, Frank Collazo...."

Frank neither smiled nor frowned. He wasn't looking for accolades on this day or any other. While Beatrice Jackson and Bones Sullivan smiled with pride, chest out, Inspector Holden remained stoic. No one seemed to notice, except Frank, that Captain Justin Smith appeared to roll his eyes.

"Frank, we're all sorry for what you've been through since the accident. It was a terrible thing, what happened to your family...." Holden was quickly cut off.

Raising his hand in a gesture that made clear to all that he wanted neither pity nor sympathy, Frank said, "For all in the group here today, I'd rather we focus on the task at hand and hope you can all refrain from any well wishes or compassionate gestures. My family and I are fine. Thank you, though, Commissioner."

Jackson winced at Frank's comments, while Holden seemed to take the rebuff in stride. Perhaps he understood Frank's crucible of pain. He felt terrible for both Penny and their child.

Bones, however, was proud of his partner. He knew Frank was hurting and that he desperately wanted to separate his job from his personal life.

"And for those who have yet to meet this up-and-coming superstar," Holden smiled at Bones. "This is Detective Jon Sullivan from the 39th District. Jon is a fourteen-year veteran of the department and was credited with collaring the East Falls Rapist last year."

All nodded in respect of his service and accomplishments, but Captain Justin Smith extended his hand to shake that of a mildly embarrassed Bones Sullivan. When releasing Bones' hand, Smith purposely looked in Frank's direction and half-smiled. His action was purposeful and yet imperceptible to all except Frank. Frank's opinion of Justin Smith was now confirmed. In Frank's opinion, Smith was an ill-humored asshole, and he officially now hated him.

"Please, everyone, let's be seated." Holden motioned the group to sit at a twelve-foot conference table in the lavishly accommodated room. "Momentarily, we will be joined by forensics experts from Manayunk.... I believe we're all familiar with Director Daanesh Patel and Chief Forensic Officer Rupali Sharma?"

All nodded in acknowledgment of the leadership team from the Manayunk Forensics Division and were anxious to hear their findings from one or all of the unsolved murders of Philly's finest, dating back to June.

With everyone seated, Commissioner William Holden had some news to share.

"For all of those at the table today, I would like to make an announcement. Many in the building already know, and it will be reported to the press later today...." Holden paused. "I will be retiring at the end of this year."

The two female Captains at the table were genuinely disappointed because they knew how far women and women of color had progressed in the department under his leadership. As for Frank and Bones, however, they barely knew the man and were content with just keeping North Philly safe from the bad guys. They neither liked nor disliked the leader of the Philly P.D.

"Who will replace you, Commissioner?" asked Jackson as Jones looked on.

Both selfishly hoped it wouldn't be a gray-haired white male from within the department. They thought a change at the top should include a change in perspective and life experiences.

Holden beamed with pride at the question. "Well, now.... I don't want to ruin the surprise and begin to name names, but we are bringing in someone with a fresh new approach to law enforcement, and while you won't hear *HER* name from me, we're bringing in someone from Portland, Oregon. Some might consider her a renegade. For me," Holden winked and smiled, looking over to Caffey and Smith. "I would call her more of an *Outlaw*.' The last little hint I'll give is this...." Holden again smiled with great pride, "The City of Philadelphia will have its first black female Police Commissioner in its history."

With that admission, both Beatrice Jackson and Cassidy Walker-Jones beamed. Frank also nodded his head with pride, remembering Penny's namesake and the woman immortalized in bronze, standing tall in the courtyard of the Municipal Services Building just across from City Hall. Penelope Denise Bryce became the first female detective in the department's history back in 1974, the very year she went missing from FalconClaw on Christmas morning.

"One last thing before I step away and let you fine gentlemen and ladies get to work." Commissioner Holden was full of surprises. "As for Frank and those from Germantown and East Germantown," Holden acknowledged Walker-Jones, Bones, and Jackson, "The Phoenix will rise from the ashes...."

All at the table were aware that The Phoenix, the outdoor shopping, dining, and residential complex, was being rebuilt after Isak Cameron and disgraced Detective Kyle Wade conspired and burned it to the ground on Easter Sunday, 2019. They all looked at each other, thinking the old man was losing it a little.

"....But apparently, it won't be called The Phoenix this time around," Holden paused. "The Phoenix Group felt a little superstitious and wanted to change the name so that history would not repeat itself."

"So, what are they going to call it, sir," Jackson perked up in her chair.

"Believe it or not...." Holden paused again and smiled.

Frank swallowed hard, hanging on Holden's next words like a man dangling out of the window of a burning building.

"They just got the new name approved through the Germantown City Council...."

Frank shook his head, knowing what Holden was going to reveal. He felt in his heart that history was indeed going to repeat itself.

"FalconClaw Park!" Holden exuberantly professed, excited that he was the one to break the news to the group. "Because Mount Royal Park backs up the original FalconClaw estate," he explained. "It seemed natural to marry the two."

Frank was sick. His life had been destroyed by FalconClaw back in 1992 when his father was murdered there, and then again in 2017 when he was shot by The Schuylkiller just feet from where his father died.

Frank Collazo's vision suddenly went dark again without anyone in the group noticing, just as it had the day before and dozens of other times since the accident. This time, instead of a loud squeal, a loud ticking caused him to wince. A white blizzard of snow blinded his vision. His psychological episode went unnoticed partly because Denny Patel and Sharma Rupali had just entered the room, and all except Frank stood to greet them.

Frank ground his teeth and clenched his fists, trying desperately to shake the visions in his head. All he could see was fire, snow, blood, his father's lifeless body, footprints in the snow, the basement of FalconClaw, and Old Man Winter looking down over all of it. Frank desperately needed his support system back. He needed Penny.

After pleasantries were exchanged, Commissioner William Holden excused himself, turning the meeting over to the rank and file. Inspector Jonathan Caffey would continue the meeting.

"Okay, everyone, in front of you is a file that includes every detail of every police killing since June."

In front of each member gathered were roughly one-inch thick brown accordion folders. "Go ahead, open them up."

Each member perused the contents, with all but one focused on the graphic crime scene photos. Frank was the only one more curious about the case details. He, like any good cop, knew that the whats, whens, wheres, and hows would almost always lead to the whys. If all those didn't add up to the *why* then the case was either unsolved or the monster was born and subsequently became a killer for no apparent reason. Frank knew better than the experts, though. He knew that monsters created monsters and that they weren't born.

Cameron St. John taught him that. Isak Cameron taught him that. The Tsykabarna that mutilated Isak taught him that.

Frank would pore over the evidence and fill in the blanks. Great minds were gathered around the table, and together, they would catch the killer. If they couldn't, then Frank would kill the killer.... Or killers.

"Justin, you're leading the city-wide investigation. Tell the group what we have so far." Caffey was likely talking to his successor as he knew he was also about to retire, and Captain Justin Smith was his logical successor.

Without saying it out loud, guys like William Holden and Jonathan Caffey would never admit it to anyone, but the Schuylkiller case, the Isak Cameron case, and now the Cop Killer case was ending more than lives; it was ending careers. The spotlight on the department and its brass was far too bright, and the burden of lost lives too heavy. The carnage inflicted on the City of Philadelphia in recent years had taken its toll on everyone, and no one more, outside of the victim's families, than it had on Frank. While the others had the luxury of retiring, further unscathed, Frank still had a job to do; get another bad guy off the street. Frank wasn't stupid, though. The job had taken many of his friends and family from him. He missed Penny, his dad, his captain, and fellow detectives, who all meant the world to him. Frank knew in his heart that he'd never get to retire. The job would claim him, too, like his father, at an age much too young to die. Frank was certain of it.

Captain Justin Smith was a former Marine and ensured that everyone knew it. 'Oorah!' flew from the lips of Smith at least once a day, and the high and tight haircut, though now completely gray, told everyone that he was first to the fight. Or at least once was. Today he led his troops from his civil-military perch, Race Street. No one dared try to out-piss him. If they did, they'd feel his wrath via ridicule, public humiliation, termination, forced resignation, or outright indignation. Smith looked across the table and knew he couldn't compete with the street credibility that Frank had earned in his career, though. However, that wouldn't stop him from ruling his new minion with an iron fist.

"Thank you, Inspector Caffey. It's an honor to head up such an important case," Smith's voice was deep and monotone. "I'd like to bring the 14th and 39th Districts up to speed in this ever-growing case. What I will share with you today has been previously discussed with ranking members of all other Districts where police homicides have occurred. While none of our brothers in arms have been lost out of the East Falls area, we all know the implication and significance of what was discovered yesterday at the Cope House.

"Frank, for the record, let me just say that I think your father was a fine cop. I'm not sure if the current or former Captains here at the table know or not, but I started my career with the force at the age of twenty, back in 1980. I first served as a uniformed officer in the 14th District...."

Frank perked up. He knew that his father worked out of the 14th for his entire career and would have known Justin Smith.

"That's right.... I knew your father, Frank. He was a good man and a good cop. Your father was an inspiration to his men. When Salvatore Collazo was killed, we all took it personally. With that being said, I'm sorry for your loss. Additionally, I'm sorry about the tragic accident involving your family this past May. You've been through a lot, and I want to thank you for your continued service and sacrifice."

Frank expressed his gratitude with a nod and was beginning to reconsider how he felt about who he initially believed was his new nemesis. His gut told him that the guy was no good, but he suddenly found himself in a wait-and-see mode.

Justin Smith then pulled a small velvet drawstring bag from his pocket. A few at the table recognized it as a letter bag from a Scrabble game. Opening the navy blue pouch, Smith emptied its contents onto the table. The sound of the wooden tiles hitting the laminate surface unsettled Frank, and he cocked his head a little to the side, again hearing the ticking in his head. While some at the table saw Scrabble tiles, Frank saw dead cops.

"I'd like each of you to pull the case file before you for Detective Bobby Lane." After everyone appeared to have the case file in front of them, Smith laid out the facts.

"Bobby Lane was a fourteen-year man who had just earned his Detective Badge sixteen months prior to his murder on the night of June 11, 2021. Witnesses have Lane intervening in a scuffle on the corner of West Glenwood and Jefferson Street. According to our investigation, a fight started inside of Stone's Beer & Beverage Market at around 9:15 in the evening. The incident spilled out onto the sidewalk where Lane was standing. When trying to break up the fight, Lane was struck and knocked to the ground."

"Incensed, as his nose was reportedly bleeding, say those witnesses interviewed, Lane gave chase to two of the instigators outside the store. A foot pursuit ultimately turned into a car chase that led the two vehicles up and down the one-way streets of Brewerytown."

"Did he call it in?" Frank knew the answer to his question from the notes in front of him but wanted edification for the others around the table.

"I was getting to that." Looking perturbed, Smith nodded in Frank's direction. "Being off duty, our victim didn't have his walkie with him, and his cell phone was found on the sidewalk in front of Stone's Beer & Beverage, presumably dropped during the scuffle."

"His name was Bobby Lane." Frank continued perusing the file.

"Excuse me?" asked Smith, looking directly at Frank, again perturbed.

Frank looked over at Smith with little expression and responded, "You referred to our fallen brother as 'victim.' I was merely reminding everyone around the table that his name was Bobby Lane."

"Yes. Of course." Smith and everyone at the table could now see the pissing contest was underway.

Denny Patel looked over to his colleague Sharma and conveyed a look that told her he didn't want to be there.

In an effort to preserve the career of her most accomplished detective, Beatrice Jackson weighed in. "What was he thinking entering into a car chase without a means to call it in?"

All around the table nodded in agreement except for Smith, whose callous gaze was fixed on Frank, who continued to read through the file, seemingly unconcerned with what Smith felt about his comment.

Bones mused aloud that Lane may have entered the pursuit, unaware he'd lost his phone.

"Yes. As it turned out, the car, reportedly with one a male and a female passenger, screwed up and turned down a one-way street," Smith referenced his notes. "It was West Harper Street. There's a map with the chase route highlighted in your file."

The group found and studied the map.

"Oh, yeah. Would you look at that?" said Walker-Jones, now donning her reading glasses. They messed up when they made that turn."

"Or, it was planned?" Without looking up, Frank softly questioned the intentions of the perpetrators. Several at the table looked in his direction, wondering if he knew more than they did.

Smith looked agitated by Frank's utterance but continued. Pointing to his photo of the dead-end street, Smith said, "You'll see a carport here," he pointed again, "and a garage here without a garage door."

The group studied the images.

"Well, what we can surmise based on very little eyewitness testimony.... a guy half a block away, likely drunk or getting there, said he saw Lane's vehicle drive down to the end of the alley/street looking for a car that wasn't there. When he attempted a three-point turn to get out of there, a car, presumably the one he was following, backed out of the doorless garage, blocking our victim," Smith quickly cleared his throat and said, "Blocking Lane in."

Smith continued. "Lane laid on his horn, likely not thinking it was the car that he'd been chasing...."

"Why do we believe that to be the case, Captain," asked Bones.

"Because it was a dark alley, he would have been looking out his side or rearview mirror, and backing lights aren't as bright as headlights. Perhaps the perp car was less recognizable to him."

"As for what happened next…. We have plenty of eyewitness testimony for the events that led to Lane's death. After laying on his horn repeatedly for what witnesses say was ten to thirty seconds, half the neighborhood was either outside to investigate or looking out their windows. The shooting was witnessed by at least six people who all said the same thing…."

The group sat captivated by the accounting of the facts.

"The passenger of the perp car exited the vehicle and began to approach Lane's driver's side. At that moment, Lane made the fateful decision to exit his car, gun in hand, and before he could raise his city-issued Glock, took three to the chest."

"My God." Jackson was mortified, her hand covering her mouth.

"Description of the shooter?" Frank looked up at Smith.

"Gray hoodie, hood pulled over the head. White male with a slim build. Baggy jeans…." offered Smith. "Witnesses say the guy looked homeless."

Frank's memory went to the homeless man near the Mad River Bar. "What about a plate number on the perp car?"

"Yes," said Smith, "As you can probably surmise, it had been reported stolen an hour before. Also, our shooter picked up Lane's gun and took it with him."

The group, curious about the details of the second cop killed, again perused the file. All were startled when Justin Smith slammed a single Scrabble tile onto the table.

"When Forensics processed the scene, they found this on the ground where witnesses say Lane's gun was picked up by his killer." Lying face up on the table was the letter H.

"First letter of the street address." Frank stole Smith's thunder.

"Yes, Detective Collazo. And just how might you be privy to that little-known fact?" Smith seemed bothered by Frank's utterance.

"The word is out on the street, Captain Smith. Nothing stays quiet for long in this department." Frank finally showed some emotion. "When a cop dies in the street, his brothers...." he made eye contact with the three females at the table, "....and his sisters take notice. Additionally, it was all over the news for weeks."

"Yes, of course," Smith huffed. "For everyone's edification, your brother in blue was murdered at 2898 West Harper Street."

"I was there this morning," Frank addressed the group, turning away from Smith and Caffey.

"Oh?" Jackson was curious. "Was that the little errand you had to run, Frank?"

"It was one of five errands, Captain." Frank was stoic.

"Why were you there, Detective Collazo?" Jonathan Caffey finally weighed in.

"You brought me here today for a reason, Inspector. I wanted to prepare myself for today's discussion...." Frank paused. "And.... I was curious."

Frank continued to the displeasure of Smith. "You see, folks, that little Scrabble piece that Captain Smith slammed down on the table a moment ago, like Bones over here." Frank motioned to his right, "Robert David Lane was a fourteen-year veteran, and I wanted to better understand his death."

"That's good initiative, Detective." Caffey was always impressed with Frank. Captain Justin Smith, on the other hand, again felt insulted.

"There's one more thing, though...." Frank looked over the file. "I spoke to a man this morning who witnessed Lane's death, and he told me something that doesn't appear here in the file."

"And what exactly is that, Collazo?" Justin Smith continued to feel upstaged by Frank.

"The killers knew their victim." Frank closed the file in his hand.

Smith's eyes went wide as audible gasps were heard around the table, everyone shuffling through the case details, looking for validation of Frank's claim.

"What are you talking about, Collazo?!" Smith was visibly angry.

"Yes, what are you talking about, Frank," asked an alarmed Inspector Caffey.

"This morning, at 8 o'clock, I spoke to a man named Dale Carnessa. He lives at 2898 West Harper Street. He told me that after the three shots rang out and Lane hit the ground, the killer said, 'Take that, Detective Lane.' The killer knew his victim."

Caffey was outraged, looking sternly at Smith. "Now's a good time to take a break," Caffey ordered. "Why don't we all stretch our legs and grab a coffee? Be back here in twenty minutes." Caffey then stood to Smith's surprise.

As the group stood and headed for the door, Caffey was ready to chastise Justin Smith when Smith asked Frank to stay behind for a moment. "Inspector Caffey, would you mind if I spoke to Frank alone for a moment?"

"For a brief moment only, Captain." Caffey furrowed his brow. "But after that, you and I will have a side meeting in the next room."

Caffey knew Smith was humiliated by Frank's discovery, but he didn't think Frank was out of line for a second, and his face showed it.

After the room cleared, Smith invited Frank to take a seat, but he declined.

"Thank you, Captain Smith, but I'll stand. I don't particularly like sitting for long stretches. It dulls the senses."

"That's fine, Collazo. Stand then." Smith looked perturbed, as if he didn't know how to handle Frank's surprise disclosure.

Frank looked at Smith as if to say, 'Whatta ya need?'

"I want you to know something, Collazo." Smith puffed his chest, which didn't measure up compared to Frank's.

"What's that, Captain?" Frank's gut was right. Captain Justin Smith was an insecure prick.

"I don't like you. You're a hero, and heroes often die in the line of duty and often take their brothers down with them."

"Kind of like my father, Captain?" Frank's breathing was subtle, while Smith was nearly panting.

"Exactly like your father. He was a hero. A dead hero, as they often are, and I didn't like him either."

"Like father like son, then?" Frank was calm and cool when others might have already taken a swing at Smith.

"That's right, Collazo." Smith was now red-faced. "A loose cannon like you will never make it to retirement age. You'd much rather go out on a stretcher than a wheelchair."

"I don't need a pin on my chest or a pension to know my worth, Captain. My worth comes from how many people I save, not by how many people report up to me."

"Lives saved, huh?" Smith got up in Frank's face. "That's funny coming from a man whose suspects never see the inside of a courtroom," he huffed.

"You're a murderer, Collazo. A vigilante disguised in blue and hiding behind a shield. You're a disgrace to this department and should be wearing prison orange and not hailed as a hero." Smith swished around the saliva in his mouth, wanting to spit it in Frank's direction.

"When you come eye to eye with evil...." Frank paused. "It's best to put it down like a rabid dog."

"Were the Clark family rabid dogs, Detective?"

The last thing Justin Smith saw before hitting the floor was Frank's eyes go red. After picking himself up and wiping the blood from his mouth, Justin Smith dismissed Frank Collazo. "Leave now, you son-of-a-bitch, or I'll have your badge!"

"It'd be my pleasure, sir. Besides, you can't get much done sitting around a table. My job is out on the streets catching the bad guys."

"You mean killing the bad guys." Holding his chin and watching Frank collect his things and head for the door, Smith yelled, "Prodigal Son, my ass!"

Frank turned to Smith, smiled, and said, "Oorah!"

Later, sitting in his car in the underground parking garage, he turned his rearview mirror toward his face. Staring into the eyes of Salvatore Collazo, Frank knew his fate was, and always had been, tied to that of his father.

Frank knew that the universe was busy connecting the dots of his life. He knew the resurrection of FalconClaw would harken old memories, old stories and shake the graves of the long and not-so-long-ago dead and buried allies, adversaries, and family members.

Detective Frank Collazo was resolute. He would face down the ghosts that wanted him dead. On his side would be the ghosts that armed him with the wisdom and strength to walk the line but never become the very monster he was trying to kill. Against him would be the ghosts that had haunted him since 1992. They were the very monsters he was born to kill.

It was good versus evil, and Frank knew whose side he was on.

Was he, in fact, the Prodigal Son? Frank wasn't even sure what that meant. What he was sure of, though, was that he would head north to see Penny.

Chapter 10 – Heredity

The telephone inside a house could be heard ringing from the driveway of 969 Trent Road in the Fairview section of Camden, New Jersey. Playing outside was a seven-year-old boy named Talon Grayson.

It was October of 2000, and little Talon finally found a home he thought he could live in forever and a set of parents he believed loved him unconditionally. Talon was on his fifth foster family in as many years after his birth mother died of an overdose when he was only three.

Talon, or Grayson, he answered to both, had a mean streak in him, and it caused four sets of foster parents before the Steineckers to surrender him back into the foster care system and at the mercy of the state.

Every child deserves to belong. That's the motto of the New Jersey Department of Children and Families, and the Steineckers believed wholeheartedly in the catchphrase and had served as a foster family for more than a decade.

Unable to have children of their own, the Steineckers had fostered no less than eleven children in ten years, coming close to adopting two of them during that time. However, things didn't work out as someone from the children's respective families always came to claim them.

Children from DCF weren't perfect, as many suffered emotionally from the scars left by a parent abandoning them or the death of a parent, and then the subsequent inability of the extended family to take them in. Many had suffered physical or psychological abuse at the hands of their birth or foster parents, or both, and Talon Grayson was one of those children.

Delores and George Steinecker were both thirty-five years old and were up for the challenge. They seemed to genuinely like Talon and felt he could grow into a fine boy with more tutelage and love. However, they had seen the dark side of the boy twice. Once, when he had badly beaten a much smaller boy in school just two months after taking him in. The other time, Talon had burned the stuffed animals left by other foster kids the Steineckers had cared for previously. The fire department even had to be called out as the tree branches hanging overhead in the home's backyard caught fire.

On both occasions, Delores and George made an exception and forgave him, blaming the aggression on a cry for help from the little boy. What they didn't know, however, was the lineage or heredity of the child. They'd made it clear to DCF that they were ready to finally adopt but needed to know more about the parents of Talon to better access possible hereditary traits, such as family medical history, extended family information, and place of birth. They just needed to know more about the boy named Talon Grayson.

The month prior, the Steineckers applied with DCF to obtain all birth records, medical history, and birth parents' names. However, they didn't know that they would receive that information today.

Delores Steinecker wiped her hands clean of the Saturday morning breakfast mess as the phone rang and yelled out to George, "I'll get it, Honey!"

"Hello," she answered in a pleasant voice. "This is Delores."

"Mrs. Steinecker. Hi, it's Carolyn McHale from Children and Family Services."

"Oh, hi Carolyn!" Knowing her office was closed, Delores wasn't sure why McHale would call on a Saturday. "Is everything all right?" Delores did a doubletake of the oversized calendar hanging on the wall in the kitchen, making sure that it was, in fact, Saturday.

"Well," McHale nervously paused, "If you recall.... You and George applied for birth records and medical history for Talon."

"Oh, my! Yes! Of course!" Delores was overjoyed. "Is that why you're calling? What a pleasant surprise hearing from you on a Saturday."

"Yes. That is why I'm calling Mrs. Steinecker." Again, Carolyn McHale seemed anxious, but Delores Steinecker couldn't detect McHale's tone due to her elation.

"George!" Delores called out to her husband, who was upstairs getting ready.

George Steinecker was a sanitation worker and was preparing for his big day. He had planned to take Talon to a local landfill to show the boy where trash went after it was picked up off the curb. After that, he would take the young boy to the truck yard where all the trash trucks were parked and let him sit inside of one. Then, he would take Talon to the Dairy Queen, where the boy would enjoy anything he wanted. George was excited, as Talon was the first foster child in his care that he actually wanted to take to his place of work.

"What is it, Honey?!"

"It's Carolyn McHale from DCF, and she's got news about Talon."

"Mrs. Steinecker...." McHale tried to regain Delores's attention.

George quickly made his way down the stairs of the tiny two-bedroom house and wore an oversized smile, now standing before his wife.

Outside, Talon heard his foster mom yell for George and thought he heard Delores say, DCF. Talon, however, didn't rush into the house, as his excitement was muted. Little Talon had been disappointed time after time, family after family, for every year of his brief seven-plus year existence. Instead, he played with his Tonka dump truck and tried not to listen.

Talon had always tried hard to remember his mother, who had died when he was barely three years old. Every night he'd stare at the ceiling, trying to jog his memories of her. All he could ever muster was the memory of bad teeth and bad breath. He was sure of it; his real mother had bad teeth. That was all, though.

Back inside, Delores couldn't contain her excitement. Covering the mouthpiece, she excitedly whispered to George, "This is it. Talon's going to have a permanent home, and we'll finally have a son."

George encouraged his wife to resume the call. Delores wanted to hear everything, wanting to savor every word from McHale. This was a big day for her and George, and she planned to remember it for the rest of her life.

"I'm so sorry, Carolyn." Delores had to catch her breath. Regaining her composure, she inhaled deeply and said, "Okay, so tell us everything."

"Well, Mrs. Steinecker," McHale paused. "I'm afraid the news I have to share with you may be a bit unsettling."

"Oh, dear." Delores's face sagged, and she placed her left hand over her heart. "Is there something in his family's medical history we should be concerned about?" She looked over at George, who had now moved closer to his wife in an effort to listen in on the conversation.

"I'm afraid that's not it, Mrs. Steinecker. It's...." McHale couldn't bring herself to share the news.

"What is it, Carolyn?!" Delores Steinecker was visibly upset and began to grow impatient.

"Well, you see.... it's about Talon's birth parents."

"What about them? Are they dead?"

"Well, yes.... They are both deceased, but it's just that...."

"Oh, I see." Delores looked at her husband.

"It's about Talon's birth father." McHale began to sound emotional.

"What is it?!" demanded Delores.

"Well, I'm afraid he's someone you may have heard of."

"Go on...." Delores felt ill.

With the next words shared by Carolyn McHale, Delores Steinecker let out a gasp followed by a wail. Little Talon heard his foster mother sobbing in the kitchen and knew he had done something wrong like all the other times. Something that he knew nothing about and wouldn't for another ten years.

The next day, a car with a state-issued license plate pulled into the driveway of 969 Trent Road. Standing in the driveway, eager to return the child to DCF, was George Steinecker. Sobbing from the upstairs bedroom window, which looked down over the driveway, was Delores Steinecker.

The couple would never again take in a foster child and never conceive a child of their own. Tragically, in April 2021, the Steineckers were killed in a home invasion. George was stabbed to death while Delores was strangled with a phone cord taken from the kitchen telephone. The killers reportedly left their DNA in the home on two cups from a local Dairy Queen. The DNA was sent to CODIS but did not match any DNA on the national registry.

Over the next decade, after being removed from the Steinecker home, Talon Grayson would move through the foster care system and live in another twelve homes. At the age of thirteen, he was charged and convicted of arson after setting fire to his middle school. After spending six months in juvenile detention, he was convicted of armed robbery with a knife and locked away for another six months. The list of offenses grew, and by the time he'd reached adulthood, he had spent nearly as much time in juvenile lockup as his father had done by the same age. He was a chip off the old block and would soon find out who his father really was.

At the age of eighteen, the state finally released Talon's birth certificate to him, and he would finally learn why no one wanted him. He would finally know why he was viewed as a pariah, a misfit, an unholy child, and why he always felt different. Why he always felt evil.

Less than one year later, after being dishonorably discharged from the Army after serving only six months, Talon returned home and finally crossed the Delaware River for good. Now, homeless in Philadelphia, he felt no brotherly love from the city that promised it. Living under bridges, train cars, barges on the river, and old deserted churches, Talon learned to fight, sell drugs, burglarize homes, knock over liquor stores, and steal cars. Now at nineteen, Talon met someone who was just like him. The two were the same age, shared the same background, had the same likes and disinterests, and the same sexual appetite. The two were peas in a pod and even looked and dressed alike.

Talon and his new girlfriend Genesis Harper began a crime spree that included knocking over Seven-Elevens and gas stations, which would go on for years. The two lovers would spend every hour of every day talking to each other but always refrained from talking about their dead parents. They would only share that Genesis's mother was a prostitute who was killed by her pimp and that Talon's mother died of an accidental overdose when he was only three. Perhaps the two never spoke of their fathers because each had never met the man. They only admitted to each other that their father was in prison most of their childhood and that he was now dead. Just another thing the two had in common.

The vile pair each had a secret they would keep from each other for another eight years. During that time, the two would separate for months at a time until they would run across each other, standing around a Burn Barrel with other junkies and homeless people. Seeing each other again would rekindle their thirst for debauchery and a life of crime. The two often referred to themselves as natural-born killers, not because of the movie starring Woody Harrelson and Juliette Lewis but because of the real-life characters on which the movie was based.

In 1958, a young Lincoln, Nebraska couple embarked on a murder spree that would shock the country. Charles Starkweather, twenty, and fifteen-year-old Caril Ann Fugate went on a murder spree that claimed eleven victims in 1958. However, Starkweather killed his first victim on December 1, 1957, a grocery store clerk.

Then, on January 21, 1958, the two walked into Fugate's home and murdered her stepfather, mother, and two-year-old stepsister.

Then on January 27, the raging maniacs killed a seventy-two-year-old man and his dog. Just hours later, they murdered a young couple, ages sixteen and seventeen.

Finally, on January 28, the couple entered a household, shot the forty-seven-year-old husband, and then stabbed to death his forty-six-year-old wife and fifty-one-year-old housekeeper.

Later that day, they shot and killed their final victim when stealing a car. After being chased by a nearby police officer, the two were shot at while in the vehicle, with Starkweather being struck. Believing that he was mortally wounded, he surrendered.

The following year Starkweather was executed in the electric chair while Fugate received a life sentence that was eventually commuted. She served only seventeen years in prison and is still alive today.

Their weapons of choice: a .22 caliber rifle, a shotgun, a handgun, and various knives.

Talon and his lover Genesis often fantasized about going on a killing spree of their own but always delayed their murderous obsession, reasoning that they had no logical victims to target. That would change in January 2021 when the two finally confessed their long-held secret.

Chapter 11 – No Absolution

After Frank exited the parking garage, he headed north. Calling Penny to let her know he was on his way to see her; he again got her voicemail. *What's wrong with Penny?* He wondered. Did the accident change her, or did it change him? *Why isn't Bonnie talking? Is she still in shock from the accident?* He was worried for his family.

Frank wouldn't push the issue, though, if he were able to see Penny today. He just wanted to see her face and to hold her hand. Whatever was causing Penny to hold back, Frank knew that he was somehow to blame. Kind of like he blamed himself after his father died. Perhaps if he were a better son, his father would have had more reasons not to put his job first.

As Frank drove north, through a city he barely recognized, he wondered what he would say to Penny. He decided to only share case details, not wanting to push her away any further. During his last meeting with her, Frank detected that she wanted to help. He believed Penny missed being a cop deep down inside and was glad to assist him in any way she could. Penny's instincts were always better than Frank's, and he would put them to work on the case.

Turning right off Morton and onto East Locust Avenue, Frank's nerves were shot. *Is she even home?* He asked himself. The drive reminded Frank of when he'd first picked up Douglas Cantrell at the airport back in 2019. His mind began to race when he remembered the date, May 14. It was exactly one year before Penny's car accident. Today, however, was November 2, 2021, and he thought that time was passing too fast. Some days, though, without mercy, passed far too slowly for Frank's fragile psychological state.

The coincidence further rattled Frank. He was growing wary of coincidences and circumstances fitting together like puzzle pieces with dates aligning; all of it rattled him. What he was really afraid of, though, was the picture he would see once the final puzzle piece fell into place. Was his life a simple roll of the dice? And if it was, would it come up snake eyes?

Now sitting in the driveway, Frank couldn't find the courage to leave his car. Before exiting, he would call his friend. On the second ring, Cantrell would answer.

"Frank? Is that you?"

"Hey, Doug. You got a second?" Frank's emotions were scattered. He recalled that it was on the night of May 14, 2019, that he finally confided in his friend that he saw ghosts.

"Of course I do. What's happening with the case since we last spoke?"

"Do you remember my new partner, Bones?"

"Yes, I do."

"Well, after the murder at the Cope House, the brass down at Race Street decided to include the 39th in the city-wide investigation because my name was left at the scene. Bones and I are now officially part of the investigation."

"That's good. So, what happens next?"

"Well, we had a meeting down there this morning, and it didn't go well." Frank lamented.

"Oh? How so, Frank?"

"Well, the special investigator heading up the case...."

"Is that the Smith guy I keep seeing on the news giving updates?"

"Yeah, that's him," said Frank.

"Go on."

"Well, let's just say.... He doesn't like me very much. Less after what happened today."

"That sounds pretty ominous, Frank. You wanna tell me what happened down there?"

"That son of a bitch brought up my father...."

"Oh, Jesus...." Cantrell's sigh could be heard through the phone.

"It wasn't just that, though," Frank grimaced. "The prick brought up Willard Clark and his family."

"I hope you let him have it, Frank!" Cantrell saw red. "Damned be the consequences!" Douglas Cantrell was not a violent man but understood the devastating impact the deaths of the Clark family had on Frank.

"I did, Doug," Frank paused. "He went down pretty hard. I'm surprised he got back up as quickly as he did."

"Man, oh man. What happened next?"

"He got up, rubbed his chin, and excused me for the remainder of the meeting."

"So, where are you now?"

Frank looked over to his right and saw the back steps of his childhood home. The steps sat empty as if a metaphor for how he felt.

"I'm at Penny's."

"Okay?" Cantrell treaded lightly, respecting Frank's wishes not to discuss her or Bonnie. "Are you wondering if getting out and visiting her is okay?"

Frank was meek. "Yes. I'm afraid she's not there."

"She's there, Frank. You need to hang up the phone and go talk to her."

"You think so?"

"Of course. I'm not even sure why you're on the phone with me right now."

Frank looked back over to the steps and was surprised to see a smiling Penny looking in his direction.

Breathless, he stuttered, "Doug, I gotta go! Penny's here!"

Frank ended the call without waiting for Cantrell's reply and exited the Dodge. Shyly, he walked around the front of the car and nervously onto the sidewalk leading to the back porch, Penny's gaze never escaping his.

"There's my guy." Penny smiled and slid over to her right, tapping the top of the stairs to her left, inviting Frank to sit beside her.

"Hey, Pen. How are you?" Frank couldn't hide his nerves. "Is everything okay?"

"Of course," Penny smiled. "Bonnie and I are doing good. We miss you, though."

"My God." Frank was caught between tears and joy. The last time he saw Penny, it was dark out, but now, in broad daylight, he could see her every feature and radiant glow. The last time he'd seen that glow was when she was pregnant with Bonnie. "Penny, you look so good. I don't know what to say."

"I wish I could say the same about you." Penny flashed a witty smile. "What's weighing you down, Frankie Boy?" she grinned. "Who'd you punch out this time?"

"How'd you know?" Frank looked puzzled, shaking his head.

"Because," said Penny. "The last time I saw that look on your face was right after you punched Kyle Wade. And besides," she looked down at his hand now in hers, "your hand is all swollen. Look at this thing." Penny placed her other hand over Frank's.

When she did, Frank's hand's throbbing pain magically disappeared.

Embarrassingly, Frank admitted what had happened downtown and was hoping for advice on what his next steps should be.

"Wow!" Penny's brows were raised, almost with pride. "Well, first off, don't be hitting anyone else," she offered. "You need to call the guy and apologize. You need to be on this case, Frankie. This case needs you, and you need it."

Frank looked exasperated. "But, Penny, he brought up the Clark deaths," Frank paused. "I don't think I'll be making that call."

"You make the call, Frankie. Make that call." Penny rubbed his hand. "Then you get your butt back to the 39th and find out what was discussed after you were excused."

Frank looked confused. Shaking his head, he said, "How did you know I was asked to leave the meeting?"

Penny blushed, "Come on. No way the guy let you stay after that."

"No, you're right. Of course, I got excused." Frank still seemed a little perplexed by her comments.

"Listen, I gotta get back in the house." Penny stood to Frank's dismay.

"So soon?" Frank's face sagged as he, too, rose to his feet.

"Yes, I have to take care of Bon-Bon."

"Um. Okay. Well, when can I see you again?" Frank kept thinking that every time he saw Penny would be the last.

"Whenever you need to," Penny smiled.

"So, tomorrow, then?"

"I would love that." Penny turned to walk into the house. "Oh, and Frank," she turned back toward him. "I have something that might help you in the case. It's in the car," she looked toward the garage.

Frank flashed a quizzical look. "What are you talking about?"

"Go into the garage and open the trunk. There's something there for you. I want you to have it."

Frank was confused. *What is she talking about?* He wondered. He couldn't imagine how anything in the car, leftover from the accident, could help him in the case.

As he stood there, lost, his phone rang. It was Bones. Swiping left, he ignored the call and looked back up at Penny, but she had gone back into the house. Staring at the back door, Frank was disheartened, but his curiosity caused him to look toward the detached garage. Now standing in front of the garage, he was almost afraid to raise its door.

After several minutes of fear and consternation, Frank reached into the Dodge, pushed the garage door opener on the rearview mirror, and waited.

As the door opened, he stood tentatively, fearing what he might find inside. Not because Penny pointed him in that direction but because of the memory of that day. The Honda Accord was sacred to him, but Frank wasn't sure why.

Seeing the Accord, Frank's vision grew dim. It was suddenly storming outside, thunderclaps abound as the rain fell in sheets, and somehow, he was in the Dodge racing passed Magnolia and then taking a hard left onto Musgrave, fishtailing wildly, nearly hitting a car as it was entering the tiny intersection. Now, on Belfield, he took a right on Washington Lane, heading right for the fifty-five-acre Awbury Arboretum estate.

Frozen in fear, still standing at the rear of the Honda, Frank looked down at his hands and saw them clutching the Dodge's steering wheel. Through the deluge of rain and the maddening sound of flapping wiper blades, washing away his sanity, and unable to understand, Frank saw Calvin Murphy's 2006 Volvo making a right onto Chew Street and to his ultimate death. Frank screamed. He didn't know what was happening. Murphy died on Halloween, the accident was on May 14, and today was November 2. What was happening? Frank felt as if he was going mad.

Suddenly, another thunderclap jolted Frank back to 454 E. Locust Avenue and the Honda Accord sitting benignly in front of him, awaiting his inspection. Tentatively walking around to the driver's side, Frank hesitantly opened the car door. Grabbing the handle, he could almost feel Penny's hand on his. Opening the door and then popping the trunk, Frank walked to the rear of the car and slowly lifted it. Looking inside, he chuckled for a second, and then he cried. His tears drenching his smile, he saw five boxes of *Little Bites* crumb cakes strewn about.

As Frank surveyed the trunk and the littered mess from its contents being violently tossed about, he saw the Scrabble board. In addition to the game and crumb cakes were the other items Penny had picked up that day. Frank was confused and saw nothing that might help him in the Cop Killer case. Noticing something among the scattered solo plastic cups, paper plates, now old bags of potato chips, and soured cookie dough, scattered by the force of the collision and its impact, he noticed something peeking from beneath a gray Walmart bag. A random Scrabble piece that had somehow been separated from the others sat alone. Face down, he reached for the solitary piece, picked it up, and held it in his hand. Refusing to turn it over and reveal its embossed letter, he put the wooden tile in his pocket instead.

Thinking it was nothing, he thought of Penny and looked back toward the house. Just then, his phone rang. It was Bones again. This time he answered.

"Bones, what's up?"

"What's up?!" Bones was jacked up on adrenaline. "You tell me, Maestro! You knocked that fucker out, didn't you?!"

"Maestro? What in the hell are you talking about?" Frank was still in a fog from moments earlier.

"You know," said Bones. "Leader of the band, the master, the teacher. You're all of it! And you're my new idol."

"I thought I was already your idol." Frank tried to joke with his partner. He hoped levity would help clear his head from the raging storm drowning his psyche and bring him back around.

"Frank, did you really hit him?"

"A little...." Frank was trying to downplay the event.

"A little?! Frank, you should've seen the guy's face." Bones was laughing through the phone. "I picked up on all his not-so-subtle jabs at you. That guy's full of shit, too. He never cared about your dad or what happened back in '92." Bones conveyed empathy. "Was that it? Did he say something about your father?" asked Bones. "Is that what pushed you over the edge?"

"Nah," Frank paused. "He brought up the Clark family deaths."

"No shit?!" Bones was shocked. "He's lucky he didn't go up to Manayunk in a body bag."

"So, how'd it go after I left? What did you learn?"

"That's why I'm calling. After the meeting, the Captain pulled Denny and me aside and asked us to join her at the 39th for a secondary meeting."

"A secondary meeting?" Frank was curious. "About the case? A meeting with who?"

"With you, dumbass," Bones smirked. "Where's your head, Bro? Cap wants you over here now."

Frank shook his head, not wanting to be a cop at that moment. Catching himself, he remembered Penny saying, 'You need to be on this case. This case needs you....' she told him.

"Fine. I'll come in." Frank reluctantly agreed to meet Bones and the others back at the 39th and to be briefed on the remaining victims in the case. And, as Frank looked down in his palm, to learn what other Scrabble letters they'd had.

As Frank began to back out of the driveway, he looked over to the back porch, hoping he might see Penny there. He didn't. Then, just before checking his rearview mirror to back out, something in the backyard caught his attention. Frank's overwrought guilt stopped the car, and there, standing alone, looking lost, was eleven-year-old Isak.

Sitting there, staring, he remembered that Justin Smith had called him a murderer, and then he remembered the night he took Isak Cameron's life. Frank often felt guilty about Cameron's death but knew little Isak wished for it.

Now on the road heading south to East Falls, Frank hoped that one day he might find some absolution from his guilt. Or would he suffer through eternity, receiving none?

Chapter 12 – Puzzle Pieces

A short while later, Frank turned onto Schuyler Street and saw Bones leaning against his car. He'd been waiting there for Frank. Frank parked the Dodge next to Bones' Interceptor and got out. Bones walked over to Frank to shake his hand. Frank's partner, being a former fighter, admired Frank for sticking up for himself under the bright glare reflecting off the Race Street brass.

"My boy, Frank!" Bones was all smiles.

"Calm down, Partner. It wasn't that big of a deal." Again, Frank was modest and wasn't exactly proud of his actions.

"Well, clearly, you left before the swelling started. That self-righteous prick could barely talk after you left. Caffey had to cut the meeting short."

"No shit?" Frank winced. He knew Caffey liked him and would be more upset with an abbreviated meeting than for defending his honor against a bully like Smith.

"Frank, you should've heard Caffey giving it to Smith in the adjacent room. He was screaming as if no one could hear him."

"Could you make out what they were saying?"

"Not *THEY*, him. It was all Caffey." Bones recounted what had happened. "We all heard enough to know that he blamed Caffey and not you for the altercation."

"So, how's Jackson feeling right now?"

"She hates the prick, too. We all saw through his BS." Like Frank, Bones had a small circle of friends, and Frank was in that circle. He would gladly get in a brawl with anyone or any number of people that messed with those closest to him.

"So, how's it gonna go up there, ya think?"

"I'm sure she'll say all the *Captain* stuff that the Department requires of her, but you need to know that she's in your corner."

"Makes sense." Frank pursed his lips and said, "Well, let's get to it then."

Immediately upon entering the district house, Frank heard a "Yo, Rocky!" coming from the direction of his Ops Supervisor, Sergeant Tommy McLaughlin, who looked back at Frank pretending to shadowbox.

"Really?" Frank shook his head. "You had to tell Tommy?"

Bones played dumb before eventually saying, "What can I say? I'm proud of my partner."

"Yeah, yeah." Frank gave him a pass.

Now upstairs, Frank and Bones walked into the Detective Room where Jackson and Denny Patel were sitting and talking at an eight-foot conference table outside of the smaller interview rooms A & B. Every time Frank looked over at Interview Room B, he thought of Kyle Wade and how, without a conscience, tried to mislead him and Cantrell as to the facts of the Cameron twins birth records. Frank hadn't stepped foot inside IRB since.

Upon seeing Frank arrive, Jackson stood and motioned for him to follow her, saying nothing as she passed him on the way to the door. Once in the hallway, Jackson pulled Frank into another room that was used for storage.

"Get in here, Collazo."

"Yes, Captain."

Squaring herself with Frank, indicating that she meant business, Jackson got to the point with her best detective. "Listen to me very carefully.... For the record, what you did this morning is grounds for termination. Hell, you could've even been arrested for assault. I'd like to say I don't know what got into you, but I can't." Jackson exhaled heavily. "I've known you long enough to know that you're a loose cannon and perhaps need some more time off."

"Captain, listen...."

"I'm not done talking yet!" Jackson put her foot down. "You compromised not only your job this morning but my reputation and that of the 39th." She shook her head in frustration.

"Captain, that prick called me a murderer and trivialized the Clark family deaths to serve his selfish ego. That was a line that should've never been crossed." Frank was adamant as he stared down his captain. "If I had to do it all over again, I would've hit him harder."

"Are you finished, Detective?"

"Yeah. I'm finished." Frank was annoyed.

"Now that I've said what I had to say, let me go off the record for a second." Jackson turned to make sure the door was closed all the way. "I wish you had hit that smug SOB harder. You've given up more for this city and this department than anyone could ever ask of anyone. You and Penny personally rid the streets of two of those twin terrors, saving untold lives while doing so. That arrogant piece of shit should've bled more. He needs to hit his knees and pray harder for more cops like you."

And Penny, he thought. Looking at Jackson, he nodded in appreciation. "Thanks, Cap."

"Don't *Thanks, Cap*, me. And don't do it again," Jackson was serious. "I need you on this case, Frank. And this case needs you."

Frank froze momentarily, hearing Penny's words from an hour earlier echo in those of his Captain. Shaking it off, he said, "I got it, Cap."

"Good. Now, let's get in there and get you brought up to speed on what you missed this morning."

As the two returned to the Detective Room, Jackson asked Frank, "How's your hand doing?"

Frank looked down at his swollen hand, examining both sides, and said, "Strangely, it doesn't even hurt. But I wished I'd broken it on that motherfucker."

"Me, too," Jackson grinned and opened the door for her best chance at getting the Cop Killers off the street.

"Okay, Bones, Denny, let's lay it out for the 39th's own Italian Stallion, Rocky Balboa!" Jackson made it clear that Frank would be hearing that joke for many months to come. And that he'd earned every bit of the harassment that he'd have to endure.

"Yo, Adrian!" yelled someone from the back of the room. "Hey, Paulie!" yelled another. As other detectives laughed and piled on, jeers could be heard coming from around the room.

As Frank sat down beside his partner, Bones whispered, "How'd it go in there?"

Frank's eyes went wide as he shook his head. "Not gonna lie, but it was brutal in there." He exhaled fully and added, "I mean, she's joking now...." he whispered under his breath, "....but she really let me have it."

"No shit," Bones looked surprised.

"Okay, Bones, lay it out for us, and then Denny will fill in the science," said Jackson.

Bones handed Frank the same accordion folder that he'd been handed earlier that morning.

"All right, Frank. We're gonna continue where we left off this morning." Bones pulled the file on Bobby Lane and looked over to Denny.

"Okay. So, as we discussed today...." Denny opened a separate file and reviewed aloud the extent of the wounds. "The slugs recovered from Lane's body reveal he was killed with a .38 caliber handgun. Likely a snub-nose revolver...."

"Close range. The science and eyewitness testimony corroborates that fact. Nothing was left at the scene to connect a suspect to the case, though." explained Patel.

"No fancy bullets?" asked Frank. "No hollow tips?"

"No. In fact, none of these murders, as we'll go on to discuss, include anything that would indicate any form of sophistication or exotic planning or methods."

"So, low-life scumbags are doing the killings?" Frank looked at Denny Patel and the others.

"So far, that's what it seems."

"Okay, Bones," prodded Jackson. "Onto our next victim."

Bones pulled another file and said, "Danny Westerfield, twenty-eight years old, is our second victim. He was a rookie cop, first on scene to a reported hold up at Jimenez Grocery located at Alleghany West & 35th, just one block east of Laurel Hill Park."

"July, right?" asked Frank, looking through the information he had. He also took note of the address and scribbled the letter A down on a nearby legal pad.

"Yep," said Bones. "July 15. It was a Thursday night at around 11:15 pm."

"So, how'd it go down?"

"Yeah, so Westerfield arrives, hangs back waiting for back-up, and is approached by the bystander that supposedly called it in."

"Except he wasn't just a bystander, was he?" Frank was guessing.

Bones shook his head, indicating that Frank was correct. "When Westerfield called in his location, he was told to standby and not enter until back-up arrived, and he told his supervisor that he was collecting some information from a witness out on the street who claims to have called it in." Bones read from his notes captured earlier in the day down on Race Street.

"The last thing the supervisor heard from Westerfield before the sound of a single gunshot was, 'Looks like a possible hostage situation.' That was it."

Denny spoke back up. "Westerfield was shot in the back of the head at close range with a .40 caliber handgun. He was dead before he hit the ground."

Frank shook his head, knowing what a .40 caliber bullet could do to a human skull. His mind flashed back to Isak Cameron and the attic of the old Sharpless House before asking, "Anyone get a description of the guy?"

"No one saw him pull the trigger, but according to two eyewitnesses, what appeared to be a white male wearing a gray hoodie fled the scene west into Laurel Hill Park and then just disappeared."

"Hoodie, huh?" Frank's pencil clawed away at his notepad. "Just like the Lane murder." He also reflected momentarily on the vagrant asking him for money out on the street near his apartment the night before.

"It appears so," Jackson shook her head.

"Scrabble piece?"

Patel slid Frank a photograph that revealed a letter tile lying in the pool of blood around the victim's head.

Frank squinted, trying to see what letter it was, when Patel slid another picture with a close-up of the same image across the table to him.

"I'll be damned," Frank sat back and exhaled heavily. "The letter A." Pausing, he added. "So, without knowing anything else.... everyone investigating the homicides believes that the letters correlate with the street the victims were killed on, is that right?"

"One hundred percent." Jackson saw the look in Frank's eyes. "What're you thinking, Detective?"

"I agree that the letters represent the location of the murders. I'm just wondering why. Why drop Scrabble pieces at each scene? We already know where the cops died." Frank sat back in his chair and pondered his thoughts.

"Go ahead, Frank. Tell us what you're thinking. What are they trying to spell out for us?"

"It's a name, not a word." Frank was sure of it.

Denny Patel spoke up. "I'm not so sure, Frank."

"Why's that, Denny?"

"Bones, continue until all the letters are revealed," suggested Denny.

Bones referenced his notes again. "Okay, At the Lane crime scene, an H was found...."

"Okay," said Frank, scribbling. "That's Harper Street."

"Westerfield was killed on Allegany...."

"That's an A," Frank kept scribbling.

"The next murder was on August 8. It was a Sunday." Bones pulled the file of Dennis Cameron. "Cameron was an eight-year veteran, first on scene. Location, South Red...."

Frank heard August 8, an eight-year veteran, and the name Cameron, and everything went quiet in his head, and his vision went dark. On August 8, 1972, Donald Ewen Cameron, the mastermind behind MK Ultra, took his life by hanging. His suicide came after being exiled to his home country of Sweden by both the United States and Canada for his involvement in CIA-sanctioned mind-control experiments at FalconClaw in the late 1950s and early 1960s.

Then, two years later, on August 8, 1974, his son, John Ewen Cameron, unable to escape his involvement in the experiments, also died by suicide after being stripped of all his licenses to practice any type of medicine, anywhere.

Frank recounted the facts which were burned in his memory. Then, on August 8, 1990, Gregory Ewen Cameron, who changed his name to Gregory St. John to escape the sordid past of his father and older brother, took his life on his son's sixteenth birthday. That son? The Schuylkiller, born Getty Ewen Cameron, later changed to Cameron Ewen St. John. He was the older twin brother of Isak Cameron.

It was during Cameron St. John's birthday party that he found his father convulsing at the end of a rope. That event and the destruction of the Cameron legacy resulted in The Schuylkiller's thirst for revenge. The bloody reign finally came to an end on August 8, 2017, when Penny Bristow killed the monster.

The Cameron reign of terror in North Philly would be silenced for good on July 7, 2019, when Frank killed Isak Cameron in the attic of the William C. Sharpless house on Wayne Avenue and West Schoolhouse Lane, finally breaking the string of eights.

"Frank! You with us, Buddy!" Jackson snapped her fingers near Frank's face.

Bones and Patel looked mildly concerned at seeing Frank completely zone out while his eyes remained wide open.

After another snap of Jackson's fingers, Frank came back around and said, "Yeah.... August 8.... That can't be a coincidence. And the name," Frank paused. "Cameron. They knew their victim just like with Bobby Lane."

All those at the table hadn't made the connection of the name Cameron, the date of his murder on 8/8, or The Schuylkiller Case. The three sitting around Frank looked at each other and were convinced he was on to something.

"St. John." Jackson nodded her head and started taking notes of her own.

Like behind the Cope House, Frank was undeniably being drawn into the spider's web. Jackson hoped he wouldn't fall prey to the venomous killers who were stalking and killing Philly cops and who appeared to be on a course to kill the city's Prodigal Son.

"Go on, Bones. Continue." Jackson needed Frank's head clear for the next victim and where he was killed.

Bones again referenced his notes. "Location was...."

"Yeah, South Redfield." Frank was starting to get antsy. "I know. I was just at all of the crime scenes this morning. What I'd like to know is why Denny doesn't think it's a name?" Frank's eyes fell squarely on Patel, who nervously sat erect in his chair, preparing to defend his assertion.

"Um, well, yeah. So, with the most recent double murder down in the Dickinson Narrows on McClellan, and then on Halloween night at the Cope House on Awbury," said Denny, "that gives us five letters."

"Hang on a second," Frank reviewed his notes. "So these fuckers took a break in September. The killings were in June, July, and August, and then two in October. Nothing in September? Are we missing something?"

"Frank, the whole state would know if a Philly Cop was killed in September," said Jackson.

Frank agreed with a consolatory nod.

"Yeah, but let's not forget.... they got three of our guys in October." Jackson's eyes narrowed, wondering when they'd strike again.

"But how did they know their victim's names?" Bones thought aloud.

"Hang on, Bonesie." Frank cut his partner off and looked over to Denny. "Let's stay focused on the letters for now."

"Frank, you got the letters all lined up, man. You were there this morning. H-A-R-M and A," said Patel.

"Harm?" Frank looked anguished. "HARM A what?"

Everyone looked confused. "What are we missing, guys?" Frank wondered aloud, purposely not mentioning the letter tile in his pocket. He would hold that one close to his vest as he wasn't even sure it was relevant to the case. Additionally, he didn't know how he would explain its possible relevance to the others.

He again thought about September and how no cops had been killed that month. Could the letter tile in his pocket represent the first letter of a street name where another yet unidentified victim was killed?

Why did Penny lead him to the trunk? Why was that single-letter tile sitting alone, away from the others? Was it the tile that Penny wanted him to find? Frank couldn't be sure.

"One thing is for sure, though," said Denny. "The next Scrabble piece is coming, and we'll have another letter to work with."

With Patel's words, Frank reached under the table and felt the protruding tile in his pocket, tracing its outline with his finger. The tile was begging to get out, but Frank once again resisted.

"What weapon was used on Dennis Cameron?" Frank again looked at Patel.

"A .40 cal."

"Jesus Christ!" Frank was disgusted. "I got money Lane's gun was the murder weapon used."

"These fuckers are collecting city-issued guns along the way." Bones was heating up. "Killing cops with cop guns! That takes some balls, right there!"

"Did they get Westerfield's gun, too?" Frank flipped through the case files haphazardly.

"Yep. A Glock 9," said Jackson.

"I'll be damned." Frank shook his head in disbelief.

"All right," Bones was a bit more animated. Almost fidgety, he said, "The names? How in the hell could they have known their victims' names?"

While everyone racked their brains, Frank's chin dropped, and the three others noticed.

"Frank?" Jackson was making sure her boy didn't zone out again. "Whattaya got, Detective?"

Frank exhaled and half smiled. "The motherfuckers knew their victim's names because they knew their victims."

"What are you talking about, Frank?" Jackson wasn't following, and Patel looked a little puzzled as well.

Bones smiled with an aha look and said, "They knew their victims because they had once arrested them."

"Exactly." Frank nodded in his partner's direction.

Captain Beatrice Jackson had a look of dread on her face. "Do any of you realize how long it's gonna take to search the arrest records for every collar our victims ever made?"

"Easier than you think, Captain...."

"And how's that?" Jackson was skeptical. "Some of these guys likely had hundreds, if not a thousand plus collars in their careers."

Bones jumped back in, following Frank's lead.

"You start with the officer with the fewest arrests, and then you cross-reference those with the other lists."

Jackson was mildly impressed. "Rummaging through her notes, she said, "One of our victims was a rookie, right?"

"Two of 'em," said Frank.

"Westerfield and Ritchie," Bones blurted out.

"Boy, I see the two of you are rubbing off on each other." Jackson looked over at Patel as if she were a proud mother.

"She's right!" said Denny. "You two are a match made in heaven."

Everyone except Frank laughed out loud, followed by Jackson summoning two nearby detectives to do the legwork connecting the hundreds of dots that were common collars between the six victims.

Frank sat quietly, looking off into space. At that moment, he thought of Penny. He missed his partner, and he missed his love.

Moments later, as the group was preparing to leave, Frank pulled Jackson aside and had a request.

"This case needs Cantrell."

"You're reading my mind, Frank?" Jackson grinned. "You think the old-timer is up to it?"

"I think so." Frank returned her smile.

Chapter 13 – Indian Queen Lane

A week later, on Monday, November 8, at just after 8 pm, Frank, Bones, and Cantrell talked over their day with some beers at Billy Murphy's Irish Saloon. The three men sat at Frank and Penny's old table next to the only window in the place, facing the Conrad Street side of the building.

Murphy's was a favorite hangout of the cops from the 39th, and the locals, like Mike Murphy, the place's manager and son of the late Billy Murphy, loved it. Mike always joked, "It's the safest place in North Philly! You'd have to be crazy to commit a crime anywhere around here. The place is always crawling with cops."

Cantrell laughed, saying, "I'm just trying to figure out which of you would win in a fight. I mean, look at the size of your arms." Reaching over and squeezing Bones' left bicep, he said, "You see these things, Frank?" Cantrell seemed almost smitten with his new friend.

While Bones blushed, Frank nodded wide-eyed and said, "Yep, every single day, unfortunately." Smiling, he added, "Doug, for the record, Bones would destroy me. He'd put me six feet under in sixty seconds or less. That's why they call him Bones.

"Oh, come on, Frank. I wouldn't tussle with you. You outweigh me by at least ten to fifteen pounds and are taller." While Bones would back down from no one, he'd never mess with Frank. Bones knew he had the killer instinct inside the octagon, but he knew that Frank had the killer instinct in the streets. Literally.

"Taller?" Cantrell couldn't help himself. He was trying to make friends with Bones, and the alcohol was getting to him. "Frank, how tall are you?"

"Six foot three and then some."

"And how much do you weigh?"

"Two thirty-ish." Frank rolled his eyes and humored his tipsy friend.

"And you, Bones?"

"Six foot three, two-twenty." Bones raised his glass to Frank. Like I said, I ain't messing with Frank over there."

"Yeah-yeah, Bonesie," Frank was dismissive. "Whatever you say."

"I still got Bones in a fight." Cantrell shot Frank a wink, chiding his buddy.

"So, how'd the two of you meet, anyways?" Bones took another swig of his Heineken and was enjoying hearing the old man joke around with Frank. He felt like he was in the company of royalty and enjoyed being around the two legends. He also liked how Cantrell seemed to make Frank more relaxed.

Bones was seeing a side of Frank that he'd never seen before. He could see that Frank felt safe around Cantrell.... less scared, too. He also felt comfortable with the man Frank had always held in high regard. Bones wished his father could have been like Cantrell.

Frank, not much of a drinker these days, held his beer, mostly for show, smiled, and said, "Go ahead, Doug. Tell him how we met."

Cantrell, always the humble one, pretended he couldn't remember. Looking up and to his left, and after a couple 'ohs' and 'ums,' he said, "I've got it. Yep, it was....um...." Cantrell looked over to Frank and asked, "When was it, actually, Frank?"

"Ha-ha, Old Man. Quit messin' with the kid."

"All right. All right. I received an email from Frank in April 2017. He was mired in The Schuylkiller case.... from what I can remember, he hadn't made any progress in the case at all...." Cantrell maintained a straight face.

A smiling Bones looked over to Frank, who was rolling his eyes, listening to his friend purposely butcher the facts.

"Yes. As I recall," Cantrell rubbed his chin. "Your partner over here was hopelessly stuck and in need of some professional help. Being the right guy for the job, I thought I should lend the poor sap a hand."

"It wasn't long after that that I was down here speaking with all the detectives on the case."

"Wait, you guys only go back three and a half years? I would have thought it was more because you're so close."

"It feels like a lot more, huh, Doug?" Frank smiled at his friend.

Cantrell's eyes went wide. "Heck! Like twenty!" he joked with a deadpan face, further razzing his friend. Douglas Cantrell was happy to be back with Frank. Like all the other times he'd been to Philly, he'd wished it was under different circumstances.

Frank was happy his friend was back in town as the banter went back and forth. Frank needed Doug for more than just the case, and Doug knew it.

"In all seriousness, though," Bones wanted to know. "How does the relationship between the two of you work?"

"Frank's my boss, and I just comment on the things that he bounces off me."

"Not quite," Frank set down his beer. I would've been killed twice if it wasn't for this guy." Frank reached over and squeezed Cantrell's shoulder.

Just then, a young couple out for a stroll passed by the large window to Frank's left, startling him. He always sat on the side of the table that faced the intersection of Conrad and Indian Queen Lane. It helped his claustrophobia and kept his paranoia at bay when he could see those coming and going. Studying the couple, he recognized them as regulars of the saloon.

Seeing Bones look out at what caught his partner's eye, Frank looked over at him and was reminded that Bones was sitting in Penny's old chair. He was reminded of how much he missed his old partner. Of how much he missed Penny. The way she would keep him grounded and focused brought peace to his life. Without her, there was none. Letting out a random chuckle, Frank remembered how Penny would ball up sugar and straw wrappers and throw them at him. His mind wandered until his good friend returned Frank's shoulder squeeze with one of his own.

"Frank, here, is being modest, Bones. It was Frank the whole way," Cantrell proudly doted over his friend. "His instincts are good. I can't think of one misstep he made in either investigation."

"Doug, over here...." Frank pointed with his thumb. "....got me into the mind of the killers. He helped me to understand what they think and what they feel. Their needs, and their desires...."

Bones interjected, "And what's that?" he looked back and forth between Cantrell and Frank, unsure who would answer first.

"To be heard," the two men chorused together, causing each to smile and look at the other with a deep appreciation for the other.

For Bones, he was looking at teacher and pupil, protégé, and mentor. *Father and son*, he even thought to himself.

"So, Frank. What made you reach out to a retired FBI guy?" asked Bones. "You could've just called one of the guys at the FBI offices on Arch Street downtown."

"Nope," Frank shook his head. "I needed the best. This guy, right here...." he again pointed with his thumb. "Cantrell helped old Frank Bruno solve the Gary Heidnik case back in 1988."

"Man," Bones nodded. "I was only three years old back in '88."

"Did you know Doug consulted on the Silence of the Lambs movie?" Frank gloated over his friend's accomplishments.

"No shit?! Was that based on a case you worked on?"

Frank and Cantrell looked at each other and chuckled at the question.

"What?" Bones had a '*What gives?*' look on his face. Sitting up in his chair, he leaned forward. "No, really. What am I missing?"

"I genuinely don't believe your young friend here knows, Frank."

"Knows what?" Bones was anxious.

"You want to tell him?" Cantrell was too modest to tout his own exploits.

Frank smiled, threw his hands up, and said, "Hell no! That's all you, Dougie Boy."

"Come on. Tell me already," Bones insisted.

Cantrell reluctantly spoke up. "Okay, okay." His hands went up in a show of surrender. "You're off the hook, Bones. Heck.... you were only...." Cantrell did the math. "....what.... around six years old in 1991?"

"That's right." Bones took another swig of his beer, highly entertained by the FBI legend.

"Well, Bones, you see, the character Buffalo Bill Gumb from Silence of the Lambs was inspired by Philadelphia's Gary Heidnik."

Bones fell back into his chair. Running his hands through his hair, he said, "No shit?! How did I not know that?"

"Because you were young," Cantrell placated the thirty-six-year-old.

After dinner and a few more beers, it was going on ten o'clock, and the boys were getting tired after a long day at the 39th District reviewing case notes. An even longer day for Cantrell, who'd flown in that morning from his home in New Hampshire.

"So, you worked with Frank Bruno back in the day, huh?" Bones, the youngest of the three by far, wasn't ready for the night to end just yet.

"I did." Cantrell nodded. "I first met him back in 1974 when he and Penny Bryce came down to Quantico to discuss a case they were working on."

After yawning and stretching, Frank dropped his elbows onto the table and folded his arms. He'd heard the story about Frank Bruno and Penny Bryce and always loved the Frank and Penny connection, then and now.

"Was that the year she went missing up at FalconClaw?"

"Yep," Frank chimed in. "It was also the same year she got promoted to detective."

"That was a sad time," Cantrell pursed his lips and exhaled heavily through his nose when remembering the woman who'd opened so many doors for all the women that came after her. "Penny had just been promoted, got her first case, came down to Virginia to collaborate, and was gone just weeks later. Without a trace." Cantrell sighed. "That was hard on her partner. Frank Bruno almost left the force because of her unsolved disappearance."

"Then he went missing, too," said Bones. "All those years later."

"That one went unsolved, too." Frank always got frustrated talking about Bruno's disappearance. "They pulled Penny and me off that case almost immediately after Belinda Mereby went missing from Strawberry Mansion." Frank ground his teeth and shook his head in frustration.

"Yeah. Such a pity," said Cantrell.

"You know, Bones. You're lucky. You're working with the modern-day Frank Bruno." Again Cantrell acted like a doting father. "Trust me. I know. I worked multiple cases with each of the Franks."

Frank almost blushed. "Come on, Doug. Give it a rest. That man was a legend."

Bones now sat erect in his chair. "You come on, Frankie. You killed Isak Cameron and The Schuylkiller. You're the most famous cop in all of Philadelphia. Every cop in the country knows your story."

"Montreal, too," Cantrell beamed.

"For the record," Frank corrected his partner. "It was Penny who took out The Schuylkiller. Not me."

"No disrespect," Bones threw his hands up. "Penny will never be forgotten. She was a legend in her time."

The reference in Bones' statement struck Frank as odd, and he corrected his partner's comments by saying, "*Is* a legend. Not *was* a legend. Get it straight, partner."

When Douglas Cantrell and Bones noticed Frank looking out the window again, they made eye contact to acknowledge each other's discomfort. Seeing where the conversation was going, Cantrell headed it off.

"You know, Bones. Frank was actually named after Frank Bruno. Weren't you Frank?" Cantrell smiled, knowing his statement wasn't true.

"No, shit?" Bones did the math in his head. "But Frank, you're forty-three. Was Bruno considered a legend in what....nineteen seventy-eight?"

"Doug's just messin' with you." Frank rolled his eyes at a smiling Cantrell. "It was Penny who was named after Penny Bryce." Frank brought the subject right back to his girl.

The three men nodded in respect for both of Philly's most famous female detectives when Frank reached for his wallet, ready to call it a night. He was ready to get back to his shitty apartment. There, he would lie in bed, stare at the ceiling, and think about Penny, just like every other night. Frank planned to call her from the car after dropping Cantrell off at his hotel. After waving for the check, he looked out the window again, and at that exact moment, a couple wearing hooded sweatshirts, hoods pulled up, came around the corner from the direction of Indian Queen Lane. Passing by the window, the male pedestrian looked through the glass and grinned at Frank. Instantly, Frank recognized the scruffy beard and bad teeth. It was the homeless guy that had asked him for money the week before.

Frank's eyes narrowed with the facial recognition, and everything went into slow-motion as the two maniacal twenty-somethings walked by. While an unsuspecting Bones checked his emails and Cantrell wiped his mouth, Frank's eyes widened when the man's grin grew into a sinister smile. The man then dragged his bloody left hand across the glass of the only window in Billy Murphy's Irish Saloon.

In the wake of the man's five filthy fingers were five long scarlet rows. Things went from slow-motion to full speed as Frank's heart rate exploded.

Jumping from the table, startling Bones and Cantrell, Frank screamed for Mike Murphy to call 911. "Get an ambulance here, Mike! Now!"

Catching all the patrons of the bar off guard that night, cops or otherwise, Frank ran for the door, which was on the backside of the bar, and emptied onto Indian Queen Lane. He knew someone was hurt, and he knew it was a cop. By the time he reached the door, the first of many blood-curdling screams could be heard coming from the street.

With the scream, the remaining few in the bar, including Mike Murphy, Frank's fellow Italian buddy, and weekday bartender Dane Mandato, filed out onto the street. Outside, looking three cars north up on Indian Queens Lane, Frank identified the area of the screams. Knowing a cop was dead or dying just north of his position, Frank sprinted south down to Conrad and took a left around the corner of the bar, hoping to catch the killers. As he passed, his eyes caught the bloody streaks on the window and the now-empty table where he and Penny used to sit.

The blood seemed to intermingle with Penny's empty chair and caused Frank's vision to go a fuzzy white this time instead of going dim. In that terrifying moment, he was back in the Dodge, heading north on Washington Lane, speeding through the Awbury Arboretum estate, desperately trying to get to his family. White-knuckled and now crying, Frank rushed to get to Penny and his daughter. Racing through the tunnel of trees, the wind and driving rain had caused branches to fall and litter his now visually impaired path. Punching the accelerator, Frank struggled to see the road in front of him. Looking to his left, despite the torrent of rain, he could clearly see two people wearing hooded sweatshirts, laughing hysterically, and walking south through the Arboretum. Shaking his head and the vision in it, he nearly missed his left turn onto Ardleigh Street.

Frank's eyes cleared again when his right hand found his Smith & Wesson, holstered under his left arm. The cold metal coaxed Frank's mind and brought him back to Conrad Street and the pursuit of the hooded pair. Ahead in the distance, Frank saw a moving vehicle.

Running toward its red taillights, the car turned left onto Crawford Street North, stopping Frank in his tracks. He then turned and feverishly backtracked toward the screams and cries for help. The Cop Killers got away in a sub-compact, in what Frank believed was a 1990s Ford Fiesta, tan or white in color. Unfortunately, it was too far away to get a plate number.

As Frank got closer to the scene, which was roughly fifty feet north of the bar's entrance, he saw the glows of more than a dozen cellphones illuminating the pitch-black street and the recently emptied tree branches overhead, thanks to the chill of what would become an early winter in Philadelphia.

Pushing his way through sobbing and terrified bystanders, Frank saw several cops gathered around one of their own. Lying on the street, after being pulled from a parked car in an effort to render aid, was patrol officer Renaldo Lopez of the 39th District. Crying uncontrollably nearby was the woman who first saw Lopez bleeding out, Esmerelda Gutierrez, a resident of Indian Queen Lane. Frank and Bones knew Lopez, an eight-year man who had hoped to take the detective test in the spring of the following year.

Phone flashlights, held by trembling hands, lit up the body that Lopez once wore and revealed to Frank that Bones was the one rendering the aid.

"Come on, Lopez!" Bones tried in vain to somehow put pressure on the most severe of the neck wounds suffered by Lopez.

Cantrell, and everyone else standing nearby, witnessed just how brutal the Cop Killers were. Renaldo Lopez had suffered multiple stab wounds to the left side of his head, neck, and chest. Frank looked around at a crime scene that was completely destroyed in the terrifying chaos that had ensued just five minutes earlier.

Frank could see by the amount of blood on the street and by the empty eyes of his fellow cop that Lopez was gone. Instead of pulling Bones off of him, Frank let him hold on to his brother in arms a little longer. Now panning the crowd, worried for his friend's safety, Frank found Douglas Cantrell leaning on the back bumper of a nearby car as the approaching sirens cried out into the night.

"Doug, are you okay?" Frank sounded panicked.

"I'm okay." Cantrell stood and grabbed Frank's arm. "Son, did you get a plate number?"

In frustration, Frank seethed. "No, those fuckers got away!"

Later, just before the sirens went quiet and the street was washed in red and blue lights, Frank looked down Indian Queen Lane and saw the red ribbons that once gave Lopez life flowing downhill as if desperate to get to Conrad Street. Just before making it to the intersection, the stream of blood took a left and down into a sewer on the street next to Billy Murphy's.

Frank thought the rats that once ran beneath the North Philly streets were now running on them. In their wake, a trail of dead cops. Frank knew that that trail would lead the Cop Killers right to his door. For the first time, Frank was glad that that door wasn't located on 454 East Locust Avenue up in Germantown.

Chapter 14 – Friends with Benedicts

A white Ford Fiesta sat just three blocks from St. Peter Claver Roman Church on the corner of 12th & Pine. Parked next to it was a police car. The officer nearby was writing a parking ticket for a car parked in front of a fire hydrant, just outside a fish place called Friends with Benedicts. Due to the time of day and poor street lighting, the officer didn't notice blood all over the dark-colored seats as he called for a tow truck.

After making the six-and-a-half mile, twenty-two-minute drive south from Billy Murphy's, the Cop Killers, covered in blood, dumped the car close enough to the church to get back on foot without being seen by many witnesses but far enough not to connect the car to the church in any way.

Now back in the church's basement, Talon Grayson carved another tally mark onto the back of his lover Genesis minutes after receiving one of his own. In the background, the murderous anthem, *Take Me To Church*, played, and the pair lay on the blanketed cement floor near a controlled fire. Though the fire was too small and the air too cold, the lovers celebrated each's flesh and blood and entered into heroin-fueled copulation, with Talon bending his lover over and yanking her light brown hair violently backward.

In their ravenous lust, the killers paid little attention to a black homeless man who slept on the floor just feet away from their tryst.

"I hate you, Genesis," grumbled Talon, pulling harder on her hair.

"I hate you more, you filthy prick." Her moans were speckled with bawdy laughter.

The killers didn't actually hate each other but recognized that they were monsters and liked it. Unable to love evil, they would mock real love and instead revel in their fictitious hatred of one another.

The two then slept for six hours before they started their day jobs of robbing local shops and vendors at the crack of dawn, shoplifting their basic needs, and mugging or maiming for their greater demands.

Later that morning, on November 9, Cantrell, Frank, and Bones were back at it in the Detective Room after sending a BOLO for the Ford Fiesta. The tow yard that had hooked the vehicle the night before reported to police that they had found blood on the car's interior in the light of day.

Detective Sergeant Robert Brooks approached Frank and the others sitting around the conference table and reported that they'd found the Ford.

"No shit?! Where?!" Frank's heart began to race as he turned to Bones and Doug.

Brooks looked at the Post-it in his hand and said, "12th & Pine, downtown." He then handed Frank the information. "Did they finish processing the Indian Queen Lane scene yet?" asked Brooks.

"Yeah. They finished this morning. We're waiting on Denny to call with details."

"Scrabble letter?" Brooks already knew the answer to his question.

"We know they found one, but I don't have confirmation of the letter yet," said Frank.

"Gotta be an I, right?"

"I got money on it." Frank was sure, as was everyone else.

Brooks looked over at Bones. "How you holding up, Bonesie?"

"This shit got real serious, real fast." Bones was trying to process the events of the night before and at The Cope House on Halloween.

"That's tough what happened to Lopez. He was a good kid." Brooks nodded empathetically. Before returning to his desk, he added, "Well, now the 39th is officially part of the case."

Frank looked at Bones after realizing that it was official. Until the murder of Lopez, no cop from the 39th District had been killed during the Cop Killer crime spree. "We knew it was just a matter of time, and now that time has come."

Bones agreed. "We were just down in the Narrows talking about this like, what, two and a half weeks ago? These fuckers worked fast to get one of our guys from East Falls."

"They're ramping it up, for sure." Frank saw the writing on the wall. "After three homicides in four months, there've now been four in just nineteen days."

"Frank," Cantrell had been quiet but now spoke up. "I don't mean to alarm you, but they're sending a message that they're getting close. Meaning, close to you."

Everyone in the city-wide investigation knew after the Calvin Murphy crime scene on Halloween that Frank would be the killer's eventual target, but hearing Cantrell state the obvious underscored to Frank that he better watch his back. Frank thought the next homeless guy to approach his car would be taking his life into his own hands.

Frank's cell phone rang, startling him. As he always had since May, he looked at the caller ID with eager anticipation, hoping it might be Penny. It wasn't. Frank looked up to Bones and Cantrell and said, "It's Denny."

Bones and Cantrell looked at each other and then back to Frank.

"Okay. We'll see you in a minute." Frank looked pleased, hanging up the phone. "Denny's parking outside. He'll be up in a minute."

"I'll be damned," Bones' brows shot up. "They must be making good progress on the crime scene from last night."

"How are you doing, Bones?" Frank hadn't given much thought to how his partner might be handling seeing a co-worker die in his arms until Brooks inquired about the scene moments earlier.

"I'm okay." Bones tried to seem unaffected, but his slack jaw and trembling hands told Cantrell and Frank that he was deeply affected.

"You sure?" asked Doug. "I mean.... a thing like that can have a profound psychological effect on a person."

"I mean, yeah, it's tough," Bones acknowledged with a slight nod. "I've been seeing Calvin Murphy's ear in my dreams since Halloween, and now this shit." Shaking his head, he added, "I mean, Jesus Christ, what in the hell is happening in this city?"

"Well, as the Captain said earlier, they've got a counselor downstairs waiting to chat," Cantrell reminded both men. "No shame in talking it through."

Denny Patel walked in at that moment carrying file folders and a computer bag. "Hey guys," Patel was happy to see the three men.

Frank walked over, assisted Patel with his things, and asked, "So, whatta we know?"

Patel set his bag down on the conference table and took a deep breath.

"Have a seat, Denny," Bones offered by pointing to the empty chair to his left.

"I think I'll stand." To those around the table, Patel appeared to be very uncomfortable.

"Denny, you're clearly rattled," said Frank, showing his friend that he was concerned for both Patel and the news he was about to share.

Patel reluctantly took a seat and pulled some loose-leaf papers from his bag.

"You guys want the bad news first, or do you want the bad news first." Denny wasn't normally pessimistic.

"Just let us have it, Denny." Frank was a matter of fact.

"Okay, here goes." Patel almost winced when getting ready to share the facts. "Lopez had semen on his shirt and jeans."

Frank and the others shook their head in confusion. They weren't expecting to hear that. It opened so many more lines of questioning.

"Okay, maybe he was fooling around with his girlfriend before he headed out to Murph's last night?" Frank was trying to separate Patel's revelation from Lopez's murder.

Cantrell, on the other hand, was intrigued. Sliding to the edge of his seat, he asked Denny to continue. "Go on, Denny."

"I'd like to say it's unrelated, but the evidence says otherwise."

"What evidence, Denny?"

"Frank, we found another letter tile."

"I know. You texted me earlier and told me that."

"It's where the letter tile was found...."

"Come on, Denny. Out with it." Bones was beside himself.

"It was in his pants, I'm afraid." Patel winced again.

Frank and Bones shook their heads in disbelief while Cantrell asked an important follow-up question.

"Was he driven to Indian Queen Lane postmortem?"

"No, he was still bleeding when we pulled him from the car." Bones was sure he was attacked right there while sitting behind the wheel.

"No, Mr. Cantrell," said Patel. The murder took place right there in the car. The blood patterns inside the vehicle suggest that the attack started from his right side, with the driver side door closed, and then continued from his left side with the door open."

Frank thought aloud before finishing his thoughts. "So, if there is semen on top of his clothing, shirt, and pants, and the attack came from his right side first, then here's what I'm thinking...."

Bones and Cantrell looked on.

"Lopez was getting a blowjob from one of the killers, presumably by the female suspect, and he ejaculates," Frank paused. "And that's when the attack started."

"His head would have been tilted back with his chin raised into the air if he was being pleasured," Bones reasoned.

"Yep," Frank squeezed his lips together in agreement. "His neck exposed to the killer," he said. "Upon ejaculation, he would have been vulnerable and not feeling threatened, forgetting where his gun was."

"If he had his gun at all. No weapon was found in the car," revealed Patel. "And as far as the number of wounds.... From what I could count at the scene.... at least twenty or more. Stay tuned."

Bones was red-faced. "Motherfuckers got another gun!"

"Neck up, in a vulnerable position...."

Bones interrupted Frank. "I'm sorry, guys. This doesn't jibe. His pants weren't pulled down when we pulled him from the car. I don't remember his pants or belt undone. You don't stab a guy to death after giving him a blowjob and then pull his pants back up for him. If anything." Bones then added, "You take his dignity after you take his life. You leave his pants wrapped around his ankles and let him be found like that."

"Bones is right, Denny. The scene doesn't fit the facts."

Cantrell saw the look in Denny's eyes and waited.

"His zipper was found down, fellas."

"Da fuck!" Bones shook his head.

"No shit?!" Frank was perplexed. "I don't remember that."

"It was," Denny said. "The photos taken right after forensics showed up capture the fact that it was open."

"Huh," Frank exhaled through his nose while squinting. "All right. So as I was saying, during ejaculation, the attack begins on his right, and blood is cast onto the driver's side window and door panel. Seeing the attack begin, the male assailant opens the driver's door and continues the assault from outside the car. After that, he closes the driver's door, and the female assailant exits the passenger side. Is that what the evidence shows, Denny?"

"Yes. Lopez's blood was also found on the inside passenger door handle and handrail. It was a real mess in there, guys."

"Fingerprints?" asked Bones.

"No, sir. Not yet," Denny shook his head. "The blood patterns indicate latex gloves were likely worn as the areas where hands would have contacted the door show smooth, sliding type blood stains."

"What kind of sadistic motherfuckers are these people?" It was now Frank who was red-faced. "It's a guy and a girl, from what I saw last night. You'd figure they were together or something." Frank visualized the two as they passed by the window. "They weren't wearing blue latex gloves when they left the blood on the window. Make sure your guys check there, too."

"They did," said Patel. "Nothing."

"Psycho friends with benefits." Bones' quip was subtle out of respect for Lopez.

"Homicidal maniacs will use every tool at their disposal, Frank," said Cantrell. "Especially sex," he added. "The male suspect may have even drawn some erotic pleasure from the act precipitating the murder."

"Well," Denny spoke up. "We might not have fingerprints of the female, but we'll soon have her DNA."

"You swabbed Lopez's penis for saliva?"

"We did. We'll know if it's male or female in a day or two. A week after that, we'll have a profile." Denny's enthusiasm was measured, though. "Not sure if you guys remember, but we have a male DNA profile, but it didn't get a hit in CODIS when we ran it."

"That was a male DNA sample, right?" Frank confirmed.

"Yes."

"Well, maybe this psycho bitch is in the national registry."

"After Captain Justin Smith and me, you'll be the first to know, Frank."

Frank rolled his eyes. "Damn, I'd forgotten all about him."

Denny stood and placed his notes back into his bag when Frank blurted out," Oh shit! What letter was on the tile?"

"Oh. Damn. Sorry about that, guys. I almost forgot. It was an I," said Denny.

"There ya go," Bones nodded emphatically.

After the men stood and said their goodbyes to Patel, Frank flipped through his notes.

"So much for HARM A something." Frank never thought the tiles would reveal a word, but he still couldn't see a name in the letters.

"So, we got H-A-R-M-A-I so far...." Bones also referenced his notes and added the letter I. "I'm not seeing anything either."

"Maybe we have to unscramble the letters." Frank began trying to make words. "ARM, HIM, RAM, HAIR, RIM. I just can't see anything yet. What about you, Doug?"

"I agree with you. If it's a message, it will likely be a name than an actual multi-word message." Cantrell looked discouraged. "I'm sorry to say this, gentleman. But I believe we're still two to three letters away from knowing what it spells. That means...."

"Yeah. Two or three more dead cops." Frank couldn't believe the amount of carnage Philadelphia had seen in the last four years.

The grizzled detective also refused to factor in the letter tile from the trunk of Penny's car. He wavered between not thinking it was part of the case and being terrified that it meant something.

"I still can't believe that a cop let a hooker into his car right up the street from a cop hangout." Bones' mind was blown.

Cantrell, on the other hand, had a theory. "Like with the other slain cops...."

Frank marveled at his friend and finished his sentence. "Maybe they knew each other, too?"

"Jesus Christ, Doug. You're a genius!" Bones jotted some notes. "So, we look into busts made by Lopez involving prostitutes."

"If he ever arrested her at all." Frank was thinking quid pro quo.

"Yeah, I'm with Frank." Cantrell nodded. "You do for me, and I do for you. That exchange has been happening for as long as cops have been busting prostitutes."

"Lopez gets a blowjob from a hooker near a cop hangout. Hmm," Frank thought aloud. "Still doesn't make sense to me."

"How many other cops knew the girl, too?" Bones was now on the same page as Frank and Cantrell. "I'll get it to the guys connecting the common-collar dots."

"Another thing, Bones. Let's try to remember what other cops were at Murph's last night. It's a good chance Lopez was meeting up there with his buddies in the district. They might know about a hooker from his past if he was." Frank looked around the Detective Room. He wondered how many cops in the 39th were or had engaged with prostitutes in their careers. He knew not one of them would ever admit to it. If they did, it could mean an end to their careers.

"Will do," said an inspired Bones. He knew catching the East Falls Rapist the year before would be his second biggest case. Bones thought that the Cop Killers were now inside the jurisdiction of the 39th District and that they likely would try to finish their reign of terror there. They were coming for his partner, and he'd do everything to ensure they would never find their target.

Later that night, Frank and Cantrell sat in the lobby of the Residence Inn across the Schuylkill from the Wissahickon train station and reviewed their notes.

"This thing's got an end date," Doug was pointed. "If those letters spell a name, then I believe that means our suspects aren't trying to get away. These two are psychopaths, and for some reason, they've concluded that there's an end date to all this killing and an end date to their lives. Frank, they've picked you for some reason, and at this moment, it's more important to figure out why they kill as opposed to their true identities. If we can do that, we might be able to find out what makes them tick.... Maybe then we can slow their thirst for blood, revenge, or whatever it is that drives them."

"Damn, Doug. Find out the *WHY* before the *WHO*, huh?"

"That's right. These two don't want to get away. And they certainly don't want to get caught before finishing what they've started."

Frank sat back on the lobby sofa and stared into the fire burning in the fireplace separating the lounge from the dining area. His mind retraced the steps of his life and the people who defined it. His father, Salvatore, Penny, little Bonnie, The Schuylkiller, and Isak. Then he thought of the ghosts that guided him, Frank Bruno, and Old Man Winter. What it all meant, he couldn't be sure. Where it would lead to, he knew for certain.

As Douglas Cantrell witnessed Frank drift from the moment, pondering his past, present, and future, Cantrell looked up and around him. The large glass atrium housing the lounge made him feel suddenly vulnerable. Who was lurking outside watching him and Frank as they spoke? He turned to see the darkness and the reflections of a hotel lobby that seemed void of life. That void included him and Frank. He knew he was near the end of his life, and for the third time in four years, he thought Frank was, too. Would he outlive his young friend? He prayed that he wouldn't.

"Frank, listen." Cantrell pulled his friend from the depths of his personal insane asylum.

"Did I ever tell you about one of Abraham Lincoln's most famous quotes?"

"You did. It was during The Schuylkiller investigation." Frank grinned with the recollection. "I also remember Googling it to see if you were just trying to be prophetic in an effort to keep me safe or not."

"And? What did you find?"

"There's no consensus among historians that such a quote was ever made. He may or may not have ever said such a thing." Frank smiled. He loved Cantrell whether Lincoln ever said the words or not.

"Do you remember the quote, Frank?" Cantrell's eyes narrowed as he tilted his head, waiting for Frank's reply.

"As I recall," said Frank. "It was just months before he was assassinated when he'd confided to a close associate that.... I believe he said, 'If a man is willing to give his life to take yours, then there is little you can do to stop him.' Does that sound about right, Old Man?"

"Yes, it does, Frank. Yes, it does." Cantrell smiled warmly, knowing that he'd made his point.

On the other side of the river, and a mile and a half northeast, in the detached garage at 604 Markle Street, another Philly Detective sat in his car pondering. From his garage, he stared at the childhood home that provided him with his best and worst memories. On this night, like many others, he'd again sleep in his car. Bones Sullivan reclined the front seat of his Ford Interceptor and zipped up his jacket; the forecast said low thirties the last time he looked. The last thing Bones saw through his windshield before the garage door went down was the light on the side door of his house flicker three times. Was it his mother saying, I love you? he wondered again. Or was it his father saying, I hate you? Bones was sure that it was both.

Back south and west a little, Frank took Cantrell up on his offer. Doug had taken the liberty to book a room for Frank that night so that he could get a good night's sleep for the first time since before the accident. Doug smiled when Frank said yes, then Frank walked his best friend up to his room to ensure he got there safely.

After hearing Cantrell bolt his door, and with his keycard in hand, Frank walked right past the room Doug had booked for him and into the elevator going down. Frank, like his partner, would also sleep in his car. On this night, however, it would be from the driveway of the home he once shared with Penny up on East Locust Avenue.

Chapter 15 – Good Cop, Good Cop

In June 2012, the summer drug addiction and rehabilitation session was beginning at the Eagle Overlook Recovery Center for Adolescents on Gray's Ferry Road, in the Devil's Pocket section of South Philadelphia. The unassuming building sat just east of Naval Square, across from an affluent neighborhood that once served as the United States Naval Academy from 1834-1845.

As part of their one-year probation, and after being released from The Juvenile Justice Detention Center in West Philadelphia the week prior, two nineteen-year-olds, who had never met, were assigned community service work and in-person classroom studies for troubled teens.

"So, what're you in for?" Talon Grayson joked with the girl sitting next to him in the court-mandated one-hour class.

"Fuck off, scumbag," said the girl sitting to his left with hair so greasy that her dirty blonde hair looked brown and wet.

"Fuck you, too, bitch!" Talon was taken aback and not used to not getting his way. "I was just trying to be nice to you."

"Yeah. Whatever." Genesis Harper rolled her eyes. "I know what trying to be nice means to guys like you."

"Well, you're not my type.... so, who gives a shit," Talon shot back, lying about his taste in girls. He had always been into doped-up skinny girls. "And you're way too skinny for me, anyway."

"Too skinny? Really? Whatever, bro," Genesis shot Talon a glare. "I ain't here to meet no man. So just fuck off."

Her words were loud enough this time to get the teacher's attention, whose face told Talon and Genesis that he didn't want to be instructing poverty-ridden adolescent drug addicts on a Saturday morning in June or any other month of the year, for that matter.

Lowering his voice, Talon said, "Yeah, well, I'm hangin' out later over at Loco Pez down the block if you wanna stop by."

"Like I said, I ain't looking for no man. Not unless you got some smokes."

"That's it?" Talon smirked. "A pack of smokes is enough to get with you? Man, I had you pegged the minute you walked through the door."

"I didn't say nothin' about gettin' with nobody.... let alone for a pack of smokes. Besides, you ain't my type, neither."

"Oh, yeah." Genesis had Talon's attention. "And who's your type anyway?"

Genesis grinned flirtatiously. "A guy with a pack of smokes who hangs out at Loco Pez after court-ordered classroom bullshit."

"Now, that's what I'm talkin' about." Talon flashed a 'yo, what's up?' look. Bobbing his head and squinting his eyes, he made sure not to smile because he feared she'd see his bad teeth.

Later that night, after getting high, Talon and Genesis had sex under a tree in the Schuylkill River Park between the Walnut and South Street Bridges.

Thirty minutes later, sitting on a park bench on the Schuylkill Banks Boardwalk, Talon said to Genesis, "Now, that was an awesome birthday present."

"Today's your birthday?" Genesis seemed stunned, shaking her head. "No shit?!"

"No," said Talon. "It was on Monday. I just turned nineteen."

Genesis' chin dropped. "Your birthday was on June 11? You're fucking with me?!" she again shook her head in disbelief. "And you just turned nineteen?"

"Yeah. Why?" Talon puffed on a cigarette, thinking it was no big deal.

"I just turned nineteen, too."

"No shit. When was your birthday?" Talon took another drag of his smoke.

"On June 11, asshole. How you like that shit?" Genesis barked. "We're both Geminis."

"No fucking way!" Talon seemed impressed, smiling in Genesis' direction. "You fuck pretty good for a kid."

"We're the exact same age, dumbass."

"Well, I'm used to older women," Talon exhaled a plume of smoke through his nostrils.

"Yeah. Right."

Genesis couldn't believe the two shared a birthday. And of the same year. She thought the coincidence was a sign. Talon was less impressed but continued his courtship with Genesis for the next six months until he found someone else. It wouldn't be long, though, until the two would be back together again. Being homeless, sharing fast food, cigarettes, an occasional joint, and dreams that would never come true, the couple withheld a secret from one another. It would be years until they shared their story, fearing rejection by the other. The confession wouldn't come until their twenty-seventh birthday. And when it finally did, it would set in motion a killing spree that would shock the City of Philadelphia and alter the life of Detective Frank Collazo and all that knew him. A murderous rampage that would take the lives of eighteen people.

Back at the 39th, it was Friday, November 19, and it had been eleven days since the murder at Indian Queen Lane, and detectives were poring over the interview results of every patrol officer in the eight North Philly Police Districts. A weeklong dragnet had been conducted, but asking detectives to police their own was proving fruitless. After more than five hundred interviews, not a single cop confessed to fraternizing with prostitutes or knowing if any of their brothers in blue had. The next step would be to interview the hookers themselves. Another week of subtly trying to get prostitutes to confess to sleeping with cops proved harder than getting the cops to incriminate themselves. One, however, did have something to say. With the promise that she wouldn't be arrested for prostitution and a request for one hundred dollars in cash, Monica Mo Jefferson, street name Money, would give up what she knew.

"Frank!" Captain Beatrice Jackson burst through the doors of the 39th's Detective Room. "We got something!"

Frank was sitting at the conference table with Detectives Robert Brooks, Bones Sullivan, Jonah Abecassis, and Collie Mitchell. Douglas Cantrell had flown home for a few days to attend his wife's annual physical examination. While his wife's cancer had been in remission since 2018, Doug and Gaye held their breath every time she went in for a checkup. He was due back that evening.

"Whatta we got, Cap?"

"We got a hooker coming up from the 5th who claims she knows someone who used to sell her services to cops."

"No shit?!" Frank looked around the table. "Reliable witness, ya think?"

"As reliable as a prostitute can be." Jackson was skeptical. "Let's see what she has to say."

"Got an ETA?"

"She's being driven up in an unmarked car now. Should be here in less than ten."

"You want to sit in on it, Captain?" Frank already knew his boss's answer.

"You're goddamned right I do. This is our only lead after two weeks of sham interviews!"

As Jackson was leaving the room, her cell phone rang. It was ORS supervisor Sgt. Tommy McLaughlin. "It's Tommy." Jackson covered the phone and whispered to those at the table.

"Yeah. Please have her escorted up to the Detective Room." Jackson looked mildly excited. "Thanks, Tommy."

A minute later, a uniformed officer escorted a drug-riddled-looking black female into the Detective Room. She was estimated by those at the table to be in her early forties.

The men and Jackson stood to meet Jefferson, who looked understandably nervous. Jackson scanned those around the table and the other detectives working around the expansive Detective Room to see if she recognized any of them.

"So, Ms. Jefferson," Frank took the lead. "My name is Detective Frank Collazo. This is my Captain, Beatrice Jackson, my Detective Sergeant Brooks, and across the table from me are Detectives Sullivan, Abecassis, and Mitchell." The men all nodded, with Jackson wearing a look of skepticism. "Please, have a seat." Frank motioned to an empty chair with his hand.

"I ain't talking to all these people," said Jefferson. "No way," she shook her head defiantly.

Jackson was having none of it. "Ms. Jefferson, you have been compensated in advance for your time here today. I suggest you get talking or lay what you've been paid on the table right now and walk back down south to wherever it is that you call home."

Cracking her gum against her cheek and chewing loudly, Jefferson surveyed the room and its occupants and said, "I'll talk, but not to all these people. And I won't talk out here in the open, neither. I know way too much, and that can get a girl in trouble. Mmm-hmm." Money placed a sassy hand on her tilted hip and threw her eyes open wide.

Frank interjected, "How about you talk to my partner and my Captain in a private room right over here?" Frank pointed to the small interview rooms over his right shoulder.

"I ain't talkin' to this one." Jefferson looked Jackson up and down and said, "Dis bitch looks like she be havin' a bad day or somethin'."

"That's it, get this woman out of my sight," Jackson had had enough of the unfolding charade.

"Hang on, Captain." Frank motioned with his hands to calm the escalations. "How about Sullivan, Brooks, and I chat with Ms. Jefferson privately?"

Jefferson noticed the smaller interview rooms, looked Jackson up and down, and nodded her approval. "But it's got to be in one of those rooms. I don't want everyone up in my business."

Jackson rolled her eyes and reluctantly agreed without words. "Call me when you're done."

"This way Ms. Jefferson." Frank turned toward IRB but quickly recollected his bad memories of the room and his late and disgraced former fellow Detective Kyle Wade and instead led Jefferson and the other two detectives into Interview Room A.

The four sat around a small round table with four chairs.

"Can I offer you some water, Ms. Jefferson?"

"No."

"A Coke?"

Jefferson looked Frank up and down and said, "Well, ain't you a gentleman?"

Frank feigned blushing and responded, "I ain't no gentleman. I can promise you that."

"A Coke will do just fine. "Some of them corn chips, too, that I saw in the vending machine downstairs."

Frank smiled. "Sure. Bones, would you mind?"

Bones flashed a look at Frank, conveying he didn't want to miss anything, and then reluctantly agreed to head downstairs.

"Don't worry, Bones. We won't begin our conversation with Ms. Jefferson until she's received her refreshments. Frank steered clear of the words interview or interrogation, not wanting to spook the potential witness before she could relay whatever information she'd claim to have.

After Bones departed, Jefferson said, "Listen. I'm a little scared. The cops down at the 5th said I can't be arrested for tellin' what I know. That was the deal."

"That's right, Ms. Jefferson. That's the deal," Brooks reassured the witness. "You'll be free to go once we're done here today. We'll have an unmarked car return you to your home."

"That's good," said Jefferson, appearing a little more comfortable in the presence of a smaller audience.

Frank concurred. "Ms. Jefferson, we just hope the information you provide us with is helpful. It can only be helpful, however, if it's truthful."

Jefferson perked up and looked at Frank like she knew him. "You that detective, ain't you?"

Frank played dumb. "And which detective might that be? We have a whole bunch working just outside that door."

"Nah," she shook her head. "You're that guy that killed all those people. You killed The Schuylkiller and them other ones, too."

"Guilty as charged." Frank didn't correct Jefferson; he just sighed heavily in agreement.

Just then, the door opened, and Bones walked back in with two lunch-sized bags of Fritos and a can of Coke.

"Here you are, Ms. Jefferson." Bones placed the items on the table in front of her and sat down to her right.

"All kinds of gentleman working up here in the 39th. I might want to bring my game up north a little." Jefferson's humor was received with three insincere smiles.

The detectives took out their notepads, and Frank began the questioning.

Turning the page, he said, "So, Ms. Jefferson...."

"Call me Monica, or Money even."

"Sure." Frank nodded, glanced at Bones and Brooks, and then back to their witness.

"We understand you might have some information that could help in a case we're working on. Is that right?" asked Frank.

"Whattaya got some sort of sting goin' on? I mean, youse guys are out in force asking every working girl to fess up their cop connections."

"Something like that," said Frank. "But don't worry, anything you tell us today will be held in confidence. In fact, your statement today will be listed as coming from an anonymous concerned citizen. Your name will not go into the file." Frank lied.

"That's good," said Jefferson, eyeballing the corn chips on the table.

"Go ahead, Monica. Enjoy the chips."

After the bag was torn open, Frank continued. "So, what can you tell us today, Monica?"

Jefferson swallowed her gum and said, "Well, I know a girl.... She used to work the streets with me down by the river. She never told me her real name, but her pimp called her Genesee. You know, like the beer." Jefferson nervously looked at the men around the table. "She used to work in a package store. That might be how she got her name."

The men around the table scribbled with each word.

"Got a description of this woman?" asked Frank. He'd seen the male and female suspects outside of Murphy's the night Lopez was killed and remembered what the woman looked like. Flipping through his notes, he read, mid to late twenties, around five foot three to five foot six, skinny, Caucasian, poor complexion, dirty brown shoulder-length hair.

"She was cute, sometimes," said Jefferson. "Got a lot of action cuz she was white and skinny. I'd say around my height...."

"And how tall are you, Monica?"

"Five foot four."

"Okay." Frank motioned for her to continue. Any detective knew that once a witness started talking, you kept them talking. "Please continue, Monica."

"She looked like a user. Her face had some pockmarks. She had dirty blonde hair when it was clean. When it was greasy, though, it looked brown."

"Eye color?"

"Brown eyes," said Jefferson.

"Okay," Frank thought. The girl he saw that night matched up with Jefferson's description. "What else can you tell us about her?"

"Well, she'd been busted by cops before and always offered up her services in exchange for not taking her in...."

"And?" asked Frank.

"Well," Jefferson popped the Coke can open. "I had forgotten all about her until word got out that that cop got killed up off of Indian Queen Lane...."

"Oh?" Frank was the only one asking the questions. Bones and Brooks knew not to intimidate the witness by making her feel outnumbered. On this day, there'd be no *Good Cop, Bad Cop*, only *Good Cop, Good Cop*.

"I saw it on the news and recognized that guy immediately. "He used to work out of the 5th. He went by Rennie back then...."

Frank looked over to Bones and Brooks with the 'Rennie' namedrop. The look on their faces represented that they all knew that Renaldo Lopez had sometimes gone by the nickname.

"So, this Rennie cop guy hooked up with this woman who went by the name Genesee, is that right?"

"Yeah, long after he first busted her," she explained. "She was his side girl after a while. The pimps went easy on her because they didn't want no extra heat coming down on their turf."

"What eventually became of this woman.... Genesee?" asked Frank.

Crunching away at the bag of chips in front of her, she said, "I ain't seen her in more than a year. She just disappeared one day," said Jefferson. "I'd heard that maybe she got her old job back. Something like that."

"Got the name of the place she used to work?" Bones chimed in.

Jefferson looked off in thought and said, "Some package store down by the river off Ridge."

"East Falls Beverage!" Brooks blurted out, tapping on his notepad. "That's by the...."

"Yep. That's it." Jefferson nodded.

"Yeah. I got it, Bob." Frank looked off again and couldn't help but think that everything was coming back around full circle. He knew the East Falls Beverage store was at the end of the block, down from the Creative Minds Daycare and the row house where Mo Cheeks lived. His mind immediately returned to his last two big cases, The Schuylkiller and Isak Cameron. Frank had been in that store with Cindy Stafford several times while dating.

Seeing that Frank had zoned out on them, Robert Brooks chimed in. "Monica, can you provide a detailed description of this Genesee woman to our sketch artist?" He leaned in, asking the prostitute like she was a friend, and he needed a favor.

"I'll do it under one condition...."

"Yeah, what's that?" asked Frank, now out of his funk.

"I get another hundred bucks.... And...." she swallowed the last of her Coke, burped, and said, "I get another one of these, too." She then turned her stare to Bones, who smiled.

"I think we can work something out." The men stood, with Frank saying, "Bones, get Monica here another can of Coke, and I'll get with the captain on the cash payout."

Monica stood and made eye contact with each man in the room. "So, I'm not under arrest, right?"

"Nope." Frank shook his head. "As agreed upon, you'll be free to go after you sit down with our sketch artist downstairs."

"Well, that's good, cuz I got one more thing...." Monica looked around and then out the door's sidelight window.

"Oh, and what's that?" asked Frank.

"One of your boys out there likes the ladies down off West Leigh Street."

"You see someone out there you recognize?" Brooks perked up, thinking that one of his guys just got implicated.

"Oh, yeah," said Monica Jefferson with a grin. "Don't tell him I said so, but the guy that was sittin' over there in the corner when I came in...." she lifted her chin, looking out the sidelight to a now empty chair. "I saw him when I first walked in, and he saw me, too. He goes by Jamie, I think. That's all I know."

"Jamie, huh?" Brooks looked at Frank.

"Yeah, he's a white boy, but he likes the black girls best." Jefferson smiled again. "Don't say nothin' until I'm gone, though, or I don't sit down with no sketch artist."

"That's a deal. But no money until we have a sketch composite worked up." Frank reminded Jefferson of the deal.

After Bones escorted Monica Jefferson out of IRA, Frank looked at Brooks and asked, "You wanna handle Jamie Baumgartner? I gotta pick up Cantrell at the airport in an hour."

"It would be my pleasure," Brooks smiled. "I personally interviewed that prick about Lopez and prostitutes. That son of a bitch lied to my face." Brooks' eyes narrowed.

"Lying to a cop," Frank was unsubtle as he smirked. "That's a crime last time I checked."

"Yeah," said Brooks. "And lying to me is even worse."

Minutes later, now downstairs, Frank stepped into the room where Jefferson was providing a detailed description to the sketch artist of a woman called Genesee. Frank said, "Hey, Bobby, I want two sketches when you're done. The one you're working up now and then one with the same likeness but wearing a hoodie."

"You got it, Frank!" said Bobby Colapietro.

Frank handed Colapietro an envelope with a hundred-dollar bill in it and said, "Make sure she gets this when you're all done here."

"Sure thing."

"Thanks for assisting us today, Monica." Frank handed her another can of Coke.

"Any time you need something from me, Detective. You let me know," Jefferson smiled slyly, revealing her rotten teeth. "It'll be on the house, if you know what I mean."

"I'll keep that in mind." Frank grinned, raising his brows.

Forty minutes later, Frank rolled up to the American Airlines terminal, where a stabbing had just taken place outside of baggage claim. Putting on his blue flashers to wade through the traffic, Frank's heart was in his throat.

Abandoning his car to get a better look at the victim, he could see that it was an elderly man who was lying on the ground next to his roller bag.

Frank began to tremble when he suddenly heard a familiar voice coming from the crowd to his right. Looking up, he saw Cantrell approaching and sighed heavily in relief. Frank realized how fragile life was and knew that if he were a target, then so was his friend. He wouldn't know what to do if he lost his best friend, Douglas Cantrell.

Chapter 16 – FalconClaw Park

Later that night, after Cantrell had checked in to the Residence Inn Bala Cynwyd, Frank met him in the lobby after parking the car.

"Frank! Over here!" Cantrell got his attention and waved him over to the same couch they'd chatted on back on November 9.

"Have you been up to your room yet?" Frank couldn't see Cantrell's roller bag.

"Yeah, I took my bag up already. Thanks for making the reservation for me." Cantrell was concerned for his friend. He could tell that Frank was in a bad place. "Listen, I thought we could chat a little before dinner."

"Absolutely, and I'm sorry for the delay. I called Joanne from the car and then spoke with Conner, too."

"How is he adjusting to life in Michigan?"

"I think he's starting to like it up there." Frank was happy that Joanne and Conner were adjusting to their new home. "Conrad, on the other hand.... Well, he hates me more than ever. And he should. I basically chased his daughter and grandson out of town."

"Oh, don't be too hard on yourself." Cantrell tried to ease Frank's burden of guilt. After several seconds of silence, he added, "You think Conrad will move up there and join them at some point?"

"Well, considering that his only two children live up there, along with his grandchildren, I'd say it's just a matter of time."

"What'd they do with the house?"

"They're not gonna sell it anytime soon just in case Joanne decides to move back. Plus, Conrad paid it off last year, so they'll just sit on it for a while."

"Maybe you can live there instead of the flat over the bar." Cantrell desperately wanted Frank to live a normal life. "I mean, just for a while until you move back to your house."

"I don't know about that." Frank displayed a look of resignation. "Like I said, Conrad hates me."

"I see," said Cantrell. "And how are you feeling about your only son being so far away?"

"You know, you're starting to sound a lot like a therapist right now."

"Is that such a bad thing, Frank?"

"I guess not." Frank looked around and felt a little more at ease since the lobby was empty and things were quiet. The burning fire had a calming effect on him, as he remembered the last time he was there, staring into the same fire just eleven days earlier. "Doug, listen. I owe you an apology. The last time...."

"I know. I stopped by your room and saw the maid coming out. She told me the room was untouched. She let me peek in, and I knew you didn't sleep there."

"I'm sorry. I left to go see Penny, and, well, I fell asleep in my car again. I'll pay you back."

"Nonsense. You already have by paying for my reservation this time around." Cantrell looked around before speaking again. "Listen, Frank. I'm worried about you."

"I'm fine, Doug. I mean it. I'm good."

"That's not true. You're hurting, and you need to start talking to me about what you're going through."

"Listen to me.... I'm okay. It's just that I'm still trying to process what happened with Penny and Bonnie."

"Oh? Are you ready to talk about it, then?" Doug thought Frank might finally be ready to open up about the accident.

"It's just that every time I see her, she seems so cold and distant." Frank wore a look of desperation and sadness.

Cantrell felt as if a breakthrough was imminent. "Go on, Son." He sat up and moved closer to Frank.

"Well," Frank hesitated. "She doesn't say much and never lets me into the house."

"Have you tried to walk in without asking her first?"

"No!" Frank's eyes flew open. "I couldn't do that. I mean," he shook his head. "She wouldn't want that. Not yet."

"Frank, you know they're having a service up at Laurel Hill for Renaldo Lopez next week. Are we planning to attend?"

Frank furrowed his brow. "Doug, I told you the last time we were there that I wasn't going back."

"And when was that? Remind me, Frank." Cantrell attempted to get Frank to face his agony by discussing the May accident. Perhaps then, Cantrell thought, his friend could begin the healing process.

"Doug, it was in May...."

Cantrell was astonished by Frank's response. He thought he was about to hear the words that both he and Frank needed to hear.

".... May 2019, it was Ali's funeral. How could I ever forget that day."

Cantrell sighed heavily. Disappointed, he fell back into his chair. Frank was lost, and he wasn't sure how to help him. He could never convince him to see a professional.

"So, you haven't been back since then?"

"Of course not. I told you then that I was sick and tired of burying my fellow cops." Frank just stared into the fire. "The next time I'm there, they'll be putting me into the ground."

"That's what I'm afraid of," Cantrell whispered, but Frank didn't hear. Feeling hopeless, he changed the subject. "So, how's tomorrow going to go?"

"We're going to start at FalconClaw Park." Frank looked away from the fire and over to Doug.

"Really?" Cantrell sat back up and re-engaged his friend. "Well, that's a surprise."

"I thought you'd feel that way." Frank smiled.

"The last time we were there, we got caught up in that rainstorm, remember?"

"Oh, yeah," Frank paused. "I forgot to tell you the last time you were here...."

Cantrell was on the edge of his seat.

"They're reopening the Mount Royal Chalet."

"No kidding?" Cantrell pursed his lips and nodded his approval. "I bet that place will look beautiful when they're done."

"It'll be soon," said Frank. "They're timing its grand opening with the grand opening of FalconClaw Park. They're trying to tie it all together. I'd heard that the grown-over path we walked on to get to the chalet has been cleared."

"And when is the grand opening?"

"New Year's Eve," said Frank.

"Hmm. New Year's Eve, huh? That's odd." Cantrell looked baffled, rubbing his chin. "You would think they'd hold off until spring with the harsh winters in Philly."

"It's been mild the last couple of years.... I'm sure it'll be okay."

Looking up through the glass panes in the atrium, Frank saw snow falling. He remembered that it was Christmas Eve night when Penny Bryce went to FalconClaw and disappeared, leaving two sets of footprints in her wake. "Right on cue. Would ya look at that?"

"My, oh my." Cantrell smiled. "I love to see the white stuff fly."

"Well, I better get back." Frank stood. "Tomorrow's gonna be a big day."

"But it's only eight o'clock. What about dinner?" Cantrell stood and looked at Frank with a sideways stare.

"Yeah, that, well, um." Frank was tongue-tied.

"You're going to the house, aren't you?"

"Yeah, I haven't seen Penny in weeks and wanted to stop by and check on her and Bonnie. The last time I went, she didn't come out."

Cantrell felt sympathy for his friend. He placed his hand on Frank's shoulder and said, "Would you send her my love?"

"I will. Penny will be excited that you're in town."

"I'm sure she will, Frank. I'm sure she will."

"Let me walk you up to your room." Frank motioned for Doug to lead the way."

"No, you go ahead. I'll be fine."

"I don't think so, Doug." Frank was adamant, especially after the airport stabbing scare. "I'll be walking you up, Old Man."

With a look of surrender, Cantrell walked ahead of Frank to the elevator bank.

Upstairs, on the third floor, Frank led the way out of the elevator, and only then did he let Cantrell proceed. After a cursory search of the room, Frank said, "I'll pick you up tomorrow at nine."

"Okay, Frank." Cantrell patted his friend on the back as he walked out the door. "Don't forget to tell Penny that Gaye and I are thinking about her and Bonnie."

"Will do." Frank turned to go. "Oh, and Doug...."

"Yeah?"

"....No delivery or room service unless they tell you the password."

"Password?" Cantrell chuckled. "What password?"

"Dinner's on me tonight, and just make sure you ask for the password."

"And you're not going to tell me what it is?"

"You'll know," Frank smiled. "I hope Italian is okay."

"That'd be fine," Cantrell smiled. "Drive safe."

"See you tomorrow."

Frank walked down the hall smiling. Waiting on the elevator, he relished his friendship with Cantrell and looked forward to getting back out on the trail with him the next day. When the elevator finally opened, Frank was startled. Looking in, he saw Old Man Winter and Frank Bruno.

Garrison Winter smiled, tipped his cap, and said, "Hello, Frank."

As Frank stepped in, Bruno stepped out. Tipping his fedora in a show of respect, Bruno simply said, "Frank."

Old Man Winter nodded to Bruno, and Frank Bruno walked off toward Cantrell's room. As the elevator door closed completely, the door to the stairwell at the far end of the hall opposite Cantrell's room opened. Stepping out into the hall was a thinly bearded male and his female accomplice, both wearing hoodies with the hoods up.

Looking down the hall, they saw no one coming or going. The twin killers were unable to see Frank Bruno stepping inside Douglas Cantrell's room.

Back in the elevator, Garrison Winter smiled and said, "Behavioral Science Unit, huh?"

Frank laughed. "I thought that would be an awesome password."

"Yes, it is," Winter shook his head. "It's perfect, Frank."

"Where'd Bruno go off to?"

"He'll be hanging out with your friend, Douglas, for the evening."

Frank looked a little startled and, with fear in his eyes, said, "Well, he's in good hands then, isn't he?"

Winter smiled. "He certainly is."

Frank was relieved. Before leaving the hotel, he stopped by the front desk and ordered his friend Chicken Parmesan with a side of spaghetti and a slice of chocolate cake from the hotel restaurant. Gazing at the young woman's nametag, he smiled. "Listen, My name is Frank Collazo, and I want to order my friend some dinner.... but you'll have to personally deliver it. Just bill it to the room." After asking for and receiving a piece of paper, he scribbled a note and then handed it back to her. "The guy in room 305 will require a password from you before he opens the door. This is it," Frank smiled. "The guy's old and paranoid and used to work for the federal government. Just give him the password when he asks for it."

The young lady behind the desk smiled and began to recite what was written on the paper when Frank cut her off.

"Shhhh! It's top secret." He looked both ways, winked, and smiled. "Share it with no one."

"Got it," said the twenty-something.

"Frank looked down at the girl's nametag again and smiled. "Penny, huh?"

"That's me," said the girl, grinning.

"Ever ask your parents why they named you Penny?"

"Of course," she smiled. "I figured you were a cop."

"How'd you know?" Frank was impressed.

"I got cops on both sides of my family. I saw you coming from a mile away," young Penny paused, "Plus, you're wearing your Detective Badge on your belt. I spotted it before you zipped up your jacket."

"You should be a detective," Frank chuckled. "So, Penny Bryce, huh?"

"Yep. First-ever female detective in the City of Philadelphia," said young Penny.

"Goodnight, Penny." Frank slipped her a twenty-dollar bill.

"Thank you, Detective Frank. Goodnight."

Thirty-five minutes later, Frank pulled into 454 East Locust Avenue and sat for a minute before exiting the vehicle. He'd lost his nerve again and hoped Winter would give him a little nudge, but turning to look, the old man had gone.

Looking up through the windshield, he noticed the snow was falling heavier. Reconsidering being there, he thought perhaps he should go. Putting the car into reverse, the back porch light came on. Frank smiled as he turned off the engine and stepped out into the snow. He hadn't seen Penny since November 2 and was relieved he'd see her tonight.

"Hey, Frankie Boy." Penny sat in her usual spot.

"Penny, it's freezing out here. Where's your jacket?"

"It's beautiful, isn't it?" Penny took a deep breath through her nose and exhaled fully, smiling.

Frank looked her up and down and was again surprised to see her wearing the same clothes she had worn the day of the accident. He chose to say nothing.

"Come on, let's get you inside. It's way too cold out here."

"No, Frank. You can't go in there. Not yet, anyway." Penny shook her head. "Let's talk out here for a moment. I don't have long before I need to get back inside. Bonnie's waiting for me."

Frank removed his black shell jacket and placed it around Penny's shoulders. "There, that's better."

"So, how's the case going?"

"It's awful. Too many dead cops are littering the streets of Philly. Some really good men." Frank shook his head solemnly.

Penny took Frank's hand and caressed it. "I'm afraid there are going to be more, Babe."

Frank cocked his head. "What makes you think that?"

"Because you haven't caught them yet."

Them? Frank thought to himself. He wasn't sure he'd told Penny that there were multiple assailants.

"Penny, how do you know it's more than one person?"

"Oh. The last time we spoke, I'm sure you used the term 'They' when referring to the suspects. It's more than one, isn't it?"

"Hmm, okay...." Frank shook his head. "Yeah, we think it's more than one."

"Male and female?" asked Penny.

"That hasn't been mentioned in the news. How did you know that?"

"I just figured, that's all."

"Just figured, huh?" Frank was confused and skeptical. It was as if Penny had been talking to someone else in the department.

"Well, listen," said Penny. "It's cold out here, and now you're the one without a jacket." Penny removed Frank's jacket and gave it back to him. "Oh, and tell Doug I said hello, would ya?"

Astonished, Frank looked at Penny. "Penny, have you been talking to Doug?"

"No. Why do you ask?"

"Because you seem to know a lot about the case and...." Frank stumbled over his words. "How did you know Doug was in town? He just got in this afternoon."

"Um.... I just figured he was helping you with the case. He's here, right?"

"Yeah. Right."

"I love you, Frankie. I've gotta get back in there. Be safe and come back soon. Okay?"

Before Frank said his goodbyes, he asked, "Is she in there?" He looked at the house, but it was completely dark. "Is my Bon-Bon in there, Penny?"

"Of course, she is. Don't be silly." Penny smiled. "She's waiting for you to come home, Frankie Boy."

"I'm here, PENNY!" Frank began to cry. "I'm right HERE! Why can't I come home?!"

"It's not time yet. Close the case, Frank." Penny smiled warmly at him. "Get the bad guys off the streets. Remember?"

Sobbing, Frank cried, "Where's your jacket, Penny!" Why are you wearing those clothes?!" Throwing his arms into the air, he cried louder and harder. "What is happening in my life?! What is going on?!" Looking back at Penny, he saw that she had gone.

The next morning, Frank passed by the front desk en route to the elevator and saw that young Penny was working. "Hey, Penny!" he smiled without breaking stride.

"Oh. Hey, Detective Frank. Good morning!"

"How'd it go with dinner last night? You know, the password thing?"

"Oh, yeah, that's right," Penny wavered. "I took the food up just like you asked, but no one ever came to the door. I waited for a second but then just brought the food back downstairs. Don't worry. It's no charge. I went ahead and credited it back to the card on file."

In a panic, Frank ran for the elevator. On the third floor, he exited the elevator and saw Cantrell coming out of room 305. Relieved, he said, "Doug, are you okay?"

"Well, of course, I am. I'm fine. Why?"

"The girl downstairs...... I ordered dinner for you last night, but she said no one answered the door."

"Oh, I must've fallen asleep. I'm so sorry. I'll pay you back for the food."

"Don't worry about it." Frank waved off his friend's offer. "I just had a little scare, that's all."

"It's been a long time since I slept that good." Cantrell looked five years younger.

After personally escorting Doug down to the lobby, Frank looked for young Penny, but she wasn't there. "My life story...." Frank mumbled beneath his breath.

Now in the car, Cantrell asked, "So, how did it go last night?"

"It went okay," Frank seemed reluctant to talk about it.

Not wanting to pry, Cantrell had just one more question. "Did you tell her that I said hello?"

"Doug," Frank looked over at his friend. "Have you been in touch with her?"

Cantrell was shocked. "Have I been in touch with Penny?" he repeated the words to ensure he heard Frank correctly.

"Yeah. Have you spoken with her?"

"Frank, what would make you think that?"

"She knew you were in town, and...."

"No kidding?" Cantrell whispered under his breath. Almost in shock, he stared in amazement.

"She seemed to know about the case, too."

I guess she would. Cantrell said to himself.

"You two went behind my back before when you planned her disappearance, but I wouldn't appreciate you doing that now. Not in light of what's been happening."

"Frank, let me stop you right there. Of course, I haven't spoken to Penny." He paused, "I couldn't."

"You promise me?" Frank looked over at his friend.

"Yes, of course." Cantrell's heart was broken. "I'll tell you this, though. You'll be the first to know when and if I speak to her."

"All right, then. Let's get up to FalconClaw."

Crossing the Schuylkill River, things were quiet in the car. Cantrell thought that it would be cathartic for Frank to return to the place where not only his father died but, right before his death, he lived. He was alive before three bullets to the back put an end to him. He took his last breaths there. That had to mean something. Cantrell reasoned in his mind. He hoped Frank took consolation in that, too.

Frank, imprisoned by his memories, was trembling at the notion of again retracing his father's last steps and final breaths. He seethed when he thought of the madman who killed his father. He thought that even as a fourteen-year-old, he would gladly have been the one to depress the plunger at Walker's execution and end a life that should have never begun.

Twenty minutes later, the Dodge came to a stop. "Well, here we are." Frank threw the gear shift into park. Looking up the hill from down on Bedford Street, he couldn't believe his eyes. Frank could hardly believe that the massive display of shops, condos, and restaurants had taken the place of the burned-out Phoenix, and FalconClaw, before that.

Frank wasn't reminded of his father, Old Man Winter, what happened to Penny Bryce, MK Ultra, or the sordid history of the mansion that once was. Instead, he saw the future instead of the past, and his spirits seemed to be lifted at that moment.

"Wow! Would you look at this place!" Cantrell was equally as impressed. "I saw it going up on the news over the last year, but, geez. This place is amazing!"

The two stared at steel, glass, and granite three-story condos with glass balconies sitting atop upscale shops and restaurants. In the foreground, the place lived up to the 'park' portion of its name, with gorgeous lamp posts lining the many sidewalks that crisscrossed their way up the hill. Placed in a way that gave one the impression they were from another time and place, the beautiful park benches were very much from the present. It made one feel that the park benches were there during the first one hundred and fifty-year run of the original FalconClaw estate when in fact, there were none prior to its rebirth. The place had exceeded The Phoenix by a long stretch in Frank's mind, and he was glad The Phoenix Group had decided to rebuild after the fire.

Walking through the original yet restored front gate, Frank was happy to see the original FalconClaw Gate Lodge still sitting just inside the main gates, to the left. A gatekeeper would reside in the outcropping of the main house and allow passage to the Crenshaw family's invited guests. Samuel Crenshaw being Penny Bryce's paternal grandfather.

Frank knew the history well enough to appreciate that the old gatehouse should stay and was happy it did.

"So, you got it in you to climb that hill, Old Man?" Frank laughed at his friend, who seemed to be sizing up the trek to the top.

"First of all, quit calling me old man," Cantrell jokingly scoffed. "You're the one that's aged twenty years in just the past four."

Cantrell immediately regretted his remark, but Frank took it all in stride.

At that very moment, snow started falling just as the wind picked up. The two men looked at each other and smiled.

"This is perfect." Frank inhaled deeply through his nose, taking in as much oxygen as he could before the climb.

"Come on. I'll race you to the top!" Cantrell got a head start on Frank.

Frank chuckled and purposely fell behind, hoping to see his friend struggle a little so that he could make fun of him.

Once at the top, the two men cheered each other on, celebrating their accomplishment, and celebrating their friendship. Doug Cantrell could always bring Frank back from the depths of hell. Smiling at his friend, Cantrell hoped he could also prevent him from ending up there.

Chapter 17 – Blue Bell Park

The day before, Friday, Money Jefferson had implicated a detective in the 39th as possibly having information about their female suspect, known to fellow prostitutes as Genesee. It was unclear if the woman had any involvement in the cop killings. Detective Sergeant Robert Brooks mentioned to Frank before he'd left to pick up Cantrell from the airport that he would question the detective about what he knew.

After the interview with Jefferson was completed, Robert Brooks looked for Detective Jamie Baumgartner, but the detective was nowhere to be found. One of his fellow detectives told Brooks that Baumgartner had just left for the weekend.

"Son of a bitch!" Brooks ground his teeth.

Trying Baumgartner on his cellphone several times and repeatedly texting his subordinate, he got no response. Brooks then alerted Frank and his captain that Baumgartner likely went AWOL after discovering he'd been implicated by the mere presence of Monica Jefferson in the Detective Room.

Later, while driving back to his place in Blue Bell Hill, just a half mile east of Bones' house and only a mile from Frank's place above the Mad River bar, Baumgartner made a few calls in an effort to reach the girl known to some as Genesee. He wanted to get out in front of the scandal he'd now be facing at work. His boss, Brooks, and Frank would have questions for him, and his answers would likely lead to his termination. He had withheld vital information about possibly knowing one of the two cop killers and had also been consorting with prostitutes, abusing his power as a Philly cop.

"Hey, Bonesie." Brooks approached Bones Sullivan, who was wrapping up his notes from the Jefferson interview. It was just after five o'clock.

"Yeah, Sarge?"

"Listen, don't you live over in Manayunk, near Blue Bell Park?"

"Yes, sir. Just west of the park. I can see it from my driveway. Why, what's up?" asked Bones.

"So, it looks like Baumgartner skipped out of here early before I could talk to him. And now the guy's gone radio silent...."

"You want me to stop by his place?" Bones' smile communicated to his boss that he'd love to. Bones loved the idea of confronting his fellow detective about what he knew.

"You know where he lives?"

"Yeah. I've been to his place before," Bones nodded in the affirmative. "He lives in a duplex on Naomi Street near the corner, just north of the park. I don't remember the house number, but I'll be able to figure it out once I get there. It's got a red door. It's distinctive."

"Do me a favor, would ya....?"

"You want me to go over there and rough him up a little?" Bones laughed, joking with his sergeant.

"No, Bonesie. I just want you to see if he's home. If he is, don't say a word about Jefferson or hookers. Just tell him I've been trying to reach him and that he needs to call me ASAP."

"Sure thing, Sarge. I'll be leaving here shortly. Look for my call...." Bones grinned, ".... And his, too."

Forty minutes later, Bones arrived at 636 Naomi Street; out front, he observed Baumgartner's black Dodge Challenger. Parking and walking up four tiny steps to a small landing area, navigating around two green plastic lawn chairs, and then four more steps, Bones opened the red screen door and loudly knocked three times.

Repeatedly knocking several more times, Bones yelled, "Let's go, Jamie! I know you're in there!" Still no answer, he tried calling Baumgartner's phone and texting.

Inside, upstairs, and peeking through his bedroom window blinds, Baumgartner knew who was at the door; recognizing Bones' car and voice, he would lay low until his fellow detective had gone.

Back downstairs, Bones yelled, "Call the Sarge, Jamie!" Turning to leave, he accidentally knocked over a potted plant from the top step, scattering its contents onto the third and second steps.

After seeing Bones' Ford Interceptor pull away, Baumgartner's phone pinged. It was a text from an unknown sender. The text read: *I heard you're looking for me. What's up?* The message was signed using only the letter G.

We need to talk. Shit's heating up at the 39th.

Where can we meet and when?

Blue Bell Park. You know where it is? texted Jamie.

Yeah. It's by your house. I remember.

Get that sweet little ass over there and meet me at the abandoned baseball field just south of the Blue Bell Field parking lot on Orange Trail. Come alone.

What time?

Meet me there at 7. It'll be dark. Just look for my car. The Challenger.

I'll be there.

Come alone.

I got it. I'll be there.

Fifty minutes later, the park was pitch dark as Baumgartner rolled up to the baseball field. The park had little lighting and was usually empty during the fall and winter after sundown.

Baumgartner parked his car under a tree behind home plate and waited. He checked his phone and saw eight missed calls and more than a dozen text messages. After a minute, he looked out toward the baseball field, made out a dark figure sitting on a bench behind the first base side of the diamond, and flashed his high beams. The tiny figure, wearing a gray hoodie, stood and approached his car from the passenger side.

From a now rolled-down window, the words "Get in," told Genesis Walker her company had arrived.

"Where's your car?" Looking for a vehicle, Baumgartner looked around and then in his rearview and side mirrors.

Now sitting uncomfortably in the car, Genesis said, "I ain't got no car. I got dropped off. What's this all about?"

"First things first," said Baumgartner. With no emotion, he proceeded to unzip his pants.

"Put your shit away. I ain't doin' that tonight."

"You will if you want to know what I know. Shit's comin' down on you. Money ratted you out to the whole detective team at the 39th."

"Ratted your ass out, too. I bet." Genesis dismissively looked out into the darkness.

"You'll get busy doing your thing if you want to know more." Baumgartner looked down toward his crotch and grinned.

Genesis lowered her hood, pulled her hair back, and did what she had done dozens of times to Jamie Baumgartner and other cops from the 5th and 39th. Two minutes later, she was done.

Wiping her mouth, she said, "Now, what's up?"

"First, you tell me what you know about the cop killings? This shit's now happening in the 39th District, and I think you know something."

"What cops? I don't know about no cops getting killed. Da fuck you talkin' about, Jamie?"

"Bullshit! Money dropped your name, and they're gonna start looking for you. When they do.... You don't fuckin' know me. You never even heard of me." Pulling on Genesis' hair minutes earlier, Baumgartner pulled it again and growled, "You understand. You never heard my name. Got it?"

"Same thing for me, asshole," Genesis pulled away from the clutches of Baumgartner. "They know my name, or what?"

"They know the name Genesee. That's all. But they'll likely be heading down to East Falls Beverage later, maybe tomorrow, to ask about you. It won't be long until they know your real name." Baumgartner checked his mirrors again, beginning to feel uncomfortable. "How'd you fuckin' get here anyway?"

"Uber. Why the fuck do you care so much?" Genesis opened the door, and Baumgartner grabbed another handful of her hair before she could step out.

"Listen to me, Genesee.... Whatever your fucking real name is. You say nothin' to nobody. You got me?"

"Yeah, I got you, motherfucker!" Standing outside the car now, Genesis spat on the ground to her left and wiped her mouth again. "You don't know me either, Jamie."

"Fuck you, whore!" The window to the Dodge went back up, and the backing lights revealed an empty park behind it.

Jamie Baumgartner again surveyed the area to ensure none of his buddies were out and about looking for him. Checking his phone again, more missed calls and text messages had come through. After making the one-mile drive back home, he circled his block three times. Seeing that the coast was clear, Jamie had to park two houses down because a beat-up Honda Civic was parked in the spot in front of his house where he usually parked.

Walking through the front door, Baumgartner kicked off his shoes and made his way through the dark house into the kitchen. Flicking on the light, he stood frozen in fear. With no time to react, he saw a slight man standing before him with a knife. Before the eight-inch kitchen knife from his cutlery set on the counter was plunged deep into his abdomen, Jamie Baumgartner saw an unrecognizable hooded man smiling, revealing several rotten teeth.

Catching Baumgartner in his descent to the kitchen floor, the rotten-toothed, bad-breathed man whispered, "You're dead cop number nine, motherfucker."

Coughing up blood, Jamie Baumgartner bled out on the floor in front of his refrigerator. Gasping for air, he clutched his killer's arms in a plea for mercy. After his eyes went wide and his breathing stopped, Talon Grayson placed a wooden Scrabble tile in Baumgartner's bloody mouth. The letter embossed on the tile? An N. For good measure, he then proceeded to slit Baumgartner's throat from ear to ear.

Ten minutes later, a beat-up, stolen Honda Civic pulled up to the baseball field in Blue Bell Park, the southernmost section of Wissahickon Valley Park, and out of the darkness came a woman, a hood casting a shadow over her face. Opening the car door and seeing blood on the sweatshirt of her man, she smiled and said, "Fuck yeah!"

As the car sped away, its occupants listened to Hozier's *Take Me to Church* on their cellphone and sang along loudly.

"Take me to church!" the two killers howled. Talon's goddess got the sacrifice that she demanded. As the car turned right onto Lincoln Drive, heading south toward the Schuylkill, the windows came down, and the two monsters sang into the night.

On Saturday morning, a scream was heard coming from 636 Naomi Street, followed by wailing and crying in the street out front. Natasha Steingart found her boyfriend, Jamie Baumgartner, dead inside. Frank, Cantrell, Bones, Brooks, and Beatrice Jackson joined a dozen or more first responders and forensics team members at the scene within thirty minutes of the 911 call.

Donning their powder blue latex gloves and shoe coverings, Jackson said, "It ain't pretty in there, boys." She had been the first of the group to go in. "I want Frank and Bones in there first, and then you, Brooksie. You can go in after. It's a tiny house."

Frank had instructed Cantrell minutes earlier to hang back due to the number of personnel on scene.

"This is unbelievable," Bones said to Frank as they made their way around the back of the house to the kitchen door. "I was just here last night."

"This wasn't random. Just like the other victims, Jamie knew one or both of his killers," Frank surmised aloud. "We're gonna need to talk to Jefferson again, along with more hookers. This shit's gotta end, and soon."

Frank lifted the inner circle of police tape, allowing Bones to go under it. Climbing the back stairs, the two avoided one of Denny's guys dusting for prints on the handle of the back screen door just as the snow began to fall.

Inside, the men met up with Denny Patel, and the three discussed the scene.

"Forced entry through the back door, no prints visible yet. The murder weapon...." Denny looked over to the deceased, using his chin to indicate it was still in the victim's body. "....came from that cutlery set right there." Patel again pointed with his chin.

"Jesus fucking Christ! Look at what that maniac did to Jamie!" Bones continued to be shocked at the depravity of the Cop Killers. "His fucking throat is cut wide open."

Frank, like Bones, was just as shocked. "I see," said Frank. "It looks like a match."

"Hard to miss the matching red handles," said Bones.

"Time of death?" Frank looked back at Denny.

"Based on the rigidity of the body, I'm guessing twelve to fourteen hours.... maybe more."

"Christ!" Bones was stunned. "He was murdered right around the time I came looking for him."

"You were here?" Patel looked surprised.

"Yeah. Brooks sent me over to make visual contact with him and to have him contact him back at the district house."

"Any signs of breaking or entering when you were here?" asked Frank.

"Not from the front of the house. I only knocked on the front door."

"Well, thank God you didn't come around back, or your fingerprints would be all over that door, and you'd have some explaining to do," said Frank.

"You're telling me?!" Bones looked somewhat relieved by Frank's comments, though still shocked by the circumstances.

"What time was that, Bones?" asked Frank.

Bones, examining his call and text history on his phone, said, "I called him at 6:07 and then texted him at 6:08. Either he was dead, or he was pretending not to be home because his car was parked right out front."

"That's valuable information," said Frank. "That helps us with the timeline."

"If I find out the killer was inside while I was here, I'm gonna...." Bones shook his head, unable to articulate what he was feeling. "Wait a second!" Bones snapped his finger. "Jamie's car was parked directly in front of his house last night when I arrived. That's how I knew he was home."

"His car's parked two houses down, now." Frank made a mental note when he arrived. "That means he left sometime after you did last night, Bones."

"Exactly!" Bones nodded with the revelation. "So, I left here around 6:10 or so, meaning he was alive during that time." After a brief pause, Bones added, "Oh damn! Another thing. I kicked over a potted plant on the front steps when I left. When we walked up, it looked like it'd been picked up."

"So, let's get with the neighbors before we leave and see if they can shine some light on when his car might have arrived back on the street. And," Frank looked at Bones, "let's check the condition of the plant and where it is."

Frank's adrenaline was starting to flow. The veins in his neck were evident to both Bones and Denny, and the two looked at each other as if to say, *Get the fuck out of Frank's way!*

Bones also felt the juices flowing. "We can also ask his neighbors if they saw another car parked on the street they didn't recognize."

"Okay." Frank displayed his determination with steely eyes. "So, Denny, that leaves us with the million-dollar question."

"It was in his mouth." Patel pulled a small evidence bag from his jacket pocket. "His gun, cellphone, and badge are all missing, too."

Squinting to see the bag's contents, Frank studied the clear plastic bag and saw the letter tile covered in blood.

Denny handed it to him, but Frank was still unable to make out the letter as the embossed typeset was covered in a tacky, deep, crimson-colored blood, nearly matching the color of the maroon tile.

Later, back at the 39th, the team discussed what they knew and what they didn't.

Around the table were Frank, Cantrell, Bones, Brooks, and Jackson.

"We now have eight dead cops and seven letters," Frank's frustration was boiling over. "We have no fingerprints, no eyewitnesses, the testimony of a prostitute, and a dead detective that could've broken this thing open by revealing the true identity of Genesee, whoever the fuck that is!" Frank slammed his hand down on the table.

"Settle down, Frank." Jackson mildly scolded her best detective. "We need you thinking clearly on this case. It's too important."

Frank took a deep breath as those around him looked on. Each person in the group knew that Frank's instincts would ultimately solve the case, and they felt he was close. They also knew that he had suffered a great deal of emotional trauma and physical scars in the last few years, including the May accident. Additionally, they knew that he lived with the fact that his father was killed by a notorious serial killer when he was only fourteen. They all prayed that he would hang on just a little while longer. Afterward, they would encourage him to step away from the profession and seek the help he desperately needed.

Collecting himself, Frank continued discussing what they had so far. Referencing his notes, he asked the team what the letters meant. What message do the letter tiles tell us? H-A-R-M-A-I-N? ARM? HARM? MAIN? RIM? RAM? RAIN? HAM? HAIR? I'm just not seeing it, guys!" Frank continued to withhold from the group the letter tile found in Penny's trunk. He still refused to believe that it could be relevant. His emotional scars prevented him from seeing the obvious solution to the jigsaw puzzle staring back at him.

Cantrell leaned over to offer Frank his thoughts as the others reviewed their notes. Whispering to Frank, he pointed out that the killers were acting in an unsophisticated way, which likely meant that they were inexperienced and new to killing. From his experience, Cantrell knew something sinister triggered a rage that would encourage someone to dare to kill so ruthlessly, deliberately, and so many times in such a short window.

As Doug had told him days before.... The *why* would reveal the *who*.

Frank excused himself from the meeting, stating he was hitting the streets. He felt far more comfortable working with a smaller group of investigators. Namely, he and Cantrell. He'd also try to work away from the district house as much as possible. The answers he needed would come from the streets.

"Where we off to, Frank?"

"East Falls Beverage. We're going to find out exactly who Genesee is. I'm pretty damn sure that's not her real name."

"That sounds like a great place to start." Cantrell was eager to get going.

As the two exited the Dodge on Ridge Avenue after Frank parked in a no-parking zone, a familiar face emerged from the package store across the street. Mo Cheeks walked out and immediately recognized Frank.

"Well, well, well!" he yelled out, pretending to be suspicious of Frank, and said, "If it ain't Mr. Detective Frank."

Frank smiled, looked at Cantrell, and rolled his eyes playfully.

"Well, if it ain't Old Mo Cheeks...."

"Hey now! Wait just a minute!" Cheeks' hand went up, correcting Frank. "We already done had this conversation once, Detective. Only my friends call me....."

"Ahh, yes. I remember." Frank smiled again, feigning embarrassment. "Maurice Cheeks. How have you been? Did you ever get the insurance thing figured out?"

"Well, I'm standing here, ain't I?"

"I thought you may have headed back down to East Lansdowne." Frank was happy to see the man who could make him smile even when cross.

"That's some racist bullshit, right there. Like my skin's too dark to live in East Falls?" Mo Cheeks looked offended.

"No! I wasn't saying that at all...." Frank was red-faced as his grin was washed away.

Cheeks broke out in a smile, and said, "Just messin' with you, Copper. By the way," Cheeks looked up and down the street. "Where's that fine looking lady you wuz with last time? Mmm-mmm! That PYT was dressed to kill....., always." Cheeks shook his head, closed his eyes, and smiled at the memory of Penny.

"She's no longer with the Department, I'm afraid." Frank wore a vacating look, almost sighing in despair.

"Greener pastures, Detective?"

"Yeah. Something like that." Frank raised a somber brow.

"So, what brings you down to Ridge Road?"

Cantrell felt like a third wheel. Cheeks hadn't even acknowledged his presence. It didn't go unnoticed by Frank either. He just tagged along as the two men walked and talked.

"Listen, Maurice.....:

"Call me Mo. All my friends call me Mo." Cheeks smiled. "Now that I remember.... you and I made friends last time you wuz here."

"That's my memory, too." Frank smiled. "So, Mo. I'm investigating homicides of cops throughout the city, and my investigation has led me down here, more precisely, to East Falls Beverage. You been going there for a long time?"

"Years. Why?" Cheeks walked and talked as the men headed west on Ridge.

"Well, there was a girl that used to work there. Her name was Genesee, like the beer. Did you know her?"

"Ahhhh.... Good old Jenny," Cheeks lit up. "I more than knew her. I got with her a couple of times. Right up there." Cheeks pointed to his second-floor bedroom. He and Frank were now standing in front of his row house.

"No shit!" Frank's eyes went wide as he looked over to Cantrell. "So you knew her well, then?"

"She didn't talk much," Cheeks grinned. "if you know what I mean?"

"Yeah.... Right. So what was she like?"

"Man, for twenty bucks, that girl would suck the chrome off a trailer. She was a dirty one, let's just say that." Cheeks shook his head when remembering.

"Have you seen her lately?"

"Hell, nah!" Cheeks waved off Frank. "I ain't seen that Ho for what it be.... Like two years now?"

"Two years, huh?" Frank took mental notes instead of written ones. With a guy like Cheeks, he knew it was best to keep things unofficial. "Why'd she leave? Do you recall?"

"Yeah, she had a possessive boyfriend, brother, whatever the fuck they had going. Shit didn't seem natural, neither. And I seen all kinds in my day. Just put off a weird vibe, those two. He knew she was hookin' and got her fired because he was always comin' round. Checkin' up on her, ya know?"

"Un-natural? Hmm." Frank's eyes narrowed. "Got a name for the guy?" he crossed his fingers.

"Let me think on dat one." Cheeks rubbed his chin and looked off. "Oh yeah, she called him Grayson.... Or some shit like that."

"Gray-son, like the color gray?" Frank wanted to be sure.

"Yeah! Like I said, Copper. Grayson was the name."

"Gotta last name?"

"Man, you cops just don't get it, do ya? Less is more. People round here.... they don't go askin' for last names cuz they don't need to know."

"Anything else you can tell me about the two? Where they're from? Anything?"

"Nah. Never asked cuz I never wanted to know."

"Well, thanks, Mo. You've been a big help."

"Big enough to buy me a twelve-pack?" Cheeks raised his brow and held it there.

"Hell yeah," said Frank. That's the least I could do for a friend."

Before returning to the beverage store, Frank said, "Mo, you mentioned brother when talking about the relationship between the two. Are they related.... you think?"

"Nah. Can't be cuz they was fuckin." Cheeks shook his head. "I just said that cuz they looked like they was twins. Fraternal twins, you know, boy-girl twins."

Frank's memory was the same. The two were similar in stature, facial features, and height.

"I'll tell you what, Mo. I gotta run now, but here's a fifty and my business card." Frank pulled the large bill from his pocket. "Buy yourself two cases, okay?"

"Hells, yeah! Now that's what I'm talkin' about. Damn, Detective Frank. You need to come round here more often!" Cheeks was all smiles.

"Thanks, Mo." Frank returned his friend's smile and motioned to the business card. "Maybe I'll come back again soon. Don't forget to call me if you think of anything."

"Will do, Detective. Will do," said Cheeks, all smiles. As Cheeks watched Frank and Cantrell walk away, he yelled, "Who knows! Maybe I'll even come see you one day!"

Frank turned and smiled at Cheeks and then entered the beverage store. Ten minutes later, Frank left empty-handed. The owner was new, and so were the employees. No one knew of a Jenny, a Genesee, or a Grayson.

As Frank turned back toward the car, he looked at his friend. "Old Mo Cheeks didn't even acknowledge your presence. What's up with that?"

Cantrell smiled. "That's okay. The last time he acknowledged me, he called me a KKK-looking mother-something."

Frank cracked up, laughing heartily at Cantrell. "That's right. I remember that."

"What did he mean when he referred to Penny as 'PYT,' anyway?"

Frank chuckled. "You don't know what that means?"

Cantrell shook his head, thinking that he probably should.

Smiling at his friend, Frank said, "*PYT - Pretty Young Thing.* It's a song from the early eighties.... Michael Jackson. Hello?"

"Of course." Cantrell shook his head in acknowledgment. "Yes, but.... *Hello* was a song by Lionel Ritchie." Secretly though, he was still confused. He'd never heard the song and never followed Michael Jackson.

Frank just shook his head and chuckled at Cantrell's confusion about songs and artists. Going from laughter to sadness, Frank thought of Penny when remembering his last meeting with Cheeks. He missed her. He needed to go home to his family.

Chapter 18 – Paternal Consanguinity

Seventeen months earlier, on the Monday morning of June 11, 2020, Talon Grayson took the SEPTA bus, got off at Broad & Christian, and walked the four blocks to the Christian Street YMCA. There, he would have his first shower in more than a week. It was a big day; he and Genesis would celebrate their twenty-seventh birthdays. They planned to eat dinner at an Arby's restaurant and see the movie thriller *Lucky* at the Roxy Theater on Sansom Street. Later in the week, the two would celebrate the eight-year anniversary of their first meeting in 2012 when they'd attended court-ordered classroom studies at the Eagle Overlook Recovery for Adolescents Center.

Talon had two-hundred and fifty dollars left from his paycheck from the Friday before. He'd recently started work at a home improvement company up in East Kensington three weeks prior. He was hired to pick up materials from suppliers and vendors and drop them off at worksites around North Philly. Normally the company wouldn't have hired someone with a criminal record, but post-pandemic, like every other company around town, it was hard to get people to work. Grayson was hired solely because he had a driver's license and could work any time, but he was also warned that if anything ever came up missing off the truck, even a single nail, he'd be fired immediately.

"God, I love curly fries," said Genesis. "I can't even remember the last time I went to an Arby's."

"That's why I brought you here," said Talon. "We always do McDonald's or BK, but today is special. Happy Birthday, Genesis." Talon slid a small box across the table and studied his girlfriend's facial expression to see if she acted surprised.

Genesis was blown away, and her chin dropped. "What's this?" Her look of surprise and gratitude brought both a smile and a sigh of relief to Talon.

"Can I open it?" At that moment, Genesis felt like a normal girl on her birthday, not someone who was homeless more than she wasn't.

"Of course. I just hope you like it." Talon again held his breath.

Timidly opening the tiny white box, Genesis pulled back the foam padding that was hiding a necklace. Her expression told Talon that she was puzzled. "What in the hell is this? A baseball bat?"

Genesis pulled out a tiny baseball bat dangling from a chain. The small bat was wrapped in fake barbed wire and covered in fake blood.

Caught off guard by Genesis' reaction, Talon got defensive. "It's a replica of Negan's bat from *The Walking Dead*."

"I know what it is," Genesis looked mildly offended. "I just thought you got me that bracelet we saw last week at Walmart."

"That was like twenty bucks. I'm not made of money, ya know?"

"The movie tonight is gonna cost more than that," Genesis reasoned as she angered Talon even more.

"Fuck this! I'll be right back!" Unable to control his temper, Talon got up, stormed away from the table, and headed for the restroom.

"Talon, wait!" Genesis knew Talon got his feelings easily hurt and tried her best to prevent the night from going sideways.

In the restroom, Talon leaned over the sink, clutching its sides with both hands. Staring in the mirror, angry at himself, he mumbled incoherently. His mouth nearly foaming in his anger, he headbutted the mirror, causing it to shatter. Now bleeding slightly from the top of his head, he ran cold water and soaked a paper towel. After the bleeding stopped, he rejoined Genesis at the table.

"How's it look?" she smiled.

Seeing the necklace around his on-again, off-again girlfriend's neck, along with her what appeared to be a sincere smile, Talon momentarily felt a little better.

"What happened to your head?" Genesis focused her gaze on the top of Talon's head, where she saw blood.

"I dropped something in the bathroom, and when I stood up, I hit my head on the paper towel dispenser."

"Jesus, babe! Can we still go to the movies?"

"Yeah, sure." Talon pressed a handful of napkins against his wound.

Later, at the Roxy, Talon told Genesis he had another surprise for her but that she'd have to wait until later. He had planned to tell her who his father was. It was a secret he had kept from her for eight years. He also knew that she had the same secret and might tell him if he told her.

Thirty minutes after the violent, bloody movie, the two were excited and sexually aroused. They decided to head down to the Schuylkill River Park, the place where they had sex on the day they first met back in 2012. After doing the deed and pulling up their pants, the two walked and talked, ended up on the Schuylkill Banks Boardwalk, and sat on the same bench from years earlier.

"Listen, Genesis. I need to tell you something," Talon hesitated. "But I've been afraid to all these years. To be honest, I'm embarrassed and hope you don't judge me." Talon Grayson had always been deeply insecure and felt judged by people and society. People never made sense to him, and he never made sense to people.

"I've got something to tell you, too." Genesis suddenly found it hard to look her boyfriend in the eye.

"You go first." Talon was trying to buy a little more time. He was ashamed of his father's true identity.

"No, you go," said Genesis, feeling the same as Talon. She had long wanted to tell him her truth.

Talon took a deep breath and began his tale. "Well, I was finally given my birth certificate when I turned eighteen. I always knew my mom's identity but never knew about my father...." Talon took another deep breath and exhaled fully. "I was only ever told that my father was dead and that he died in prison. I figured if he was anything like me, he was probably a piece of shit."

Genesis closed the space between her and Talon and slid closer to him. She was also beginning to feel more comfortable about sharing the truth about her father. "Who was he?" she felt her heart race.

Talon choked up a little before whispering the name in Genesis' ear.

In shock, Genesis gasped as she fell backward, attempting to get away from Talon. The look on her face was what he had expected, but he was still unprepared for her reaction.

Lying on the ground crying, Genesis looked up at Talon and screamed. "Oh, my God! This can't be happening!"

Talon tried to console her, kneeling down to comfort her and tell her he was sorry. "I knew you would feel this way, Genesis. That's why I never told you." He reached for her hand.

"Get away from me! Now!" she growled as if possessed. "I'm going to be sick!"

"Okay! All right, already." Talon felt terrible, and Genesis made him feel guilty for being born. "I get it. You don't have to make me feel worse than I already do."

Genesis rose, stumbled to the railing, and vomited into the Schuylkill River.

Talon rolled his eyes and thought that while his news was shocking, Genesis was being way too dramatic.

"Give me a break," he said. "He's dead and gone. He isn't my father! He never was! I never knew the man, Genesis."

With the face of a crying ghost, Genesis turned and looked at Talon and said, "We have the same father!" she wailed. "Your father was my father! You're my fucking brother!"

Talon felt every muscle in his body constrict, and his face go numb. Unable to speak, he stumbled backward onto the bench and then onto the ground. His life was over. The only woman he'd ever loved, the only person who accepted him for who he was, was his half-sister. They could never be together, he thought. He would never find someone else like Genesis.

Climbing to his feet, Talon ran. Unable to scream, he raced silently south down the boardwalk and disappeared under the South Street bridge. As he did, Genesis screamed out for him.

"Talon!" she cried out into the night. "TALON!"

Talon heard nothing except his breaking heart. After another twenty minutes of wandering aimlessly, Talon found himself on Gray's Ferry Avenue and in front of the building that once housed the Eagle Overlook Recovery Center, where he met Genesis. Now able to speak, he screamed. His agony echoed across the Naval Square and up and down Gray's Ferry, the row houses muffling his pain. A group of nearby homeless men were alarmed, causing one to approach Talon.

"You all right, buddy? It'll be okay." The man rubbed his back as Talon hunched over, crying. Looking back at the other two men and nodding, the homeless man attempted to grab Talon's crotch.

Shocked, Talon fell backward in retreat and fended off the much larger man. The homeless man continued his assault and encouraged the other two to assist him.

Suddenly, Talon saw his dead father in the face of his attacker and fought back. Blow after blow, his anger and desperation could be felt in his strikes. The two other approaching homeless men saw that Talon now had the upper hand and wanted nothing of the rage they were witnessing, so they fled. Now unconscious on the ground, the homeless assailant was defenseless and could not stop the frenzied onslaught of a man who had nothing more to lose. A man who was cursed at birth. A man unwanted by his girl, society, mother, and the foster parents he thought loved him.

Talon Grayson stomped to death the homeless man in front of the building where he met the love of his life. Looking up at the weathered outline where the word EAGLE once was, like an eagle, and like his name, he would use his talons to kill again. The man at his feet would be his first kill, but in his bloodlust, looking at his hands, Talon knew he was like his father, and in killing more, he would become him.

Seventeen months later, Frank quietly screamed in his sleep, lying in his Mad River prison. Covered in sweat, he squirmed in his bed, trying desperately to get to Penny and Bonnie at the scene of their accident. Now on Ardleigh Street, his tires spun on the wet surface, fishtailing again as he reached East Upsal. Now heading north, Frank saw his father kneeling next to a wooden fence, a hammer in his hand. Through the pouring rain, he saw his father crying. His head slumped in anguish, down on one knee, and with a hand gripping the fence, Salvatore Collazo wailed. He knew the countless nails in the fence would define him as a father and permanently scar his only child.

Witnessing the misery, Frank screamed. "Dad!" He slammed his hands down onto the steering wheel, nearly losing control of the Charger.

Waking from his nightmare and lying in a puddle of his own making, Frank dragged himself into the dark bathroom just as a train ran south over the Schuylkill. Clawing at his ears, trying to silence the screams of his father, Penny, and Bonnie, Frank looked in the dark mirror and saw the man he was becoming. Frank saw his father, Salvatore Collazo, staring back at him, crying. Crumbling to the floor between the sink and the toilet, Frank sobbed. He cried in defeat. This world was no longer for him, but before he left it, he would see Penny and Bonnie one last time and get the bad guy and girl off the street. Frank would kill the Cop Killers.

Ten hours later, Frank was awakened from his fetal position on the bathroom floor by a loud banging on his apartment door. Covered in dirty bath towels, a robe, and a shower curtain, he was shivering violently, and outside, a blanket of snow covered the ground. It was nine o'clock on Sunday morning, November 21, and two people stood outside his door, pounding away in fear, caring little about the other occupants in the building.

Frank stumbled to his feet and retrieved his Smith & Wesson from the bedside table, then, without caution, made his way to the door. Without looking through the peephole and disregarding his own safety, he opened the door and pointed his gun. Standing in the tiny hallway were his friends Candace Weatherby and Douglas Cantrell.

Looking Frank up and down, Weatherby blushed while Cantrell said, "Oh, Frank."

Frank looked down and saw that he was completely naked. Even the cold couldn't disguise his Italian ancestry, and Cantrell quickly took off his trench coat to save Frank from embarrassment and the cold. He also thought of Candace and wanted to save her from a vision she wouldn't soon forget.

Candace could hardly look away, but while impressed by Frank, she also saw a shell of the man she first met in Montreal. She was worried for him and had made the trip from Canada to support her friend and help in any way she could.

"Let's get you covered up, Frank." Cantrell pushed past Weatherby, who remained frozen in the hallway.

Frank raised his hands and let Cantrell lead him back into the bathroom.

"Candace, give us a second, would you?" Cantrell led Frank into the tiny bathroom.

"Of course." Weatherby closed the apartment door behind her and made sure that it was locked.

Cantrell found a robe on the floor in the bathroom and helped Frank put it on.

"Frank, are you okay, Son?" Doug was devastated at the condition of his friend. "I tried calling incessantly last night and then for two hours this morning...."

"What is she doing here?" Frank now seemed fully cognizant.

"It wasn't my idea. Candace called me last week and said that she's been trying to contact you for months but that you never returned her calls," Cantrell pleaded his case. "She's worried about you, Frank.

We're all worried about you. Just look at yourself in the mirror. You look awful. You're going to kill yourself if you don't get some help."

The last thing Frank wanted to do was look in the mirror again.

"But why is she here right now?" Frank cocked his head. "If Penny were to find out I had a woman in this apartment, she would freak out."

Cantrell shook his head. "Frank, we're getting you to a doctor tomorrow. This madness has got to stop."

Standing just outside the tiny apartment's bathroom door, Weatherby could hear every word the two men said. Dread befell her face when hearing Frank speak of Penny. She had been worried sick for him since first hearing about the accident.

Candace Weatherby made the trek to Philadelphia and hoped to apply her recent criminal justice degree to the Philly P.D. and the case Frank and Cantrell were working on. She had recently earned an Associate's Degree from the University of Montreal, finishing the two-year program in just eighteen months. Inspired by her friends, Cantrell and Frank, Candace desperately wanted to follow in their footsteps and had recently begun interning for Detective Lieutenant Benoit Pelletier and Detective Sergeant Pierre Labrec in the City of Montreal Police Department. Her background in history and her knack for knowing what stones to overturn quickly made her an asset to her colleagues in Montreal, and she hoped she could assist Frank and the case in any way she could.

Walking out of the bathroom, Frank apologized for not being prepared for company. "Yeah, about that...."

"You don't owe me any apologies, Frank," said Candace. "And it wasn't Doug's idea that I come down here. I was worried, and I wanted to help."

"Candace." Frank tried hard not to insult the well-intentioned woman standing in his apartment. "Meaning no disrespect, you're a

Historian and an Archives Manager at Ravenscrag. How could you possibly help?"

"Well, isn't that condescending of you?" Candace reached into her bag. "If you would have returned any of the messages I left, you would have known...." She pulled a lanyard from her bag. Dangling from the end of it was an employee I.D. for the Montreal Police Department.

Cantrell sat back and didn't feel the need to come to Weatherby's defense. He knew the fiery, intellectual bombshell could handle herself with Frank or any other man, woman, or otherworldly being. He knew that even he couldn't match her smarts, and with looks that could open doors to go along with her genius, perhaps she could help with the case.

Frank studied the I.D. and smiled, again trying not to offend Weatherby, and said, "Intern?" Pursing his lips and shaking his head, he gave a shot at compassion. "Candace, we are staring down two lunatics that have brutally murdered what we believe to be eight cops. All but two were seasoned with ten to twenty years on the force. And...." Frank wanted to be clear, "they were all licensed by the City of Philadelphia to carry...." He paused intentionally, "GUNS."

Handing the I.D. badge back to Weatherby, Frank tightened his robe, smiled, and said, "Now, what's for breakfast? I'm starving."

The three had decided to return to the hotel for breakfast due to the weather since Cantrell and Weatherby were both staying there. Forty-five minutes later, the three sat around a table and ate. Frank reluctantly let Cantrell brief Candace on the case for the next sixty minutes.

"If you gentleman will excuse me, I need to powder my nose."

"Of course," Cantrell, followed by Frank, stood out of respect. "She's something else, isn't she?" Like with Bones, Cantrell was smitten.

"She's something, all right...." Frank again rolled his eyes.

"Come on, Frank. She only wants to help."

"Doug, she could be killed." Frank looked exasperated. "And Jackson would never let her near the 39th. I'll lose all credibility if I ask my captain to consider it. No way, Doug. Not going to happen." Frank was exhausted, and it showed.

"She's not a Philly cop and wouldn't be a target. Additionally, you could call Benoit Pelletier with the Montreal Police and ask him to vouch for her to Jackson."

"Doug, you're starting to lose my respect. You're biased. You're fond of her. I get it.... she's fuckin' awesome, but collateral damage is a real thing," Frank paused. "And in case you haven't noticed, the two psychos we're hunting down want me dead. That puts you at risk, and her, too. Don't forget that!"

Cantrell felt rebuffed. "Well, if you don't want me here...."

"Oh, gimme a break! Of course, I want you here. I need you here. I just don't need her here," Frank was frustrated with his good friend. "Plus, I would need clearance from my good buddy, Captain Justin Smith."

"Is that the man you knocked out?" Cantrell winced.

Frank raised his brows and nodded.

Cantrell pondered how to get Frank to buy into her helping out when Frank blurted out, "Plus, she saw me naked. Completely naked!"

Cantrell smiled and nodded politely to the nearby adults sitting with their children. Looking back to Frank, he smiled and said, "I did, too."

"Ha-ha, Doug. You're a funny man."

"Keep it down a little," Cantrell motioned with his head to Frank at the families sitting on either side of their table.

Just then, Candace Weatherby walked up and said, "The killers are related, and they know Frank somehow."

"Yeah, we got that they're likely related, but they don't know me." Frank was again being dismissive.

"They know you, Frank. Or at least know of you." Weatherby took her seat.

"Candace, come on." Frank shook his head and rolled his eyes, trying this time to be condescending. "Everybody in this city knows me. It's not a stretch to think that they know of me."

"Excuse me, folks," Cantrell looked over to the table next to theirs and asked," Does this man look familiar to you?" he said, tilting his head in Frank's direction.

The husband and wife looked at each other and shook their heads no. "I've never seen that man before today," said the wife.

"I haven't either," the husband added. "Should we?"

Cantrell smiled wide and looked at Frank and then back to the table next to his. "No. I was just conducting a social experiment. That's all. Thank you for your time."

Candace smiled and said, "I guess not everybody knows you after all."

Frank smirked at Candace and Doug and then questioned the same family, "Excuse me, folks. Sorry to keep bothering you, but may I ask where you're from?"

"Texas," chorused the couple. "We just got into town yesterday."

"Thank you," said Frank smiling politely. "I rest my case," he said to Cantrell and Weatherby.

"Frank, you know what we meant," Doug pleaded with his eyes.

"Whatever." Frank wasn't amused as he looked back over to Weatherby. "Okay, Candace, why do you think they know me?"

"The killers may not know you personally but can relate to your story. I know just about everything there is to know about you professionally. It's all out there in the public record. The suspects in this case are somehow relating to your story. They know your father is dead, and my guess is that their father is dead, too. Maybe he was a cop killed in the line of duty or killed by a cop. I'm feeling a real familial connection between the killers and you."

"Feeling a connection, are you?" Frank smirked. "So, now you're educated in psychology, too?

"Believe it or not, I minored in psychology back in the day."

Frank tossed his napkin on the table and said, "Of course you did." Standing, he said, "Now it's me who needs to powder my nose."

Chapter 19 – Visual Snow

39th District, Jackson's office, Monday, November 22, 2021 – The week of Thanksgiving.

"You're going, Frank!" Beatrice Jackson was a matter of fact. "And you're off the case until you do!"

"Come on, Cap!" Frank was livid. "I don't need to see a shrink. I'm fine, goddammit!"

"You're not fine. You've been zoning out since the Isak Cameron case. Don't think I'm not noting all of your episodes. You're losing your shit right in front of your fellow detectives. And let's not forget what happened down on Race Street."

Frank shook his head in disgust. "So, whatta I have to do?"

"See Dr. Archibald Riley twice a week," said Jackson. "I've already set it up. Tuesday and Thursday, five o'clock, every week for six weeks, and once he signs off on you, the department will drop the mandate, and you'll no longer need to go."

"Mandate? Department?" Frank stood from his chair and walked away from his boss. Turning back toward her, he said, "So, the department is behind this? This isn't just you worried about one of your guys?"

"Frank, you know therapy has to be sponsored by the department if we're gonna pay for it. And besides...."

"Justin Smith is behind this, isn't he? I knew it!"

"Well, when a subordinate strikes a superior, there better be some mental health issue, or you would, of course, be fired," Jackson explained what Frank already knew.

Frank exhaled in disgust.

"Frank, you've got PTSD from the accident, the Cameron case, The Schuylkiller case, the Willards, and.... The loss of your father."

"First of all, don't talk about my family to me." Frank was red-faced. "I'm not going there with you."

"Fine, Frank. Whatever you say, but to be clear.... Unless you attend therapy, you're off the case."

"Captain, you know very well I'm at the center of this investigation. Those fuckers are coming for me...."

"Yeah, you're right! And I want your head clear when they finally find you. A dead Frank Collazo is not what any of us need right now. Just do what you're being asked to do and help us get the lunatics off the street. We need you, Frank. I need you."

Frank begrudgingly agreed. "I'll do it under one condition."

"Here we go," Jackson rolled her eyes. "The man's got conditions. I can't wait. Come on," she sat back and motioned Frank to bring it on.

"Candace Weatherby from Montreal, do you remember her?"

"Yeah, she's on the case." Captain Beatrice Jackson shrugged her shoulders nonchalantly.

Frank was taken aback. Shocked, he said, "Wait. What? I'm confused."

"Yeah, Justin Smith was contacted by the Montreal Police Department this morning.... He approved it. He called a little while ago."

"But it's only 9:30." Frank looked at his phone.

"Well, he got the call from Detective Lieutenant Benoit Pelletier this morning at eight. Pelletier gave his recommendation, said she played a vital role in the Isak Cameron case on the Canadian side, and that she's an understudy of Douglas Cantrell." Jackson was surprised Frank didn't know. "You do know she works for the Montreal Police Department, don't you?"

Frank's eyes rolled up, and his head fell back. "Those bastards went behind my back."

Jackson laughed. "That old Cantrell is wily, just like the coyote. First, he hides Penny up in New Hampshire, and now he's got a rookie cop down from Montreal. Gotta love that guy."

"Love-hate relationship," Frank mumbled.

"What's that?"

"Nothing, Captain. Nothing at all."

Twenty minutes later, Frank walked into the Detective Room and found everyone gathered around the new girl on the case. Seeing Frank walk in, Weatherby smiled at him and went back to talking with Bones and the other detectives on the case. Bones barely noticed Frank enter the room.

"Doug, can I speak with you for a moment in private?" Frank, already heading toward Interview Room A, demanded the meeting.

"Sure, Frank." Douglas Cantrell looked like a schoolboy who'd just been summoned to the principal's office.

Once inside the tiny room, Frank motioned for Cantrell to sit, and Doug obliged him.

"You're not going to sit?" Cantrell was nervous.

"No, I'm not." Frank pulled out a chair, placed his foot down on it, and leaned forward with his forearm resting on his knee. "Whatever the hell you're up to, I don't appreciate it."

"Well, I...." Cantrell stuttered. "Um...."

"Don't play naïve with me." Frank stood erect and pointed his finger in Cantrell's direction. "You were already making calls to Montreal before you asked me what I thought about Candace joining the case yesterday. Justin Smith heard from Pelletier at 8 am this morning. That means you were already in contact with him last week."

"You got me, Frank." Cantrell stood up. "Big tough guy, Frank Collazo.... Whoopie. Captain America can do it all by himself. All the fame, all the glory, and a bullet with his name on it!" Cantrell would not be bullied. "You're going to get yourself killed, and I won't sit by and let that happen."

"So, you're gonna save the day, huh?" Frank shrugged off his friend's concerns. "I can handle myself.... Thank you very much!"

"That's horseshit, Frank. You're a shell of your former self. Since The Schuylkiller case, you've been on the decline and getting closer and closer to meeting your maker. Your instincts are good, but your execution is sloppy." Cantrell now pointed a finger in Frank's direction. "You're suffering, and it's going to get you killed. You need to see a professional or just retire already. How many family members are you willing to lose in the pursuit of 'getting the bad guys off the streets?' Those are your words, my friend!"

"So, you put Jackson up to it, then?" Frank was in disbelief.

"Up to what?! I don't know what you're talking about!"

"She's got me seeing some shrink over at Temple on Tuesdays and Thursdays, or she's taking me off the case!"

Cantrell's eyes widened. "I assure you that I knew about any of that."

"Whatever!" Frank threw his hands up in frustration.

"Whether you think so or not, that's a good thing, Frank. It could really help you. It might help you see things through a different lens. It could save your life."

"And how's that, exactly, Doug?" Frank was sarcastic.

Cantrell sat back down in an attempt to lower the temperature in the room. "Frank, you want to die. You're positioning yourself to do so. You want nothing more than to face death and accept it. I have to stop that from happening. People die, Frank. Someone always dies first. Every relationship has an expiration date.... Sound familiar? You once told me that." Cantrell pushed Frank's chair out, hoping he would sit down. "We all try to extend relationships for as long as we can. That's what we do as humans. But no matter what we want or how hard we try, the relationship ends before one or both are ready."

Douglas Cantrell wanted nothing more than to break through to Frank and get him to accept what happened back in May, but he needed Frank to sort it out himself. Or by talking to someone about his loss.

"How philosophical of you, Doug." Frank was unrelenting. "You might be able to get into the head of a serial killer, but not me," Frank huffed.

"You're not all that different, Frank...."

"And what the fuck is that supposed to mean?" Frank was stunned by the comparison.

"I don't mean it that way...." Cantrell struggled for his words. "You are singularly focused on an outcome that's not lawful. You play God from time to time, to hell with the outcome. People die once they enter your sights, and you've been lucky so far...."

"Is that right? Lucky, how?"

"You've been in the sights of multiple killers, Frank. It's just a matter of time. You're walking on a tightrope, and somebody is holding a pair of scissors." Cantrell was metaphorical. "I don't want to lose you, too, Frank?"

"Too?" Frank cocked an eye. "What does that mean?"

Douglas Cantrell rose to his feet and closed the distance between him and his friend. Standing directly in front of Frank, he said, "I'm going to walk out that door right now." He motioned with his eyes. "I'm going to take Candace Weatherby by the arm, and the two of us are going to leave. If we don't hear back from you by the end of day tomorrow, we'll each be on a plane back to our homes. Cantrell teared up. "We'll sit in our homes, Frank. And we'll wait. We'll wait to get the word that we've lost someone we care about. We'll wait until we hear that the bad guys got another good guy. We'll wait.... and then we'll grieve. We'll grieve for a friend, and we'll grieve for ourselves because we'll be less of who we are without you in our lives."

Cantrell placed his hand on Frank's left shoulder and squeezed. "Goodbye, friend. I hope my phone rings tomorrow night before I go to sleep. If it doesn't, I'll fly home on Wednesday and be with Gaye for the holiday, and I won't come back. Together, she and I will wait. I wish you all the strength and wisdom that a man I used to know possessed. Goodbye, Son."

Douglas Cantrell turned and left the room, closing the door behind him. In his wake was a man so lost and confused that not even the fiercest love from his best friend could save him. Frank looked out the sidelight window with a tear in his eye. He watched as his friend Doug whispered to a sitting Weatherby, who was clearly taken aback by his words. Frank watched as a disappointed Candace Weatherby stood, collected her things, and walked out of the Detective Room, looking back to IRA before she did.

Frank sat down in the tiny room and dropped his head into his hands. Sitting there, he wondered where it all went wrong, and then it came to him. Twenty-nine years ago, Frank Collazo went to a baseball game without his father. Twenty-nine years ago, he lost his dad. Twenty-nine years later, he was losing his mind..... and his life. Was death what he wanted all along?

Later that night, Frank sat in his car, the snow falling heavily. As his wiper blades chased away the flakes, he stared out at the Residence Inn and thought about going in. Frank instead put the car into drive and drove off into the darkness. He was going to see his girl. He only hoped that she was home.

As Frank drove away, two vagrants, a man and a woman, stood outside the hotel and looked in through the atrium glass, both donning hoods. In their sights were two people just sitting down to have dinner, an old man and a young woman. However, no one could see two men walking into the hotel, wearing trench coats and fedoras. One appeared to be in his forties, while the other wore snow-white hair. Sitting in the lounge, directly between the bad guys outside and the good guys inside, were the ghosts of Christmas past. Old Man Winter and Detective Frank Bruno would let nothing bad happen on this night.

Outside, a frigid blast flew up behind Talon Grayson and Genesis Harper. "Did you feel that?" Talon asked Genesis.

"The wind? Of course, I did. It's fucking freezing out here." Genesis crossed her arms.

"No, not the wind," said Talon. "It was something else...." He looked around in fear, feeling as if he was being watched.

"I don't know what you're talking about," said Genesis. "Let's go in there. It's too cold out here."

"Fuck that shit!" said Talon, pulling on the drawstrings of his hood. "Tonight's not the night. We're outta here. Let's go!"

The next day at 4:55 pm, Frank stood outside of an office on the campus of Temple University. Looking at the business card in his hand, then back up to the building name and number, Frank walked in and checked in at the reception desk. The nameplate on the sign outside the door displayed the name Dr. Archibald Riley – Head of Psychiatry, matching the name on the business card.

Fifteen minutes later, Frank sat in a plush office that looked and felt straight out of the 1800s. Surveying the room with its dark woods, and floor-to-ceiling bookcases filled with hundreds of books, Frank looked up above the oversized mahogany desk and saw what appeared to be a stuffed falcon. The feathered creature looked to be presiding over the room, its furnishings, occupants, and every past, present, and future spilling of the guts by Rice's patients. Looking again at the ravenous yet majestic bird, Frank couldn't help but stare at its talons, four on each foot, each appearing to be one to two inches long. For a brief moment, his eyes closed, Frank was transported back to FalconClaw.

Frank's vision suddenly became blurry, like television snow when a channel went offline. It had happened since his father died only once or twice a year until The Schuylkiller came into his life; after that, it would happen more often. When it occurred, Frank would try shaking the snow from his vision by squeezing his eyes tightly closed as hard as he could and shaking his head violently back and forth. The event would usually result in a migraine headache that would keep Frank down for hours at a time.

As his vision escaped the howling blizzard in his head, it was replaced by FalconClaw, the 1992 version of the estate. It was the very adaptation that filled so many of his nightmares. Frank was defined as much by the old mansion that used to sit up on the hill overlooking Bedford Street as he was the man who took his father's life, Vincent Charmaine Walker. The two, the man and the mansion, lived together, rent-free in Frank's head, and always would.

"So, you must be the legendary Frank Collazo," came a voice from beneath the Falcon.

An embarrassed Frank was startled back into full consciousness. Abruptly standing to meet the esteemed doctor, he said, "Um. I'm sorry, I didn't see you come in."

"Yes, I noticed," said the hefty man somewhere between sixty and the grave. "If I may, where did your memories take you off to just then?"

Frank wittingly said, "Well, that's a little forward of you. Shouldn't you, at the very least, offer me a drink before we confess all of our sins to each other?"

The man chuckled, setting down his time-worn, brown leather notepad on the desk. "Yes, yes. I thought as much...." Riley smiled and shook his head slightly, purposely not finishing his sentence.

Frank waited, thinking the man seemed peculiar, then said, "Thought as much? Did you want to finish your sentence?"

"Why, yes, you remind me of a young man I used to know some decades ago. He was a man so full of life one day and wondering how it would all end the next. The young man had quite the sense of humor, too," the Head of Psychiatry at Temple University recalled. "A witty young man who'd lost his father as a boy and wondered what it all meant. Was it a divine plan or an irreverent mishap? The young lad struggled with that question for years."

Frank was suddenly confused. *Surely this couldn't be the man heading up Temple's Lewis Katz School of Medicine's psychiatric department,* he thought.

"Pardon me," said Frank. "I'm Detective Frank Collazo, and I'm supposed to meet with Dr. Archibald Rice..... am I in the right place?"

"Yes, young man. That's me, unfortunately....."

Frank cocked his head, unable to get a read on the quirky, seemingly unrefined doctor who appeared completely out of place in the opulent setting.

"Sometimes, I will jump into a conversation without first introducing myself. I am Archibald Rice, and yes, you are in the right place. Please, call me Archie." The man looked around the room and then off into a memory. "I hate being called doctor, such a formal term for such an informal world. Wouldn't you say?" Rice's gaze once again found Frank.

"I guess." Frank's eyes were still wide, trying to grasp the interaction thus far.

"Yes, well, here we are. I am thrilled to be here with you today, Frank. May I call you Frank?"

"Yes, of course," said Frank. "Detective is such a formal term for such an informal world. Wouldn't you agree, Doctor?" Frank maintained a straight face.

"Ah, yes. As I said, you do remind me of that young man."

Frank's eyes widened slightly. "So, Doctor, if I may? Can I ask you a question?"

"Why, yes, please do, Frank."

"I was wondering why the Head of Psychiatry for all of Temple University was assigned to meet a middle-aged cop from East Falls who appears to be losing his mind. Surely you have bigger fish to fry?"

"Yes, yes," the good doctor pondered. "Before I answer your question, please join me over here on the couch?"

"That's a bit forward of you, don't you think?" Frank maintained a straight face while continuing his joke from earlier.

Archibald Riley laughed, causing his belly to jiggle and pop one of his shirt buttons open. "Oh my. You are the funny one. You and I will create such good memories." Riley wiped a laughter tear from his eye. "Yes, I do have to be careful these days when having a female patient in my presence. You can't just ask a woman over to your couch. I'm always keenly aware of a woman's struggles in today's and yesterday's society, both in and out of the workplace. But today, I have a strong young man in my office, and am very excited to get to work. So, please, join me on the couch if you wouldn't mind."

"Were you planning to answer my question, Doctor?"

"Yes, of course. I will the moment you come over here and sit down." Riley motioned with his hand to a red velvet chaise lounge while he turned to find his well-worn brown leather armchair. "And please, call me Archie."

After a fleeting moment of wanting instead to turn and leave, Frank joined the good doctor.

Both, now sitting, Archibald Riley explained, "When I saw your name come across my assistant's desk, I immediately recognized it and quickly became intrigued. As you know, we have a relationship with the Philadelphia Police Department and see hundreds of law enforcement officers annually. And while I normally teach and mentor our staff and students, when I saw your name, I thought to myself, what a wonderful opportunity to learn about a man with such a storied history."

Sitting, not lying on the red sofa, Frank smirked and said, "Storied?"

"Oh yes, Frank!" Rice's face lit up. "Nearly all humans have the same story. You know, the usual, lost their job, broken heart, the passing of a loved one, stressful job, down on their luck.... While I don't want to trivialize such events, as they shape one's psyche, your story is riveting."

"Riveting?" Frank again smirked. "More like tragic, no?"

"Even in tragedy, young Frank, you can find redemption, salvation, and, believe it or not, happiness and the will to live."

"Will to live?" Frank shook his head. "Man, you're just full of one-liners today, Doc. Not sure who you've been talking to about me. Or, what's written in your fancy leather journal, but I don't have a death wish."

"Don't you, Frank?"

It was at that point that Frank knew he should probably lie down.

After forty-five minutes of mostly get-to-know-you questions, the two men stood to say goodbye.

"That's an interesting falcon you have mounted on the wall."

"It's a Peregrine Falcon, the fastest of all Falcons," Riley looked proudly at the magnificent bird looking down over the room.

"Did you kill it yourself?"

"Oh, heaven's no," Riley shook his head emphatically. "I would never take the life of any creature." The good doctor caught himself, knowing that Frank had taken the life of Isak Cameron. "That is if I could help it."

"How fast?"

"In a predatory dive, it has been clocked at over two-hundred miles per hour, believe it or not."

"And why a falcon?" Frank couldn't help but wonder. What were the chances, he thought, that a falcon would coincidentally be hanging in the office of his shrink?

"My father once worked at FalconClaw. I'd been there once while attending Temple. When they closed it down, they had an estate sale, and my father bought the falcon at a ridiculous price, but it was something he just had to have. I remember him saying that it called out to him. It once hung in the office of a Mr. Dean Travers, the former administrator of Heavenly Gates back in the early seventies."

Frank shook his head and thought Old Man Winter and Frank Bruno must be hiding around the corner. The coincidences were just too many.

As Archibald Riley opened and held the door for Frank, his new patient turned and said, "Archie, you mentioned that I reminded you of a young man..... Is that right?"

"Yes, you do, Frank."

"How did you know him? And is he still around?"

"Why, yes, he is." Riley turned to look at his office, smiled, and looked back at Frank. "That young man grew up to be the Head of Psychiatry at Temple University. Coincidentally, this is his office."

Frank was solemn. "So, that young man lost his father, too?"

"He did," Riley was stoic.

"How old were you when he passed?"

"I was fourteen, Frank. Just like you." Riley paused. "He took his own life. It took many years for me to forgive him, but I finally did. And I'm better for it."

Frank nodded and said, "Thank you for your time today."

"Next Tuesday, then?"

Frank cocked his head. "No Thursday?"

"Thanksgiving is a big day in my house, Frank." Archie Riley rubbed his belly. "So, unfortunately, I won't be coming into the office, I'm afraid."

"Yes, I understand. So, next Tuesday, then. Five o'clock sharp?" Frank smiled and turned to go.

"I can hardly wait," chuckled Riley, another button popping on his shirt.

Across town, two vagrants were stalking their next victim at a place called Rocky Tops. It was just a block from FalconClaw Park. It was a place where Talon would pick up flooring and granite countertops for his new job. Standing guard in the supply yard was an off-duty Philly cop named Daniel Moncrief. He was trying to make a few extra bucks to support his young family, a wife and one-year-old twins.

Chapter 20 – Unholy Union

The day after Talon Grayson murdered a homeless man on the streets of Philadelphia back on June 11, 2020, he fled across the Delaware River to his hometown of Camden. He felt in his heart and mind that he and Genesis were finished. How could they not be? Genesis was his half-sister, both having the same biological father.

Two days later, Talon stood in front of 969 Trent Road and just stared. Seconds later, a woman appeared at the side door and looked out.

"May we help you?" she yelled from the half-open screen door.

Talon immediately recognized the woman as Delores Steinecker and chose to say nothing, unsure of how he felt. Anger, love, resentment, and yearning had all crossed his mind. At that moment, if he were only wearing his hoodie, he would've pulled his hood up to disguise himself from his former foster parent, but it was June, and his black AC/DC T-shirt provided him with no cover. Not sure of what to say or do, Talon turned to leave.

Now two houses down from his former home, he looked back to see the woman, who was now standing in the front yard, watching as he walked away. The woman yelled out to Talon, thinking that she recognized him.

"Talon!" she yelled, now on the sidewalk nervously clutching a dishtowel. "Talon! Is that you?"

Frightened, Talon began walking faster.

"Talon!"

As Talon got further away, the woman lowered her head, thinking she had mistaken the stranger for the one foster child that would never escape her memory. After Talon Grayson, Delores and George Steinecker never fostered another child.

Talon, now running, fled with tears in his eyes. The tears soon dried, however, and were replaced with bitterness. "That was my home!" he growled beneath his breath; teeth clenched. "They took it away from me!" The young man was angry. He had just killed a man the day before and felt the need to kill again.

After being homeless for nearly four months, it was now early October 8, and Talon was broke and desperate. Having no money since abandoning his job with the home improvement company in Philly, Talon was missing Genesis and becoming angrier and angrier every day. Homeless shelters kept kicking him out after he became increasingly violent with other homeless people. Additionally, his Tracfone had been cut off after running out of minutes two months earlier, and Talon had been unable to contact Genesis. He loved her but hated the situation. *How could it ever be appropriate to be with her?* He kept asking himself.

Repeatedly looking at the phone and the last text Genesis had sent him back on June 28, seventeen days after he last saw her on the boardwalk, the text read, *Call Me.* Talon would stare at the last words she sent him, whether sheltering under a bridge, in an abandoned building, or from inside a burglarized home. Talon stared at her words, and he longed for her. It was time, he thought. It was time to return to Philadelphia and find his love.

Hitching a ride, he crossed the Ben Franklin Bridge hoping the last four months had allowed the case of the murdered homeless man in front of Naval Square to go cold. After all, he thought, the police weren't rolling out the Special Victim's Unit for the death of a homeless man.

Talon's first stop would be seeing his former employer and requesting his job back. Without phone service, he would never find Genesis by simply walking the streets. He hoped that she had the same number.

The next morning, after begging for his old job, Talon's former boss reluctantly agreed as he was again short-staffed. After asking for a pay advance and being declined, Talon would have to work two weeks before getting his first paycheck. When he finally did, he went to a local Walmart to get his Tracfone reactivated.

For several days Talon couldn't get ahold of Genesis. Believing she didn't love him anymore, he thought of ending his life. Before he did, though, he would go to all the old places they would hang out. Afterward, he would make his way over to the Twin Bridges and jump off at their highest point towering above the Schuylkill River.

After spending Halloween day down by the Schuylkill River Park, sitting on the same park bench where he'd learned Genesis was his half-sister, Talon decided he would take the chance and revisit the scene where he killed the homeless man. It was the place where he'd first met Genesis. It was now nightfall, and Talon pulled his hood up, trying hard not to be identified by anyone who may have witnessed the murder more than four months earlier. Walking up and down Gray's Ferry for hours, finding nothing, neither satisfaction nor Genesis, Talon would go upriver to the Twins, where he would end it all.

Along the way, the temperature fell rapidly, and Talon sought temporary relief from the cold and the two-mile walk north. Before crossing the South Street Bridge, he saw a barrel fire under the bridge, with several people standing around it. He thought it could be his refuge. Approaching the circle of homeless, and the amber glow that silhouetted their figures, Talon studied one of the people and noticed the small frame of a woman. She appeared to be wearing the unmistakable gray hooded sweatshirt that Genesis had always worn.

Walking up from behind, he quietly crept up on the woman and touched her right shoulder. Alarmed, a young black woman turned back, saw Talon, and recoiled in fear.

"Get away from me, mothafucka!" said the girl, pretending she wasn't frightened.

The four other men around the fire shouted at Talon, staring him down and threatening him, telling him to 'beat it.'

"But.... I, I, I just wanted to get warm for a minute. I didn't mean nothin' by it," Talon pleaded with the girl.

"Get lost before you end up in the river, white boy!" said a large black man standing beside the girl.

Talon sighed and turned to leave. When he returned to the top of the bridge, he looked to his right and down the Schuylkill River Boardwalk, where he'd been three hours earlier. Squinting to see, he thought he saw a slight figure sitting on the familiar bench. Looking to his left and the other side of the South Street Bridge, the direction he was headed, he looked back to the right and decided he'd take the chance.

Now on the boardwalk, his spirits were lifted when he thought he recognized the person sitting alone as Genesis. Afraid to sneak up unannounced, Talon quietly called her name as he approached.

"Genesis," he almost whispered. "Genesis," this time louder.

The sound of the river and the gusting wind muffled his words. Losing confidence, his approach waned. Stopping in his tracks to stare, the girl on the bench turned to her left and saw a man she knew so well.

"Talon?" she stood. "Talon!" she screamed when seeing that it was him.

Tears in his eyes, Talon ran to Genesis, and she met him halfway. Standing on the boardwalk, both crying, the two hugged.

"Why did you leave me?!" Genesis cried. "Where did you go?"

"I.... I.... I went home," Talon cried.

Genesis cried, too, pounding on Talon's chest with both fists. "I am your home! And you are mine!"

"I love you, Genesis!" Talon sobbed. "I love you!"

"We're family, Talon." Genesis wiped her tears. "Where you go, I go," she vowed.

"I have a hundred dollars," said Talon. "I know a place over on Samson where we can get warm."

"No. Keep the money. I have a place we can go."

"Where's your sweatshirt?" Talon rubbed Genesis' shoulders to keep her warm.

"Those people under the bridge took it from me."

Talon seethed. He would see them again as he looked back toward the South Street Bridge.

"I'll get you another one. Forget about them. Let's go." Genesis took Talon's hand.

The two walked the one-plus mile to St. Peter Claver Roman Church, on the corner of 12th & Lombard, and along the way, Talon shed his hoodie and gave it to Genesis. Passing through the broken gate of a wrought iron fence, Genesis led Talon to the church's underbelly, a modern-day catacomb for many homeless waiting their turn to die and be rid of a society that wanted rid of them.

The church had been abandoned since 2014 and was home to Genesis and several other homeless men and women from time to time for the last few months. Once in the basement of the historic church, which was awaiting its demolition, Talon and Genesis built a small fire in an old wire basket using small wooden crucifixes and tattered bibles. After getting warm, the two entered into their ritualistic and now unholy union of the flesh, with the haunting lyrics of *Take Me to Church* filling the cold, dank air. After they finished, they spoke of their father and his sins. One deed, in particular, captured their imagination more than the others. At that moment, one man became their muse and would serve as their reason for being, their reason for killing.

It was Halloween night, 2020, and in just one year, the ravenous butchers would amass a death toll of ten cops by Halloween 2021, earning the name Cop Killers by the press. After learning who their father was, they studied his misdeeds and idolized the man and his nefarious accomplishments. While their journey began separately on June 11, 1993, it would end together, but only after completing the circle.

Back to the present, it was Tuesday evening, November 22, 2021, and Frank found himself back at the Residence Inn hotel after meeting with Archibald Rice. Sitting in his car, he pondered if he should go in or not. It had been a little more than twenty-four hours since he and Doug had their fight, and Frank was nervous about seeing his friend. Looking at the hotel through the flurries, he was petrified that perhaps Doug had decided to leave a day early, worried that he may have lost his only true friend.

Instead of calling, Frank entered the hotel, nodded to young Penny behind the counter, and took the elevator up to Cantrell's floor. Now standing in front of room 305, he took a deep breath before knocking. After several taps on the door and several seconds of waiting, Frank's heart sank. Doug was gone. Exhaling fully, with an emptiness he'd experienced far too many times in recent months, he turned to go. Now at the elevator, Frank pushed the down arrow when he heard a door latch release.

Standing in a white robe and slippers and drying his hair, Cantrell yelled out to his friend, "What took you so long?"

"Jesus!" Frank sighed in relief. "I thought you'd gone home."

"Not before you came to apologize, first," Cantrell smiled.

"That's why I'm here." Frank walked to Doug's room and hugged his friend. "I'm sorry, Doug."

"Well, come on in, now that we have all that nonsense sorted out." Doug waved Frank in, continuing to towel dry his gray hair. I was just getting ready to meet Candace downstairs for dinner. Will you join us?"

"Umm, well, I was gonna go see Penny, but I guess I have time for dinner."

"Bones will be joining us. Will that be okay?"

Frank cocked a curious brow and began to feel a bit territorial. "Bones? Why is he coming here?"

"Well, apparently, he made quite the impression on Candace, and she made quite the impression on him. He's coming over to discuss the case and update us on what we missed today. We weren't sure we would see you before we left tomorrow. As I recall, our group meeting ended abruptly yesterday." Cantrell not so subtly reminded Frank that the argument the two had had prematurely ended the case review.

"Wait, so you're leaving tomorrow?"

"After I told Gaye about what happened yesterday, she made me promise to come home for Thanksgiving," explained Doug. "I'll return on Sunday if you'll have me."

"Sunday?" Frank was trying to reconcile the case, Doug leaving, Candace and Bones, and a Thanksgiving holiday that might not include Penny and Bonnie. "Um, okay. Of course, I want you back here. I just wish you didn't have to leave."

"Come with me, then." Doug's eyes grew bright with the thought. "Gaye would love to see you. It would be nice."

"Geez." Frank wasn't sure he should go. "I mean, the case and all," he hesitated. "And what about Penny?"

"Frank, I'm quite certain Penny and Bonnie would want you to go." Cantrell lowered his head as if subtly pleading with his friend.

"Let me talk it over with her later. Would that be okay?"

"Of course. I was thinking of inviting Candace, too?"

"Yeah, sure, whatever." Frank was still in a fog. Thinking of Penny, his head began to fill with the fuzzy white snow again.

"Why don't you head downstairs and meet up with Candace and Bones? They're in the bar waiting for me," said Cantrell. "I'll meet up with you after I get dressed."

"You want me to just wait for you here?" Frank had always worried for Doug's safety at every turn and preferred to wait in the room.

"No, you go on ahead. I'll meet you downstairs in ten minutes. After I get dressed, I need to make a quick call home, and then I'll join you."

Getting off the elevator, Frank saw Bones and Candace walking out of the hotel bar, each with a drink in their hand. They didn't seem to notice him as they walked toward the hotel restaurant. Seeing them together rubbed Frank the wrong way. He wasn't jealous but rather fond of both and wanted nothing more than for those he cared about to be happy. While he didn't know Candace well, only chatting with her several times to keep in touch since he'd returned from Sweden the year before, he was sure her intentions were good.

Bones, on the other hand.... Frank chuckled while standing in the lobby. He couldn't be sure of a guy who slept in his car when having a perfectly good house to sleep in at night. After second-guessing himself regarding the two, he smiled and walked to the restaurant to join them.

Strolling up from behind, he joined them as they waited to be seated. "There they are," Frank pronounced, "Mr. and Miss America!"

Candace turned, saw Frank, and smiled. "I beg your pardon," she said. "That's Miss Canada." She paused and added, "First Runner-Up, actually."

"You're too modest, Candace," Frank joked.

"Wait," Bones joined in on the conversation. "You were Miss Canada?"

Candace rolled her eyes back, half flattered and half humbled. "As I said, First Runner-Up."

"Wow! Who would've thought?" Bones was fooling no one. He was taken by her beauty the minute he laid eyes on her. He was guarded, however, unsure how his pseudo-big-brother Frank might feel if he displayed interest in Candace outside the case.

"Sure, Bones. Whatever." Frank patted his friend and partner on the back. "Don't get your hopes up, though." Frank was expressionless. "She's married with five kids."

"Oh," Bones looked confused. "I had no idea."

"Right this way," the young hostess addressed the group.

Turning to follow the girl, Frank leading the way, Candace turned toward Bones, rolled her eyes again, and shook her head, mouthing the words, "He's just kidding."

A sigh of relief washed over Bones' face, and Candace took notice.

Minutes after sitting down, Candace asked where Cantrell was. That was all it took for Frank to panic mildly. Looking toward the hostess station and beyond it to the lobby, he didn't see his friend. After several more agonizing seconds, he spotted Doug exiting the elevator. Smiling, he saw Doug chatting up the bellboy outside the elevator and shook his head when he saw Cantrell tip the young man for no apparent reason.

Frank wandered off for a second and remembered all the time he and Doug spent together, good and bad. Doug was his friend for life, and knowing that something came after, he was sure he and Doug would always be friends, even after death.

Frank stood to greet Cantrell as he approached the table, smiling. Frank returned his smile and asked, "Did I just see you tip the busboy, Doug."

"What's that?" Doug looked lost for a moment. "Oh, yes. What a fine young man. He's studying over at Temple. He wants to be in the FBI one day."

"Yeah, but why did you tip him?"

"Well, you know, Frank. College can be expensive."

"No, I wouldn't know. I never actually attended college." Frank's mind went to Archibald Riley for a moment. He thought that Doug and Archie would get along great.

After exchanging pleasantries with Bones and Candace, Doug shook out his napkin, placed it on his lap, and whispered to Frank. "Speaking of Temple, how did it go today?"

Frank, wanting to be discrete about his session, whispered, "We can talk about it later."

"So," Cantrell enthusiastically addressed the group. "I have an invitation I'd like to extend to my friends gathered around this table...."

Bones, Frank, and Candace all looked at each other. Frank suspected what Doug had in mind.

"Well, before coming down from my room just moments ago, I was on the phone with Gaye, and she thought it would be a great idea to open our home to the three of you for Thanksgiving dinner." Cantrell beamed at the thought of hosting his friends.

Frank shook his head and smiled, knowing full well that Gaye had nothing to do with it.

"Is that right?" Frank asked, grinning.

Cantrell looked to his left, smiled, and winked at his friend. "So, what do you say, folks? Thanksgiving dinner at Doug's?"

Candace appeared to love the idea after celebrating the Canadian Thanksgiving the month before. Bones, almost seeking Frank's permission, looked over at his partner. He wasn't sure they should be out of town for any amount of time, considering that the Cop Killers were on the loose.

"I think it's a great idea," said Frank, looking directly at Bones and Candace when he did. "I, unfortunately, won't be able to make it as I have a pressing matter to attend to." Frank didn't mention Penny or Bonnie, but the three around the table immediately thought of them.

"I'm not so sure it's a good idea," said Bones. "I mean.... to be out of town? I'm pretty sure I can't go."

"Nonsense, Bones. I'll clear it with Jackson tonight. You're going." Frank was adamant. "I think you guys should all get on a plane tomorrow and enjoy your time at Doug's. Penny and Bonnie spent some time up there in the summer of '20 and had a wonderful time."

Doug looked at Frank, and his heart bled for his friend. "Are you sure you won't join us, Frank? Gaye would love to see you."

"I'm the investigative lead on the case out of the 39th, and I'm damn sure the captain won't permit me to go. Additionally, I don't want to step away from the investigation. Not even for a day."

"I completely understand, Frank. I know Gaye will, too."

"So, an airplane, you said. Is that right?" Bones looked nervous, swallowing hard.

"Yes, it's just a one-hour and forty-five-minute flight each way." Doug was hopeful Bones would go. He'd feel strange taking only Candace with him. He wondered what Gaye might think.

Candace looked over at Bones and smiled at him. "Bones. Have you ever flown before?"

Bones again swallowed hard and said, "I almost did, once," his eyes as wide as an owl's.

The three laughed at Bones, with Cantrell saying, "So that's it then, I'll book the flights after dinner."

Candace smiled while Bones looked a little pale.

"Don't worry, Bonesie. I'll hold your hand." Candace Weatherby reached for Bones' hand atop the table.

Frank noticed the gesture and said, "Bonesie? I'm sorry, Candace, but only good friends get to call him that." Frank's heart went cold for a second. Seeing Bones and Candace sitting next to each other reminded Frank of him and Penny at the Ritz on Easter Sunday, 2017. Frank's next memory had his vision turning to snow again as he saw the face of the young valet who parked his car that fateful night. Frank remembered his name was Matt. He then remembered finding the young man's body and severed head in the trunk of his car just as Penny screamed for her mother, Bonnie Ross, as Dante's Inferno consumed her and four others. The next thing he heard was Cameron St. John laughing wildly.

Cantrell noticed Frank's blank stare and kicked him under the table, recognizing that he was having another episode.

Snapping out of his funk, Frank said, "As I was saying, Candace. No more nicknames for our boy here until you get to know him a little better."

"Yeah, Candace. What were you thinking?" Bones feigned annoyance. "Only my close friends call me that." Bones winked at Frank and grinned.

"Well, who knows...." smiled Candace, "Perhaps a little field trip up to New Hampshire might remedy the predicament we find ourselves in?"

All at the table laughed. Thinking of Penny and Bonnie, Frank hoped he'd see them both on Thanksgiving Day.

Chapter 21 – Ellery & Bedford

At 9:40 am, the day before Thanksgiving, Frank gave his friends a ride to the airport. Bones and Candace would return to Philadelphia on Friday, while Cantrell would return on Sunday evening.

"Remember, no Ubers," Frank said to all three of them as he said goodbye on the curb outside Terminal F – American Airlines departures. "Trust no one." Frank hugged Cantrell.

Turning to Bones, Frank joked, "Be careful with this one," he said, turning his gaze to Candace. "She thinks she's a cop. Don't go solving any crimes up in New Hampshire, or we'll never get her back down here."

"Oh, I'm coming back, all right," said Candace. "You just make sure you don't solve this one without me."

"Fat chance," said Frank. "I can't solve cases without Miss Canada – First Runner-Up." Pausing, he added, "Take care of my boy, Bones, over here. He might look tough on the outside, but apparently, his kryptonite is air travel."

Bones sighed heavily and said, "Is it too late to change my mind?"

"You'll be okay, Bonesie. Just stay close to Candace."

As the three headed off to ticketing, Frank, for a fleeting moment, wished he was going. Pursing his lips and shaking his head, he felt like his friends were going off to a college that had rejected him. He felt alone, and he felt scared.

Driving up 95 North and stuck in rush hour traffic, Frank looked out over the Dickenson Narrows and reviewed the case details in his mind. Something was missing. Why was there no one killed in September? What did the letter tiles spell out? Frank was convinced that there was a dead cop out there somewhere that no one knew about. He was beginning to rethink the Scrabble tile in his pocket. Perhaps it did, in fact, mean something. Frank was stubborn, though. He would keep it in his pocket until another cop turned up dead but hoped that he'd never have to take it out. His instincts told him that the piece likely meant nothing. *How could it?* He thought it was too random. He knew, however, that Penny's instincts were better than his, and she was the one who had led him to the trunk of the Accord.

Forty-five minutes later, he ended up at the 39th, but the place was a ghost town. Every detective, except for the rookies, were off until Monday unless, of course, there was a break in the case. En route to the Detective Room, Frank passed through the Ops Room and was asked if he'd seen Officer Daniel Moncrief, whose wife had been calling incessantly. Frank shook his head 'no' and kept walking.

After studying the case files for more than two hours, nothing jumped out at Frank. Closing the folder in his hand, he leaned back in his chair, stared up at the ceiling, and exhaled in frustration. He just wanted to go home to his family, like everybody else.

With his confidence waning, and out of inspiration and lacking motivation, Frank grabbed his keys and went for a ride. Fifteen minutes later, he was parked near McMichael Park, at the corner of West Coulter and Netherfield Road. There, he sat and stared up at the old Clark Family Home. Frank wasn't sure what brought him there. The night Richard Clark got a hold of his gun and killed himself on his front lawn was still fresh in Frank's mind. But it wasn't Clark that he was thinking about. It was Penny. Penny was there during all of his toughest times. She had supported and nurtured him and given him a reason to live. Now, she seemed more like a ghost, only appearing when summoned. Cold and distant, and emotionally unavailable, Frank was tortured with the why. Why was she acting the way she was? Why couldn't he go into the house? The mounting questions were smothering him.

Next, Frank went to the old Sharpless House, just five minutes north, on the corner of Wayne and West School House Lane. Parked between the house and the Germantown House apartment building, Frank got out of his car to get a better look at the third-floor attic window, which from the road, was obstructed by trees. Looking up, he could almost see the eleven-year-old version of Isak staring down at him. The wind rustling through the trees overhead convinced Frank that Isak was indeed up there. He wished, at least. He wanted to go in there to see his friend. He wanted to cry with him again. Frank pressed his lips tightly together, looked again at the window, and nodded to a boy who wasn't there.

Never had Frank been so alone, and his thoughts were becoming unhealthy. Feeling for his M&P strapped to his left chest reassured him that if things didn't get better soon, he could trust that the same gun used to set Isak free might also free him from his prison. Like Isak, Frank's life ended when he was just a child. And Frank wanted nothing more than to be that child again. The one with a baseball and a bat. The one with a father.

Unaware of his surroundings, Frank found himself suddenly driving again. He was lost when studying the street signs and intersections; nothing looked familiar to him. With another left and another right, Frank pulled into a vacant parking lot on Ridge Avenue, directly across the street from the Laurel Hill Cemetery. Feeling dizzy and sick to his stomach, Frank couldn't understand what had led him there.

Shaking his head, his instincts told him he was there for a reason and should go in. But something inside was screaming, *No!* Frank was suddenly frightened and knew everything would change if he entered the cemetery. He felt that he would never be the same again, and life as he knew it would be over.

Laurel Hill Cemetery was once known as the cemetery of the elite and was a popular burial place for Civil War generals, including General George Meade, the victorious general at Gettysburg. Even Adrian Balboa and her brother Paulie, the fictional wife and brother-in-law of Rocky Balboa, were buried there. Frank was able to make out their gravesites from the street. He chuckled when he thought of Bones.

To Frank and many of his brethren, though, it was better known as the place where cops killed in the line of duty were laid to rest. That made it an unwelcoming presence in his eyes. Though he hadn't been there since the funeral of Ali Ashfaq, he felt as if he'd been there more recently. The feeling unsettled him, and he couldn't understand why.

Sitting in his car, he stared at the grand pillared entrance. Frank was prepared to leave when his phone rang. Hoping it was Penny, he held his breath momentarily before looking at the caller ID. It was Cantrell.

"Doug? You guys made it in okay?"

"We did, Frank. It feels good to be home. I wish that you had come with us."

"Not gonna lie, Doug, that feeling crossed my mind as I pulled away from the airport. I think the time away would have done me good."

"So, where are you now? At the 39th?"

"No. I'm actually up at Laurel Hill."

"You're at Laurel Hill right now?" Cantrell was suddenly short of breath. "And, what took you there today, Son?"

Frank sighed. "I'm not really sure, Doug. It was as if the car drove itself here. Something's telling me to go in, but I'm afraid to for some reason. I can't explain it."

"Perhaps you should, Frank. You can drive around the place a little. Maybe it'll come to you why you're there."

"Yeah. I don't know about that." Frank was against the idea. "I think I'm just gonna drive over to Penny's and say hello."

Douglas Cantrell desperately wished he was there with Frank at that moment. He knew Frank was close to a breakthrough and was kicking himself for leaving him to work through his pain alone.

"Frank, listen to me. Whether you decide to drive through or not, would you please call me tonight when you get home?"

"Yeah, well, um.... I don't want to upset the party over there. You guys settle in and have a good time. Don't worry about me. I'll be fine."

"You're like a son to me, Frank. I'm always worried about you."

"I'll be fine, but thank you for being my friend. I love you, Doug."

"I love you, too, Frank."

"Talk to you later."

"You better call me tonight."

"Roger that, Doug. I will."

As soon as Frank hung up, his phone rang again. Not recognizing the number, he thought he should ignore the call thinking it was a cold caller. Being the good cop he was, though, he answered it just in case it was information pertaining to the case.

"Hello?"

"Yes, is this Frank Collazo?" said a familiar voice.

"Yes. Who's calling, please?"

"Frank, it's me, Archibald Riley. Archie."

"Oh?" Frank sat erect in his chair as if Riley were there with him. "Dr. Riley, what can I do for you?"

"Frank.... Please call me Archie."

"Okay, Archie. Is everything all right?"

"I was calling to ask you the same thing. How are you doing?"

Frank sighed. "It hasn't been a good day for me, I'm afraid. I dropped off my friends at the airport. They went away for the holiday."

"Such a bummer," said Riley. "What are your plans for Thanksgiving?"

"Outside of a frozen turkey dinner, I don't have any."

"Well, I'd invite you over, but we have a rule in this house.... it's my wife's rule. No patients allowed over for the holidays."

"I can only imagine. You must have hundreds of them."

Riley chuckled. "Thousands over the years."

"So, why the call if you have so many people in your care?" Frank asked. "Why do I get special treatment?"

"I know we just met, but you've made quite the impression on me. You came to mind when packing my things for the long weekend, and I thought I would call to check in."

"Well, I'm flattered, Archie." Frank was indifferent to the call but thankful he was talking to someone who seemed to care.

"So, what are you doing right now? Chasing the bad guys around town?" Riley tried to keep things light, understanding the immense pressure that Frank was under.

"I'm actually up at Laurel Hill Cemetery. Not sure why, though, to be honest with you."

"Oh? Is that right?"

"Yeah, I just sort of ended up here."

"Did you go in and visit any loved ones or friends? Fellow fallen officers?" Riley gently probed. Like Cantrell, he felt Frank was on the verge of a breakthrough.

"Nope." Frank was adamant. "Not going in there, not today, not while I'm still alive."

"But Frank, it can be cathartic to visit the grave of a loved one. Perhaps you should take the first step and drive through those hallowed pillars.

"No thanks, Archie. I'm good."

"Well, you let me know if you need to chat before our visit next Tuesday. This is my cell that I'm calling from. Please save it in your phone so that you'll have it."

"Will do, Dr. Riley. Sure thing."

"You have a Happy Thanksgiving, Frank."

"I'll try. You have a Happy Thanksgiving as well."

The two hung up, and Frank wondered what to do next. Bedford Street was calling him, and he would answer that call.

Just minutes into his drive north to Old Germantown, Frank's cell phone rang again. Frank was annoyed, shaking his head in frustration, knowing the caller wasn't Penny. He was sick of the well wishes and holiday cheer and just wanted to wallow in his despair.

Looking at the caller ID, Frank saw that it was his captain.

Fourteen hours earlier, off-duty Philly cop Daniel Moncrief arrived for work at his night job. Moncrief worked out of the 39th and lived just eight blocks from FalconClaw Park. It was Tuesday night, just after 10 pm, and he was arriving for an eight-hour shift. Moncrief would act as a security guard for a company called Rocky Tops. The company sold granite for countertop installation, ceramic tile, stone, and tile flooring, and had an expansive outdoor inventory of sand, natural flagstone, bluestone, slate, and tons of Wissahickon Schist. Moncrief would patrol inside and outside of the business from ten at night to six in the morning. He'd then sleep for a few hours before returning to work at noon on Wednesday. After that, he would be off for Thanksgiving and Black Friday.

Due to the holiday, builders and contractors weren't shopping for stone or flooring, so Rocky Tops was closed for the long weekend and wouldn't open again until Monday, with no one scheduled to work the retail side of the business until then. Moncrief would leave at 6 am, and the next overnight guard wouldn't arrive until 10 pm on Wednesday.

Rocky Tops had begun using off-duty cops from the 39th & 14th Districts two years prior due to vandalism and graffiti artists destroying and spray-painting their outdoor inventory. All of which was too large and too heavy to keep indoors. Though the outside inventory was fenced in, with CCTV surveillance, the owners took no chances, and Daniel Moncrief had been employed there three nights a week for the previous two years.

Moncrief's wife had given birth to twins the year before, and the two were expecting another baby in the spring of 2022. Every bit of moonlighting money would help, as a uniformed officer's salary with his tenure was only seventy-one thousand dollars a year. With his wife, Denise, a stay-at-home mom taking care of the babies, making ends meet in America's sixth-largest city was increasingly difficult.

Rocky Tops sat just feet from the intersection of Ellery & Bedford Street. The place was nestled between two vacant buildings due to be bulldozed because of the area's rapid expansion due to what the Germantown City Council called the *FalconClaw Renaissance*. The past year had seen more and more developers buying up land for the purpose of expanding the live-work-play district. Because of this growth, Rocky Tops' business was booming.

The place and the nighttime security guard were familiar to Talon Grayson, whose employer regularly purchased ceramic tile, granite countertops, and flat stone for outside patio and sidewalk improvements. It was where Talon and Genesis would commit their well-planned final act before stalking and killing their muse, Frank Collazo.

At just after 2 am, Moncrief, monitoring the premises through close-circuit television from inside the manager's office, noticed activity on one of the outdoor cameras in the southwest corner of the lot near the large slate slabs. It was an area that had been vandalized by graffiti artists dozens of times.

Moncrief noted on paper that the single intruder was wearing a hood, seemed small in stature, and appeared to be female.

Without further hesitation, he grabbed his gun, a city-issued 9mm Glock, and made his way out the back of the building. Moncrief had eyes on the intruder as he methodically zig-zagged through the stone yard, maneuvering around pallets of cobblestone, flat-stacked stone, and Tennessee fieldstone. Approaching with his flashlight off, not wanting to lose the element of surprise, he had yet to unholster his gun, thinking it was just some teenage kid. Now, just feet away from the intruder, Daniel Moncrief could smell and hear the familiar sound of spray paint being discharged from an aerosol can. Waiting until the last second, Moncrief turned on his flashlight and saw the back of a slight figure standing before him, hands raised in the air, an aerosol can in one of them.

"All right, kid, turn around towards me and keep those hands in the air where I can see them." Moncrief was now holding his gun.

The intruder slowly turned and slightly revealed to Moncrief what she'd painted on the six-foot slab tile.

Smiling, hands still extended, Genesis Harper said, "Just out havin' some fun, mister."

"Where are all of your buddies?" Moncrief was fishing, believing from the CCTV that the woman was alone.

"Got nobody with me, sir," said Genesis, still smiling.

"Go ahead and drop the spray paint and step away from the slab so I can see what you did there."

"Sir, yes, sir." Genesis dropped the can and side-stepped to her right.

Not fearing for his safety and thinking the vandal might run, Moncrief's weapon remained holstered as he reached for his cell phone to call the police. His flashlight fixed on the woman and about to dial the front desk of the 39th, Moncrief panned his light on the graffiti and saw a single letter, painted in red, two-feet tall. It was the capital letter E.

Trying to process what he was seeing, dread befell his face as he recognized the single letter as possibly the mark of the Cop Killers.

"Don't you move." Moncrief was measured in his tone and his movements. Putting his cell phone back in his pocket, he reached again for his belted sidearm, keeping his flashlight steady, and pointed at the young female standing just ten feet from his position.

"I won't, officer," said Genesis flashing a sinister grin. "I'll stay right here."

The term 'officer' made the hair on the back of Moncrief's neck stand up as the young woman had referred to him as 'sir' or 'mister' when first addressing him. He now believed that the vandal and possible cop killer knew that he was an off-duty officer.

"I want you to interlock your fingers behind your head, turn around with your back to me, and get down on your knees," quietly ordered Moncrief, his gun now drawn. "And do it slowly," he added.

Moncrief momentarily took his eyes off his suspect and didn't notice her eyes focus in on an area just over his right shoulder.

"Don't move, motherfucker," Talon Grayson whispered to Moncrief, placing the barrel of his stolen gun behind the right ear of his next victim. "Put your hands out to your side, arms fully extended. If you try anything, you'll never see your twins again.

Moncrief exhaled slowly and closed his eyes. He knew now that the man behind him knew him or at least knew of him, just like every other dead cop who fell victim to the Cop Killers.

"This here's a .40 caliber. You fuck around with me, and I spray paint these stone tiles with your brain."

Kneeling, Moncrief softly said, "I don't want to die tonight, man. Maybe you just let me walk away, and...."

"Shut up, bitch," said Talon. "Turn off the flashlight and put it on the ground along with the gun."

"You got it, partner. I'm following orders. No need to get antsy. No need to hurt anybody." Moncrief remained calm when slowly placing his gun on the ground.

"Now, kick the gun away from you, towards my friend," quietly ordered Talon.

"You got it." Moncrief followed orders. "Just know that I got little kids at home and another one on the way."

His eyes adjusting to the darkness, Daniel Moncrief saw something shimmer in the woman's right hand. The street light coming through the nine-foot, barbed wire fence reflected off something metallic in her hand. Swallowing hard, he knew it was a knife. Thinking of his wife, kids, and unborn child, he would not go down without a fight. Swinging wildly, trying to strike the assailant to his rear, he struck Talon, knocking him to the ground. Fighting for possession of the gun in the male assailant's hand, he had to ignore the young female momentarily and win one fight at a time.

On top of his attacker and fighting for the gun, the much bigger Moncrief had gained a measure of control and thought for a brief moment that he might survive the attack.

His moment of hope was quickly dashed when he felt a sharp blow to the back of his neck. Thinking that he had been hit with a rock, his flashlight, or a fist, the cold night air passed over a three-inch wound in his neck, followed by a dark red river gushing to the ground beneath him. Falling back and holding his neck, now in a frenzied panic, Moncrief's face grimaced as he felt the life quickly leave his body. Blood was everywhere, and resigned to his fate; he no longer had the will to defend himself from his attackers, who placed the gun firmly against his belly and pulled the trigger. Shock filled Moncrief's teary eyes as he looked on in horror at his smiling, black-eyed killers.

The cold, damp night air, along with Moncrief's winter jacket, muffled the sound of the gunshot, giving the killers comfort that they wouldn't have to flee immediately. The bloodlust that followed would be a message to all that the Cop Killers were nearing the end of their reign. The depravity and brutality shown to Daniel Moncrief would serve as a precursor to their final act....and their grand finale.

Back to the present, Frank answered his cell phone, unsure why his captain was calling. "Captain, everything okay?"

"Frank, there's been another killing. Ellery & Bedford! Get there as fast as you can! It's one of our guys."

"Who is it?"

"It's Daniel Moncrief, Frank. It's Danny."

"Fuck!" Frank felt ill. The ORS Sergeant had just taken up a collection for Moncrief and his wife to help with baby food and diapers when it had been announced that Moncrief and his wife were expecting another child. "I'll meet you there, Captain!" Frank hit his blue flashers and floored it.

His engine screaming north, Frank's vision went fuzzy again with snow, and the landscape grew dark. The sound of pounding rain and windshield wipers flapping ravaged Frank's senses. Running a red light at Lowber Avenue, he narrowly missed a family of four splashing through a crosswalk. Looking in his rearview mirror, he made sure they were all right.

Back to the road and the torrent of rain, lightning bolts lit up the Chelten Hill Cemetery to his right. As Frank looked over, the world around him slowed, and he saw people standing out front waiting to get in. As he looked closer, he saw nine dead cops, seven uniformed and two in plain clothes. The last one was saying goodbye to his pregnant wife and one-year-old twins.

What Frank saw next stole his breath, sending him into a dizzying spiral. From up the street, he saw Penny smiling and waving as she and Bonnie approached the fallen cops as they walked into the cemetery one by one. Though it was pouring rain, they seemed to be warm and dry. Confused and squinting to get a closer look, Frank saw a cut on Penny's hairline, and blood was running down her face and across her smile. Frank gasped for air, now looking down to see Bonnie. Squinting again, Frank could see that Bonnie's eyes were closed, but his little girl was walking beside Penny, holding onto her mother's hand.

Frank screamed for Penny and Bonnie as he lost control of the car. Screeching tires and the sound of honking horns woke Frank from his hallucination. Shaking his head and smelling burning rubber, he heard nothing. Looking around, he saw vehicles scattered along the road before him, with people exiting their vehicles to see if everyone was okay.

Frank just sat and cried. He couldn't understand what was happening to him. He didn't understand what his visions were trying to reveal.

"Hey, buddy! You okay?!" A pedestrian approached Frank's Dodge and tapped on his window, looking to see if Frank was hurt; his voice muffled and low. Standing back to inspect the car, the man saw no damage to Frank's vehicle and moved on to assist others involved in the near collision.

Now in control of his senses, Frank looked up to see the street sign, Bedford & Pine. He was just three blocks down from Ellery and the crime scene.

Chapter 22 – Rocky Tops

Looking ravaged, Frank arrived at the scene in front of Rocky Tops to an unprecedented number of units on scene. Officers from the 39th and 14th had all made their way over to Ellery & Bedford, curious about the radio chatter regarding the death of one of their own.

Frank parked his Dodge a block away and walked through the freezing drizzle. Getting closer, the wind picked up, causing a strand of yellow police tape to tear away from a telephone pole and flap violently in the gusts. The change in weather sparked a greater urgency in the forensics team to preserve as much evidence as possible before the degrading weather washed or blew it away. Frank noticed the scurrying of white-clad technicians coming and going from several unmarked white vans.

Nodding to all personnel who had acknowledged his arrival, Frank methodically made his way through the crowd, saying little to anyone. When entering the front entrance of Rocky Tops, Frank observed a civilian crying while being questioned by two uniformed officers and a female plainclothes detective whom he didn't recognize. Frank assumed the civilian was one of the managers of the establishment.

"Too many fucking people in this place," Frank mumbled under his breath as he made his way to the back of the building and the exit to the exterior stone yard. Frank recognized three cyber-forensics personnel from the Manayunk division near the rear entrance and thought that Denny Patel and his captain must be out back. The scene reminded Frank of the Cope House murder back on Halloween. He again muttered, "Too many people."

Now outside, Frank observed the stone yard in the dwindling daylight. It was just after 4 o'clock, and the wicked skies were trying hard to hide what little was left of the late November afternoon. Looking around, Frank saw large floodlights on poles in each corner of the sizeable lot. Looking back down, he tried to guess Moncrief's route through the maze of palleted stone en route to his ultimate demise. Looking back up, his eyes led him to his captain, who was standing with Denny Patel under a blue tarp while several techs processed the scene behind them. Frank noticed that the blue tarp, which served as a tent over the crime scene, aided by the wind, seemed desperate to break free from the nearby barbed wire fence as the wind grabbed ahold of it. Frank also observed that the seven-foot light poles, erected by the Forensics team to illuminate the scene, also looked as if they wanted to come down. Looking at his captain, Jackson turned to meet him.

Walking several steps toward him, as if trying to shield him from the horrific display that awaited the grizzled detective, Jackson warned, "Frank, listen, it's bad."

Frank could tell by the look on Jackson's face that this particular murder would be unlike any other that he had seen. Frank reminded himself that he saw former, disgraced fellow detective Kyle Wade dismembered by a raging Isak Cameron and couldn't imagine the scene could be worse than that.

"Here, Frank, you might need this," Denny Patel handed Frank an Emesis bag, also known as a barf bag.

Donning blue latex gloves pulled from his pocket, Frank declined Patel's offer with a subtle shaking of his head.

"Frank." Denny looked the legendary detective dead in the eye and said, "Take it."

Frank looked over at Jackson, who nodded in agreement with Patel and quietly repeated Denny's words. "Take it, Frank."

Frank's eyes widened in acknowledgment, and he took the plastic-lined, paper bag.

Denny then lifted a strand of police tape which was attached to two fenced-in, stacked-stone pallets. Once under the tape, Frank saw what he hadn't before; yellow evidence tents littering the area and sitting benignly next to various rocks covered in dark sticky blood. Frank began to prepare himself for what might lie beneath the white sheet covering his fellow brother from the 39th District. He couldn't know that the carnage left behind, presumably by the Cop Killers, would haunt him until his dying days.

"Go ahead," Frank said to a nearby tech, who was waiting for his approval to unveil what he believed was the ninth victim in the Cop Killer rampage.

Taking a deep breath, he stared into the eyes of the forensics tech and rapidly nodded as if psyching himself up to absorb the visual blow. "Do it," he said.

As the tech pulled away the sheet, Frank fell back against a one-ton pallet of cobblestones and gasped for clean air. His eyes teared as he struggled to open the barf bag in his hand, readying it for what was inevitable.

Trying but failing to look away, Frank witnessed Daniel Moncrief's head completely flattened by a large, blood-covered cobblestone that sat where Moncrief's head once was. A high volume of blood was splattered outward in every direction, and in its still-drying, syrupy pool were chunks of skull bone and brain matter. The butchery didn't stop there, though. As the white-clad technician pulled the sheet further down, it revealed what were once blueish gray, now crimson red, flat, triangular slate stones impaled into the chest and abdomen of Moncrief. *Six.* Frank reluctantly counted to himself. Without the arms and legs clinging to the carnage, one would never know that it was a human being lying dead there. A human being that, right before his death, lived there.... and had a wife and children.

The scene left Frank speechless, but in his mind, he knew that he would take joy in killing not one but both Cop Killers. No matter the risk or consequences, he would murder both. To hell with his oath and any ethical standards he swore to uphold. He would die before another cop died at the hands of the Cop Killers. He would kill the yet unnamed savages even if they killed him while in the act.

"Cover him up," Frank directed the tech.

Before turning to his captain and Patel, Frank looked up at a white sheet draped over a large slab of flat stone propped up against a metal post. Staring, a massive gust of wind tore the sheet from the stone and revealed to Frank the capital letter E, retraced in blood, now dry and dripping from its corners. The spray-painted letter was retraced with the sticky residue that once gave Daniel Moncrief life.

Frank could feel the wooden letter tile in his pocket, yearning again to get out. And in eighteen short hours.... it would.

Now turning to his captain and the head of the Forensics division, Frank walked right past them and said in a coarse, monotone voice, "No more cops are dying. Starting right now!" Three steps later, Frank doubled over and began vomiting into his barf bag.

After composing himself, he headed back inside Rocky Tops. There, Frank would gather more information from the other detectives on scene. Just before he arrived, Robert Brooks, Jonah Abecassis, and Collie Mitchell showed up and reviewed CCTV footage and collected names of all vendors, regular customers, and Rocky Top employees.

Back inside, Frank saw a visibly shaken Jonah Abecassis, who had just viewed the footage of the murder from the night before.

"How's he doing?" asked Frank, looking concerned for the junior detective.

"Frank, I, I.... I've never seen such brutality in my life. I'll be seeing that playback in my head forever." Robert Brooks looked shell-shocked. "I mean, what the fuck?" he shook his head in dismay.

"Brooksie, listen to me," said Frank. "Don't go out there unless the captain mandates it. And when we review the scene later, back at the 39th, you gloss over the pictures. Do you understand me?"

"Yeah, Frankie, I got it," Brooks was stunned.

"Where's Collie?" Frank looked around.

"He went outside ahead of Jonah. They're both messed up by what they saw on that tape." Brooks tried to shake off the images of Moncrief's remains. "Frank, what we're dealing with here is pure evil...."

"Two of them, right? A guy and a girl?"

"It's like they were enjoying it.... No, wait," Brooks caught himself. "That's not the best way to describe it," he paused. "It seemed as if it was ritualistic. Like they were bathing in the moment."

"Well, that's a sick fuckin' way to describe it, Bob." Frank was disturbed.

"Frank, you told me not to go out there to see what's left of our friend.... Well, you don't need to see that video, buddy."

"That's not Danny out there anymore, Bob. Now show me the tape." Frank walked toward the manager's office, where the DVR rack was kept.

Brooks went wide-eyed again and whispered, "Here we go," shaking his head and following Frank into the room.

Minutes later, as Frank watched, he was spellbound. Rarely was a murder caught on tape, and when seeing the events that led up to Moncrief's killing, he wanted to jump into the monitor and save his fellow cop. "Fuckin' Christ!" his heart was pounding.

"So, here's where Danny spots something on camera 13." Brooks pointed to cameras 1 and 13, camera 1 being the camera in the manager's office which provided a view of Moncrief sitting at the monitoring station witnessing the events unfolding outside. They could see Moncrief lean toward the monitor for camera 13, indicating that he saw movement.

Looking at camera 13 more closely, Frank saw the movement that first alerted Moncrief to the intruder. He also observed that the exterior flood lights were off. "Damn, if he'd only called it in prior to going out there, he could've been home with his family. And why in the hell aren't those outside lights on?" Frank was puzzled. "Either of those things could have saved his life."

"The female perp doesn't look very big," said Brooks. "I could see why he didn't immediately call it in."

"Look at that...." Frank was engrossed ".... he's literally walking toward his eventual death." He shook his head as he watched Moncrief exit the rear of the building and slowly creep toward the female intruder.

"Look at her," said Brooks. "That's the letter E she's spray-painting?"

Frank was solemn. "It's painted in blood, now." Taking a deep breath, he continued watching, unable to look away.

"So, that's the missing letter, huh?"

"One of them." Frank's eyes narrowed, again reminded of the tile in his pocket.

"Okay, watch this over here." Brooks pointed to camera #7. "Here's where we first see our male assailant. This is what Moncrief never saw on the cameras because, at this point, he's outside."

Frank watched as a hooded man, who'd been hiding behind a tool shed on the west side of the stone yard, crept up from behind Moncrief with what appeared to be a gun in his hand.

"I guess he didn't turn on his flashlight because he didn't want her to know he was approaching." Brooks attempted to narrate Moncrief's intentions.

"Yeah, I would've done the same thing," said Frank.

Frank and Brooks watched until Moncrief took the shot to the belly, and then Frank stood to leave. "I know what happens from this point on."

"Smart man, Frank." Brooks agreed that he didn't have to watch it.

"Make sure Mitchell and Abecassis have access to counseling," said Frank. "You, too, Brooksie."

"Yeah, Roger that, Frank. And what about you?"

"I'm good." Frank thought of Archibald Riley and was happy that no one in the Detective Room knew he'd been mandated to see him.

"Oh, and Frank. What you didn't see was that they emptied his pockets. They got his cell, and they got his wallet and badge."

"Yeah, these fuckers are collecting badges," said Frank. "An arsenal, too."

"I've got a car parked in front of his widow's house. They know where he lives now."

"Thanks, Brooksie." Frank turned to leave. "Oh, and Bob..... who had the grim task of breaking the news to his wife?"

"Jackson sent one of her Lieutenants over to his house."

"Which one?"

"Sonya Middlefield."

"That's good. She's the right person for the job." Frank shook his head and walked away.

Brooks sat, slumped in the manager's chair. It was the same chair that Daniel Moncrief sat in minutes before being brutally murdered, he thought. He quickly stood and vacated the room.

Outside, Frank made a call that he hoped he wouldn't have to make just eight hours earlier.

Sitting in his car, shielded from the cold and wind, Frank called Bones.

As the phone rang, Frank remembered his vision from earlier. The sight of Penny and Bonnie walking toward a cemetery rattled him. *And why were Bonnie's eyes closed?* He wondered.

"What's up, Frank?" Bones was in a good mood. After all, he survived his airplane ride and was on a mini vacation.

"Bones, we've got a problem, buddy."

"Oh shit. What is it?"

"They got another one of our guys."

"Which District?"

"The 39th, Bonesie."

"Awe fuck!" Bones was beginning to take the case personally. "Who was it?"

"It was Danny." Frank felt terrible delivering the news.

"Moncrief?!" Bones was rattled. He thought things were getting too close to home. First, Jamie Baumgartner and now Daniel Moncrief.

"Yeah, Bones. He's gone. It's bad, man."

"Oh my God, the twins. His wife, Tricia." Bones sounded devastated.

"Where?"

"He was moonlighting at...."

Bones and Frank chorused together, "Rocky Tops."

"Jesus Christ, Frank!"

"This one was as bad as it gets. These fuckers are making a statement." Frank rubbed the back of his neck. "They got him good."

"All right. I'm getting on a plane."

"No, listen. Stay the night and catch the first plane tomorrow morning. The airport will be packed tonight but not on Thanksgiving."

"You sure, Frank?"

"Yeah. I'll tell the captain you couldn't make it out tonight." Frank wanted Bones to have one night away from his shitty house and his shitty life. He knew what Bones had been through as a child and how he was haunted by it every day. "Just make sure you and Candace come straight to the 39th from the airport. Text me your itinerary when you have it, and I'll have a unit pick you guys up in the morning."

"Okay. Will do." Bones paused and added, "Oh, what about Doug?"

"Have him call me tonight, but he should stay home for the weekend."

Just five minutes after Frank hung up with Bones, his phone rang. It was Cantrell.

"Doug....?"

"Frank. My God, what happened?"

"An officer from the 39th was moonlighting up by FalconClaw Park and was murdered just after 2 am last night."

"FalconClaw Park, huh?" Cantrell thought all the crime scenes had been breadcrumbs, and they had now led his friend back to FalconClaw.

"Okay," Cantrell sounded steadfast. "I'm on a plane in the morning with Bones and Candace...."

"Whoa! Wait a second, Doug. You're staying home this weekend. You need to be with Gaye for the holiday. Just come back on Sunday as planned, and I'll pick you up from the airport."

"Frank.... Well, I, I think that it's best that I...."

"Listen to me...." Frank put his foot down. "I'll call you if I need you, but let us line up all the evidence while you're away, and then you can help us come up with something on Sunday. You're not coming back to Philly tomorrow, Doug. That's that."

Cantrell didn't want to argue with his friend. He knew Frank was already on the edge and didn't want to push him over.

"You got it, Frank. My plane lands at 11 am. American Airlines. I'll text you my itinerary."

"Doug, please share a wonderful Thanksgiving with Gaye. She deserves it..... you both do."

"And what about you....?"

"Me? I'll be at the 39th working the case." Frank sighed. "Sounds like Chinese food for the gang and me."

"Watch your back, Son. Those animals are getting close."

"You know what they say....?"

"What's that, Frank?"

"Keep your friends close..... and your enemies closer."

Douglas Cantrell dreaded hearing those words. He knew Frank was on a one-way mission. A kill or be killed journey from which he'd likely never come back. Cantrell loved Frank like a son, and he didn't want to lose his boy.

Now eight o'clock on Thanksgiving Eve, the team had all assembled at the 39th except for Bones and Weatherby. Brooks would lay out the facts, and Frank would delegate tasks.

"All right. So, first of all, on Monday, we're setting up a Go Fund Me page for Tricia Moncrief and her children. Unfortunately, Danny wasn't tenured, so his life benefit won't last more than five years. I urge all of you to give as much as you can. On top of losing her husband the way she did, that woman has one-year-old twin girls and one on the way. Do what you can."

Frank was surrounded by six detectives, Captain Jackson, Denny Patel, and Rupali Sharma from Manayunk.

"Secondly, thank you all for doing what's necessary as we head into the holiday weekend. Tomorrow we'll only need half of you here as we try to put all the puzzle pieces on the table and see what picture we can get from them. Those off tomorrow will work on Friday, and those working tomorrow will get Friday off."

"Frank, what's the status on Bones, Cantrell, and the new girl from Canada?" asked Robert Brooks.

"Yeah, I spoke to all of them earlier," said Frank. "Some of you may know that Cantrell had invited Bones, Weatherby, and myself up to his house in New Hampshire for Thanksgiving to return on Friday, but I decided it was best to stay behind. And I'm glad I did." Frank looked worn out from the day and the things he'd seen, and not just at the crime scene. Penny and Bonnie were weighing heavily on his mind. "I insisted Bones go. I thought he could bond with Cantrell a little and get a feel for Candace Weatherby and what her contribution to the case might be."

"What is she, Frank, some kind of Wizkid or something?" asked Collie Mitchell.

"Yeah, pretty much," Frank nodded. "She was a huge asset on the Isak Cameron case, helping to trace his familial ancestry. In doing so, we were able to identify our killer. She knows her stuff."

"So, how does that help us here?" asked Jonah Abecassis, sitting beside his partner Mitchell.

Frank shrugged his shoulders and said, "Don't know. That has yet to be seen. We don't know what we don't know. After this weekend and studying every last piece of evidence, maybe we can figure out how she can help us."

"So when will they be back?" asked Detective Cassidy Winston, who was brought in from the 14th District to help out and provide information from the ongoing investigation of the Halloween Night, Cope House murder of Detective Calvin Murphy.

"Thanks, Cassidy," Frank acknowledged his sister in blue from the 14th. "For everyone's edification, Cassidy will be working the case out of the 39th going forward. She's on loan from the 14th and will assist with their ongoing investigation from Halloween night." Frank paused, trying to remember her question. "Oh, yeah.... So Bones tried to get a flight tonight but couldn't because of the holiday. He offered to drive, but they're getting some bad weather up in the New England states, and it's a six-hour drive anyway. Long story short, he secured a flight tomorrow morning, and we'll have a car pick him and Weatherby up from the airport. He should be here by 10 am."

"Cantrell will rejoin us on Sunday afternoon," said Jackson.

Frank added, "He wanted to come sooner, but Doug's getting up there in age and only has so many more Thanksgivings left to spend with his wife. I insisted he stay home for the holiday."

"Okay, so our goal tonight is to ensure everyone's on the same page and ready to put it all together this weekend. By the way, does anyone know where we stand on the common arrests made by all our victims...." Frank was cut off mid-sentence.

"Tommy, Billy," said Brooks to the two detectives that Jackson had assigned the task of cross-referencing arrest records for all the victims. "You guys got your information together for when we meet tomorrow?"

"Yeah, got the files right here," said rookie Detective Billy Washington.

"Hold on to them until tomorrow. It's getting late," said Jackson.

"All right, everyone," Frank stood. "Unless the captain needs anything else, you're free to go. Brooksie posted the updated schedule for Thursday through Sunday. If your schedule changed due to today's events, I want to thank you in advance for working on Thanksgiving," Frank was grateful. "Missing a holiday sucks, but losing a spouse is life-altering. Think of Tricia Moncrief, and pray for the soul of our lost brother, Danny."

"Goodnight, everyone," said Jackson, closing the meeting. Turning to Frank, she waved her head, pulling him to the side for a brief one-on-one.

"Yeah, Cap?"

"Frank, how are you feeling?"

"I feel good, Captain."

"Don't bullshit me. You're as good as I got, but you've had a rough year, and now this, the whole family, and the holiday thing. What I'm trying to say," she paused, "is that Brooks and I can run it tomorrow if you need a day or so...."

Frank quickly interjected, "Captain, are you losing your mind? Of course, I'll be here tomorrow.... and every day after that."

"All right. Just saying," Jackson threw her hands up. "Listen, how'd it go with the Temple guy on Tuesday?"

"It went fine." Frank was apologetic. "I'm sorry that I overreacted to the mandate. He seems like a good guy. Sorta like another Cantrell," he nodded.

"We can all use a few more Cantrells in our lives," Jackson's smile was subdued as she shook her head.

"Yeah, you're right about that."

"Listen, why don't you go ahead and get out of here? I'll secure everything and lock up." Jackson saw that Frank was exhausted.

"No. No. I got it, Cap. I have something that I have to take care of before I leave."

Jackson's eyes narrowed. "You sure, Frank?" She was worried for her best detective. "Well, all right. Goodnight then."

"Goodnight, Cap." Frank walked her to the door and locked it behind her.

Hearing the deadbolt turn over, Jackson looked suspiciously back at the door, hesitated, and then turned to leave.

With Jackson gone, Frank looked around one last time. He had a memory of Penny for every table, chair, corner, desk, and window in the Detective Room that evoked memories of Penny. He missed his girl, and he missed his partner.

Turning off the lights, Frank walked to the one spot in the Detective Room that gave him the most peace. Standing in front of, and staring out the Schuyler Street window, Frank remembered every case he'd ever worked. Looking out to the left, he saw the Time Out Sports Bar. Laughing, he remembered taking Penny there for a beer after she first got her detective badge. During their toast, their eyes met, and each knew there was something between them, but it would have to wait as they were both married.

Looking to his right, down at the street sign on the corner denoting the intersection of Schuyler & West Hunting Park, he thought of his former captain, Roz Sumner, and smiled. Sumner's mother's maiden name was Schuyler, and she took pride in coming to work at the 39th every day. Looking to his left and down at the sidewalk in front of Time Out Sports, he remembered seeing the charred remnants of where his beloved captain died.

Thinking of Penny and taking one last look around the room, Frank was resolute. Drawing his Smith & Wesson, the only friend he had left, he released the safety. Pulling back the slide to see if there was a bullet in the chamber, Frank placed the barrel in his mouth, closed his eyes, and thought of being with Penny and Bonnie again. When he did, Frank saw Penny standing there in the dark with him, shaking her head slowly.

"No, Frankie. It's not time to come home yet. Get the bad guys off the street, then come home to your family."

Weeping, Frank opened his eyes, and Penny was gone. Hitting his knees, Frank cried uncontrollably. "Where are you, Penny?" He spewed saliva. "Where did you go, Baby?!"

Chapter 23 – The Missing Letter

Later that night, Frank sat on the back steps of his old house, waiting for Penny. He didn't notice the cold as it dipped into the low thirties with wind gusts that made it feel even colder. Staring at the scarred fence, Frank wished he'd seen his father there. Looking around, he felt alone and wished someone would step out of the shadows and tell him he was still alive and that he was worth something.... anything.

Checking his cell phone for missed calls or texts, there were none; he stood to leave. Noticing that it was after 11 pm, he thought it best to head back to his claustrophobic hell and get some sleep. He knew tomorrow would be a big day and needed to be sharp. Anything less could result in Frank or someone around him being killed. He was no longer worried about himself anymore, and he'd be damned if another cop was going to die. He'd give up his life to make sure that didn't happen.

Walking to the Dodge, Frank was stopped in his tracks. Behind him, whispering in the howling wind, was Penny's voice.

"Hey, big man. Leaving so soon?" Penny said, "I thought we could talk for a minute."

Frank, almost afraid to look back, fearing she wasn't really there, took a deep breath and turned around. Seeing Penny temporarily filled his heart but then drained it again, knowing he couldn't be with her. "Hey," he said, looking desperate, depleted, and forlorn.

"Hi, Frankie," smiled a jacketless Penny. "I'm sorry I haven't been around. I've missed you. Bonnie has, too."

"How is she? I had a dream about her today.... It freaked me out. I saw her walking down the street with you, but her eyes were closed."

"I remember," said Penny. "You were driving in the rain."

Frank looked puzzled and concerned. "What do you mean?"

"I saw you driving north on Upsal. We both did."

"Penny, what are you talking about? What were you doing there?"

"Were you trying to get to Bonnie and me, Frank? We're you trying to get to the accident?"

"What is happening? What are you talking about?" Frank walked over to Penny and gently grabbed her by the shoulders.

"It's okay, Baby." Penny gave Frank a soft, reassuring smile. "We're okay. You don't have to hurry."

Frank grabbed Penny and held onto her tightly. Looking her directly in the eyes, he teared up and asked the question he'd been terrified to ask.

"Are you dead, Penny? Did you leave me? Where is Bonnie?"

"Oh, Frank. Don't worry about things like that." Penny patted Frank's chest with her right hand in an effort to comfort the man she loved. "You have a big day tomorrow. Get some rest, and don't forget about what I told you.... You know, the trunk...." Penny smiled warmly and took his hand. "Don't forget. Everyone's counting on you tomorrow."

Frank looked at the garage and remembered the letter tile in his pocket. Looking back at Penny, he saw her standing at the back door, ready to walk into the house. "Where are you going?" Frank panicked.

"I've got to get the house ready for you, Frankie. You're coming home soon. We can't wait." Penny's glow was radiant.

"But, I...." Frank was speechless.

"Oh, and Frankie...." she nodded reassuringly. "Don't you be mad at Doug. Promise."

Before Frank could speak, Penny was gone. Not understanding what she meant, Frank shook his head to clear the noise and reached for the Scrabble letter in his pocket. Pulling it out, he saw the back side of the tile, the letter begging him to reveal itself. He knew he could no longer conceal the letter from his fellow detectives.... or himself.

Twenty minutes later, Frank saw a homeless man wearing a gray hoodie near his place above the Mad River. Slowing down, he stopped the car, got out, gun at the ready, and approached the man who might or might not be one of the Cop Killers.

"Hey, buddy," Frank spoke loudly as he approached. "You live around here?"

Hearing Frank approach him from behind, the man pulled down his hood and said, "I don't live nowhere.... And what's it to ya, anyway?"

Frank ruled out the man as a threat, as he looked to be in his mid to late fifties and had mostly gray hair. "Sorry, brother." Frank felt foolish and, for some reason, felt the need to make up for his paranoia. "Listen, I'm looking for a young couple that hangs out around here. A guy and a girl, always wearing hooded sweatshirts.... Late twenties. You seen anyone like that around here?"

"I don't know no one or nobody."

"Well, if you see them, you steer clear. They aren't very nice." Frank touched the man's shoulder in a show of compassion.

"Whattaya, some kinda queer or something?" said the vagrant, taking a step back and looking Frank up and down.

"Not at all." Frank recoiled his arm. "Listen, it's pretty cold out here. How about I get you a room for the night? You can get a hot shower, and I'll give you money for breakfast in the morning?"

"You sure you ain't gay?" The man again looked Frank over head to toe.

"No." Frank grinned a little, shaking his head. "Just looking to help a brother out, that's all."

"Yeah?" Still skeptical, he asked, "And you ain't gonna try nothin'?"

"No. No, I'm not." Frank smiled warmly.

"How much ya think that would all cost, anyway?"

"Not sure," said Frank. "About a buck-fifty."

The homeless man's eyes went wide. "A hundred and fifty, you say?"

"Roughly." Frank squeezed his lips together and nodded.

"Well," the man looked both ways and said, "How about you just give me the cash, then?"

Frank chuckled, shook his head, and reached into his pocket. Counting what he had left in cash, he handed the man one hundred and seventy-six dollars. "Here, just take it all. I won't be needin' it."

"That's mighty kind of you, friend. I never liked this neighborhood before.... But now I do. Maybe I'll come round more often." The man smiled, revealing his four missing teeth and rotten others.

"Be safe, and remember what I said about the two strangers wearing hoodies. You steer clear," said Frank, patting the stranger on the shoulder.

"Steer rhymes with queer, you know?" the homeless man grinned at Frank. "You sure you ain't no faggot?"

Frank shook his head, unable to conceal his smile. "Like I said.... Just tryin' to help you out a little."

"Yee haw, motherfucker!" the man celebrated as he walked away from Frank. "Got me some beer money. Woo-hoo!"

Frank yelled as the homeless man walked away, "Don't go flashing that around town now." Turning back toward his car, he shook his head and laughed again.

The next morning Frank grabbed a hot shower and, when stepping out of the tub, went to wipe the steam from the mirror. Pulling his hand back, he reconsidered, not wanting to see the man who might be looking back at him.

After putting on his pants, Frank reached for his socks and realized he had slept well for the first time in months. He felt energized and singularly focused. Before walking out of his apartment, Frank felt the outside of his pocket for the familiar one-inch square wooden tile, and it was there. Looking content, he headed out.

It was now 9:40 am, and nearly the entire team had assembled in the Detective Room. The text Frank received from Bones fifteen minutes earlier stated they were en route and would be there by 10.

Jackson approached Frank, who was standing alone looking out the Schuyler Street window. "How you feeling today, Frank?"

After a second, Frank looked surprised when he turned to look at the person at his side and saw that it was Jackson. "Oh. Sorry, Cap. What was that?"

"I said, how are you feeling?"

"Believe it or not, I feel great. I slept straight through the night. No dreams, no nightmares, no nothing. Just a black sea of tranquility."

"A 'black sea of tranquility?'" she shook her head, never not amazed by Frank. "How poetic of you. So, how do you think today's gonna go?"

"Pretty good, I think," Frank nodded. "I asked Bobby Colapietro to join us today. I hope that's okay."

"Of course, but why?" Jackson cocked a brow.

"Yesterday, when Brooks and I watched the playback of the attack on Danny, there was a fleeting moment when you could see the faces of each killer." Frank looked both ways for effect. "I may have seen the male assailant over near the Mad River bar. I want Bobby to sketch what I tell him I saw and then sketch what he sees on the tape. Additionally, we have his first two sketches of who Monica Jefferson described as the girl named Genesee."

"Hmm. I see." Jackson nodded her approval. "Well, let's see what he comes up with."

At that moment, the door opened, and the remaining attendees walked in. It was Bones and Weatherby. Sitting around the conference table, the group assembled nearby and collectively said, "Yo, Bonesie!" Frank smiled, happy to see the two, but his expression changed when another person came through the door. It was Cantrell.

Wanting to be upset, Frank instantly remembered what Penny had said the night before. 'Don't be mad at Doug,' he recalled. Frank was confused. He asked himself, *how could Penny have known that Doug would show up unexpectedly? How could she have known that he told Doug not to come back?*

Realizing that he was glad to see his friend, he walked towards Cantrell with a straight face. "Doug....?"

"Now, Frank...." Cantrell held up his hands, which were full, holding his jacket and leather satchel, "....I can explain."

"Doug, I'm so happy you're here. I'm sorry Gaye has to celebrate the holiday alone, though."

"Comes with the territory when you're chasing bad guys. Please don't feel bad for either Gaye or me. Feel bad for all the spouses and children of the fallen officers. We have to put a stop to this, Frank. The more resources we can throw at this, the better off we'll be. I'm one of those resources."

"That you are, Doug. That you are." Frank placed his right hand on Cantrell's shoulder and squeezed. "Here, let me help you with your things."

After several minutes, the assembled team was briefed by Robert Brooks and Frank. Sitting around a conference table meant for eight was Beatrice Jackson, Jon Bones Sullivan, Candace Weatherby, Douglas Cantrell, Frank, Brooks, sketch artist Bobby Colapietro, Collie Mitchell, and Jonah Abecassis.

"All right, guys," Brooks started the meeting. "Looks like everyone is here. So, listen up. We're gonna work through the day until we come up with something...."

"And every day after that," added Frank.

Brooks continued. "We'll have food brought in later. I hope Chinese is okay. That's all that's open today, sorry to say."

"Guys," Frank caught himself, looked to Jackson and Weatherby out of respect, and said, "and ladies. I want to thank you for missing out on your Thanksgiving holiday. But frankly, we've gotta put an end to what's been going on since June."

Brooks spoke back up. "So, here's how today's going to go. We're all gonna watch the playback of what happened to Danny Moncrief up at Rocky Tops early yesterday morning. I want to be very clear, though, it'll be tough to watch, but we all signed up for this." Pausing, he added, "Except for Bobby and maybe Ms. Weatherby. Please excuse yourself if you feel uncomfortable or ill at any point."

"For everyone's edification, though," Frank jumped in. "What you won't see in today's meeting is what happened post-mortem. That will be seen by the detectives on the case ONLY. And only if you feel like you need to. Trust me, today's evidence includes pictures of Moncrief's body as it was found. You may likely feel that the pictures alone will suffice. As Bob stated, this is going to be a tough day for all of us, so buckle your chin straps."

"Frank. Go ahead and tell everybody why Bobby's here," said Jackson.

"Like the Captain said, we brought in Bobby Colapietro from downstairs to work up some sketches on our killers." Frank addressed Bobby directly. "Bobby, we want you to sketch what little facial features you can extract from the videotape."

"Tell him what else you want him to sketch, Frank." Jackson wanted to reveal to everyone at the table what Frank had revealed to her minutes earlier.

"Well, back on November 1, I was approached by a homeless guy over by where I'm staying, and I think it may have been the male killer that you'll be seeing on the tape shortly."

Some in the room gasped, while others whispered, "No shit," under their breaths. Cantrell feared for Frank's safety even more so as he was on the phone with Frank the night he was approached; it was the night after the Cope House murder of Calvin Murphy. He and the others now believed that the killers were likely stalking Frank.

What those around the table couldn't see, except for Candace Weatherby, was that Bones was clenching his fists. Bones Sullivan was fiercely loyal to Frank and wanted to ensure he was there the next time his partner crossed paths with the killers. Weatherby stared at Bones' fists until they unclenched and then looked into his eyes. Looking at Frank and then back at Bones, she could see that the two would have each other's backs no matter what. She, too, hoped they were together if and when they confronted the Cop Killers.

"Okay, so before we get to the video evidence, I want to review what we know about the night in question," said Brooks. "As many of you know, Danny Moncrief was beloved around here. And if you never got the chance to meet the man," Brooks looked at Weatherby and Cantrell, "then you missed out on knowing one of God's better children."

"So, what we know from the video, eyewitness testimony, Danny's wife, Tricia, and the evidence at the scene is as follows." Brooks referenced his notes. "At around 9:50 pm on Tuesday, Moncrief, who moonlighted at Rocky Tops to make ends meet, arrived for his ten o'clock shift. He was scheduled to work until 6 am," explained Brooks. "After walking the store, the grounds, and the property's perimeter, Moncrief settled into the manager's office and had some food he'd brought. After nodding off for thirty minutes or so, between 1:30 and 2 am, he began viewing the live CCTV camera footage, which you'll all see shortly. Then, at precisely 2:03 am, the footage will reveal that Moncrief saw something on the video. We now know it was the female assailant spray painting the letter E on a large stone slab."

When Cantrell heard the letter E, he immediately pulled his notes from prior meetings and added the letter to the rest of the letters found at each scene on Scrabble tiles.

"So," Cantrell raised his hand politely. "So, the letter was spray painted instead of a Scrabble tile?"

"Yes," said Brooks. "No wooden tiles were recovered from the scene."

"Interesting," Cantrell mumbled. "I wonder why they changed their M.O.?"

"Could've been because of the inclement weather," said Frank. "The wind was blowing pretty good that night. Or, perhaps, they just forgot to leave it in their haste. It was messy, and they wanted to ensure the letter was found.... Who knows. Maybe it'll show up somewhere amongst the pallets of stone and rock."

"Yes, I see." Cantrell looked off, imagining the scene. "By spray painting the letter, they knew it would easily be found and wouldn't have blown away. My guess is red paint. Would that be accurate?"

Frank had a momentary flashback, remembering how the red letter was retraced in Moncrief's blood.

"Yes, Doug, it was red spray paint."

"Other things to note are as follows. Like the other victims, Danny's gun, cell phone, and wallet were stolen," Brooks said.

"These killers are amassing an arsenal of guns," said Jackson, with Abecassis, Mitchell, and Frank all nodding in agreement.

"Hmm." Candace Weatherby was skeptical. By subtly shaking her head, she told the others she had doubts.

"Ms. Weatherby?" Jackson addressed Candace's perceived skepticism. "Do you disagree with that conclusion?"

"Um," she paused, not wanting to step on any toes. "I think our suspects are homeless or off the grid. And if they are, they're likely selling the weapons to finance their minimal needs. It seems from the other murders that they're either using a .40 caliber, a knife, or both in the attacks. I don't know yet what weapons were used in this attack, but my guess would be one or both."

"Huh," Jackson looked impressed with Weatherby. "Brooksie, you want to share with everyone what weapons were used?"

"Well," Brooks raised his brow, impressed with the girl from up north. "Other than the rocks, which were readily available to our killers, the murder weapons were a knife and a .40 cal."

"So far, so good, Montreal." Jackson had a new nickname for their young visitor. Keep it up," the captain nodded her approval. "And you might be on to something with the sale of the stolen guns. They would fetch a pretty penny out on the street." Jackson looked over to Mitchell. "Collie, you and Jonah get on that tomorrow. I want our guys from all the districts involved to ask around if anyone is selling the specific guns taken from each victim."

Bones, proud of his new friend, added, "Cop guns would fetch even more." He made eye contact with everyone around the table.

"What do you mean, Bones?" asked Frank.

"Well, if they marketed the gun as stolen from a cop, criminal buyers might pay a little extra. Just for vanity purposes."

"Yeah, but that would implicate the seller in the cop murders. No?" asked Collie, doubting Bones' notion.

"It might not matter," Cantrell spoke up.

"Oh? And why's that, Mr. Cantrell?" asked Jackson. All eyes went to the famous criminal profiler.

"Because our killers have a death wish. They don't care. They're going out in a blaze of condemnation, not glory. They don't care who knows. You'll notice they are on a rampage as of late. After starting slow, one killing a month for three months, and none in September, they've killed six cops since October 21. They're getting more daring and more vicious with each kill. My guess is they have an end date. Our killers are near the end of their murderous run and will likely try to take out Philly's prodigal son, Frank, by year's end. After that, my guess is that they won't be taken alive. Or they'll commit suicide in some ritualistic fashion."

Frank nodded in the direction of Candace and Cantrell.

"I believe the grand opening of FalconClaw Park is on New Year's Eve." Cantrell looked around the room. "That's the end of this year. By design, they chose Rocky Tops for their final kill before..... they attempt to take Frank's life."

Several around the table shook their heads with the revelation, while others seemed skeptical of Cantrell's hypothesis.

"FalconClaw Park, huh? End of this year?" Jackson tossed her pencil onto the table in both surprise and admiration. "Okay, let's get FBI and Montreal over here, a badge and a gun all ready. These two are breaking the case while we're all sitting around mired in the evidence. Damn!" she shook her head.

All at the table were impressed. None more than Frank of Cantrell and Bones of Candace.

"Okay, but I'm curious about why it took so long for Moncrief's body to be discovered," Jonah Abecassis wondered aloud.

"We have evidence to support how it went undiscovered from roughly 2:30 am for some twelve-plus hours...." The group leaned in, hanging on Brooks' next words.

"After the killing, the killers confiscated Moncrief's phone, as we detailed moments ago. At roughly six in the morning, when Moncrief was due to get off work, a text message was sent to Tricia Moncrief stating that Danny was going straight to work instead of coming home first. It wasn't until later in the morning that Moncrief's wife started calling his cellphone with no answer and then calling downstairs looking for him yesterday morning."

Frank remembered being asked by ORS Sergeant McLaughlin if he'd seen Moncrief around the District house when he'd walked in after dropping off Cantrell and the others at the airport.

"So, you're suggesting the killers didn't want the body to be discovered until much later? Why?" asked Abecassis. "And who discovered the body?"

"They needed time to get away," offered Cantrell.

"But why not get rid of the CCTV evidence if they had the extra time?" asked Collie Mitchell.

Before Brooks could answer, Cantrell said, "They wanted the footage to be seen. They would have had no interest in getting rid of evidence documenting their most brutal attack. They were sending a message, as I've stated all along."

Brooks jumped in, answering Abecasis' question from moments earlier. "Rocky Tops was closed for the holiday beginning Tuesday at 6 pm. It was an employee that found him...."

"But I thought the place was closed until Monday? Why would an employee have been there?" Cantrell's eyes narrowed with suspicion as he cocked his head to the side.

"Well, according to her testimony, the young woman, Carolyn Ratcliffe," Brooks looked down at his notes, "came in to retrieve her wallet, claiming that she'd left it the day before. After that, all hell broke loose." Brooks paused, "You guys know. You were all there." Brooks looked at everyone except for Cantrell, Weatherby, and Colapietro.

"They knew his schedule," said Candace.

"They knew Moncrief," said Cantrell. "They knew the place would be closed for the long weekend. That lines up with the other victims, too."

"Yeah, we figured as much," said Brooks. "Collie and Jonah will share what they have on common collars from all the victims later."

"If I may...." Cantrell held up his index finger. "Does the Ratcliffe woman make a good suspect?"

"No, we spoke to her family after interviewing her at the scene. They vouched for her whereabouts the night before, but we're bringing her in along with the seven other employees who work there," said Brooks. "We'll be cross-checking work schedules to see who might've been in close contact with Danny." Brooks brought Bones, Cantrell, and Candace up to speed. "We have them all coming in on Sunday for thirty-minute interviews. Eight employees in total."

Candace sighed and shook her head again.

"Whattaya thinking, Montreal?" Jackson liked her instincts.

"I once dated a guy who worked at a place that was similar to Rocky Tops...."

"And?" Jackson prodded.

"Well, eight employees may work there, but they likely work with dozens of vendors, contractors, home improvement companies, and local laborers. Not to mention regular customers," suggested Candace. "Many of whom may have crossed paths with our victim."

Jackson's eyes went wide.

"She's right," said Bones. "We're gonna all have to divide into subgroups and then divide and conquer to get them all on record regarding who knew Danny and might've had a score to settle."

"Less of a score, I think...." Cantrell was thinking out loud.

"Whattaya thinking, Doug?" Frank turned to his friend.

"This wasn't revenge or to settle a score," said Cantrell. "This was all about opportunity. The killers picked Officer Moncrief because he was a cop out of the 39th that worked close to FalconClaw Park. More precisely, FalconClaw. Again, this was a message being sent to Frank. The breadcrumbs have led Frank to FalconClaw. You're next, I fear."

"Frank? FalconClaw? New Year's Eve?" Jackson was rhetorical in her questions. "Jesus Christ!" The good captain shook her head and was beginning to realize that every dead cop since June was the result of some twisted nutjobs that wanted to kill the legendary Frank Collazo. She thought silently that by ending the reign of The Schuylkiller and Isak Cameron, Frank had unwittingly unleashed a new kind of evil on North Philly.

Frank stared off into space while everyone else at the table looked at him as if he were a dead man walking.

"Okay." Brooks tried to end the awkward moment of silence and get everyone's eyes off Frank. "Let's talk about the letter E."

Frank was nervous about the change in subject. He knew the letter in his pocket would change everything. He had since the day Penny led him to it.

"Should we watch the tape first, Brooksie?" Frank's question was more of a suggestion.

Brooks, like everyone, knew that the letters would likely be the catalyst to determining who the killers were, and he knew Frank did, too. He wasn't sure why Frank would suggest delaying the letter aspect of the case.

Shaking his head, Brooks said, "The letters are the one thing that connects all our victims. This letter is going to spell something out to us.... Literally."

"All right," said Jackson, looking anxious. "Time for a word scramble."

Frank again looked apprehensive and nervous, almost pale. Cantrell noticed and was worried for his friend.

"So far, we have H-A-R-M-A-I-N and now E," said Brooks.

Everyone at the table either referred to their notes or wrote the letters down on their notepad.

Cantrell said, "I live in New Hampshire, which borders Maine, so I see M-A-I-N-E jumping out at me."

"I see H-A-R-M," said Jackson.

Frank's left eye started to twitch, and his breathing began to shallow. Trying to speak, he had trouble as his mouth went bone dry. Cantrell and Brooks, who bookended Frank, noticed his hands beginning to tremble. Slowly, each man and woman looked at him, then at each other, and all grew concerned.

"Frank, are you all right, Son," asked a now distressed Douglas Cantrell with butterflies in his stomach.

With every worried eye around the table looking at him, Frank didn't speak. With an unsteady hand, he reached beneath the table and into his pocket and pulled the Scrabble tile he'd found in the trunk of Penny's car. Frank had been in denial for weeks. He knew in his heart what the letters would spell, and he had confirmed it the day before, causing him to consider taking his life. Every cop that died in the wake of the Cop Killer rampage died because of him. Every torturous moment of his life since he was fourteen.... Every moment of unbearable sadness.... It had all come full circle.

Cotton-mouthed and unable to speak, Frank struggled to raise the hand that would turn the case on its heels. Slowly returning his trembling hand to the top of the table, his pasty white lips and pooling eyes let everyone know that whatever was in his hand would set the next phase of the case in motion. It would go from cops being hunted to cops on the hunt.

As a solitary tear ran from Frank's left eye, he stared blankly, straight ahead. Turning over his tightly clenched fist, he slowly opened it. When doing so, he revealed the letter that had sat alone in the trunk of the Accord since the day of the accident back in May. The letter that had been missing since the first cop was killed? It was the letter C.

Douglas Cantrell gasped at the sight of the tile, immediately turning to Frank in time to see his eyes roll back into his head and to catch his friend as he fell back toward him. On the other side of Frank, Brooks took a second to process what he saw. Studying the letter, he didn't see Frank lose consciousness, and only at the last second, when seeing panicking eyes from those around the room, was he able to turn and help his fellow detective as he collapsed to the floor.

Everyone at the table jumped and hurried to Frank's side. Only Cantrell and Brooks saw the letter clearly and were able to make the connection.

Holding the back of Frank's head away from the wooden floor and trying to comfort his friend, Cantrell cried, fearing the worst for Frank.

"What happened?" Jackson hovered over those trying to assist the fallen detective.

"Turn him on his side!" Bones yelled. "Turn him on his side." He knew that an unconscious Frank could possibly swallow his tongue.

Candace was the first to dial 911. Hearing her on the phone, Bones said, "Fuck that!" and asked Mitchell and Abecassis to help him get Frank downstairs to the nearby firehouse and the ambulance they had on site.

"Frank!" Bones implored his partner. "Wake up, buddy!" he repeatedly slapped his face.

Frank's 230 lb. limp body wasn't cooperating with three thirty-something, physically fit, full-grown men struggling to raise him from the floor.

"Guys, don't move him!" Jackson yelled. "Wait for EMS to get up here!"

"What is happening?" Bones feared for his partner.

"What was in his hand?!" Jackson demanded. "What was it?!"

"The letter C!" Brooks wiped his near-drooling mouth. "The letter C." He finally made the connection and could now understand why Frank collapsed.

"The letter C?" Jackson looked puzzled, as did Mitchell, Abecassis, and Colapietro.

"CHARMAINE!" Cantrell fell back onto the floor and wept for his friend. He knew Frank would have to live with the guilt of nine dead cops. But what he didn't know yet was that there was a tenth and eleventh victim.

Still not connecting the dots, even though keenly aware of the 1992 murder of Salvatore Collazo, Jackson looked around the room and hoped someone could solve the mystery of the letter C.

Candace Weatherby, the lone historian in the room, stood, turned toward Jackson, and said, "Charmaine. Vincent Charmaine Walker – FalconClaw – 1992."

Chapter 24 – And so it Begins

It was late April 2021, seven months before Frank's collapse. Genesis Harper and Talon Grayson sat in their favorite spot on the Schuylkill Banks Boardwalk, planning out how they would die.

"What was it like killing that man?" Genesis had often fantasized about killing someone since she was eighteen and learned her full name was Genesis Harper Walker, the daughter of a prolific serial killer. "I always wondered if I would become a serial killer like our father."

"It was amazing," Talon said. "To know that after someone lived for so long, avoiding diseases, car accidents, and drug overdoses, that they could die beneath the heel of my boot in just seconds. I felt like God. No, I felt more powerful than God."

"No shit? How?" Genesis stared at her man, proud of him and his accomplishment.

"Well, it was like God gave the man life, and I took it away, and God couldn't stop me."

"Fuck!" Genesis squirmed in her seat. "You're starting to turn me on, Grayson."

"It was better than sex. I'm tellin' you." Talon stared wide-eyed out at the Schuylkill River. "I wondered, too, why our father killed his first victim, but since killing that motherfucker on the street, I know why he killed again and again. It felt good."

"I wanna kill somebody!" Genesis perked up in her seat.

Talon looked at his half-sister and said, "You know we're going to hell, right?"

"Fuck yeah!" Genesis flashed a sinister grin. "I say we kill as many cops as we can and then kill each other so that we'll always be together."

"I'm serious," said Talon. "This world is not for us. We were born sick. It's just like the song, Genesis. We were born monsters."

"I think that, too." Genesis spun on the bench, now facing the river like Talon. "I need to feel the way our father felt when he killed. I need to feel the way you felt. I need to kill, Talon."

"You will. I'll teach you."

"When?" Genesis turned back to her man. "When can we do it? Who can we kill?"

"I know just the people." Talon's eyes narrowed. "They deserve to die." Talon spit out toward the river, the western wind coming off the Schuylkill blowing it back in his face. Wiping it away. "Those motherfuckers need to die after what they did to me."

"Who?"

"The Steineckers."

"Holy shit!" Genesis jumped from the bench and crouched down in front of Talon. Looking up at him, she said, "Are you fucking serious? Can we do it?! Can we?!"

"They still live in the same house." Talon cradled Genesis' head as he kept staring, the sound of the moving river causing his senses to go numb. "I went there. I saw her."

"Where? Who?" Genesis stared into her brother's eyes, head cocked.

"Before I found you. Before I killed that guy....." Talon looked his girlfriend in the eyes. ".... I saw the bitch who threw me to the wolves, and she saw me." Talon didn't share his confusion about how he really felt about the Steineckers with Genesis. He still loved them but hated them for giving him up. In his mind, they were at fault for the man he'd become, not his birth father.

"Delores Steinecker needs to die, along with that bastard who handed me over to the state. I'll never forget that day, and neither will he." Talon wore a vacant look.

"Why didn't you ever tell me this?" Genesis couldn't believe it. "I always wanted to kill every fucking family that took me in just to give me up."

That fucker was supposed to take me to the landfill and then to the Dairy Queen. Talon said to himself, his heart beginning to race. "Not me," said Talon. "Not all of 'em, just those two."

"I wish I could find the motherfucker who molested me when I was eight. I would cut off his dick and feed it to that son of a bitch." Genesis had kill in her eyes.

"I loved them, and they said they loved me every night for almost a year. They lied to me, Genesis. The Steineckers need to die."

"When can we do it?"

"My boss is on vacation the day after tomorrow. We can take the van across the river and stake out their house. They used to go to bed early, and I bet they still leave a key outside under a fake rock by the water spigot." Talon was starting to fantasize about their deaths. "If that key is there, that's our way in."

"Are we really going to do this?" Genesis started to feel a little nervous.

"Genesis, this is our destiny. We were born to kill," he looked at her. "Just like Charles Starkweather and Caril Fugate." Talon's mouth watered. "But they lived...."

"But *WE* have to die." Genesis' eyes narrowed. "We have to kill spectacularly and die that way, too."

After a minute of silence with both pondering the future, Genesis said, "We need to outdo the Natural Born Killers."

Talon's eyes momentarily went black. Shaking his head methodically from side to side, he said, "No, Genesis. We have to outdo our father."

"He killed eleven," said Genesis.

"Yeah, and the last one was a cop." Talon smiled.

Genesis began to fantasize, too. "I can think of three pigs that need to die right now." Genesis racked her brain, recounting the names of the cops who had threatened her and then used her for sex.

Talon nodded in agreement. "Yeah, I can see it now. If we kill enough of them, maybe they'll call us the Cop Killers."

"God, that makes me wet just thinking about it." Genesis squirmed in her seat again.

"Who was the cop he killed up at FalconClaw?" asked Genesis.

"The name was Collazo. Salvatore Collazo."

"Isn't that the guy's name that took out The Schuylkiller?"

"Yeah. Our father killed his father on Halloween back in the early nineties."

"Wait a second!" Genesis was shocked. "Our father killed Frank Collazo's father?"

"I know, right?" Talon grinned. "We should kill him."

"But that guy's famous...." Genesis was on the edge of the bench.

"Yeah, I know."

"Could you imagine how famous we would be if we killed him?"

"Yeah," Talon smiled. "His bitch is famous, too."

"We could kill her, too." Genesis shook her head, smiling.

"I tried to kill him once, you know?"

Genesis thought Talon was bullshitting her. "No way! What the fuck are you talking about?"

"No, I'm serious. I used to stalk that fucker. One day back in the summer of 2016, I got lucky. It was like it was fate or something. I was working cleaning pumps at the Queen Lane Reservoir...."

"Holy shit! I remember when you worked up there."

"Whatever!" Talon shot Genesis a dirty look. "That's the summer you fucked me over and was fucking that asshole, Ronnie Blake."

"I never even liked him. Just keep telling me the story."

Talon shook off his jealousy and continued. "Well, I just got off work and walked down Fox Street to a gas station to get some smokes. And I couldn't believe my eyes. That some bitch was pumpin' gas when I walked up." Talon's heart raced with the memory.

"So, what happened?"

"Well, I had a gun in my backpack that I stole from one of the security guards at work right before I got out of there. The dumbass probably still doesn't know who took it...."

"So, what the fuck happened?!" Genesis punched Talon in the chest. "Come on! Tell me already!"

"Yeah, so I hid behind the dumpster on the side of the gas station, and I took a shot at him while he stood there pumping gas."

"Holy Fuck! Did you hit him?" Genesis couldn't believe what she was hearing.

"No," Talon shook his head, almost looking sad. "I was actually aiming for the gas pump but put a bullet right through his back windshield. That's why I was behind the dumpster, just in case it blew up."

"So, what'd you do after you missed?"

"I was scared, so I tossed the gun in the dumpster and went inside to get some smokes."

"You fuckin' stuck around?!" Genesis was amazed, punching Talon again. "You're a fucking legend!"

"Yeah," Talon shrugged. "I tried to blend in. I didn't want anyone to see me fleeing the scene."

"So, did you ever see him again after that?"

"No, and to be honest, I was scared shitless after the whole thing."

"Why didn't you ever tell me?" Genesis was confused. "I mean, that shit's big."

"Because I would've had to tell you that my last name was Walker, and I wasn't ready for that yet."

"We need to have sex right now." Genesis jumped on Talon's lap.

Two nights later, Talon and Genesis sat in Talon's work van, three houses down from 969 Trent Road, and waited. The two would be baptized in the blood of the Steineckers before the night was over. With a twisted sense of symbolism, Talon took Genesis to the Dairy Queen down the road before heading to the Steineckers. The day the call came through that caused the Steineckers to surrender Talon back to DCF, George Steinecker was supposed to take Talon to the Dairy Queen after touring a landfill. Talon would have his Dairy Queen.... And his revenge.

Before getting out of the van, armed with knives, Talon looked at Genesis and said, "And so it begins."

An hour later, just after midnight, Talon, and Genesis, covered in blood, ran back to the van and headed back to Philly. In the days that followed, they would plan their killing spree and target cops they had previous encounters with. They would take their own lives only after their body count exceeded that of their father's, and it could only end with the two of them murdering Philadelphia Police Detective Frank Collazo.

Seven months later, Talon and Genesis had sex in the basement of St. Peter Claver Baptist Church and would wait until things quieted down. Talon quit his job with the home improvement company Vinyl, Carpet, and Windows, fearing the heat would be on and the police would look at any vendors who worked with Rocky Tops. Talon had singled out the company after repeatedly seeing the company vans around town bearing the moniker VCW in big black letters on the side. Talon thought he would be the perfect fit and felt right at home riding in a van that bore his father's initials.

Back at the 39th, everyone was relieved when Frank regained consciousness on the floor of the Detective Room after two paramedics from Engine 59 rendered aid. Proud, Frank refused to be taken to the hospital. He was humiliated and wanted to leave. With a reluctant nod of approval, Jackson signed off on it. Bones would drive him home and stay with him until he knew he was all right. Cantrell and Candace, both worried sick, would see Frank into Bones' car and then head back upstairs and wait for word.

Forty minutes later, Bones went through Frank's refrigerator and said, "Jesus, Frank! You've got hotdogs in here older than me. Where in the hell is all the food?" Grabbing a half-full bottle of Gatorade and closing the fridge, which sat just feet from the raggedy couch Frank was sitting on in the tiny studio apartment, Bones added, "How do you keep your weight up? No wonder you fainted. You're malnourished."

After Bones handed him the drink, Frank said, "We both know that's not why I passed out."

Bones felt out of place talking about Frank's mental health. He loved his partner but saw him as more of a big brother and didn't want to cross any boundaries that might upset him or potentially damage their relationship.

"Sounds like you want to talk, Frankie." Bones tiptoed around the subject but was willing to listen and wouldn't pry.

"Is she gone, Bones?"

Frank looked just like he did when he was a little boy coming to grips with the loss of his father. Now, just like then, it took months for him to believe that his father was gone. And he still wasn't sure whether Penny and Bonnie were dead or not.

Bones looked mortified. "Well.... Um.... I...."

"Bones, you are one of only two friends I have left in this world. I need you to be straight with me. Is she gone?" Frank prepared himself for the truth, pleading with his eyes he needed to know. "Is Penny dead? Is my little girl gone, too?"

"Frankie, you sure?"

"Just tell me something that makes sense, Bones! I'm going out of my fucking mind." Frank clutched his hair with both hands and pulled," growling in frustration as he did.

Bones sat down to the left of his friend on the couch and began to tell him what he needed to hear. "Penny and Bonnie died on May 14, Frank." Bones placed his right hand on Frank's left shoulder.

Frank clenched his teeth and fists and sat quietly as his heart began to break.

"It was on Cheltenham Avenue in front of the Enon Tabernacle Church. There was a bad storm, and a construction van rear-ended Penny causing her to lose control of her car and collide head-on with another vehicle."

"And?" Frank ground his teeth, fighting back the tears as he stared at the empty wall opposite the couch. "And?! Tell me!" his hands began to tremble while his left eye twitched.

Bones saw what he and the others witnessed back at the 39th an hour earlier. Using his foot, he pushed the empty coffee table away from the couch in case Frank fainted again.

"Tell me, Bonesie! What happened next?" Frank's face was now frozen, and tears ran from both eyes. "You tell me! Goddammit! You tell me the truth!"

"You tried to get there to help them, but there was nothing you could do."

"Did I make it there before they died, Bones?" Frank began to lose control. His chin quivered violently, and the tears continued to stream.

"Yeah, Frankie. You made it there on time...." Bones didn't have the heart to tell his friend that little Bonnie had passed away before he could get there.

Frank gasped and seemed almost relieved. Falling into Bones' arms, he collapsed into a heap of sorrow. Frank cried for his Penny and his Bonnie. And he cried for himself. Like the loss of his father, he'd lost his family for the second time in his life. In his anguish, he desperately searched for comfort in the fact that he made it to his family before they died.

Bones held his friend tightly and took solace in being there for Frank when he finally realized his family was gone.

"I miss her, Bones!" Frank wailed. "I miss Penny and Bonnie!"

"I know, Frankie." Bones rubbed Frank's back as he held his friend. "They're in a better place now."

Frank recoiled. "She's still at the house!" He pulled away from Bones with a look of sudden concern. "I have to see her!" Frank jumped up, grabbed Bones' car keys, and headed for the door.

Bones leaped from the couch in pursuit of Frank, intercepting him as he ran across the tiny apartment. "Frankie, you're no good to drive, man!" Bones wriggled himself between Frank and the door, struggling in the tiny hallway.

"Bones, let me go! I need to see her!" Frank screamed, reaching for the door. "I need to see Penny!"

"I can't let you go up there, Frank. Your heads not right!" Bones struggled with a desperate man who had lost everything.

"Let me go, you motherfucker!" Frank pulled on Bones' jacket, ripping his zipper and scratching his neck.

Slightly hurt and lost in a moment of self-preservation, Bones lifted Frank skyward and slammed him to the floor. Struggling feverishly, the two men found themselves in the living room, with Frank lashing out at the man who would deny him his family when *they* needed him the most. And when *he* needed them, Frank thought as he fought with Bones.

Striking his friend and partner several times to break free, Frank had lost all control. Bones, not hitting back, maneuvered himself under his friend, used his legs to control his lower body, and got Frank in a rear-naked choke. Bones cried for his friend, grunting, "Don't make me choke you out, Frank!"

Frank ignored the warning as he tried in vain to escape the grasp of Bones, a trained MMA fighter and boxer who had put many men to sleep, some even bigger than Frank.

Frank flailed for a few more seconds as Bones administered a Blood Choke. Not cutting off Frank's airway, Bones cut off Frank's blood flow to the brain by applying pressure to the carotid artery in his neck.

After a few more seconds, Frank lay unconscious on the floor, with Bones rolling his friend onto his side.

Now leaning back against the couch, Bones caught his breath and cried for his friend. Wiping blood away from his nose and mouth, he saw a lost soul at his feet and didn't know how to bring him back.

Three minutes later, Bones emerged from the kitchen area with two cold, wet towels. Nursing his wounds with one, he placed the other under Frank's neck to revive him. After a few more seconds, Frank's eyes opened, and he stared blankly at the floor beside him.

Sitting up, he stretched out his neck and then his jaw. "What the fuck happened?" Frank looked around and saw broken furniture, a hole in the drywall, and Bones sitting on the couch nursing a bloody nose.

"You kicked the shit out of me, that's what," muffled Bones through the bloody wet towel.

"Oh, shit!" Frank grimaced when he noticed the big scratch on his friend's neck as it peeked out from behind the dishtowel he was holding. "Did I blackout again?"

"Yeah, something like that." Bones inspected the towel after pulling it away from his nose.

Frank stood up, and then plopped down next to his partner, and asked, "What can you tell me about the accident?"

"Frank, I'm not doing this again," Bones was reluctant. "You just beat the shit out of me, and I'm not up for round two."

"I get it, Bones." Frank was now lucid. "Penny and Bonnie are gone, but that was no accident. What more can you tell me?"

"It was a hit-and-run, Frank. The van was found a mile away from the scene. It'd wrecked off the road, and the driver was long gone," explained Bones. "The final accident report said that the van was stolen, and the driver fled after it crashed to avoid apprehension. Nothing in the accident report states that it was intentional."

"What can you tell me about the van?"

"Just that it was a ...." Bones' eyes flew open wide.

Frank's eyes met with Bones, and the two chorused, "Construction van."

"Holy shit, Frank!" Bones was in disbelief.

"Rocky Tops," the two again chorused together.

Thirty minutes later, the door to the Detective Room burst open, startling everyone inside. Jackson looked both surprised and concerned when she saw Frank, thinking he should receive medical care instead of returning to the 39th. Candace and Doug were also concerned but breathed a sigh of relief and stood to welcome their friends.

"Frank, are you okay?" Looking at Bones, Cantrell knew they'd had a fight.

"Bones, what happened to your neck? Is that a black eye?" Candace looked concerned. She also looked at Frank and felt the same as Cantrell; the two had been in a fight. "You're jacket's ripped, too."

"We're okay," said Bones. "We got jumped outside by like, I don't know, twenty guys, and I had to save Frank."

"He's not lying." Frank maintained a straight face.

"What in the hell are you two doing here?" Momma Bear Jackson was worried for her guys. "Frank, you need to see someone. We need to get you to the hospital for some medical attention. You're looking a little rough, too, Bones."

"Penny and Bonnie are gone, and it was no accident. Penny was the first cop killed and represents the letter C. She and Bonnie were murdered on Cheltenham Avenue. Now let's get to work!" Frank blew past everyone in attendance, sat at a nearby desk, and booted up a computer.

Cantrell and Jackson looked at Bones with shock and amazement. It was the first time they had heard Frank accept that Penny and Bonnie were gone.

Seconds later, Frank called out to Candace Weatherby. "Candace! Get over here!"

Chapter 25 – Archibald Riley

Minutes later, Frank gave Candace her marching orders. "Candace, listen to me. I need you to research everything there is to know about Vincent Charmaine Walker. Where he lived, his favorite food, favorite movie, his entire family tree, girlfriends, wives.... I wanna know what kept that motherfucker up at night. All of it. The people we're dealing with are fascinated by the man who took my father's life, and they're fascinated with me. I need to know why. You get busy doing what you came down to do.... You break down the history surrounding that man between Halloween 1992 to the time he was executed. You find me something I can use. If you do, you will have earned your stripes and the right to sit beside the men and women of the 39th who pound these streets every day, risking their lives."

"I'll do my best, Frank." Candace flashed a look of determination.

"Anything you need...." Frank was clear. "You get with Bob Brooks or me. By using the police database, you'll have clearance and access to the DMV, criminal background information, and birth records. You name it. Don't hesitate to ask."

"I won't let you down, Frank." Candace Weatherby knew that it could cost him his life if she did. "Oh, and Frank...." she smiled.

"Yeah?"

"What's the DMV?" Candace looked embarrassed that she didn't know.

Frank smiled, "It's the Department of Motor Vehicles."

"Yes. Of course, it is." Candace blushed.

"Okay, then." Frank turned away and looked for his brothers in blue.

"Brooks, Bones, get over here." Frank motioned to the two cops he trusted the most. "Listen, Bob. I need that list of all common collars ASAP. There's got to be a connection in there somewhere. But I can tell you this, though.... The list doesn't have to be complete because it's likely that one or more of the victims weren't killed because they had arrested our perps but rather because they were in the wrong place at the wrong time or knew them but never actually arrested them." Frank's eyes narrowed, thinking of Danny Moncrief, and he said, "Danny didn't have to die. That's on me, and I'll make sure his wife and kids don't have to suffer with the question of who did this for very long."

Brooks nodded in the affirmative.

"Bones, listen...." Frank turned to his partner with steely eyes and said, "Track down Monica Jefferson and get her back in here. My gut's telling me that she knows one or both of our killers, whether she knows it or not. That woman could possibly hold the key. I want the Genesee woman she told us about to be brought in for questioning. I got a bad feeling about that one."

"You got it, Frank." Bones looked eager to get started. "I'm on it."

Frank was determined. "Oh, and Bones, before you do anything, I need that accident report ASAP!"

"Will do." Bones turned to leave.

"Frank," Brooks made sure that Bones was out of earshot. "What happened to Bones's face? Did you guys get into it or something?"

Frank shook his head, maintained his straight face from earlier, and said, "Nah. It's just like Bones said. There must've been like twenty or thirty guys that jumped us up in the Yunk. Poor Bonesie.... I had to save the guy."

"Yeah, sure, Frank, whatever." Brooks shook his head, grinned, and walked away.

Five minutes later, as Frank headed for the door, Bones yelled out, "Yo, Frank, where you going, buddy?"

"There's somebody I gotta go see."

Frank was gone, and Bones knew exactly where he was going.

Twenty-five minutes later, Frank turned left into the driveway on East Locust Avenue, the place that had tortured him since he was just fourteen. He knew his father wasn't there, and taking that turn reminded him of that every day for the previous twenty-eight years.

That all changed when Penny had Frank's childhood home remodeled while he recovered from the bullet he took to the chest from Cameron St. John, The Schuylkiller, back in 2017. With Penny's considerable gesture, he could call it home again. It was a home that restored his sense of family and made him nearly whole again. But now, each time he returned, he couldn't be sure if Penny would be there or not. And that broke his heart again and again.

The house looked as dark as the late afternoon November sky, and as Frank pulled in, he was scared. Throwing the car into park in front of the garage, the back of the house was pitch black. Apprehensive, he opened his car door, and the cold rush of air chilled him to the bones and made him stop and reconsider going further.

Frank could feel it.... Penny and Bonnie weren't in there. They hadn't been since they died at the scene of the accident on May 14. An overwhelming feeling of sadness numbed his senses, the cold no longer affecting him. Turning to the house, Frank knew he was alone but would walk to the steps and hoped Penny would come out.

His back to the scarred fence, he stood on the sidewalk in front of the back steps. Staring at the backdoor, he prayed. He prayed to a God he hadn't believed in since 1992 when he was paternally orphaned by a psychopath named Vincent Charmaine Walker. The ghosts that had saved him time and time again in the previous four years served as his only bastion of hope. They were the thread that held him together as he sunk deeper and deeper into his own personal netherworld.

Standing in fear, he regained his senses, and the cold once again wreaked havoc on every bone in his body and what was left of his tattered soul. Frank wanted to walk right up those steps and right through the back door of the home that once housed his daughter and the only woman he'd ever truly loved. Instead, he stood frozen.

Standing and staring, his left eye began to twitch again, and his hands shook. Clenching them into fists in an attempt to convince himself he wasn't sick, tremors ran up his arms and pervaded his soul. The visual snow that had impaired him time and time again was now a blizzard, and he was blinded by it.

Suddenly Frank felt the cold steering wheel of the Dodge in his hands, and he was passing the cemetery on Upsal. Unable to stop his car and save Penny and Bonnie from joining the other slain detectives, he carried on to the place where Penny's Honda Accord struck a cement truck head-on. It was a place where he would see them one more time. One last time before they died.

The rain was fierce, and with visibility low, the row houses that lined Upsal looked like stone walls to Frank, walls that imprisoned, not protected. He didn't see the red traffic signal when he approached Forest Avenue. When he did, Frank closed his eyes and gunned the Dodge. With his eyes still closed, he saw Penny again. She was looking back to see if Bonnie was okay after the collision. Her eyes were closed. Terrified, Frank opened his eyes again and found himself hydroplaning over Williams Avenue, his stomach turning. Nauseous, he knew that the Upsal/Limekiln split was fast approaching. Frank knew he would be dead if he didn't have the green. Before the fork in the road, the six-road confluence had caused many accidents in broad daylight, but the raging Nor'easter was consuming the last of Frank's sanity, and he'd surely never run the gauntlet unscathed. He was desperate to make it to Cheltenham Avenue and the Enon Tabernacle Baptist Church, the place where Penny and Bonnie died.

Another cold wind blew Frank from his torment, and he was again standing on the dark sidewalk, still staring at the back door of 454 East Locust Avenue. Lowering his head, he returned to the Dodge and found the same oldies station as he had the previous month. Tuning into FM 98.1, Firefall's *Always* came on. Frank would ride out the storm in his head by reclining his seat and taking in the heart-breaking lyrics.

Frank sang along, heartbroken. When he reached the chorus, the line *I want you more than life* pervaded the empty place inside him, and his destiny was drawn.

Frank, eyes still closed, began to cry. Holding them tightly closed, he saw Penny and Bonnie. He remembered the last time they were all together eating breakfast. He remembered them getting into the car and heading off to Walmart. He remembered seeing the two interact and how Penny cared for her little girl. Frank remembered all the times Penny made his pain go away. Frank's lips quivered when he realized she wasn't there anymore and that he'd have to suffer through his torment.... Alone.

Frank woke up freezing early on Black Friday and headed into the 39th District house unshowered, unshaven, and wearing the same clothes he'd worn the day before. He'd hoped to get there ahead of the others as he felt guilty for leaving early the night before.

Turning down Schuyler Street, he was surprised to see Bones', Brooks', and Jackson's cars parked down the side of the building. He assumed that Cantrell and Weatherby were in there, too.

Walking in, Frank was greeted warmly. Everyone knew that the night before must've been hard on Frank as he'd finally come to terms with the fact that Penny and Bonnie were gone. And everyone could see he was wearing the same clothes.

"Hey, Frankie, we got something to go on regarding the common collar aspect of the case." Brooks was holding a manilla file folder and seemed eager to share it with him.

Frank motioned Bones over with his head, and Jackson joined the three at the conference table. Cantrell was on his laptop at a vacant detective desk near Candace Weatherby.

Removing the contents from the envelope and sitting down, Brooks said, "Okay, here's what we got." Passing papers to each of the other three at the table, Brooks revealed the following.

"Nine dead cops in all, but our historical arrest records reveal that four of the cops have zero common collars with the other five." Brooks pointed to the names of the other five slain cops and their commonalities with each other.

"Now, if you look at this breakdown," Brooks again pointed, "Five of the victims had eight common collars in their careers; three had six; and two of our victims had five common names in their arrest history."

Brooks then passed out individual pages for each of the dead cops to those around the table.

"Look at this," said Jackson, sifting through the files. "There's a Walker on my list for Officer Dennis Cameron out of the 18th District. Talon Walker. Does he appear on anyone else's list of arrests?"

"That'd be crazy if he were somehow related to Vincent Charmaine Walker, wouldn't it?" asked Brooks.

Frank felt a surge of electricity shoot up from his sternum to his head. He grimaced at the thought. "I followed Vincent Walker's life until his execution when I was twenty-two and never knew him to have had siblings." Frank wasn't convinced of a familial connection, but the last name Walker was too coincidental to ignore, in his opinion.

"Yeah, but he could have cousins, kids, aunts, uncles, you name it," said Bones.

The four looked through the information, and no other dead officers had arrested a Talon Walker.

"I got nothing here," said Frank, "but....."

"I got a Walker here," said Brooks. "A Robert J. Walker was arrested in 2006 by Sergeant Timmy Falcone out of the 3rd downtown."

"I gotta Richard Walker over here. He was arrested by Detective Bobby Lane out of the 8th when he was a rookie cop back in 2000," said Frank.

"Yeah, Walker's a pretty common name but worth seeing if they're somehow connected or not," said Robert Brooks.

"I got one more here," said Frank. "A Peter Walker on Calvin Murphy's list from 2014, out of the 14th."

"Well, we gotta run 'em all." Jackson sighed.

"Fuck! Here's another Walker. Arrested in 2020 by Westerfield." Bones looked a little discouraged.

When the four were done tallying, they'd had a total of twenty-one Walkers on their list, with only one female. Frank kept staring at the name Talon Walker, though. He knew that birds had claws, except for the ravenous ones, they had Talons. That name unsettled him as he thought of FalconClaw.

Now looking over his shoulder, he yelled for Candace. "Hey, Candace! Come over here for a second, would you?!"

Jackson, Bones, and Brooks all looked on, thinking that Frank had made a connection.

Weatherby got up and walked the ten feet to where the three detectives and their captain were sitting and said, "Yeah, Frank?"

"Whatta ya got so far on Vincent Charmaine Walker?"

"Not much. I'm starting at his birth and going forward," said Candace. "Troubled kid from the very beginning.... Both parents were drug addicts. His father died of an overdose while his mother was murdered by her pimp five years later."

"That's good work, Candace," said Frank with a nod of approval. "But I want you to start at his execution and go backward to Halloween 1992."

"Sure." Candace was cordial. " I can do that. Anything else you want me to look into?"

Frank said, "Yeah. One more thing. Look into any arrests made on a Genesee woman. Age 23 – 35 years old."

"Will do, Frank." Candace Weatherby jotted the name and walked away.

After an hour of sorting and comparing notes, the four at the table disbanded and went their separate ways. Captain Beatrice Jackson looked to Frank and, with her eyes, told him to stick around. Once no one was within earshot, Jackson asked, "Frank, how are you feeling?"

"I'm okay. Why?"

"Because you look like hell." Jackson looked him up and down, adding, "You look like you slept in your car last night, and you stink." She shrugged politely.

Frank lowered his head, discretely smelled his right armpit, and, slightly embarrassed, said, "Yeah.... Another rough night, I'm afraid."

"We all miss her, Frank." Jackson was empathetic. "Bonnie, too. Nothing or no one could ever replace them, but we need to get you better." Jackson looked around before saying, "Justin Smith wants you off the case, and he's looking for any reason to remove you. When's your next appointment with Riley?"

Frank was lost in thought with Jackson's words about his family when his captain repeated herself. "Frank, when's your next meeting with Archibald Riley?"

Shaking off his thoughts, Frank said, "I'm sorry, Captain. Tuesdays and Thursdays at 5."

"Well, you make sure you keep those appointments." Jackson had a hard exterior but a soft heart. "Two reasons...."

Frank looked on.

"I want zero reasons for Captain Justin Smith to take you off the case. And...."

"What's the other?"

"I want you to get the help you need." Jackson's look softened. "I care for you, Frank, and what you've been through.... No one should ever experience the loss that you have."

Frank tried to remain calm and collected, but inside he was broken.

"Frank, I realize you're putting on a courageous front for all of us, but even superheroes have weaknesses."

"No, I'm with you, Cap. I like Doctor Riley so far. I'll make sure I don't miss any of my appointments."

Three days later, at 4:54 pm, Frank stood outside of Archibald Riley's office on the campus of Temple University. Looking at the business card in his hand, as he had the first time he was there, he pulled the door open and walked inside. Five minutes later, he once again found himself in Riley's office alone, staring at the stuffed falcon high up on the wall behind Archibald Riley's desk. It seemed to Frank that the falcon had a story to tell but never had the chance.

Looking around the room, Frank realized that in the eyes of the esteemed psychiatrist whom he was about to meet for the second time, he was no different than all the others who had walked through the doors before him, a sick person reaching for a lifeline.

Suddenly the door in the back of the room opened, and in walked Riley.

"Frank!" the spirited doctor said with a larger-than-life smile. "Why, whatever brings you in today?"

Frank shot Riley a quizzical look. He looked up and to his left, wondering if he had the wrong day. "Forgive me, but.... We do have an appointment today, right?"

"Yes, of course we do. That was merely a silly attempt at humor."

Frank's face went cold. "You'll have to forgive me, doctor, but I'm not really in the joking mood considering recent events."

Riley's face went sober, remembering that Frank had lost a colleague since he last saw him.

"Yes, of course, Frank. I apologize for my misstep," Riley was humble. "It's just that seeing you here in my office again brings me great joy. And again, please call me Archie."

Frank shook his head, not understanding why his presence gave Riley joy, and he didn't care enough to give it any more thought.

"Yeah, well, maybe we should get started." Frank sat down on the red velvet couch and tried to ready his nerves, knowing that Riley would likely extract some painful memories.

"Straight to it, then, huh?" Riley took his seat adjacent to Frank.

Frank repositioned himself awkwardly, not knowing whether to sit or lie down. Looking over to Riley for guidance, his brows went up, conveying his confusion.

Riley grinned. "Whatever makes you comfortable young man."

Frank leaned on the backrest and stared at the ceiling. He found the couch to be comfortable and hoped he didn't nod off during their session.

"So, Frank," Riley readied his pencil. "Can you tell me what's transpired in your life since we last met?"

"Wow." Frank's brows shot up. "That's a loaded question," he thought aloud. Loaded as in a double barrel shotgun in one hand and the loss of his sanity in his other. "A man died because of me, Doctor Riley. He was a good man, with a wife, two children, and another on the way." Frank stared with empty eyes.

"Because of you, Frank?" Riley scribbled in his journal. "And why because of you?"

Frank seemed irked all of a sudden, glaring over at Riley. "Because the lunatics killing cops have their eyes set on me. Our investigation has revealed that I'm their reason for killing."

"Hmm.... Interesting. And you know this for sure, or is it simply a hypothesis at this time?"

Frank again looked irked, flashing Riley a crooked eye conveying his displeasure. "Of course, we don't have proof of that, but our evidence shows that the killers are working their way up to their final prize.... Me."

"I understand, Frank," said a compassionate Riley. "Please note that our conversation falls under patient/doctor privilege regarding your investigation, and I will not share anything you disclose with anyone else." Riley paused, "So please feel free to share whatever you'd like."

Frank settled back into the soft cushion and again found a peaceful escape from his troubled life. He was tired. He was tired of running toward something other than his pain. Frank was tired of being tired, and he was tired of being alone in a world that wasn't meant for him, and he not meant for it. He was tired, and he just wanted to rest.

"Frank, is there anything else you can tell me about your weekend?" Riley had hoped Frank had broken through his denial while at the cemetery and had finally come to grips with the unbearable fact that his family was gone.

"My wife and daughter died this weekend." Frank was melancholy.

"This weekend?" Like every other Philadelphian, Archibald Riley knew very well that Penny Bristow and her daughter Bonnie had perished in the terrible two-car accident on May 14. He understood that Frank had been in denial since the accident, and coming to terms with their deaths over the weekend had him only willing to accept that they had just died. "How can you be sure that Penny and Bonnie are no longer with us, Frank?"

"Because I asked Penny, and she didn't deny it."

"So, you spoke to Penny, then?" Riley thought Frank's disclosure was significant.

"Yes, I speak to her all the time." Frank seemed to sink even further into the cushion, and Riley noticed that he took great comfort in his own words.

"Frank, have you ever been hypnotized while in therapy before?"

"No, and I don't believe in that type of treatment." Frank was single-minded.

"You don't believe in the practice.... or in the notion that it can be helpful to the patient?"

"Both." Frank was unflinching. "You can't hypnotize me. It won't work. You'd just be wasting our hour together."

"Would you consider allowing me to try?" Riley saw an opening and felt confident Frank would, at the very least, afford him the opportunity.

Being as relaxed as he was, Frank was too tired to oppose the good doctor. He'd simply let him do his job and would happily leave after the hour was up. "You go ahead and do your thing, Doc."

"That's good, Frank." Riley sat his journal on a nearby arm table and repositioned himself at the edge of his seat.

Frank couldn't possibly understand what was about to happen. When he left the office of Dr. Archibald Riley on this day, Frank Collazo would see the world through a different lens. He would have a new peace in his life. But that peace, he knew, would only be a bridge over a raging river filled with his tears. He would look forward to crossing the bridge, knowing his family would be waiting for him on the other side.

Chapter 26 – The Accident

May 14, 2021, six and a half months earlier.

Penny rinsed out the coffee pot in the kitchen sink, looked out the back window, and saw Frank struggling to crank the lawnmower. It was the first cut of the season after a long winter and wet spring. After the fourth pull of the starter cord, the engine came to life, and Penny smiled when she saw Frank's proud look of accomplishment. Studying the man, she shook her head and chuckled, seeing that he had already worked up a sweat, partially soaking his ten-plus-year-old gray Philly P.D. T-shirt.

It was the first nice day of spring. The sun was shining, but rain was once again in the forecast. Frank was anxious to get the yardwork out of the way so that he could enjoy time with Penny and Bonnie before the Cantrells came in on Monday.

As Frank revved the engine on the lawnmower to ensure it remained running, Penny looked over at little Bonnie and said, "You wanna go to Walmart, Bon-Bon?"

"Yeah," was all that came back from a smiling Bonnie. She would be three on June 11, and Penny was going to walk down the toy aisle to get some gift ideas and see what toys Bonnie reacted to the most.

Drying her coffee mug, she said, "Just yeah, Bonnie Girl?" Tossing the towel onto the counter, Penny walked over to the highchair, wiped Bonnie's mouth and cheeks with a baby wipe, and commented, "You sure did make a mess of those Animal Crackers, didn't you?"

"Daddy going, too?" Bonnie studied her mother's face, hoping she'd say yes.

"No, Honey. Not this time." Penny unstrapped her little girl and lifted her out of the chair. "Just the ladies today. Daddy's got to cut the grass before the rain comes."

"Okay, Mommy." Bonnie looked a little sad. "Just the ladies today," she echoed her mom.

Outside, as Frank traversed the yard time and time again, the scarred fence kept getting his attention. It was as if it was calling out to him. Frank was sure his father would appear as a sense of foreboding overcame him. He couldn't escape the feeling that something bad was about to happen.

Several minutes later, as Frank cut crisscrossed lines in the backyard, the back door opened, and Penny walked out with Bonnie in her arms. Setting her daughter down on the back porch, Penny yelled out to Frank, but he didn't hear her.

"Stay here, Baby Girl," Penny instructed Bonnie. "I have to go talk to Daddy for a minute."

"Ok, Mommy." Bonnie sat down on the top step and waited as Penny walked out onto the freshly cut grass.

"Frankie!" Penny yelled out as she approached him, getting Frank's attention.

Frank cut the engine and wiped his brow as Penny approached. Looking at Penny with sweat dripping from his forehead, he said, "Heading out then?"

"Yeah, I've gotta pick up a few things at Walmart and then hit the Fresh Grocer. Do you want anything special for dinner tonight?"

Pulling his collar up over his face with both hands, Frank cleared the sweat from his face and said, "I want those *Little Bites* crumb cakes if they have 'em. Check both stores for me."

"They never have them," Penny shook her head.

"Well, if they do, get every box they have because Doug likes them, too."

"You two are like children." Penny looked back at Bonnie, who was sitting, just staring at her mom and dad.

Frank smiled at his daughter and waved. Bonnie smiled and waved back at her dad, wanting nothing more than to run to him.

"Okay, we'll be back in an hour or so. Text me if you think of anything else."

"Doug likes *Stouffer's* lasagna for lunch," Frank grinned. Pick up two, okay?"

"Sure, Frankie." Penny kissed him and made her way back to Bonnie.

"You know you messed up the lines I made in the grass, right?" Frank shook his head, looking at Penny's footprints across the lawn, and pretended to be mad.

"Yeah-Yeah, Frankie. Whatever!"

Bonnie stood up as her mother approached and said, "I want to kiss Daddy goodbye. Can I?"

"Of course, Honey," Penny smiled. "Just make sure you jump over all the pretty lines that Daddy made. Mmm-kay?"

Bonnie skipped through the grass without a word, jumping every line as if playing hopscotch.

Frank noticed and smiled, winking at Penny and kneeling to meet his daughter. "Hey, Bonnie girl. Just you and Mommy going to the store?" Frank tried hard not to get dirt or sweat onto Bonnie's pink Dora the Explorer jacket.

"Just the ladies, Daddy." Bonnie leaned in for a kiss.

"I love you," Frank said, kissing his best girl. Pulling back, he spotted gray clouds over Bonnie's shoulder. "Tell Mommy to go slow because it's gonna rain, okay?"

"I will, Daddy." Bonnie kissed him again, turned, and ran toward her mom, shouting, "Go slow, Mommy! It's gonna rain!" She jumped over every line along the way, getting her parents' attention.

Penny looked at Frank, smiled, and winked. Mouthing the words, *I love you*, she scooped up Bonnie in her arms and headed for the garage.

Frank smiled, mouthed the words back to her, and admired his best friend, lover, and his only daughter's mother. Nodding his head and exhaling through his nose, he watched with satisfaction as Bonnie's little head hit her mother's shoulders and knew Penny would always be there to protect their little girl. Looking up, Frank felt the first raindrop fall on his face and thought he'd better hurry.

Two hundred and one days later, Frank found himself lying on Archibald Riley's red velvet couch for the second time. Shaking his head and thinking about the case, he knew that hypnosis would never work on him.

"Okay, Frank, lie back, close your eyes, and relax." Riley felt encouraged. He knew if he could first get Frank to recall the source of his pain, he could then help him to deal with it.

Frank closed his eyes, and his memory went back to that day.

Trying to beat the rain, Frank kept looking over at the scarred fence, hoping to see his dad. He couldn't escape the overwhelming feeling that his father was nearby. Suddenly, the skies opened, and Frank groaned, knowing he wouldn't finish the lawn until the next day.

After stowing the lawn mower back into the detached garage, Frank sprinted for the back door. In his haste, he spotted Old Man Winter and Frank Bruno near the scarred fence, talking with his father, Salvatore. The strange scene caught him off guard, and he couldn't process the unexpected appearance of the three men chatting in the pouring rain.

Garrison Winter methodically turned toward Frank and slowly nodded with a somber look. His father then turned to his son and lowered his head in a show of empathy. Looking then at Frank Bruno, he saw the legend tip his hat to him, wearing a look of chagrin. Still processing the moment, Frank's heart sank. He immediately knew something was wrong. His mind raced, and he thought of Penny and Bonnie. Looking toward the fence again, the ghosts that had guided him for the previous four years had gone.

Soaking from the rain, Frank dragged grass clippings from his boots through the back door and into the kitchen. Locating his phone on the table, he frantically dialed Penny's cell, but after five rings, it went to voicemail. Still unsure if he was imagining things, he looked out the back door, hoping to see Winter again, but instead, he saw a deluge.

"Come on! Come on!" Frank groaned aloud in frustration, trying Penny's cell again. Again, he got her voicemail.

Forty minutes earlier, Penny buckled Bonnie into the Walmart shopping cart and headed for the food section to check on Frank's crumb cakes. Outside, she heard a crack of thunder and knew that the rain was coming. Now inside, looking up at the skylights across the ceiling, Penny saw the darkened skies and a sudden flash, followed by a massive thundercrack. Like Frank, she, too, felt a sense of foreboding.

As Penny passed the row of checkouts, two people entered the store, both wearing hoodies, with the hoods down. A man in his late twenties grabbed a shopping cart and entered the store. His greasy brown hair, ratty goatee, and bad breath led the way. To his left, a frail-looking young woman with equally greasy hair, also in her late twenties, held onto the buggy as it passed between the checkout stations and a four-way metal rack full of hooded sweatshirts. The two looked over, thinking of when they could afford new ones. Ahead, in the distance, their deadly stares found their target, who was emptying a shelf of *Little Bites* crumb cakes into her cart.

After picking up several other items, Penny continued to the back of the store, occasionally stopping to inspect things that caught her eye. Each time she did, her stalkers stopped, too, maintaining a distance that wouldn't cause Penny to feel she was being followed.

Now in the toy aisle, Penny looked for a Scrabble board while little Bonnie leaned out of the shopping cart and tried to reach for a Love *Diana Doll* dressed in a pristine angel costume. Penny immediately knew that she would get the toy for Bonnie's birthday. Thinking the expression on Bonnie's face was adorable, she pulled out her phone, opened the camera app, and snapped a quick selfie of her and Bonnie. In the picture's background, pretending to shop, were her two stalkers.

After fifteen more minutes of shopping and one Scrabble board in her cart, Penny checked out while Talon and Genesis each grabbed a pack of gum and checked out two lanes down. Now outside, the rain began to fall, and Penny laughed and said, "Come on, Bonnie girl, we've gotta make a run for it!"

Bonnie gripped the buggy handle tightly and laughed with her mother. Penny, lost in the joy of being a mother, didn't see the homicidal maniacs, their hoods now up, climbing into a white home improvement van labeled on both sides with the moniker VCW.

Just as she backed out of her spot, the skies opened, and she decided to put off her trip to the grocery store until the next day.

Penny exited the parking lot through the deluge and took a left on Cheltenham Avenue as the white van followed, two cars back.

Driving southeast, she gripped the steering wheel tightly at ten and two and looked back to see Bonnie strapped into her car seat in the middle of the Accord's back seat. Bonnie stared out at the rain contently when Penny caught her eye in the rearview mirror, causing her to smile. Penny momentarily felt relieved until her eyes went over Bonnie's head to see a white Ford van following too close for conditions.

As Penny looked back to the road in front of her, she saw what appeared to be a large truck approaching from the distance in the westbound lane. With visibility low, she moved from the passing lane to the right lane, preparing to turn south onto Limekiln Road. Looking in the rearview mirror again, she saw the white van barreling down on her, and she braced herself, accelerating to lessen the impact.

"Do it, Talon! This is it! There's a truck coming! Do it!"

Genesis' words goaded Talon, and he pressed down on the gas pedal, quickly closing the distance with the Accord.

Now in front of Enon Baptist Church, the van trailing Penny struck the back of her Accord, causing it to fishtail wildly over the rain-drenched road. Penny swerved from right to left, trying to regain control of the car when it crossed the double yellow lines and into oncoming traffic. With no center median to obstruct her path or slow her down, Penny regained her footing and attempted to brake hard, but her foot accidentally slammed down onto the gas pedal instead of the brake. With her heart now frozen in fear, she looked helplessly at the oncoming traffic and couldn't avoid the large white cement truck in her path.

The truck, too big and heavy to avoid the Accord, collided with it head-on. In a haze and bleeding from her forehead, everything went quiet for Penny. In near shock and not knowing where she was for a moment, Penny gasped when she finally realized what had happened. Unable to turn, she struggled for the rearview mirror and positioned it so she could make eye contact with little Bonnie again. To her surprise, Bonnie smiled back at her as if the accident had never happened. Relieved, Penny struggled for her breath. Looking down, she saw the steering wheel pressed against her chest. Looking up again, she closed her eyes and hoped Frank would get there soon.

Without pain, she opened her eyes minutes later and heard nothing. Vague shadows frantically circled the car as the rain intensified, its avalanche colored in blue and red. She and Bonnie stared at each other in the mirror for what seemed like an eternity. Unable to move and pinned behind the wheel, Penny smiled warmly at her little girl.

Sprinting out the back door, Frank ran down the driveway to the street, where the Dodge was parked. Using his key fob to unlock his door, he shortened the distance to the driver's door by leaping over and sliding across the front left corner of the car. Pants soaked, he threw the car into gear and did a U-turn, spinning the tires while getting the car moving north.

Back to the present, Frank relaxed on the sofa, quickly realizing how tired he was. Moments earlier, he'd hoped he didn't nod off but was quickly losing the fight as his eyes grew heavier.

"That's good, Frank. Now just keep your eyes closed and think of a quiet place that you can go to and relax for a little while." Riley studied Frank's eyes and witnessed rapid eye movement beneath his eyelids. The REM indicated to Riley that his patient was approaching a trance-like state and would soon become susceptible to his questions.

Riley's cadence was steady and calm in a smooth and melodic voice. Lowering his volume, he whispered, "That's right, Frank. You're now in a quiet place where no one can hurt you. Your arms and legs are heavy, and you're unable to move," said Riley. "Can you hear me, Frank?" Riley whispered again.

"Yes." Frank was nearly inaudible.

"Frank, I want you to raise your right hand. Can you do that for me?"

"I can't," said Frank. "It's too heavy."

Riley observed a tear running from the corner of Frank's right eye down onto his ear. He recognized that Frank's trance was deepening and could now begin probing his memory of May 14.

"Frank, what do you see? Where are you?"

"It's raining," Frank's voice cracked. "I need to get to Penny. She's in trouble." His breathing was now labored.

"And where are you, Frank?"

"East Germantown, heading north."

"Where are you driving to?"

"I need to get to Penny and Bonnie. They're hurt."

"Can you feel their pain, Frank?"

"They're hurt. I can feel it."

"And how does that make you feel?"

"I'm scared. It's hard to breathe." Another tear ran from Frank's eye.

"What do you see, now?" asked Riley.

"I see rain on the windshield," Frank's voice trembled. "The wiper blades.... They're too loud."

"Frank, I'm there with you. Keep driving."

"I will," Frank gently sobbed. "But please help me get to my family."

"I want you to take me there.... Please take me to them, Frank. I want you to tell me what you see along the way." Riley's voice was calming.

"I'm passing Magnolia Street.... I have to turn left at Musgrave!" Frank was terrified.

"You're doing fine. Keep driving, Son."

Frank's heart seemed to race, and Riley observed his chest rapidly expanding and contracting.

"What do you see now?"

Almost in a panic, Frank cried, "I see Zion church and the baseball field across the street from it! It's raining so hard!"

"You're okay, Frank. Just keep on going."

"I'm on Belfield now. It's dark.... It's so windy. I see Chew Street, now Washington Lane!" he huffed, a puddle of drool pooling in the corner of his lips as he expelled saliva.

"It's okay, Frank. What do you see?"

"I'm in a tunnel of trees. It's so dark. It must be the Arboretum." Frank seemed to sway on the couch. "I see True Light Church.... there's Upsal!"

"Good, Frank. Good."

"I'm on Upsal.... I see the cemetery now!"

"Can you see the road, Frank?"

"It's so dark! The rain....! It's hard to see!"

After several seconds of panic and labored breathing, Frank cried. "I'm on Limekiln now. I can see the light at Cheltenham! I'm almost there!"

"Good, Frank. You're doing good.... You're going to make it there, Son." Riley's voice seemed to slow Frank's breathing.

"There's traffic. I need to get through!" Frank began to sob openly. "I see emergency vehicles up ahead! So many lights! Something's happened!" Frank was beginning to panic. His words slurred through his tears. It was as if the couch restrained him as he tried to get up. "There are fire trucks! Police! And ambulances! They're hurt! They need me! My family needs me!"

When the rain and traffic prevented Frank from getting closer to the accident, he abandoned his car in front of the Bethel Deliverance

Church and ran. Frank Collazo ran the two-hundred yards to Penny's Accord through pouring rain.

As Frank sprinted past the intersection of Vernon and Cheltenham, the rain blurred his vision. Running on the sidewalk, a wall of trees to his right and backed up traffic to his left, he was able to make out a downed fence and a white Range Rover smashed against a tree, firefighters attending to its victims. At least six vehicles had rear-ended each other behind the large white cement truck, which covered and obstructed both westbound lanes. Still running at full speed, Frank was almost blinded by the red and blue flashers emanating from numerous emergency vehicles, with the deafening sound of a third ambulance riding up the sidewalk behind him.

As Frank made it to the epicenter of the accident, he screamed when he saw Penny's silver Accord. The hood and engine were pushed back into the car's cockpit in mangled pieces, causing Frank's reality to slow and things to go quiet in his mind. Racing to get to Penny, police on the scene, in yellow raincoats and hats, intercepted him as he got closer. With his screams matching the thunder overhead and his tears diluted by the rain, Frank cried for Penny and his little girl.

"That's my wife and daughter in there! Penny!" Frank screamed. "I'm a cop! Let me through!" he wailed as the officers could barely contain him.

"Hey! That's Frank Collazo!" yelled an officer near the Accord who witnessed the screams and pleas. "Let him through!"

When Frank finally broke free, the firefighters pulled away from the car as their jaws of life had successfully separated the crushed door from the car's twisted frame.

When an EMS worker and fireman tried to restrain Frank, the same nearby cop looked at another EMS worker who shook his head from side to side, indicating that neither passenger in the car could be saved.

"Let him see his wife and daughter!" yelled the cop.

As Frank broke free for the second time, he ignored the sharp, jagged metal and kneeled next to Penny, who was barely conscious, with the car's steering wheel smashed against her chest.

"Penny," Frank cried. "Penny, I'm here! I'm here, Penny!"

Penny murmured through the rain and distant car horns, "Frankie? I knew you would make it, Frankie," she gurgled as blood seeped from her mouth, painting her lips the color of certain death. "I knew you would come."

"Penny!" Frank cried. "Penny, you'll be okay! I love you, Penny!"

"I love you too, Frankie," she managed to whisper, coughing up blood.

"Officers, firefighters, and EMS workers now realized who the victims were. They all stood shaken as the woman who had taken down a monster three years earlier was now dying in her husband's arms. The famous Frank Collazo, who took out the monster's twin, was now brought to his knees, unable to save two fragile lives, one already gone and the other quickly slipping away.

Aided by the driving rain, Frank gently wiped the blood away from Penny's face. With each stroke of his hand, the blood he'd pushed away was replaced by more blood and more rain. Then, to his horror, Frank saw his daughter in the back seat for the first time. Little Bonnie was slumped in her car seat, not moving. EMS had already determined she was dead and focused their efforts on the driver.

Frank, unable to get through the crumpled back door of the Accord, reached through the shattered glass and touched his daughter's tiny head. He sobbed uncontrollably, remembering her telling her mom to "Go slow, Mommy. It's gonna rain."

Lifting Bonnie's limp head, he found her little eyes closed and her angelic face as white as an angel's. Frank cried for his daughter. With Penny still holding onto life, he was pulled away from the vehicle so workers could continue the extraction of the victims. Frank screamed, fighting those trying to help, "I LOVE YOU, PENNY!"

Through the rain, Frank thought he could see Penny mouth the words, "I love you, too," as she slipped away.

For some of the workers on the scene, the loss of life and Frank's shattered heart were too much, and several broke down, using the rain to conceal their tears. A legend and her daughter were now dead, and another legend lay broken in the street.

Penny Bryce Ross Bristow and Bonnie Ross Collazo died in front of the Enon Tabernacle Church on Cheltenham Avenue on a dark, rainy, late afternoon. It was Friday, May 14, 2021. And for all intents and purposes, Frank Collazo died there, too.

Sobbing uncontrollably in the arms of Dr. Archibald Riley on a red velvet sofa, now drenched in tears and heartache, Frank Collazo finally made it to the scene where his family died. All he wanted now was to somehow go to the place where they both now lived.

Chapter 27 – Vinyl, Carpet, and Windows

"I can't believe it's December already," said Bobby Colapietro, the 39th District's sketch artist.

"Yeah, that's something all right." Frank's mind wandered, thinking about Christmas without his family. Bonnie's fourth Christmas would've been the first that she was old enough to fully understand the holiday and its festivities. Frank also thought of his son, Conner. He would love to see him for the holiday, but it was too dangerous to bring him down, and because of the ongoing murder investigation, he couldn't leave town.

Colapietro smiled and handed Frank the sketch he'd been drawing.

"Well, I'll be damned," Frank shook his head, not in surprise but confirmation. "That's her, Bobby. That's her."

"Yeah, as you were describing her, it felt like I was re-sketching the same woman I did when Monica Jefferson was sitting with me." Colapietro pulled out the sketch he'd made two days earlier of the woman caught on tape during the Rocky Tops murder of Danny Moncrief. "I think you got your girl here, Frank."

Frank studied the three drawings and said, "No doubt about it. We now have something to put out there to all Districts and across every news channel in Philly and South Jersey."

"I've also sketched our male suspect from the Rocky Tops footage, but before I share it with you, I want to capture what you remember about the homeless guy up by the Mad River Bar. I want to ensure that I don't influence your memory in any way."

Frank nodded in the affirmative.

"Let's do that now," said Colapietro. "Maybe then we'll have two sketches to show the world."

It was December 1, and the Detective Room was abuzz with activity, and no one was thinking about the upcoming Christmas holiday.

After the brutal murder at Rocky Tops ruined everyone's Thanksgiving, no one was getting their hopes up for a quiet holiday with their families. The sense of foreboding around the district house was palpable.

As Frank and Bobby Colapietro worked in IRA, Candace, and Bones sat at the conference table and reviewed what she had so far. The two had formed a good partnership. Since their partial stay at Cantrell's house, and the subsequent flight back, Bones had grown fond of Candace, but he wasn't sure the feeling was mutual. He would avoid making his feelings known until the case was closed.

Candace seemed to be all business, completely wrapped up in her objective of unearthing everything she could about Vincent Charmaine Walker. She, too, seemed to like Bones, but like him, she had no intention of revealing it to anyone.

Cantrell was back in his cubicle over by the Schuyler Street window. He was working the phones calling field agents, letting them know that the moment he had sketches in his hands, he'd forward them to all field offices. Cantrell, like Candace, was working the Charmaine Walker angle but was looking at all serial killer cases in the tri-state area dating back to 1992. He searched for similarities between the Cop Killer murders and other known cases. Though he was coming up empty, like Frank, his mind kept going back to Vincent Charmaine Walker. The killers had, after all, invoked his name in their killings. Cantrell was spooked by the Scrabble letter tile aspect of the case as he and Gaye played the game almost every day when he wasn't in Philadelphia, which was more and more in the last two years.

Across town, the two maniacal lovers were getting itchy. Since ramping up their body count in the last month, they were bloodthirsty for more, even though they'd completed their taunting of the investigators by utilizing the Scrabble tiles.

"That was the best idea you ever had." Talon looked over at Genesis, who washed her armpits with her hands with water from a bottle.

The two killers were in their lair, in the bowels of St. Peters Claver Church. While the twilight washed the outside of the church, the church's basement was as black as the hearts that called it home.

As her evil shadow danced on the walls, Genesis said, "She handed the idea right to us. That stupid bitch bought a Scrabble board right in front of us. It was fucking poetry." Genesis poured water into her hand and stuck it down her pants to wash away her lover's passion. "You hurt me, by the way. That was too rough," she winced at the burning.

"I need to kill again, Genesis. I'm sorry that I took it out on you," Talon's eyes didn't match his words. There was no 'sorry' in his gaze. "I do everything angry lately. Eat, kill.... and that. Everything." He shook his head in frustration. "Why do we have to wait to kill that motherfucker?"

"Because his death has to be as memorable as his father's," said Genesis as she sniffed her fingers. "Not just where and how he dies, but when." She picked up her favorite knife and walked over to Talon. "You fuck me that hard again, and you won't be around to see Collazo die. You got that?" Genesis showed both sides of her blade to Talon, waving it just inches from his face. It was the same knife that had fileted Calvin Murphy up at the Cope House on Halloween.

"Get that shit out of my face." Talon pretended not to be terrified of his incestuous half-sister. Since their killing spree had started, Talon always took a back seat to her, unable to match her voracious thirst for killing.

"You heard me, bitch!" Genesis pulled back her blade.

"I hate that they don't know we've been to the hotel up in Cynwyd," Talon felt cheated. "I want all of them to know that we're close and getting closer."

"They'll know soon enough." Genesis put her shoes on.

"Let's give them a sign. Let's cause some hell up there," said Talon. "I want to scare the old man and that bitch that's always there with him."

Genesis seemed distracted. "I'm going out for a few hours."

"Out?" Talon's eyes narrowed with confusion. "Out where?"

"I'm meeting an old friend." Genesis pulled her hoody over her head.

"So, you clean up right before heading out, huh? Who you gonna go see? Your ex, Ronnie?"

"No, asshole. I'm going to see an old friend I used to pal around with when I worked at East Falls Beverage. I heard she's lookin' for me."

"Take my hoodie, then. It's cold as shit out there." Talon removed his sweatshirt and tossed it to Genesis. "Don't get in no trouble tonight. They had cameras up at Rocky Tops. They might know what we look like."

"I hope they do. I hope they got pictures of us layin' all around their office." Genesis, feeling invincible, layered up, pulling Talon's hoodie over hers. I want to be on America's Most Wanted."

"Dumb ass!" Talon laughed. "That show ain't been out in years." He pulled a dirty blanket over his shoulders. "Don't go killin' anyone tonight, either. That includes your mystery friend."

Genesis tucked her knife into the front of her waistband, a gun in the back, and asked, "Why you always wearin' three T-shirts, anyway?" Genesis looked Talon up and down and said, "It ain't because of the cold, is it?"

"I always have." Talon looked off, remembering the Steineckers, this time fondly. "One time, my foster parents took me to see a shrink, and he said it had something to do with my obsessive-compulsive disorder. He said it was just me trying to hide my anxiety and depression from the world by layering up."

Genesis looked at her man with great affection. "I hate you, Talon."

"I hate you more, Genesis." Talon loved his sister. He loved his wannabe fraternal twin.

It was now after 6 pm back at the 39th District, and no one considered going home. Detective John Branch yelled from the Hunting Park side of the Detective Room, "I got something!"

All heads looked up. None higher or faster than Frank's.

Branch zigzagged around the maze of cubicles and asked, "Where's that list of common collars?"

"Whattaya got, John?" asked Frank.

Branch found one of the many printed-out lists of common collars lying around the room. Holding up a 'wait a second' finger at Frank, Branch examined the list and said, "I'll be goddamned!"

"Whattaya got, Branch?" Captain Beatrice Jackson was getting impatient with everyone hanging on Branch's next words.

"I found an unemployment claim from last summer for a Talon Walker." Branch looked at his Captain and then at Frank. "You care to guess what the name of the company his claim was against?"

"Branch. Get talking already," demanded Frank. "We're all a little tired, ya know?" The look in Frank's eyes made it clear to John Branch that he better get to the point and fast.

"Vinyl, Carpet, Windows," revealed Branch, wanting to smile and take some credit for the discovery, but he wisely didn't.

Frank gazed over at Bones with a look of amazement.

Jackson snapped her fingers, looking at the list of collars sitting next to her, and yelled to her detective across the room, "Abecassis! Get me the mugshot for Talon Grayson Walker and the arresting officer...." She referenced her common collar list. "Timmy Falcone, back in 2015."

"Got it, Cap!" Jonah Abecassis ran back to his desk.

"That's our link, Bones." Frank's eyes went wide as he sat down in his chair. He could almost feel the road to salvation being paved beneath his feet. He closed his eyes and saw Penny and Bonnie; this time, they were smiling, waiting for him. "That connects Rocky Tops with a vendor and the name Walker."

"Holy Shit!" Candace Weatherby looked up from the laptop she'd been working on all day. Standing up, her face white as a ghost, all eyes now on her, she pronounced, "I have a birth certificate for a Talon Grayson Walker, born June 11, 1993. Mother's name, Carla

Grayson...." Candace's eyes were drenched in shock. "Father's name...."

Frank knew, and with a look of determination, he was ready for the hunt. "Vincent Charmain Walker," he cut off Candace. "Vinyl, Carpet, Windows. VCW. I'm gonna kill those motherfuckers!" Frank collected his things and headed for the door, Cantrell following closely behind him. Stopping and turning, Frank yelled, "June 11 is my birthday and Bonnie's birthday."

Everyone in the Detective Room stood stunned. They now knew the inspiration behind the cop killings and why Frank was the killer's muse. What they didn't know, though, was who his female accomplice was.

Out in the hall, Douglas Cantrell caught up to Frank. "Frank, are you okay?"

Frank was pacing the floor by the stairs going down. "I was right, Doug. They're coming to get me. All of those cops are dead because of me."

Doug saw no fear in Frank's eyes, and that concerned him. The last thing he wanted was another one-way trip to hell for his friend. Cantrell knew Frank was on the road to perdition and would make it his goal to derail him from another Isak-like showdown in the attic of some historical home or the basement of the beast, the new FalconClaw. He had to save his friend, but he wasn't even sure if that was possible. Doug knew Frank had two more monsters to rid from the streets. After that, he feared his friend would seek out Penny and Bonnie.

With Doug at a loss for words, Frank added, "What those motherfuckers don't know, however, is that I'm coming for them. It's over for them, Doug. This case will be over soon."

Douglas Cantrell lowered his head and let Frank walk away without saying a word. Cantrell was scared and knew in his troubled heart that each day forward would be one less with the man he loved like a son.

Just south of the 39th District, Monica Money Jefferson met Genesis in the public lot under the Twin Bridges an hour later. Exhaling a plume of smoke from a cigarette burned down to the butt, Money said, "Shit's getting hot. The cops pulled me in and questioned me. That interrogation lasted for hours," she exaggerated. "They're looking for you, Genesee."

Genesis looked skeptical of Jefferson. "Whatta you sayin'?"

"I'm sayin' that they were looking for you. I didn't tell them nothin', though." Money Jefferson acted nonchalant. "I mean, them bitches even tried to pay me for info. Course I didn't take it," she lied.

The mortified look on Genesis' face turned to one of self-preservation. She knew Money was lying. No prostitute from the streets turns down easy money. "Money, you listen to me good." Genesis turned to her and looked her dead in the eyes. "You give them my real name, and I will kill you. Do you understand me?"

Money backed up with a look of disdain. "Get yo' shit up out of my grill. I don't even know your real fuckin' name." She shrugged and acted like she wasn't scared. She was, though. She'd seen Genesis pull a knife on another hooker and threaten to kill her. She'd figured Genesis was carrying a weapon. "Even if I did, they wouldn't get shit out of me."

"I need cash. You got any? Like twenty bucks," asked Genesis.

"Girl, it's freezing out here." Money squeezed the collar of her jacket tightly around her neck and said, "Business is slow these days if you ain't figured that out yet."

"So, why'd you wanna meet me, anyway?" asked Genesis.

"People are talking over in East Kensington," Money looked her sorta friend up and down. "They say you tryna sell a gun that belonged to a cop."

"What of it?" Genesis seemed annoyed.

"Well," Money paused. "They say it came off a dead cop.... A murdered one. That sound about right?"

"Your sources ain't no good. They got the wrong person." Genesis wasn't convincing.

"All right, all right." Money looked to leave. "Where you stayin' these days, anyway? We never see you round no more."

"You got a lotta questions, Money." Genesis was suspicious and somewhat angry. "Best you just stop askin' them."

"I'll be seeing you around, Genesee..... whatever your real name is." Money walked away, flagging down a potential John who slowed his vehicle to check out the two women. She didn't tell Genesis that another rumor was circulating on the streets, that the cops were looking to talk to her again. She was hoping to get another hundred dollars but knew she'd need to come with more information.

Watching Money walk away, Genesis looked flustered. She felt the heat, and the gun in her waistband made her feel vulnerable. She had to get rid of it soon. Genesis knew that Money Jefferson couldn't be trusted and might pass along information to the cops that could derail her and Talon's grand plans.

Looking across the street at the Creative Minds daycare, she thought of the right person to sell the gun to.

Later, back at the 39th District house, after Frank had returned, detectives cleared out and headed home. All that remained around the table were Frank, Bones, Cantrell, and Weatherby.

"Let's shut it down for the night, guys." Frank checked his texts and voicemails out of habit; there were none.

"Where we eatin'?" asked Bones.

"I gotta run an errand. I'll pass on dinner." Frank desperately wanted to see Penny and Bonnie.

"I'm pretty beat," said Doug. "I'm just gonna grab something from the hotel when we return."

"I'm actually starving," said Candace, looking to Bones as if to accept his pseudo-invite. "You buying, Bonesie?" she smiled.

Frank rolled his eyes and said, "Doug, it looks like those two have a dinner date," he smirked. "You need a lift to the hotel?"

"If you wouldn't mind." Doug gladly accepted the offer.

"Billy Murphy's okay?" Bones asked Candace.

"Well," she paused and sighed. "Other than the hotel, it's the only place I've eaten. So, sure. That would be fine."

Candace stood as Frank and Cantrell walked out the door. Reaching for her jacket, Bones grabbed it off the back of her chair and, without asking, held it open for Candace to slip her arms into.

"Thank you, Bones." Candace pulled her hair over her right shoulder and placed her arm into the right sleeve and then the left. "Rugged cop with sterling manners. I like that."

Bones nearly blushed. "My mom raised me well." He flashed back for a second and remembered how hard his mother had to work to save her youngest child from becoming like his father.

After turning off Schuyler onto West Hunting Park South minutes later, Doug asked Frank how he felt.

"I'm okay, Doug. As good as I can be, I guess." Frank turned right onto Wissahickon Avenue.

"Frank, I want to ask you something...." Cantrell seemed a little nervous. "Gaye and I have been talking...."

"What's on your mind, Doug?"

"I.... *we* were wondering about your plans after the case is solved."

"I haven't thought much about it, to be honest with you."

"Well, it's just that.... Gaye and I were wondering if you'd like to stay with us for a while. It might be the perfect break from all of this madness," Cantrell paused for an answer.

Frank turned his head halfway and said, "But what about my family? I can't just leave them."

Doug felt remorseful. "I think Penny and Bonnie will follow you wherever it is that you might go."

"But we have a home, Doug. I can't ask them to leave our home." Frank's glare out the window was dispassionate.

"I'm not suggesting a move to New Hampshire." Doug compromised, even though he would welcome Frank to live with him and Gaye. "Just a little visit," he paused. "Just give it some thought, would you?"

Crossing over the City Avenue Bridges, Frank looked at his friend and tried hard to sound sincere. "I will, Doug. I will." In reality, though, Frank had no intention of going to New Hampshire.... ever.

Cantrell looked into Frank's eyes in that brief moment and knew Frank was never leaving Philadelphia. *Not for a second*, he thought. Douglas Cantrell again wondered how many more days he would have with his friend. He was powerless to stop what was coming. He knew that the case would end tragically for everyone involved.

"Will you see her tonight, Frank?"

Frank was pessimistic, looking at his old friend as he took a right onto Monument Drive. "I sure hope so, Doug. But I'm pretty sure that she won't be there."

As the car rounded the curve at the Righters Street entrance to Laurel Hill East Cemetery, Frank asked, "You know how many people are dead in there, Doug?" He looked over at the headstones and monuments shrouded by the night.

Doug looked over at the terrifying sight of the cemetery at night. "I have no idea, Frank. How many?"

Frank's eyes narrowed. "All of them," he said as they approached the hotel.

Doug couldn't seem to raise a smile. For him, things were getting worse and worse. Again, powerless to change what was about to happen, he lived in the 'here and now' and said, "Say hello to them for me, would you?"

"Who?"

"You know who I'm talking about, Frank. Tell them that Gaye and I miss them very much, and we hope they're okay."

Frank pursed his lips and nodded, slowing the car in front of the hotel's entrance. "I sure will, Doug. Goodnight."

The car stopped, and Cantrell got out, hoping for a parting word, but Frank just looked straight ahead, eager to leave.

As the Dodge pulled away, Doug stood there with a tear in his eye. He had lost Penny and Bonnie, and now he had lost Frank, too.

Back over in East Falls, Genesis Harper Walker stood in front of an old friend's apartment and rang the bell. Seconds later, a tall skinny man opened the door to see who his uninvited guest was. "Well, well, well. If it ain't old Jenny from the Block," said a smiling Mo Cheeks, looking Genesis up and down.

Chapter 28 – They Looked So Happy

After ten minutes of looking for a parking spot, Bones parked illegally in front of a fire hydrant near Billy Murphy's Irish Pub. Pulling a dirty Philly P.D. T-shirt from his back seat, he left it on his dashboard should anyone think of ticketing or towing it. The city tag on the car would've also prompted anyone concerned to simply walk into Murph's as it was a cop hangout. Plus, everyone knew Bones drove the 39th District's only Ford Interceptor in the fleet.

"So that's how it works here in the States? Park where you want?" Candace smiled as Bones found a solution to the parking problem. "You cops just do as you please?"

Bones blushed a little in embarrassment. "No, that's not how it works. I just wanted to get you in there. You mentioned that you were starving, if I recall."

"Nah," Candace said. "That was just an excuse to get you to take me to dinner." She winked.

Bones swallowed hard. He wasn't sure if she was serious or not. Trying to play it cool, he half smiled and said, "Let's keep it professional, Weatherby."

"Booooo. Party pooper." Candace laughed it off. "I was just joking anyway."

Bones shook his head again, unable to determine when she was serious and when she was just joking. Opening the door on the side of the pub, he said, "Age before beauty," and encouraged her to go first with a waving hand gesture.

"Oh, really?" Candace was impressed by Bones' sense of humor. "Aren't we the little jokester tonight."

"Was I joking?" he raised his brow and grinned.

Now inside, Bones motioned to Chris Overcash that he and Candace would take the table by the window. Frank and Penny's old table, and the one that he, Frank, and Cantrell sat at the night of the Renaldo Lopez murder.

Back at 454 E. Locust Avenue, Frank sat in his car staring at the closed garage door, knowing the Accord sat just on the other side. His heart broke again when he thought of the accident.

Reluctant again to get out of the car, thinking Penny wouldn't be in the house, he was beginning to think that he would never see her again. That thought alone caused him to think of the unthinkable. Looking at his gun, unholstered and lying on the passenger seat, always at the ready, he clenched his teeth and erased the notion of ending it all from his head.

Looking over at the house every few seconds, Frank looked for a reason to exit the Dodge. Looking back toward the garage, he gasped in a moment of terror when he saw the garage door was now wide open, with Frank Bruno standing next to the driver's side of the Accord. Clutching the wheel in shock, Frank caught his breath as his heart began to race.

Trying to understand the situation, Frank knew that Bruno was there for a reason. He thought that the Ghost of 1974 was trying to tell him something. Was this his reason for exiting the car? He determined it must be.

Hands trembling, he slowly reached for the door handle, his eyes never leaving Bruno, afraid his guardian angel would vanish. As he opened the door and began to step out, he witnessed Bruno tilt his head to the rear driver-side door and say, "It's in there."

Again, startled, he knew Bruno to be a man of few words since he first met him in the basement of FalconClaw in August 2017, when the legendary detective warned him of the arrival of The Schuylkiller. Frank didn't dare enter into a conversation with the ghost but followed his directions and walked to the car door. As he got closer, Bruno began to fade away. Before he did, though, another whisper of his voice hung in the air. "It's there, Frank. Find it."

His hands trembled as he reached for the door handle, knowing that Penny had touched the handle hundreds of times. Remembering the last time he opened Penny's car door, he hoped to feel her hand on his again. Before pulling on the door handle, Frank waited for a touch that wouldn't come. Closing his eyes in disappointment and fear of the unknown, he pulled and heard the click that never came the night of the accident when he tried in vain to get to his daughter, Bonnie, who lay dead in her car seat.

Seeing the top of little Bonnie's head, and her wavy hair, he opened the door fully and reached for her. Looking again, he saw an empty car seat. Stepping back in tears, he reconsidered going in. In the instant, just before she died, his little girl had lived there, but now it was her gravesite. The empty car seat, a makeshift headstone.

With the courage to lean in, Frank had no idea why Bruno had led him to the back seat of the car. "Something must be in here," Frank whispered.

Overcoming his heartbreak, he rummaged through the seat and pulled crumbs and pieces of Fruit Loops cereal from the crease. Frustrated as he reached around the car seat, his eyes went to the floorboard and the opening under Penny's seat. Leaning down to feel for what might be there, Frank's face was positioned between the seat and the center armrest, and that's when he saw it. Something shiny and plastic caught his eye. It was Penny's cell phone.

Struggling to get his hand into the tight spot, Frank grunted, barely touching it with his fingertips. Forcing his hand deeper into the narrow space, he was able to grip the phone between his index and middle fingers. Pulling it slowly from its resting place, Frank tried to count how many times he'd called the phone since May 14. Now firmly in his hand, Frank stood between the open door and the back seat and frantically attempted to turn it on. He knew full well that the battery would have died six months ago.

Racing back to the Dodge, not concerned with what might be lurking in the darkness, Frank jumped into the car and plugged Penny's phone up into his charger. His anxiety building, impatiently watching as the power percentage went from zero to three to five, he desperately pressed the power button, holding his breath until it turned on. Smiling through his tears, he saw the lock screen image of him, Penny, and Bonnie, taken in the backyard during an Easter Egg hunt in early April. Swiping up, alert pop-ups began to appear on the home screen; 367 missed calls and 916 text messages were waiting to be reviewed. Only then did Frank realize how much he had tried in vain to reach Penny before realizing his messages would never be returned.

Frank wept, his nose running, as tears ran amuck over his cheeks. Clicking on the photo app, he opened it and tapped the camera folder. Frank laughed and cried when he saw the last image taken; It was a selfie of Penny's face pressed up against Bonnie's in the toy aisle at Walmart. "They looked so happy," he cried out loud. The image, while heartbreaking, knowing that they would both be dead just minutes later, gave Frank some comfort and peace of mind. He saw the love and warmth in each of their faces, and then he saw something else.

Using his thumb and index finger, he zoomed in on the picture and saw a couple staring at Penny and his daughter in the distance. Zooming in further, he saw the Cop Killers. While he had never met or seen the female face to face, he remembered the face of the male as the homeless person who'd approached him near his Mad River apartment.

The most beautiful picture he had ever seen of Penny and Bonnie was tainted by evil and the two people that would take the lives of his family. Frank sat in that car and wept.

Back over on Ridge Avenue, Genesis looked up at Cheeks and said, "You gonna invite me in, or what?"

Cheeks held the door open and stepped aside, letting a woman he knew only as Jenny or Genesee walk under his arm and into his home. Before shutting the door, Mo Cheeks stuck his head out, looked up and down Ridge smiling, and then closed the door behind him.

"Now I wasn't expecting no company tonight," Cheeks paused, still smiling, so you know..... I didn't get no shower or nothing."

"That's not why I'm here. I don't hook anymore," said Genesis, rubbing her cold hands together.

"Oh, is that right?" The smile ran from Cheeks' face. "Then what is it exactly that I can do for you?"

"I need money." Genesis wore the look of someone who felt deserving of whatever Cheeks could give.

"You need money?" Cheeks rolled his eyes and said, "Yeah, don't we all?" He walked over to his worn-down recliner and took a seat, grabbing the beer from the cup holder built into the arm of the chair. "So, you just show up at my door after what.... two years flashing them puppy dog eyes askin' for money?" he smirked. "Yeah, well, that ain't how it works."

"I ain't asking somethin' for nothin'...."

"Now we're talkin'." The smile returned to Cheeks' face as he slid to the end of his chair.

Genesis tried hard not to roll her eyes, not wanting to offend a potential buyer. "Like I said, I ain't here for that."

"I never heard no hooker turn down money for sex," Cheeks scoffed at the notion. "Then whatta you sellin' if it ain't that little ass of yours?"

Genesis reached back and pulled a Glock from her waistband, causing Mo Cheeks to sink back into his chair and throw his hands in the air.

"Whoa! Whoa now!" Cheeks tried calming his guest. "Now, we don't want to do nothin' that would cause me to be dead, you understand?"

Genesis rolled her eyes this time and said, "I ain't here to hurt nobody. I'm here to sell," she said. "I'm looking for a buyer." Genesis spun the gun in her hand and handed it to Cheeks, handle first.

Cheeks looked apprehensive as he reached for the gun keeping his eyes locked on Genesis' looking for a deadly twinkle.

Taking the gun slowly, he immediately dropped the clip into his lap and drew back the slide, ensuring no bullet was in the chamber. Setting the gun down on the table lamp beside his chair, he examined the clip to ensure no bullets were inside it.

Feeling relieved, Cheeks asked, "How much?"

"A hundred bucks."

Picking up the Glock and reinserting its clip, he handed it back to Genesis and said, "Too rich for my blood, Jenny."

"How much then?" she asked him.

"Fifty. But before I buy, I need to know where it came from."

"One of my regulars gave it to me in return for a trick."

"That right?" Cheeks looked at her sideways. "Well, you just got done telling me a few minutes ago that you don't hook anymore, so why don't you start tellin' me the truth?"

"I found it. I stole it. I sucked some guy off for it.... What's it matter to you? Either you want it, or you don't." Genesis was starting to get frustrated.

"Yeah, I want it...." Cheeks shot the girl he knew as Jenny a sly grin. "And I might even want the gun, too."

Genesis rolled her eyes again. She shook her head and said, "I want a hundred, then."

"Now that's what I'm talking about!" Cheeks smiled.

Fifteen minutes later, Genesis Harper Walker walked out of Cheeks' apartment with one less gun and one hundred more dollars.

Back at Billy Murphy's, Candace and Bones laughed. Dane Mandato had come in for Trivia Night, and the small crowd that showed up for the event was gathered along the back wall near the ATM machine, providing Bones and Candace a little privacy.

"So, what happened next?" Candace laughed at how Bones was telling his story.

"That's just it...." said Bones, laughing. "The guy just got up and left without saying a word."

Candace's face went straight. "That's the stupidest joke I've ever heard."

"C'mon. That's funny. You just don't get it because you're Canadian." Bones swallowed the last of his Blue Moon. "Okay, it's your turn."

Candace looked across the mostly empty bar and said, "Okay, here goes." Looking left and then right, she started telling the joke.

"Okay, so it's like two in the morning, and a bar is closing down, patrons are filing out one by one...." Candace smiled, a little tipsy.

"Okay?" Bones followed.

"So, the bartender is wiping down the bar.... It's a long bar, like an L-shaped one. Well," she said, starting to chuckle. "The bartender looked down and saw a snail sitting on the bar."

"A what?" Bones laughed.

"A snail," Candace said. "So, anyway, the bartender says, 'Hey, wait a minute! Aren't you a snail?'"

"So, the snail waves his finger at the bartender and pronounces, 'You're damn right I'm a snail, and I want a beer!'"

"Hang on. Wait a second." Bones threw up his hands and laughed. "Did you just say that the snail waved his finger at the bartender?"

Candace cut Bones off. "Yeah, yeah! I get it.... snails don't have arms, hands, or fingers. Just pay attention. This is a good one."

"So, the bartender.... tired from a long night, barks at the snail and says, 'We don't serve snails here, and we're closing for the night. Get your ass out of here before I throw you out!'"

"So, the snail's pissed. He's having none of it," said Candace, her face hurting from smiling so much. "He barks back at the bartender and shouts, 'I'm not leaving until I get a beer,' he says with his little hands on his hips."

Bones just sat back giggling, also tipsy from the five Blue Moons and the shot of JD that he'd consumed. "Go on," he prodded Candace, trying to envision the little snail with hands on hips.

"Well, after a few more minutes of back and forth, the bartender got so angry he slammed an empty bottle of whiskey down onto the snail, sending it flying across the bar and out the front door as the last of the patrons left."

Candace started cracking up. "I'm gonna pee my pants!" she said, wiping laughter tears from her eyes.

"So, what happened next?" Bones laughed along, dying to hear the punchline.

"Okay, okay," Candace composed herself. "So, it's three months later, and the same bartender was wiping down the bar again, and as he looks down, he sees the same snail from three months earlier."

Bones hung on Candace's words.

"So, the snail looks up at him, red-faced, and says, 'What in the hell did you do that for?!'" Candace snorted through her uncontrollable laughter.

Bones, on the other hand, sat perplexed. His eyes wide, he shook his head and said, "I don't get it."

"Get it?!" Candace again wiped her tears away.

"No, I don't." Bones was confused.

"He's a snail! It took him three months to crawl back into the bar!" Candace snorted again, trying to regain her composure.

Bones' eyes narrowed, still not fully understanding. "Yeah, yeah, yeah. I get it now. Ha-ha."

"Come on! That was funny as hell!" she paused. "You'll use it."

"Yeah. Maybe not." Bones squinted and shook his head. "That's a Canadian joke. That won't fly around here."

"That's not a CANADIAN joke," said Candace. "That's a FUNNY joke!"

"Oh, I thought it was French with the snail and all."

Candace rolled her eyes. "Oh, brother."

After things quieted down and the crowd thinned, the two nursed a glass of water. After paying the bill, Bones asked, "So, whattaya got on Charmaine Walker?"

"I'm presenting tomorrow," she said. "I've essentially chronicled Walker's entire life."

Bones looked out the window, remembering the Cop Killers passing by, wiping Lopez's blood across the glass. "This whole thing is fucked up. I just can't wrap my head around it. They taught us all about Vincent Charmaine Walker in the academy, and now here we are, chasing down his son."

Candace looked at Bones apprehensively and said, "His daughter, too."

Bones' jaw dropped. "What did you just say?"

Candace looked frightened. "I don't know for sure. I have to do some more digging in the morning, but I learned today that Walker was connected to another woman around the time of his arrest. She visited him while he was in jail. Her name was Vivian Harper. She's dead now, but when I looked into her background...." Candace's face was drenched in fear. "She had a daughter.... Bones." Candace reached across the table and placed her hand in his. "The daughter was named Genesis."

"Genesee." Bones sank back into his chair and ran his fingers through his short-cropped hair, his eyes wide in disbelief. "I'll be goddamned!"

"Bones, there's something else...." Candace looked nervous.

"What is it, Candace?"

"Her birthday....." A tear ran down her cheek. "Genesis Harper was born on June 11, 1993. Same as Talon Grayson Walker's date of birth."

"Oh, my fucking God!" Bones stood abruptly. "I need to call Frank!"

"Bones, no, wait!" Candace was concerned. "I need to be sure. I'm waiting on an email from the Pennsylvania Department of Health. We need to be sure before we announce it."

Bones threw a twenty-dollar tip on the table and said, "You've got until noon tomorrow. I'm not sitting on this one!"

"Okay. Okay." Candace seemed out of breath, her heart racing.

Thirty minutes later, fully rehydrated, Bones opened the passenger side door of the Ford and held it for Candace. Shedding a tear, Candace turned and looked Bones in the eye. "Bones. Am I in danger?" she cried. "I'm scared."

Bones took Candace into his arms to comfort her. "Not as long as you stay close to me. I'll look after you."

As he held Candace in his arms, Bones surveyed Indian Queen Lane looking for anyone who might harm her. Like always, but more so now, Bones would stand between death and those he cared for.

For the first time in his life, Bones felt something other than worthless. And he was about to unleash his inner beast.

Chapter 29 – Monsters are Born?

The second day of December reminded everyone of where they were, bringing with it gray skies and flurries, and the drop in temperature matched that of the mood for all those on the Cop Killer case.

Bones pulled up to the Residence Inn Bala Cynwyd and saw Cantrell chatting up the front desk agent through the glass door. While Cantrell smiled and joked, Bones saw a frightened Candace Weatherby standing quietly nearby. Like the night before, he knew she was scared. She had quickly become a key player in the investigation, bringing her both fear and consternation. She thought she might be seen as a Philly cop and, like the others, now had a target on her back.

Bones texted Candace to let her know he had arrived, and moments later, she and Cantrell made their way out the door. Just as before, Bones walked around to open the passenger side doors, this time motioning for Doug to sit in front. Cantrell, always the gentleman, waved off the gesture and got into the back of the Ford.

Cantrell observed his companions in the front seat; both seemed quiet and preoccupied, neither making much eye contact. Like a black-tie chauffeur, Bones seemed to be all business, while Candace seemed scared. Cantrell had detected her fear in the elevator ride down from their third-floor suites overlooking the Schuylkill.

Ten minutes later, the snow fell heavier as the Interceptor turned left into the parking lot behind the 39th District house. Winter was in the air as December made itself known. As Bones, Cantrell, and Weatherby exited the car, they knew the month would not go as they'd hoped, and more cops would likely die. Walking into the Detective Room around 8:30, they felt late as every detective employed in the 39th was already busy at work.

After hanging his jacket, Bones looked over at Candace, who was checking emails on her phone. Sensing his gaze, Candace looked up and gave him a cringeworthy nod. He knew Candace had received confirmation of her assertion from the night before that Vincent Charmaine Walker had two children just months after his arrest and conviction. On June 11, 1993, just seven and a half months after Vincent Charmaine Walker murdered Salvatore Collazo in the basement at FalconClaw, two separate women gave birth to twin freaks. Different mothers, but the same evil father, bore twin terrors.

While society would consider them monsters created by their circumstances, Talon Grayson Walker and Genesis Harper Walker were born monsters, and they would savagely embrace their heritage.

Bones was resolute. Turning, he eyed his Captain and his partner and waved them to the hall. Standing near the stairs, Frank and Jackson joined Bones, with Frank asking, "Whattaya got?" as Jackson looked on.

"Frank, I understand Candace is presenting her research on Charmaine Walker's bio today. Is that right?"

"Yeah, right after lunch."

"Well, you might want to pull everyone together and let her share what she's got right now."

"Oh? And what's that, Bones?" Jackson looked alarmed.

"I want her to tell you, but let's just say we might have the real name of our Genesee person of interest."

"Bones," Frank was having none of the theatrics. "You tell me right now what you have!"

Bones shook his head, not wanting to break the news, but he would out of respect for Frank and his captain.

"Vincent Charmaine Walker fathered two children out of wedlock, impregnating two women just before killing your father. And get this...." Bones looked at Frank, then to Jackson, then back at his partner. "They were born on the same day....."

Frank nodded, thinking that the universe was talking to him. "June 11, 1993," he said.

"You got a name there, Bones?" Jackson was purposely sarcastic, impatient to hear the facts.

"The Genesee woman...." Bones shook his head methodically. "Her real name is likely Genesis Harper Walker. Half-sister to Talon Grayson Walker."

"Jesus Christ," Jackson was dumbfounded. "It's like fraternal twins but with different mothers. Born on the same day and with the same biological father. A serial killer at that," she shook her head.

"Monsters are born?" Frank's eyes narrowed. Questioning himself, he looked off into blank space, shaking his head in astonishment. Frank couldn't process the notion as he'd always believed monsters created monsters and weren't simply born. It was their circumstance, not their genetics, he always believed.

Jackson looked at her boys and said, "Well, let's head back in there and let Montreal tell everybody what she found. After that, I've got to get your buddy on the phone and tell him what our friend from the Montreal P.D. came up with." Jackson looked at Frank when she said it.

Frank was in a trance and didn't pick up on the subtle jab by his boss regarding his relationship with Special Investigator Captain Justin Smith.

As Jackson and Bones walked back into the Detective Room, Frank stood, still shaking his head. Everything he'd believed about serial killers was wrong.

Seconds later, Frank walked in and saw Bones whispering to Candace. He saw her face turn ghost white. Frank could tell that she was terrified that she would be the one to break the news to the remaining team.

"Can you do it?" Bones asked Candace.

"Ah.... Um...." Candace stood frozen in fear. "I think so."

Bones looked at Candace and said, "Remember on the plane when I was scared, and you held my hand?"

"Yes," she answered timidly.

"I'll be right beside you," said Bones. "Just pretend I'm holding your hand."

"Okay. Okay." Candace shook out her hands and her nerves along with them. "I can do it," she told herself, exhaling fully.

Beatrice Jackson yelled for everyone in the room to gather around. "Let's go, everyone. I need all of you at the front of the room."

Including Jackson, Frank, Bones, Cantrell, and Candace, sixteen people from the 39th were working the case, and they all had their eyes fixed on the woman their Captain affectionately referred to as *Montreal*.

"Montreal, here...." Jackson turned slightly to acknowledge Candace Weatherby, standing to her left, "has some rather troubling news to share about our killers."

Jackson turned again to Candace and whispered. "Knock 'em dead, Montreal. I have to make a call to the brass downtown." Looking Candace directly in the eye, she said, "You did good, kid. Real good." She then turned and walked away.

Candace smiled humbly and then turned to see all eyes on her. She felt naked in front of a room full of men, and her face showed it. Looking over to Bones, standing just feet away, she was assured that she was in the company of people who cared for her and had her back.

Summoning the nerve to speak, Candace said, "Um.... We believe that our killers are brother and sister."

Some in the group audibly gasped.

"I just received confirmation moments ago...." Candace paused as her voice cracked, "....from the Pennsylvania Department of Health, that Vincent Charmaine Walker fathered two children prior to his arrest in December 1992," she revealed to the group.

The group was speechless. Disbelief flashed in the eyes of nearly all members of the task force.

"Yesterday, as you all know...." Candace was gaining confidence. "....it was revealed that Talon Grayson Walker is the biological son of Vincent Charmain Walker and that he was born on June 11, 1993. Well, we now have proof that a woman named Vivian Harper gave birth to a daughter on the same exact day, June 11, to a child named Genesis Harper Walker.... The father's name listed on that Birth Certificate.... Vincent Charmaine Walker."

Frank spoke up. "We believe this woman is the person of interest that we've been trying to track down since a person with a similar name, Genesee, was first brought to us by an acquaintance of hers named Monica Jefferson." Frank paused, allowing the group to react.

The name Genesis Walker was chorused throughout the room as the faces staring back at Candace and Frank went from dismay to outright shock.

"We also have something else...." Frank paused while powering up the fifty-inch TV mounted on the wall between Interview Rooms A and B. Frank took a deep breath and looked for strength before sharing something personal with a room full of people. As the TV booted up, an image of Penny and Bonnie at Walmart appeared on the screen, and muffled gasps could be heard around the room.

"This is the last picture ever taken of Penny and our daughter, Bonnie. This selfie was taken by Penny just minutes before she and my daughter were murdered." Using the clicker in his hand, Frank clicked over to the next image, revealing a grainy image of two people in the background over Penny's left shoulder. "Those are our Cop Killers! And that was no accident."

Several around the room shook their heads, squinted for a better look, or turned to see others' reactions in the room.

"Frank, how can you be so sure that's them?" asked Collie Mitchell. "I mean, it's pretty fuzzy."

"The two match the general description of our killers, are both wearing hooded sweatshirts, and are staring directly at my family moments before they died." Frank was certain and made his feelings clear.

Bones and Cantrell stood together on the Schuyler Street side of the room, both devastated by the image.

"Have you contacted Walmart regarding their CCTV footage, Frank?" asked Detective John Branch.

"I did...." Frank's face displayed his disappointment. "They keep the footage on file for six months. Frank looked around the room and noticed some doing the quick math. "It's been six months and eighteen days."

Whispered curse words could be heard. The assembled team gathered around the front of the room were all frustrated and tired. The image on the screen of Penny Bristow, her daughter, and their killers reminded everyone on the case that this was about Frank and his family. All felt empathy for Frank, and all took it personally, too.

"I'm going up to the Walmart today on the off chance that they may be able to recover the footage." Frank turned off the television. "Meanwhile, I've sent Denny Patel the image, and his team will see if they can unblur it by using special deblurring software called FOTOR."

"Believe it or not, the FBI uses the same software," Cantrell spoke up.

"Captain Jackson is in her office as we speak, letting Race Street know what Candace has uncovered," announced Frank. "After lunch today, Candace will review what other information she has on the father of our killers." Frank purposely didn't say the name of the man who took his father's life.

As the larger group disbursed and went about their duties, Cantrell and Bones approached Candace; both shaken by the news.

"I had never seen Frank's family before," Candace wiped away a tear. "They were beautiful."

"Penny was the most beautiful person I have ever met. And that little girl," Cantrell fought his tears. "She was an angel."

"And now they're both angels," Bones said under his breath, thinking about his best friend and partner.

"Congratulations, Candace," Doug changed the subject to recognize Candace's achievement. "You did it. You really did it. You broke the case."

Bones added, "We're all proud of you, Candace." But his look conveyed that *he* was proud of her.

"I'm sorry, guys. It's hard to be proud of myself when you see the human toll that comes along with this type of work." Candace couldn't erase the image of a smiling Penny and Bonnie from her mind. "I'm just thankful I was able to assist the department somehow." Candace seemed sad, thinking her time in Philly was ending. "I guess my work here is done."

Bones and Doug looked at each other, their faces expressing their shock.

"Candace, this case is far from over, and you've proven yourself more than capable. We need you until our suspects are in custody." Bones wasn't ready for Candace to leave. His heart was in his throat, worried about how she would respond.

"Candace," Doug spoke up. "You're not leaving here until I do, and I'm not leaving until the bad guys are off the street." Cantrell was no longer joking around. "Now, if you need to get back up to Montreal, that's one thing. Or, if you've been told by the good captain that your services are no longer needed, that's another. But to be clear, these men and women in this building and the good citizens of Philadelphia need someone with your talent and expertise looking out for them. Until the killers are caught, our work here is not done."

Bones added, "Candace, your hard work likely saved lives. If I have my way, you're staying."

"I, um, just assumed that the historical aspect of the case was closed and that I'd no longer be needed here."

"Bullshit! You're staying." Bones was impassioned and having none of it. "I.... *We* need you here," he caught himself.

Cantrell noticed Bones' Freudian slip and smiled. He'd noticed a budding relationship burgeoning in the previous two weeks and thought it'd be good for both of them to have someone to lean on and count on.

Minutes later, Frank walked into the Detective Room after being summoned to Jackson's office. He motioned for Candace to join him in the hall. Bones stood up to join her and his partner, but Frank motioned for him to stay put. The look on Bones' face conveyed concern but also his desire to protect and look over his new friend and the object of his newfound inspiration.

Candace went from beaming to petrified as if summoned to the big boss's office to be reprimanded for doing something wrong. She looked at Bones as if to ask, "What going on?" and then walked submissively to the hall, fearing the worst.

"Hey, Frank. What's up?" asked Candace passively. "Is everything okay?"

"Not sure. But Captain Jackson needs to speak with you." Frank was stoic.

"Will you be in there with me?" Candace hoped, figuratively crossing her fingers.

"I will." Frank turned and started down the hall.

"Do you know what it's about?" Candace tried to keep up with the long strides of Frank.

"It's about your stay here in Philadelphia."

The wind left Candace Weatherby's sails. Her fears were coming true. Moments ago, she was worried that she would no longer be needed on the case, and now she was sure of it.

After knocking on Jackson's door, and being told to come in, Frank, followed by Candace, stood before Beatrice Jackson's desk. The two waited for Jackson to finish typing an email, and for Candace, every second was agonizing.

Hitting send and looking up, Jackson invited her guests to sit in the chairs in front of her desk. Once they did, Jackson proceeded.

"Ms. Weatherby, after speaking with the powers that be down in the Police Commissioner's office, we've decided to offer you a monthly consultation fee, and we hope that you will stay on with the department for the foreseeable future while we continue our efforts to wrap up this case."

Candace looked over at Frank, who was now grinning, and then back at Jackson and tried desperately to conceal her joy, not wanting to seem unprofessional.

"Well, I was considering wrapping things up here and heading back at the end of the week," Candace paused. "But I would like very much to stay on and see this through to its conclusion. But I think your department will need to contact my superiors with the Service de Police de la Ville de Montréal to seek their permission."

Frank laughed out loud, catching Jackson and Candace off guard.

"What's so funny, Detective Collazo?" Jackson asked out of respect for Candace.

Frank said, shaking his head and smiling, "Candace, I've known you for two years now, and that's the most French-Canadian thing I've ever heard you say."

"You caught me," Candace smiled. "I was hoping no one would notice that I was actually from Canada. I was doing my best to fit in with *YOUSE* guys," she said in her best Philly accent, causing Jackson and Frank to bust out laughing.

After the laughter subsided, Jackson said," We've already been on the phone with Montreal, and they said you're an independent contractor and can do as you please. In fact, they were thrilled that you were contributing to our case and encouraged you to stay on until the case is closed."

Jackson added, "I'll put the financial offer in writing and have it to you by the end of the day. But you may want to consider returning to Montreal to take care of loose ends now that your stay has been extended and maybe get a few more outfits."

"Oui, ça peut être une bonne idée." Candace smiled, joking with her friends.

"Translation, please?" Jackson smiled at Weatherby, pleased with her sense of humor during stressful times.

Candace smiled again and said, "Yes, that might be a good idea."

Frank shook his head in amusement and stood. "We've got a lot of work to do. We need to get back."

No longer smiling, Candace went back into professional mode and said, "Yes, of course."

Now in the hall, Frank looked down at his Canadian friend and said, "Nice work, Candace. You saved lives today. I'm happy you're here and grateful you're willing to stay longer."

"Thank you, Frank. That means a great deal coming from you. This experience has humbled me." She paused before adding, "I'm so sorry about your beautiful family. They seemed very lovely."

"Yes, they were," Frank nodded his appreciation.

Before entering the Detective Room, Candace stopped Frank and confessed, "I'm frightened."

"We all are, Candace. It comes with the territory," said Frank. "You'll be fine as long as you don't find yourself alone. That includes midnight ice bucket runs, snacks in the lobby, sitting near the fire on the outdoor river walk. Anywhere. Make sure you're always with Bones, Doug, or me."

"Now I'm even more scared." Candace became emotional.

"Listen to me." Frank clutched her shoulders. "I'm going to kill both of those people, and when I do, like them, I'm gonna disappear. Between now and then," he added, "unless they get me first, you'll be safe."

Candace was terrified but not surprised by Frank's words. She knew what he was capable of but saw something in his eyes she didn't see during the Isak Cameron case. His family was dead, after all, and she knew he was on a path from which he might never return. She was scared, not only for herself but for Frank.

Unable to articulate her fears, she simply said, "Thank you, Frank. I won't let any of you down. I feel like I belong here and plan to stay as long as it takes."

Frank smiled to try and ease her tension and, without looking down at her, said, "I'm sure Bones will be happy about that."

Candace's eyes widened with Frank's comment. She felt that perhaps everyone knew she had a crush on Bones. Instead of replying to his comment, she said nothing, promising herself to be more on guard regarding the feelings she was forming for Detective Bones Sullivan.

Later, in the Detective Room, Bones pulled a now more relaxed Candace aside and asked, "So, what happened earlier when you spoke with the captain?"

Feeling safe in Bones' presence, and with a straight face, Candace replied, "It looks like I'm heading home this weekend."

"What?!" Bones was shocked and disappointed. "You've got to be kidding me. We need you, Candace."

"Yeah, well...." She shot Bones a "Whattaya gonna do?" look and added, "The Captain said I needed to grab some more clothes and tie up any loose ends because the department would like me to stay on until the case was closed." Candace broke out a smile.

A flood of relief washed over Bones' face. Exhaling fully, he said, "That's great news."

"Yeah, but," said Candace. "They want to transfer me down to Race Street to work the case from there."

"What?! That's crazy!"

Candace smiled again and said, "Clearly, you have difficulty finding humor in Canadian jokes. "I'm not going anywhere, Bonesie, but I do have to get back to work. I'm presenting after lunch."

"I'm gonna kill her," Bones whispered while watching Candace walk away.

Turning, he saw Frank looking back at him with a blank stare. Smiling at Frank and seeing no reaction from his partner, he realized Frank had zoned out again.

Frank witnessed Bones and Candace developing a professional and personal relationship, reminding him of how he and Penny began theirs. He missed his girl and looked forward to reuniting with her and Bonnie.

Frank skipped out on Candace's presentation. The last thing he wanted to hear was the life story of the man who stole his father from him. Vincent Charmaine Walker killed his father, and now Frank was determined to kill the bloodthirsty, misbegotten, fraternal twins.

Before leaving the district house, Frank put out APBs for both Talon Grayson Walker and his evil twin, Genesis Harper Walker.

Later that day, Frank had an appointment with his new friend, Dr. Archibald Riley. As he walked through the parking lot, his phone rang. Hoping it was Penny, knowing that it wasn't, he looked down at the caller ID and saw that it was Mo Cheeks calling.

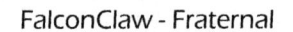

Chapter 30 – The Neighborhood of the Dead

"Mo, is that you, brother?" Frank was surprised to hear from Mo Cheeks after seeing him two weeks earlier. *Why is he calling?* Frank wondered.

"Yo, Detective Frank. How you doin', my brother from uptown?"

"I've been better, Mo. What can I do you for?" Frank remotely unlocked his car and brushed the accumulated snow off the driver's side window.

"Two-hundred bucks! That's what you can do me for, Big Money!"

Frank stood outside his car and knew Cheeks had something for him. "That's a pretty big sum. Whattaya got for me, Mo?"

"I got a dead cop's gun. That's what." Mo Cheeks spoke as if it was just another day. But he knew he had something of value to Frank, and the Philly P.D. Mo had heard on the street that a hooker was trying to sell off a dead cop's gun, and he knew it had to do with the *Cop Killer* case. He was certain the gun he bought off a woman he knew as Jenny had something to do with the case police were working on.

Though Cheeks was surprised that the seller was Genesee, he didn't let on to her. He was good at pretending.

"Mo. Where are you right now?" Frank got in his car and started the engine, intending to drive down to Ridge Avenue.

"Just got off the bus at West Hunting & 21st. You around the station?"

Frank shut off the engine and stepped out of the Dodge. "Mo, please tell me the gun's not loaded." Frank walked toward the Schuyler Street gate of the district house's parking lot and took a right toward West Hunting.

"Ah, hells no!" exclaimed Cheeks waving Frank off as if he were standing right before him. "I ain't tryin' to get shot or nothin'. Man, you crazy?"

Frank spotted Cheeks walking west toward the 39th and said, "I see you now, Mo." Frank waved him over and ended the call.

"Yo! Yo! Detective Frank!" Cheeks was all smiles.

Frank was cautious, knowing that Cheeks had a gun on him, and in light of all the cops that had been murdered, he was taking no chances. Extending his hand to shake Cheeks' he was ready for anything.

"Mo, it's good to see you again." Frank smiled, shook his hand, and purposely held on an extra few seconds. "Listen, without showing it to me, I need to know where the gun is concealed on your person."

"Okay. Okay." Cheeks recoiled, not taking kindly to the lack of trust or the extra-long handshake. "Yeah, and I thought we was friends." Cheeks stepped back and looked Frank up and down.

"Mo, there are dead cops from almost every police district from Central Philly up to Germantown, and you're approaching one of those districts right now, carrying a gun." Frank made his position clear. "I am your friend, but the minute we walk into the district house, I'm going to pat you down. Does that seem reasonable and fair?"

"Hmmm. I guess so, Detective Frank." Cheeks looked at him sideways. "Just don't confiscate nothing that ain't already paid for," he paused. "And I don't know nothin' bout no contraband, neither."

After entering the station's front door a minute later, Frank asked Cheeks to turn and place his hands against the wall. Frank then patted him down and located the gun.

Without removing the weapon, Frank said, "Okay, Mo. We're going to leave the gun in place until I can get some latex gloves and an evidence bag." Frank was leery about issuing his next command, fearing he would turn Mo Cheeks against him. Remembering Willard Clark's father, Richard, and how he gained access to his firearm and killed himself on his front lawn, Frank would take no chances.

"Mo, I can't let you walk into a police station with a gun, and because of its evidentiary value, I can't remove it from your pocket without gloves...."

"I know the drill," Cheeks said. "Man, I've had so many city bracelets on me it ain't even funny." Mo turned around, put his hands behind his back, and let Frank cuff him.

Relieved, Frank had the front desk person buzz him in, signed in Mo Cheeks and one firearm, then placed him in one of the three holding cells on the first floor of the 39th. Frank then buzzed upstairs and summoned Bones and Jackson to the first floor.

"Whattaya got, Frank?"

"I'll tell you once you come down. Just make sure the captain is with you." Frank paused and said, "It's big, Bones. I'll be in interrogation room number three." He then walked over to a nearby supply closet and retrieved a pair of blue latex gloves and a brown paper evidence bag.

Minutes later, Captain Beatrice Jackson and Bones walked into the room to find Frank and a black male late fifties to early sixties, in their estimation, standing handcuffed.

Jackson looked Cheeks up and down and said, "Let me guess, jaywalking?"

"No, this guy's done nothing wrong," said Frank, reaching for his key to the cuffs. "In fact, my friend here, Mo, is here to help us."

"How's that?" asked Bones.

"Bones. Captain. This here is Maurice Cheeks, of East Falls, originally from East Lansdowne." Frank donned Carolina blue latex gloves. "His friends call him Mo, me being one of them, but you'll both refer to him as Mr. Cheeks."

"All right. I'll bite," said Jackson. "And why exactly is Mr. Cheeks in our custody today?"

Frank reached into Cheeks' left front jacket pocket and retrieved a Glock 9mm. Releasing its clip and setting it on the table, he drew the slide to ensure no bullet was chambered.

"Now I told you it wasn't loaded." Cheeks huffed.

Jackson and Bones looked at each other and, without words, conveyed that the unloaded gun sitting on the table was relevant to the Cop Killer case.

Frank removed the cuffs, pulled a chair for Cheeks, and said, "Have a seat, Mo."

"Don't mind if I do." Mo Cheeks rubbed away the uncomfortable feeling of cold steel from his wrists and sat down.

"Bones. Captain," Frank nodded. "I have reason to believe that this gun may be relevant to our case." The three sat down at the table. "Mo, please tell us how you came to be in possession of what you've referred to as a 'dead cop's gun.'"

Cheeks made eye contact with the three cops around the table and began his story. "Yeah. So.... It's like this. I get an unexpected visitor at my place down on Ridge last night. It was late, and a former acquaintance of mine shows up at my door askin' for money. I thought she was making house calls..." he chuckled, "You know, with the weather and all."

"So, this is someone you knew well, then?" asked Jackson.

"Ah, hells no!" Cheeks waved off the suggestion. "I don't even know the bitch's real name." Mo looked over at Jackson, thinking he'd disrespected the only lady at the table. "No offense, Your Honor."

"I only know her by her street name, Genesee." Cheeks tapped the table with his index finger. "The bit...." Cheeks caught himself. "The woman used to work up the street from me, and you know, we may or may not have had relations a time or ten."

"So, she needs cash and offers you a gun. Is that right?" Bones asked.

"Yeah, that's right. A dead cop's gun." Cheeks looked Bones over and said, "Well, ain't you some heavy-handed looking white boy? Where you from? The Midwest or something?"

"Philly, through and through," smiled Bones. "Tell us more."

Frank interjected. "Mo, tell us why you believe this gun was city-issued."

"Well, first, let's get our financials agreed upon." Cheeks tapped the table again. "Your boy, Frank, over here offered me two-hundred bucks for the gun, and I'd like to get some reassurances I'm gettin' paid."

"Is that right, Frank?" Jackson half-smiled. "If this gun proves to be meaningful to our case, I'm sure we can accommodate your request. Tell us more about it, Mr. Cheeks."

"So, I hear shit. I used to work the streets.... did a little pimpin' back in the day. My ears still work.... People tell me shit all the time." Cheeks started to act business-like. "I'd heard through an acquaintance that a hooker, never did get a name, was looking to move some stolen merchandise, the merch being a gun taken from a dead cop's hand."

"And then what?" asked Frank.

"And then," Cheeks leaned in. "Whattaya know.... a self-proclaimed retired hooker shows up at my door looking to sell a gun."

"How much was she asking?" Jackson was curious.

"Three hundred bucks," Cheeks lied. "I told her that was too rich! Told her she needed to come down in price and then come clean about the dead cop rumors."

"Did she say she knew who or where the gun came from?" asked Bones.

"That ain't how it works round here, farm boy." Cheeks shook his head in Bones' direction. "Nobody givin' up nobody out on the street. Except for maybe the lady that come round here a couple or so weeks ago."

"And who might that be, Mr. Cheeks?" asked Jackson.

"Mo Money Jefferson." Cheeks looked at the three cops sitting around him and said, "But I ain't namin' no names." Pausing, he added, "We all know who I'm talking about..... Don't be playing Cop with me." Looking directly at Jackson, he said, "Speakin' of which.... If I'm gettin' two hundred for the gun, I want what Money got for my testimony here today."

"How do you know she got paid?" asked Jackson. "We don't pay for information, Mr. Cheeks."

Mo rolled his eyes. "We both know that ain't the truth, Your Honorable One." Cheeks looked back at Frank, not a fan of his Captain.

"It's a deal, Mo," said Frank. "Now tell us more about Genesee so we can get you paid."

"We go back a ways. She used to hook for a while, and then she worked at East Falls Beverage," he paused. "That's how I got to know her, and then after Frank, here, shows up out of nowhere, two weeks later, so does Genesee. Now that some shit right there," exulted Cheeks. "That gun killed one of your cops. I'll bet money on it!"

"Mo, let me ask you a question," said Frank. "Are you saying that Monica Money Jefferson's been talking about getting paid for ratting out someone to the cops?" Frank shook his head. "That violates every street code there is. That would've put her in danger, no?" Frank asked.

"Damn right," said Cheeks.

"You know this Jefferson woman pretty well, then?" asked Jackson.

"I seen her around before," said Cheeks.

"Seen her lately?" asked Frank. "Cuz we'd love to ask her a few questions.

"You mean a few more, don't you?" Cheeks let the three cops know that he knew what was going down. The Philadelphia P.D. wanted to bring her back in, and they were now desperate to get to her before someone else did.

"Mo, let me ask you something. If I showed you a picture of someone we believe to be Genesee, would you be able to confirm if it's her or not?"

"I don't see why not. I mean, I know the woman intimately," Cheeks chuckled.

Jackson's body language told Frank to wait on Denny and his team to come up with a clearer picture, but Frank thought he had nothing to lose.

Opening the picture on Penny's old phone, Frank zoomed in with his fingers and said, "It's pretty blurry, but...."

"That's her," Cheeks cut Frank off. "And that's her nasty boyfriend, too. That motherfucker always gave me the creeps."

"But the picture's poor quality," said Bones. "How can you be so sure?"

"That's them. No doubt abouddit," Cheeks nodded emphatically. "Like I told Frank. They're some kinda weird twins. Grayson's his name... I'm pretty sure they're boyfriend and girlfriend.... Pretty sure about that. They always wore those ratty-ass hoodies. Like it was their thing or something."

"Which is it?" asked Bones. "Boyfriend/girlfriend, or twins?"

"Could be both, knowing those two." Cheeks looked at the picture on the phone again and nodded. "Yep, that's them."

Bones, Frank, and Jackson all looked intrigued.

Downtown, in the bowels of a church, the twisted anthem of sibling killers, lovers, and homicidal maniacs, echoed through the now unhallowed grounds as the two worshipped each other again. In the wake of their lurid tryst, they planned out their next murder. Killing two birds with one stone, they would lure Money Jefferson to the West Laurel Hill Cemetery, just yards from the Renaissance Hotel in Bala Cynwyd, and kill the stool pigeon, Genesee, while sending a message to the cops living at the hotel by the shores of the Schuylkill.

"So, how do we get that bitch up there?" Talon asked his half-sister.

"I've been thinking about it all day," said Genesis. "That hotel is high-end, lots of business travelers. They're lonely and got money to spend."

"Yeah? And?"

"We get her up there to turn a trick for a wealthy client, and then we lure her into the cemetery just up the road."

"How do you get her from the hotel where the trick is supposed to happen to a pitch-dark cemetery?"

"You got a brain in ya?!" Genesis snapped at Talon. "I can't think of everything."

"Why you always given me shit lately?" Talon was worried that Genesis was on a power trip and might not need him anymore. "We're in this together, ain't we?"

"That's what I'm sayin.' You're smarter than me. You planned the Steinecker murders, and that went off without a hitch. I need help."

"Yeah. And you planned every single one since," Talon muttered.

"Talon." Genesis took his hand. "We're almost to the end. Our legacy is almost made. Then we end it for good. We go down in history. Now help me, Baby."

Talon racked his brain. "I got it!"

Back at the 39th, Mo Cheeks negotiated his price, and Frank, against Jackson's better judgment, personally guaranteed the money.

"Mo, you can't say anything to anyone about this?" said Frank. "That's the deal."

"If you do, Mr. Cheeks....." said Bones.

"And this gun comes back as a murder weapon used against a slain officer...." Jackson finished Bones' thought. "We'll arrest you for aiding and abetting, tampering with evidence, and a few other charges we'll come up with."

"I don't need no threats from Your Honor or Corn Fed over here," Cheeks knew the drill. "I work for my boy, Frankie. From now on, I deal with only him."

"Very well," said Jackson, picking up the evidence bag. "Frank, you take it from here. Bones and I will see you upstairs when you're all done with Mr. Cheeks."

"Roger that, Cap. See you upstairs."

After the door closed, Cheeks said, "Man. I like the good old days when it was just you, KKK, and little Miss Hottie. Now those were the days. Whatever happened to the precious little lady?"

"The Cop Killers murdered her and our daughter." Frank looked cold and agitated.

Cheeks was shocked. "Oh, damn! You think Genesee and Grayson are the Cop Killers, don't cha?" Looking into Frank's eyes, he asked, "You gonna kill 'em, ain't ya? Just like the others you killed. I can see it in your eyes, Detective Frank."

"Kill, or be killed," said Frank, now opening the holding room door. *Or, kill and be killed,* he thought to himself.

Now at the front door leading to the street, Maurice Cheeks shook Frank's hand and asked him, "Will I ever see you again?" Cheeks had a strange feeling that he might not.

"I'll have an envelope dropped off later at your place. What was the number again? 4036?" Frank tried to remember.

"That's right, Detective Frank. Good memory. And I even trust you, too."

"Thank you, Mr. Cheeks." Frank squeezed his hand tightly and said, "You did the right thing."

Squeezing Frank's hand tightly back, Cheeks said, "You be safe out there, Frank. And like I said, my friends, call me Mo."

"I'm happy to call you my friend, Mo." The two looked out at the driving snow. "Listen, it's snowing pretty good out there. Why don't you let me have a unit take you back down to Ridge?"

"You tryin' to get me killed, Detective Frank?"

Frank liked old Mo Cheeks. Softly smiling at his friend, he said, "You take care, Mo. I'll be seeing you around."

As Mo Cheeks crossed Schuyler en route to the bus stop on 21st Street, he turned and looked back at the 39th and thought to himself that he'd never see Detective Frank Collazo again. And that made him sad.

One week later, on Friday, December 10, Frank and Bones joined Candace and Cantrell for dinner at the hotel. The snow fell heavily, and things were quiet, with no new case revelations in the previous week. The footage at the Walmart was recorded over, and Denny Patel and his team had little success enhancing the selfie that seemed to capture Penny and Bonnie's killers.

At the same time as the four were enjoying dinner, the cell phone of Money Jefferson rang. It was a friend she'd spoken to the day before about a possible client who was staying at the Residence Inn.

"Yo, what's up, girl?" Money answered the phone. "We still on about tonight?"

"Yeah, I'll have my guy pick you up at your mom's house at 9," said Connie Parks.

Parks was an on-again, off-again friend of Monica Jefferson for more than two years, but unknown to Jefferson, she also knew Genesis and wasn't happy Money was getting paid by the police to rat out her friend.

In the days prior, Genesis had contacted Parks and asked her for a favor in exchange for fifty dollars. Parks was happy to help. The plan was for Parks to tell Money she was hired to meet a former client at the hotel who was in town on a business trip. A high roller from

Texas. Parks would then tell Money that she was roughed up by a john the night before and was in no condition to meet the high-paying client. Parks would tell Money she'd get four hundred of the five hundred dollars offered, giving the remaining hundred to Parks for the referral.

"Okay, what's your guy driving?" asked Money. "And what's his name?"

"A silver Mazda 6. His name's Kevin. He ain't much to look at, but he'll have your back."

"Nine o'clock, then?" confirmed Money.

"Yeah, and look good, Money. Smell good, too. The better you look, the more you'll get paid," advised Parks. "I've connected with this guy before. He's a little older, but he's a nice guy. He's real gentle."

"So, I get the five hundred, and then what?"

"I'll swing by your mom's tomorrow and pick up my share."

"And this ain't no set-up, right?" Money knew Parks fairly well but knew that no one in her profession could be trusted completely.

"This guy ain't no cop," said Parks. "Like I said, I've been with him several times in Bala Cynwyd, and he's just looking for some pleasure. He works for some chemical company in Texas, I think."

"Okay, nine o'clock, then. I'll be ready."

"Kevin will pick you up afterward. Just text me later and let me know how it goes," said Parks.

After hanging up, Connie Parks smiled, looked at Genesis, and asked, "How'd I do, Genesee?"

Sitting at a kitchen table in Parks' two-room flat in Sharswood, Genesis said, "You did great," smiling at her longtime friend.

"How about that fifty now?" Parks smiled.

"Yeah, about that." Genesis smiled while reaching into her purse.

Instead of cash, Genesis Harper Walker pulled out a knife. Three days later, twenty-eight-year-old Connie Michelle Parks would be found dead in her flat, with exactly fifty stab wounds to her head, neck, and torso, with two letters carved into her belly.

At 9:03 pm that evening, Monica Mo Money Jefferson looked out the window and saw the silver Mazda parked in front of her mother's house in Brewerytown. Feeling apprehensive, she thought of bailing on her friend but desperately needed the cash. Four hundred bucks was a week's worth of walking the streets, and she knew the hotel was nice, too.

"Mom! I'm heading out! Be back before twelve," Money said to her mom.

"Be safe, Monica. I love you, Honey," said Gladys Jefferson to her only daughter. She couldn't know she'd never see her daughter again, only a year after losing her husband to a heart attack.

Money stepped out onto the porch of 2528 West Girard Avenue, pulled up her collar to shield herself from the howling wind, looked out at the Silver four-door, and then mapped out her walk from the porch to the street. Not wanting to get her pant legs wet, she would try to walk in the footprints she'd made in the snow after getting dropped off in front of her house earlier.

Before getting into the back seat of the car, she tapped on the front door window on the passenger side to ensure she had the right car. And to get a look at a man she'd never met before.

Once the window came down halfway, Money asked, "You gotta name?"

"It's Kevin," smiled a man with bad teeth and wearing a black hoodie. "You Monica?"

"That's me." Despite her fear and apprehension, Money got into the back of the sedan and settled in for the twenty-minute ride, making little eye contact in the rearview mirror with the creepy guy named Kevin.

Ten minutes later, without a word from either passenger or driver, Money spoke. "We almost there?" she asked as the Mazda exited Belmont Park and passed the Hayes Manor Retirement Home.

"Yeah, about five minutes," replied the man, his eyes appearing black to Money in the rearview mirror.

"So, how do you know Connie, anyway?"

"Um, we went to high school together back in the day."

"Yeah? And where was that?" Money asked as she knew where Parks went to high school.

"Ah," the driver stuttered. "Over on the Westside."

"The west side, where?" Money was feeling more and more anxious.

"Um. Gimmie a second, I gotta return this text," he lied. Turning right onto Righters Ferry, he knew he was almost there and needed to stall another two minutes.

Seeing that the car was approaching the hotel, Money felt a brief sense of relief, thinking they'd be there in just a few minutes. "So, where did you go to school again?" she repeated her question.

As the car took a quick left on Monument Ave, and just before making the quick right back onto Righters and the hotel at the bottom of the hill, on the banks of the Schuylkill, it continued straight into the West Laurel Hill Cemetery and veered to the right.

"I went to the school of.... you're under arrest for prostitution. Now sit back and remain seated. The man flashed a stolen Detective Badge to Money Jefferson without looking back.

"I fucking knew it!" Money Jefferson pushed and kicked the back seat of the stolen Mazda 6. "Mother fuckin' Parks set me up! Goddamnit! Let me out of this fucking car!" she demanded.

"Calm down, Miss Jefferson, let me pull up here and turn around," said the person impersonating a cop. "You'll be going to jail tonight, but it's not the end of the world."

The sedan drove slowly down a small road with a fence to the right, Righters Ferry beyond it, and a steep hill to its left littered with headstones hithering and yonning as if out of place, somehow not belonging. In the darkness, the headstones, umbrellaed by eighty-foot tall, four-hundred-year-old trees, seemed to be sliding down the steep hill to consume her. Further down, tiny tombstones turned into larger ones, and then mausoleums appeared out of the blackness, giant ones dating back to the 1700s.

Lying in their final yet reluctant resting place were the wealthiest and most famous of Philadelphia's uppermost class of society. On this night, however, someone not belonging to their class would join them.

Horrified, Money Jefferson saw the terrifying crypts jutting from the side of the hill, half buried, half exposed, and thought of jumping from the slow-moving vehicle. It was as if the dead were clawing out of the hilly, root-entangled catacombs, desperate to breathe in air again. At that moment, Monica Jefferson wanted to go to jail. *Anywhere but here*, she thought.

As the car approached a giant cathedral-like mausoleum adorned with gothic-shaped doors, the road curved and would take the car back in the direction it came. Money felt no sense of comfort, though, and as the car nearly completed its turn, she shrieked in horror when seeing the woman she'd only ever known as Genesee emerge from the pitch in front of the fortress of the dead.

Standing on the bottom step of a towering two-hundred-year-old stone staircase, which ran from the neighborhood of the dead below to the sprawling fields of the dead high above, was a bloodthirsty killer looking for her revenge.

Money screamed and yanked on the handle, releasing the door. Falling from the car, she landed at the base of the giant stone staircase to hell and at the feet of one of her killers, Genesis Harper Walker. From behind, Talon Grayson Walker took Money by her hair and dragged her up the stairs, the winter wind, the hills of the dead, and the towering trees, muting her desperate cries for help.

Further down the hill, Frank stood on the Riverwalk between the hotel and the Schuylkill, nursing his broken heart. A frigid gust came up off the river, and Frank thought he heard another weary soul leave its earthly body en route to who knows where.

With the second blast of frozen air, Frank's attention went up to the historic Pencoyd Bridge, which first opened in 1900 to support the Pencoyd Ironworks and local industries from the Schuylkill Branch. Now a part of the Cynwyd Heritage Trail, it connected Manayunk with Bala Cynwyd. Atop the bridge, looking down over Frank Collazo and the river below, Old Man Winter and Frank Bruno presided over the wintry cold and Frank's sorrow. They wanted Frank to know that his work wasn't done. The ghost of Frank Bruno tipped his hat while Garrison Winter just nodded. Both disappeared as the next gust of wind stole Frank's breath and shattered psyche.

The next morning, Monica Jefferson was found dead halfway up the staircase, beaten, bludgeoned, and stabbed dozens of times. On her stomach were carved two letters matching those found on her recently departed friend. The letters carved into her flesh? FC.

The letters would connect the two deaths of Jefferson and Parks and put Detective Frank Collazo on a path that would take him home.

Chapter 31 – God Speed

When the past comes calling, it blows cold.

Frank stood over the body of Monica Money Jefferson, the snow around him sprayed with her blood. The snow around her, melted when the life ran from her body.

Detectives, uniformed officers, crime scene investigators, and police photographers stood in horror, processing the scene, while Bones and Cantrell stood by Frank's Dodge looking up at him. Like everyone else at the scene, Frank knew the message carved into the victim's belly was for him.

Money Jefferson's body was found with her hands over her head, pants covered in blood, her belt open with pants unbuttoned partially, and her legs spread as wide as the stone stairs and once-white denim jeans would allow. Her body was found under a gothic cathedral arch, on a landing fourteen steps up the forty-five-step staircase. Though she was clearly put on display, it was most certainly the actual crime scene, as the amount of blood indicated to all that the victim fought for her life and died there.

A tourist first found the body just after sunrise. The long shadows of lifeless trees standing tall over Righters Ferry Road could not conceal the horror that lay just inside the wrought iron confines of the eighty-acre, one-hundred-and-fifty-four-year-old cemetery.

Frank remembered the previous evening when standing on the Riverwalk between the hotel and Pencoyd Bridge; he could've sworn he felt someone die. Before seeing Garrison Winter and Frank Bruno up on the bridge, Frank could somehow sense Money Jefferson's death. Her soul cried out to him as it rode the wind coming up off the Schuylkill, just as it had when Kyle Bender and Cindy Stafford were found hanging from the train trestle beneath The Twins. Then, like now, Bruno and Winter were standing nearby, just feet down the trestle.

Frank was sick of the death, and he was ready to once and for all track down the Cop Killers and put an end to their reign. This was it for him; no more would die.

As a police photographer took the last few pictures of Jefferson before others placed her in a black body bag, the coroner stood impatiently by as another gust of twenty-degree wind blew down the long-haunted stairs. Frank looked up and could still see the letters carved into her belly. While everyone at the scene, unlucky enough to view the etchings of a madman and madwoman, believed the letters FC were initials for the name Frank Collazo. Frank, however, knew them to mean FalconClaw. He knew the killers were sending him a message; one final breadcrumb.

Frank knew the killers were telling him they were aware that he and the others were at the Residence Inn at the bottom of the hill and were summoning him to where their father killed his father. He was more certain now than ever before that the killers were fulfilling what they believed was their depraved destiny and walking in the footsteps and out of the shadow of a man named Vincent Charmaine Walker.

"We're done here." Frank looked determined as he strode past Bones and Cantrell.

With wrinkles gathering on his forehead, Cantrell looked at Bones and echoed Frank's words. "Well, I guess we're done here." The two men then joined Frank in the Dodge.

"Where to, Frank?" said Bones from the front passenger seat. "The 39th?"

"No. I need to make a stop first." Frank wasn't into talking at the moment. He first needed to see the place he would eventually come face to face with the maniacs. The two, known to the locals and the press as *The Cop Killers*, would now be quietly referred to by Frank as his *destiny*.

After putting Isak Cameron out of his misery in July 2019, Frank swore he would never kill again. Now, he was sure that he would. He was equally sure that he would see his wife and daughter very soon, and he took solace in the thought.

With little conversation, Frank drove past Rocky Tops and pulled the car over a block later in front of FalconClaw Park. Without a word to Cantrell or Bones, Frank exited the car and crossed the slushy street heading toward the original entrance of FalconClaw at 888 Bedford Street. There he stood, staring up the hill.

Seconds later, Bones and Cantrell were at Frank's side, also looking up. Both were unsure of what they were looking at.

Frank said, "Can you hear that, fellas?"

Both confused, unsure of what Frank was hearing, Bones and Cantrell looked at each other and shrugged.

"Are you referring to the traffic behind us, Frank?" Cantrell turned one ear to the goliath up on the hill known as FalconClaw Park.

"Whattaya hearing, Frank?" Bones was starting to worry for his friend.

"It's calling out to me. This is where it ends, fellas." Frank nodded with resolute, narrowing eyes.

"For the Cop Killers, you mean?" Bones beat Cantrell to the question.

"Yeah, sure, Bones." Frank knew it was where he would end, too, but not before killing the killers that stole away his present and future. He would bring a violent end to the misbegotten offspring of the man who stole his past.

Frank inhaled the cold deep, oxygen-rich air through his nostrils, exhaled fully, and said, "Let's go!"

Back in the car, no words were spoken. Bones and Doug were mortified by what they'd just witnessed and silently thought the same thing; Frank was losing his mind.

Back at the 39th District house, Frank was summoned to Jackson's office upon entering, with all eyes in the Operations Room glued to his every move. The cops on the first floor knew something that Frank didn't, and all seemed on edge.

ORS supervisor Sgt. McLaughlin instructed Frank to go straight to Jackson's office without first stopping by the Detective Room. Frank, only mildly concerned, said, "Sure thing, Tommy."

Behind him, Cantrell and Bones followed closely and looked as uneasy as every other cop lining Frank's route.

Upstairs, Frank said, "I'll see you guys shortly. Make sure you contact the Head of Detectives for each district involved in the case and see if they have any updates. Brief them on what happened at Laurel Hill West and tell them I'll call them when I get a report from Denny and his team."

"Yeah, sure, Frank." Bones began worrying that he would never see Frank again after the case was closed.

Frank heard a familiar voice speaking with his captain as he neared her office. Sighing with annoyance, he tapped on the glass portion of the door and waited.

Seconds later, Jackson opened the door, which Frank found odd because she always just yelled for him to come in. Making eye contact with Frank, she attempted to warn him that she had company and that he wouldn't be happy.

Jackson turned and led Frank into the room, revealing who the uninvited guest was. Seeing the dress whites, and shoulder Captain's bars, Frank feigned a smile and said, "Well, if it isn't the old silver fox, Captain Justin Smith. What a pleasure seeing you again, sir."

"Yeah, right, Collazo." Rolling his eyes, Smith instructed Frank to have a seat. "I'm in a hurry, so let's make this quick."

"No thanks, Captain. If you remember from the last time we met, I don't like....."

"Yeah, yeah, yeah." Smith wore a look of disdain. "You don't like sitting for long stretches."

"Exactly." Frank raised his brows while pursing his lips in a show of sarcasm.

"Let's get on with it because I have a city-wide murder investigation to tend to." The former marine stood square with Frank, again ensuring his chest was puffed out as far as it would go, sucking in his slight gut for good measure.

Frank shot Smith a 'What gives?' looking to illustrate to his nemesis that he, too, was in a hurry.

"You're off the case, Collazo!" Smith reveled in the news. "Two more people are dead because of you, and it stops right now. Take old man FBI with you, as well. That old man has contributed next to nothing to this case, and his services are no longer needed." Smith paused and said, "The girl from Montreal can stay, though."

Frank chuckled while Jackson said, "Pardon me, Captain. But Cantrell has contributed a great...."

Justin Smith dismissed Jackson's comments with a wave of his hand, his eyes fixed on Frank. "Did you find humor in what I just said, Collazo?"

Frank's smile was exaggerated. "You do know that Douglas Cantrell is working pro bono, don't you?"

"Great," smirked Smith. "That means he won't have a problem leaving then."

Frank nodded his approval and then slowly yanked at the Detective Badge on his belt with his right hand, removed it, and placed it on Jackson's desk. His actions cause both Jackson's and Smith's chins to sag. Frank then crossed his chest with the same hand and pulled his city-issued Smith & Wesson from its shoulder holster. Dropping the clip into his left hand, then quickly drawing back the slide, he launched a hollow tip bullet into the air. Jackson and Smith watched as Frank caught it mid-flight.

"I quit," said Frank, making no qualms about it.

"Frank," Jackson looked mortified. "You can't quit!"

"Captain Jackson, Ma'am, it's been a rough year." Frank sighed in resignation. "Hell, it's been a rough few years for me."

As Smith stood with egg on his face, Jackson asked her best detective, "What will you do?"

"I'm tired. I'm going to go home and take a nap. After that, I'm not sure. I'll probably go visit my son up in Michigan." Frank nodded.

"Yeah, well, best of luck with the investigation. I'll be pulling for both of you."

"Now hang on a second, Detective." Smith swallowed hard. He knew that Chief Inspector Jonathan Caffey and Police Commissioner William Holden would be pissed. Frank Collazo was a hero and a legend within the department and all of Philadelphia and South Jersey. Frank and Penny were household names from West Deptford, up to Trenton, over to Allentown, and back down to Philly. Smith would have some explaining to do once he got back down to Race Street.

"This isn't what I came up here for," he pleaded. "You're a good cop. We need you in this department, just not on this case."

"Yeah, sure. Whatever." Frank turned his gaze to his former captain and said, "Let's grab lunch sometime after the holiday."

Jackson was bewildered. "Yeah sure, Frank."

Frank extended his hand to shake Jackson's, and she reciprocated, holding onto his hand for an extra couple of seconds as if to say, 'Please don't go,' her eyes pleading with him.

As Jackson finally released Frank's hand, Smith extended his. Frank looked down at the open hand and then into his eyes, turned, and walked away.

"Don't you go into that Detective Room, Collazo!" Smith raised his voice as Frank's hand found the door handle. "And I'm gonna need that bullet in your hand."

"Fuck you, Smith," Frank turned and added. "I'll keep this one as a memento from my time with the department," he smiled. "Oh. And be sure to send Chief Inspector Caffey and Commissioner Holden my warmest regards."

Smith exhaled in disgust.

Seconds later, Frank walked into the bustling Detective Room, and when he did, the room fell silent, with all eyes on the broken man and tired legend.

"Hey guys, I have an announcement to make...."

Everyone knew Frank had just left a meeting with the brass from Race Street, and all were expecting the worst possible news. His badge less belt and empty holster brought comfort to no one.

"As of this moment, I'm officially retired." Frank gave an apologetic smile to his fellow detectives.

One by one, everyone in the room, weighed down with heavy hearts, came to shake hands and hug their longtime colleague goodbye. Cantrell, Bones, and Weatherby stood by, speechless and scared.

After the farewells and well-wishes ended, Frank motioned for his three friends to join him in the hallway.

Bones was the first to the door, wondering what had just happened.

Now in the hall, the three, looking shell-shocked, gathered around their inspirational leader.

"What happened, Frank?" Bones spoke first.

"Listen. I'm going to head home and collect my thoughts, but at three o'clock, I want to meet up with you guys back at the hotel to talk about where we go from here."

Cantrell was beside himself. "Frank, I don't want to be here if you're not here." Doug looked at Candace and Bones and said, "I'm sorry, guys. I'm only here because of Frank."

Candace felt lost and completely out of place and just nodded with tears in her eyes. Her dream of helping solve the Cop Killer case was dashed. She, too, was here for Frank, and just as she felt days earlier, she believed her time with the Philly P.D. had come to an end.

"It's okay, Doug," said Bones. "We'll power through without you." He then looked over at his partner and said, "Frank, please tell me you have a plan. This case needs you, and I'm not sure Brooks or I are up to the challenge." Bones was shaken-up. "I mean, fuck, man!"

At that moment, the door to Jackson's office opened down the hall causing the four to cease their conversation. As Jackson and Smith walked out, Frank played the part, shook hands with Bones and Weatherby, looked at Cantrell, and said, "You're with me, Doug."

"Right," said Cantrell. "Let me get my things first."

As Doug hurried back into the Detective Room to retrieve his personal effects and laptop, Frank looked at Bones and Candace, winked, and whispered, "Three o'clock."

Bones nodded imperceptibly to his partner as Jackson and Smith approached and said, "All the best, Frank. Stay in touch."

Candace, looking baffled, leaned in to hug Frank and whispered, "See you later," into his ear and walked off with Bones.

Before heading down the steps, Justin Smith looked at Frank, now standing alone, and said, "You let me know if you change your mind, Collazo. I meant what I said in there."

"You bet, Captain." Frank would've loved to punch the insincere prick in the face again.

As Smith disappeared into the stairwell, Beatrice Jackson approached Frank and said, "Please tell me you'll think it over and reconsider. Smith wasn't just appeasing you. This department does need you."

"I'm done, Cap. It's been a pleasure serving you and the 39th, but every relationship has an expiration date, and today's the end for me and the Philly P.D."

"You got what you need at home to go along with what you're holding in your hand?" Jackson lowered her stare to Frank's closed right hand, remembering the bullet there.

"In my trunk, too." Frank winked at his former captain.

"If you need anything, call my cell phone. You got it?"

"Roger that, Cap." Frank smiled affectionately at a woman that he admired greatly. "I'll be sure to do that."

"Call me Beatrice, now that we're former co-workers," she grinned and nodded. "Oh, and listen...." She looked both ways, leaned in, and whispered, "I can't give you a get-out-of-jail-free card should something go down. But I can damn sure keep you in the loop. Look for my call. If it comes, take it."

"Much appreciated, Beatrice." Frank shook his head and smiled. "That's gonna take some getting used to."

"You call me, Frank. Information goes both ways."

Suddenly the Detective Room door opened, and Cantrell walked out. "I think I got everything."

"Mr. Cantrell...." Jackson extended her hand. "It has been my great pleasure working with you. I finally finished watching the *Mindhunter* series last night and continue to be impressed by your contributions over these many years."

Juggling the items in his hands, Cantrell shook Jackson's hand and joked, "And it only took you two years to finish it?" he grinned. "Couldn't hold your attention, huh?"

"I loved it. I just wished I had saved it for my retirement. Hard to enjoy the finer things in life when you're always chasing the bad guys."

"Tell me about it," smiled Cantrell. "Call on me anytime, Captain."

"I hope I don't have to." Jackson smiled at Cantrell and then turned to Frank.

"You giddy up now, Frank," she winked.

"Hi-Ho Silver, Captain!" Frank smiled and walked toward the stairs, Cantrell in tow.

Jackson's smile quickly ran from her face, and she stood stunned. Tearing up, she knew that Frank would never call her and that she would likely never see him again. Jackson knew Frank was in *Lone Ranger* mode, and considering how many dead cops had lined the bloody streets since May, she wasn't hopeful. She hoped her hero and everyone's legend found peace in his journey.

"Godspeed, Frank Collazo," she whispered. "Godspeed." Jackson turned toward her office. Saying goodbye to a legend, she shed another tear as she did.

Chapter 32 – The Devil's Gate

After dropping Cantrell off at the hotel and instructing him to stay in his room, Frank returned to the Mad River, parked in his old spot behind the bar, and just sat there. Rolling down his window, the cold air rushed in and heightened his senses. He waited for another CSX freight train to pass over the Schuylkill River as if it were an old friend. He hated the sound but found comfort in its familiarity.

Closing his eyes, he daydreamed of a time when he and Penny might meet again. He couldn't wait until they each took one of Bonnie's hands and walked alongside their precious daughter.

Frank's cell phone rang just as the Schuylkill Valley Metro passed over Lock Street and onto the trestle behind the Mad River bar. The call was from a private number. Frank gave it little importance but thought he should answer it anyway.

After swiping right, he said, "Hello," but couldn't hear anything over the train's roar. Hanging up, he rolled up his windows, thinking the caller would call back.

Thirty train cars later, his phone rang. Once again, from a private number.

"Hello?"

"Hello, Detective," came a male's voice over the line. "Long time since we saw each other last." The voice trembled as if the caller were nervous.

The caller had Frank's attention, and he sat up straight and said, "And when was that, exactly?" Frank noted the exact time. It was 10:58 am.

"Early November, I think. Not really sure, but I remember you just fine."

"Listen, I don't know who this is, but I don't have the time. I'm a little busy right now hunting down cop killers." Frank knew exactly who he was speaking with and wanted to keep him talking. Cantrell had always told him that serial killers love to talk.

"Well, I just wanted to say hello before I killed you." Again, the caller's voice seemed shaky to Frank.

"Talon, you seem a little nervous right now. You gonna be okay, young man?" asked Frank, trying to control the conversation and the psyche of the caller. "You do know they make medicine for that, right?"

"Shut up and listen to me," said Talon. "We want to meet up with you. Soon."

"Is that right?" Frank laughed under his breath. "Let me guess. I should leave my guns at home, right?"

"By all means, bring them along. They can't save you, Collazo," said Talon, his voice cracking from frayed nerves.

"Well, I just wanted to let you and your sister know I'm going to kill both of you." Frank was calm and cool. "You're going to be remembered not for how you killed or how many, but rather by how you died and who killed you. Both you and your sister Genesis will die at my hands. Just like it was always meant to be."

"It's like we're old friends, then," said Talon, trying to keep his wits. He was terrified. He was talking to a righteous killer, and Genesis stared at him as he spoke. She prodded him to get under Frank's skin.

"Yeah, well, you won't feel that way when I put three in your back like my father did to yours."

"We'll see about that, Junior." Frank was almost blasé. Numb, while waiting weeks for first contact, he could feel his senses begin to sharpen. He would attempt to agitate his prey into careless missteps allowing him to direct their every move.

"So, we both have daddy issues, is that it?" Frank said, hearing Genesis Walker in the background. "Listen, your incestuous sister sounds like she wants to talk to a real man. Why don't you go ahead and put her on?"

After a few seconds of garbled words and a tense exchange between Talon and Genesis, a woman's voice came on the line.

"Listen here, Collazo, you fuck! I'm going to filet your ass just like I did all the others. Shallow wounds this time so that you die slowly. I want to watch you bleed out." Genesis, unlike Talon, sounded stone-cold and unafraid.

Frank feigned a yawn into the phone. "What was that? I couldn't hear you over your rapid heartbeat. You and your illegitimate twin must be terrified over there. I now know who you are and will begin searching for you."

"Trust me, dickhead!" Genesis spewed teenage insults. "You're a dead man!"

"Listen here, you genetic defect." Frank was calm in his delivery. "I'm going to kill you and your inbred twin. Then I'm going to sit back and use him as a footstool while I watch rigor mortis set into your joints. It's going to be fun putting an end to your sorry ass existence."

"We'll see about that, motherfucker!"

"I'm terrified, little Genie," Frank's giggle was raspy. "I will be seeing both of you very soon. Sleep tight in your little sanctuary because when I find the two of you, your new home will be at the base of my feet, swimming in piss and blood as I watch both of you die."

"Be ready for my next call, pig!"

"Just make sure you call me and not your brother Talon. It was unsettling hearing fear drip from each of his timid words." Frank's directive dripped with sarcasm. "Oh, and make sure you guys shower before we meet. I can smell the two of you through the phone. It's fucking awful."

The call ended without another word from the Cop Killers, and Frank again noted the time. Clicking on Bones' number from his previous call directory, he anxiously waited for his now former partner to pick up.

"Hey, is everything okay?" Bones sounded uneasy, though he tried not to show it to those within earshot.

"Bones, where are you?"

"In the Detective Room with Brooks and Candace."

"Listen to me very carefully. Walk out of the room and into the storage room opposite the stairs."

"Yeah, sure thing, Rick. Let me check on that for you." Bones concealed who he was talking to from the others. Following Frank's instructions, he entered the long-vacant room that once served as the Detective Room. "Okay, I'm alone, Frank. What's going on?"

"Bonesie, I just heard from the Walker twins." Frank's heart rate was steady. He would not be rattled by the scum of the earth, twenty-something killers. "And I need you to do me a favor."

"Of course. What is it?"

"I timestamped the call with the twins, and my guess is that they have no idea that a private call can be traced." Frank paused. "I'll text you the information regarding my number and the start and end time of the call. Have Denny Patel get AT&T's mobility department on the phone. Have them get cell data from the tower closest to me and then determine who the caller was and from which cell tower the call originated. Then get your ass over here and make sure you're locked and loaded. We're going to geo-locate these fuckers and end this fiasco."

"Jesus Christ, Frank." Bones' adrenaline was rushing. "You don't think Denny will take your call?"

"Denny's by the book. He won't take my call because he won't cross any lines laid down by his superiors. He's got to know I'm a civilian by now. And I can't blame him."

"Everybody knows about it, Frank. Rumor has it you got fired."

"We'll talk about that later. Just get on the phone and find out what tower that call originated from. I'm heading over to the hotel now. Candace and Doug are in more danger now than they ever were before, and we need to make sure they're armed," said Frank. "Those sick fuckers know that we're on to them, and they're going to get desperate. Their element of surprise is gone. They're going to make mistakes, Bones. And if we're out hunting, Doug and Candace are vulnerable. Those fraternal fuckers know where they sleep at night. They've likely been to the hotel before."

"Should we send them home while we ride out the investigation?" asked Bones.

"That would be best. Let's meet at 3 pm, as planned, and we'll figure it all out."

"Roger that, Frank." Bones was up for whatever Frank had in store. He knew his partner was on the verge of a full mental breakdown, but an impaired Frank Collazo had better instincts than ten good cops. "I'll get with Denny and see you at the hotel later."

"Watch your back, Bonesie," cautioned Frank. "Like Doug and Candace, you're in danger, too."

"I welcome it," said Bones.

After Frank armed himself from the small arsenal in his trunk, he immediately called Joanne up in Michigan. She answered after one ring, happy to hear from him.

"Frank, are you okay?"

"Yeah, Jo. How have you been? How's Con Man?"

"He's good. The question is, how are you?" Joanne was worried sick. "You haven't returned any of my calls or texts since the funeral. We're beside ourselves with what's going on down there. They aren't saying much on the news."

"I'm really sorry about that. I've just been so busy."

"Conner says you text him from time to time, but he misses his father. He's worried sick about you, Frank. And Christmas is coming soon."

"That's why I'm calling," Frank paused. "I was thinking of making a trip up there."

"Oh my gosh! When?!"

"In a week or so." Frank wanted to see his son for the last time. "Would you be okay with that?"

"Of course, Frank. Conner would love it, but I'd like to see you, too." Joanne was emotional. "We all miss you so much," she began to cry. "We miss Penny and Bonnie desperately. I can't imagine how you're living with their loss. It's just awful."

"I'm like the walking dead over here. It's been impossible. But I know they're waiting for me...." Frank took a deep breath. "Somewhere out there.... they're waiting for me, Jo."

"Frank, I don't like the sound of that." Joanne sniffled and cried. "Please get up here, fast. We're desperate to see you."

"I'll call in a day or two. Please tell Conner that I'll be there soon. Tell him I love him. Take care."

"You take care." Joanne was beside herself. "You make sure you get here, Frank."

"I will, Jo. Goodbye."

"Goodbye, Frankie," she cried.

After hanging up, Frank backed out of his usual spot just as another train roared across the tracks heading south. Frank closed his eyes, took a deep breath, and recognized it as a metaphor for where his life was heading. He was a runaway freight train, and things would go south soon. He promised himself that before things got too crazy, he'd see his son again and the mother of his only remaining child, too.

Ten minutes later, and right before Frank walked through the doors of the Residence Inn, he looked up to his left, hoping to see Bruno and Winter up on the Pencoyd Bridge. They weren't there. Frank squeezed his resolute lips together and squinted. He had work to do, and whether or not they were at his side, he would get the job done and then make his way back home to his family up at 454 East Locust Avenue in Old Germantown. This time for good.

Now in the lobby, Frank passed Lisa Bass, who ensured the stay of his friends at the hotel was more than cozy. Bass was the GM of the new hotel and had made fast friends with Doug and Candace, making them feel at home during their extended stay.

"Well, hello, Frank," Bass walked out from behind the desk when she saw him. "How's it goin'?"

"Good, Lisa," a tired Frank forced a smile. "Did you make sure that our friend Doug stayed in his room while I was away?"

Bass chuckled. "That old coot is sitting right over there next to the fireplace."

Frank looked over, saw Doug reading a book, and shook his head in mild frustration. "Thanks, Lisa."

"You got it, Detective Frank."

Frank nodded, realizing that he was officially no longer a detective with the Philly P.D.

Frank noticed that Doug was immersed in his book and could sneak up behind him as he sat on the blue sofa in front of the fire.

Squeezing Doug's shoulder caused Cantrell to jump from his seat in fear. Turning to look, he saw Frank, who wasn't smiling, and said, "Jesus, Frank! You trying to give me a heart attack?!"

"No, sir. I'm trying to save your life," said Frank. "Doug, these lunatics could be right outside, and nothing could stop them from walking through that front door." Frank paused. "They're here, Doug. There is no safe place safe."

Cantrell could see in Frank's eyes that his friend believed that hell had opened up and released two of its mutinous flock. He knew that the end was no longer near but rather that the end was tragically here. It was that finality that caused him to believe that he would lose his dear friend.

"Frank, I'm scared," said Doug. "Not for me, Son, but for you."

"Don't worry about...."

"Frank, stop. Listen to me," Doug pleaded, cutting off his friend. "You've written yourself a one-way ticket to the great beyond, wherever that might be, but you can come back from this. I know you can. This doesn't have to be the end."

"Doug, I love you. And I couldn't imagine how my life would've turned out had we never met. But I want to make it very clear to you." Frank was blunt. "After I kill the Walker twins, I will find my family. We will be together again. I will see them again."

Feeling that Frank had made up his mind, Douglas Cantrell stood and said, "Then I won't be here for it. I won't stand by and watch you give up a life with so much more to offer...."

Now it was Frank that cut off his friend. "Doug, was your father murdered when you were just a child? Did serial killers murder your wife and daughter?"

"No, Frank." Doug couldn't possibly know what Frank was feeling; he just knew that the world would be better with him in it.

"I have lost everything. Am I to wait around for you to die of old age?"

"Frank. Come on...."

"You see, Doug. I may have more to offer life, but life has nothing more to offer me." Pausing, he added, "Don't you see it? Every time life gives me something.... it takes it away in the most brutal fashion."

"No, it doesn't!" Doug raised his voice, getting the attention of those checking in and of Lisa Bass, who lifted her chin to see what was happening in the lounge.

"Doug...."

"What about Conner? Is he supposed to lose his father around the same age you were when you lost yours?"

Frank was tongue-tied. "Well, I...."

"Let that one sink in before you go running headfirst into certain death."

"Penny and Bonnie's death will not go unpunished. I deserve to see them again, and their killers deserve to see their father in hell."

"I'll have none of it. I will not be a party to you orphaning your only son, as your father orphaned you." Doug picked up his book and sweater and said, "I'll be in my room.... packing."

Frank let his friend walk off and plopped down in front of the fireplace where he'd first sat with Cantrell a month and a day earlier.

Staring into the flames, he was in a trance. A minute later, his phone rang. Bones would awaken a sleeping giant with the news he had to share.

"Frank, where are you right now?!" Bones fishtailed off Schuyler onto West Hunting Park, heading south. His dash-mounted blue flashers on.

"I'm at the hotel. Whattaya got?"

"Frank, you packin'?"

"Yeah. What's going on, Bones?" Frank's heart rate was catching up to his partner's.

"I'm en route. Meet me outside in ten minutes. We're heading downtown."

"Bones, what the fuck is happening?! Spit it out!"

"As soon as I hung up with you, I called Denny..... You're not gonna believe this. That guy got on the phone with AT&T wireless techs, and less than thirty minutes later, he called me with a location. Frank, they've triangulated the signal to a location downtown."

"Where?" Frank was now standing outside waiting for Bones.

"There're so many cell towers hiding in plain sight downtown that they narrowed it down to an old, abandoned church at 12th & Lombard!"

"Saint Peter's Claver." Frank's head turned to the Pencoyd Bridge, and there they were. Frank's guardian angels were watching over him. Their presence told him he was on the right path.

"Frank, you there?" Bones yelled into the phone. "Frank?!"

Frank shook off the vision and said, "Yeah! Yeah, I'm still here."

"I just turned onto the City Avenue bridges. I'm hanging up. See you in a minute."

Frank pocketed his phone and looked up at the bridge again, and they were gone.

Inventorying his weapon in the middle of the parking lot, ensuring that a round was chambered, he frightened two businesswomen returning to the hotel from a midday meeting across the street.

"Sorry," said Frank, smiling and waving to them. "I'm a cop."

The ladies rushed into the hotel, unsure if he was.

"Lisa will calm them down." Frank was sure of it.

Flashers now on to alert Frank of his arrival, the Ford Interceptor came flying out of the twin arched tunnels that emptied Righters Ferry traffic at the hotel's base. Just as he did, the Interstate 76 westbound traffic slowed overhead.

Bones pulled up, and Frank jumped into the Ford.

"Who knows about this?" asked Frank.

"Nobody but you, me, and Denny," said Bones, heading back up Righters Ferry. Two hundred yards later, Frank looked through a black wrought iron fence and saw the yellow police tape from earlier in the morning. Seeing the wicked staircase between the fence posts, Frank thought he saw Money Jefferson standing under the giant arch presiding over her final resting place. Looking closer, he saw her lift her chin as if to say, "Hey."

Frank thought it was a shame that a woman guilty of many things, but undeserving of her death, would have to suffer all eternity in a place where the dead lay restless by day and mingle unencumbered by night.

Shaking off the vision, Frank asked, "Where's Candace?"

"Surrounded by cops at the 39th," said Bones. "What about Cantrell?"

"Packing his bags back at the hotel."

"Packing his bags?" Bones looked over at Frank, surprised. "He's leaving, huh?"

"Yep," Frank shrugged. "He said he wouldn't be a part of my preordained demise."

"His words, or yours?" Bones look over.

"All right. Those were my words, but you know what I'm sayin'."

Flashers on and riding the shoulder to get through a slowdown on 76 as it ran south past the Philadelphia Museum of Art, Bones said, "Frank, I won't sit idly by and watch you die, either. Where you go, I go," said Bones. "And if you're with me.... well, I like your chances, Bro."

"Well, I'd like to say you can sit this one out, Bones, but I know you're itchin' for a fight."

Frank, listen to me," said Bones as the deep rumble strips took miles off the Ford's tires. "If it comes down to two on two, I want that bitch Genesis!"

"Yeah, and why's that?"

Because I saw the tape of what those two did to Danny at Rocky Tops. That bitch basically pushed her brother out of the way and pounded on Danny's head long after he was dead. That whore's gonna meet God about two seconds after she meets me. I'll fucking tell you that right now."

"I ain't gonna stop ya, Brother." Frank shook his head as he looked out over an old train yard that butted up against Drexel Park and Powelton Village.

Bones reached over, opened the glove box, and gave his friend a gift. It was Frank's shield, this time on a ball chain. Tossing it into Frank's lap, he said, "I know you're retired, but we're out of our district, and if shit goes down in that church, I wanna make sure you have some sort of immunity."

Frank chuckled. "Yeah.... I might actually need some immunity where I'm going," he softly mumbled.

Flashers off, Bones exited 76 onto the South Street Bridge and continued on South Street heading east, as Lombard was a one-way heading west. Ten blocks later, they pulled into a parking spot around the corner after first passing the church.

Both men looked out all sides of the car while inventorying their weapons and discussing a plan of attack.

"You sure you don't want to call for backup, Frankie Boy?"

"You're my backup, Bones. And I'm yours." Frank tsked through clenched teeth, smiled, and winked.

"I wouldn't have it any other way."

"Whatever goes down in there? I love you, Bones, and your dad was a real dick." Frank looked into the passenger side mirror and saw two men in trench coats and fedoras approaching from the sidewalk to his rear. Keeping his eyes on the men until they got close enough for him to turn and see them; they were gone when he did.

"Don't go getting all sentimental on me now."

"I wouldn't think of it." Frank again looked in the side mirror.

Seconds later, Frank asked, "You ready?"

"Yeah, but where the fuck did all this snow come from? The street was clear a few minutes ago, and now it's buried.

In a matter of minutes, it had gone from a steady snowfall to blizzard-like conditions.

"I know where it came from." Frank knew his guardians were nearby.

"So, the gate we passed behind the church, then?"

"That's our way in." Frank zipped up his jacket and opened his door. The shield Bones had returned to him was lying face down on the passenger side floor.

"And away we go!" said Bones, exiting the vehicle.

Frank squinted in the face of twenty-mile-an-hour wind gusts while standing on the snow-covered sidewalk. "Keep your gun in your belt until we get inside. We don't need to be fumbling for it should we get ambushed along the way."

"Roger that." Bones patted the front of his jacket and beltline to show Frank he was ready, then smiled.

As the two men rounded the corner, they saw the four-foot, black, wrought iron fence they'd passed ten minutes earlier. Upon further inspection, Frank found a gate latch beneath the snow accumulating on the one-inch-thick fence. After Bones jumped the fence, Frank lifted the latch and walked through it. Bones watched his partner and said, "That's the Devil's Gate you just walked through. You know that, don't you, Frank?"

Frank chuckled, "Is that why you jumped it?"

"No." Bones, slightly embarrassed, smiled at his partner. "I didn't see the gate, actually."

Frank nodded in appreciation of his partner and said, "That 'Devil's Gate' thing.... That was a damn good line, though."

Standing in the alley between the church, and the building to its rear, the two men looked for a way inside.

The back of the church was lined with four sets of four-foot-tall windows and two steel doors. "These windows are all barred," said Bones, as loud as his whisper would allow.

"I got it!" Frank pulled a small dumpster away from the church's back wall and revealed a basement window that had been kicked in months earlier.

"Since you can't watch my front," said Frank, "watch my back." Frank then squeezed down through the window feet first.

Bones, right behind him, asked Frank to watch his front. Frank rolled his eyes and shook his head. No matter the situation, Bones always tried to keep it light.

With the two men inside, Frank pulled out a mini mag light and said, "Don't turn yours on yet. I don't want to alert anyone to our arrival."

Bones shrugged and said, "You don't have to worry about me. I left mine in the car."

Frank shook his head again as the two men drew their sidearms.

"It's hard to see down there, Frank. You sure you want to go in there dark?"

"God damned right I do."

Creeping down the long dark hall, ceilings short enough to make a middle schooler crouch, the men trudged forward, gun barrels leading the way. The stench of evil, rat droppings, and incest pervaded the men's senses, slowing their approach.

Tugging quietly on locked door after locked door, the two could smell the still burning embers in a makeshift fire pit in the center of a large room that, in Frank's estimation, was twenty feet by twenty feet and ten feet tall. Bones checked all the remaining doors, which were locked, and determined that the open area was the only place the homeless could shelter.

Both convinced that the area was clear, Frank turned on his flashlight to reveal an unholy shrine. Before the men was a basement cathedral filled with red-eyed rats scurrying about, candles burned to their wicks, hay, balled-up newspaper, and filthy blankets scattered across the floor. The smell of dried seminal fluid and rancid body odor made the two men gag.

"This is it, Bones," Frank whispered. "This is their lair."

"How do you know? It could be just some homeless people that live down here."

"They are homeless, buddy." Frank's beam of light searched for a cavity in the walls or floor, where he knew they'd find the Cop Killer's stash.

"I'm not so sure, Frankie Boy." Just as he said that, Frank got his attention.

"Bonesie, over here." Frank waved over his partner. "Look at this!"

Frank turned and illuminated a loose stone in the wall at the base of an interior window that likely led to an old office or classroom back in the day. "Here, hold this." Frank handed Bones the flashlight.

Bones was surprised when seeing his partner pull the stone from the wall. "Holy shit!"

Reaching into the wall, Frank pulled out two police badges, one on a ball chain, and one torn from a light blue police uniform, the fabric still clutching the badge. As Frank dug deeper, he pulled out a gun and another badge.

"We gotta call this in, Frank."

"Yes, *YOU* do, Bones."

Back up on street level, ten minutes earlier, two vagrants, a man, and a woman approached the Devil's Gate. Seeing two sets of footprints in the snow leading to the entrance of their unholy shrine, they fled when they noticed only one set walking through the gate and the other presumably jumping the fence. Both killers knew no homeless person would've jumped the fence knowing the gate lock had been broken for years. They knew Frank Collazo was closing in on them and knew he had brought his friend with him.

The Cop Killers would search for a new home as their underworld would soon be flooded with uniformed officers from the 3rd and 17th Districts. Later that night, Captain Justin Smith would be on the local news telling viewers, "The noose is tightening around the necks of our killers."

Chapter 33 – FalconClaw

Later that night, back at the hotel, Frank and Bones discussed what was found in the basement of St. Peter's Claver as the four watched Justin Smith brief the press with an update on the case. Smith mentioned nothing of Jon Bones Sullivan or Frank Collazo in his statement to the media.

Frank turned off the television and turned to the group. "Candace, I'm not sure if Doug has told you, but he'll be leaving for New Hampshire in the morning. It might be a good idea for you to go back up to Montreal, at least for a couple of weeks. It's just not safe down here, especially if Doug won't be here in the hotel with you."

Candace looked confused and almost frightened. "I'm not leaving! We're too close to finishing this thing." She turned to Cantrell. "Doug, don't leave yet."

Cantrell had reasons for leaving that Candace wasn't aware of. He knew Frank as well as any living person, and he thought it was selfish of him to give up and not work through his loss. There were people that cared for him, and no one more than Douglas Cantrell.

"Well, think it over, and we can talk tomorrow." Frank turned to Cantrell. "Doug, what time do you fly?"

"Eight o'clock." Doug was purposely brief.

"Okay, I'll swing by at six to pick you up. It'll still be dark outside, so stay in the lobby until I come in to get you." Frank looked awkwardly at his friend, wanting to hug him.

"Well, it's getting late. We should go." Frank walked toward the door with Bones in tow.

The elevator ride down was quiet, but once downstairs, Frank and Bones chatted briefly before going their separate ways.

"What's next, Frank?"

"You gotta few minutes before we get out of here?" Frank motioned Bones over to the couch near the fireplace.

"Sure, Frank."

The two men sat down and stared at the flames for a minute before speaking. It was as if they took solace in the crackling sounds and the warmth emanating from the fire. Bones would like nothing more than to stay at the hotel and be near Candace, even if it was in the room next to hers, without her ever knowing. Anywhere but the home that took another piece of his soul each time he walked through its doors.

Frank remembered the day Penny took him back to his childhood home that she had remodeled for him after he recovered from the gunshot wound he suffered in the basement of FalconClaw, courtesy of Cameron St. John. Frank remembered their first winter there, their first winter as a family, with little Bonnie on the way. Penny lit a fire almost every night; she wanted their new life together to be warm, satisfying, and safe. Frank felt like he had failed her in that regard. He believed that if he had been driving the car that day, if only he had gone with them, then perhaps maybe he could have steered the Accord clear of the oncoming truck. Frank punished himself every day for failing to keep his family safe. He felt the only way to salvage what little was left of his worth was to avenge the murder of Penny and Bonnie. Frank wanted his family more than life. So be it if he lost his life avenging theirs.

"Listen, man. The Walker twins want a showdown up at FalconClaw, and I'm going to give it to them." Frank looked around to ensure no one was listening. "I want you there, Bones, but I can't ask you to go with me."

Bones looked perplexed. "Where you go, I go. You forget that, Partner?"

Frank shook his head in frustration.

"Bones, I'm not coming out of there alive, and I can't risk you dying trying to save me."

"Sounds like you don't want to be saved, Frankie Boy. Is that what I'm hearing?" Bones was troubled by Frank's admission but not his words. He knew Frank longed for his family and entertained the notion that death might somehow bring them all closer.

Frank was stuck. He didn't want to lie to his friend. In his assertion, he thought Bones was right on but didn't want to come out and say it. "It's not that," Frank shook his head again. "It's just...."

"Frank, you got me all turned around." Bones continued to be confused. "You say you don't believe in God, and yet you somehow believe that dying will bring your family back together with you. Which is it? You either believe in heaven, or you don't?"

Frank again looked around the lobby. He didn't want anyone to hear what he was about to say. He wasn't even sure that he wanted Bones to hear it. "Bones, do you believe in ghosts?"

"You mean like spirits that come around and make their presence known to loved ones? Stuff like that?"

"Yeah, kinda."

"I mean, sure, but I've never experienced anything like it before." Bones lied. One of the reasons he would sometimes sleep in his car was because the side porch light on his house would sometimes flicker, turning off and on when no one was there. He always thought it was his mother welcoming him home or his father telling him to stay away.

"Do you remember when I mentioned that I saw Penny before?"

"Yeah. But I'll be honest with you, Frank. That shit scared me. Not that ghosts existed, but the thought that you saw one. I thought you were starting to go a little crazy."

"Listen to me, man. I see Penny all the time. We talk to each other."

Bones felt uncomfortable again, just as he had in October when Frank first told him about it. "Frank, you're hurting, man. People suffering from losing a loved one see what they want to see...."

"It's not just her, Bones." Frank searched for the right words. He knew the conversation would be hard on his friend. He desperately hoped not to drive him away.

"Whattaya mean? You mean you see Bonnie, too?"

Frank nodded, but his face suggested there were more.

"Frank, tell me. Who else do you see?" Bones wanted to believe his friend. If Frank were telling the truth, it would change everything he believed in. But if Frank saw something that wasn't there, then his friend had gone crazy. Bones didn't know which one terrified him more.

"Okay, brace yourself, Bonesie. You're not gonna believe this."

Bones took a deep breath and then leaned in.

Frank looked both ways and said, "I see Frank Bruno and a man named Garrison Winter. He's from the 1920s...."

Bones shook his head, not knowing what to say.

"I see Isak Cameron, too. And his brother, The Schuylkiller...."

Bones was both shocked and intrigued. He could see in Frank's eyes that his friend wasn't crazy. "What about your mother or your father? Do you see them?" Bones started to think about the blinking porchlight again. Perhaps it was his mother or father trying to communicate with him.

"I've never seen my mother since she passed, but I see my father from time to time." Frank thought of his father and back to his childhood.

Bones tried to fight off his emotions, but a tear ran down his left cheek. He was frightened. "Frank, I think my parents try to communicate with me. They turn the porch lights on and off sometimes. I don't know which one, but I'm not crazy. I see the lights blink. That's why I hate going home after dark."

"You're not crazy, Bones." Frank squeezed his friend's shoulder in a show of empathy. He knew what Bones felt and wanted him to know he wasn't alone in his private hell. "It might be your mom welcoming you home or telling you to come inside."

Bones let go of another tear. "I think it's my father telling me he hates me." Bones dropped his head into his hands.

"They guide me, Bonesie. They help me to solve cases."

Bones looked up at Frank, alarmed by his words, now openly crying. The notion that his mother might still be looking after him all these years later ripped his heart out. "What are you talking about? What do you mean, they guide you? You believe they might be looking out for you?"

"Penny led me to the Scrabble tile. She told me to look in her trunk. I found the letter C there. I carried it around with me for weeks before looking to see what letter it was. Penny was trying to tell me that she and Bonnie were the first victims in the case."

"Her trunk?" Bones was mystified. "Why didn't you tell me about this sooner? That letter C altered the course of the investigation."

"I couldn't tell you because I didn't want to believe she was dead. She would be there when I went back to the house sometimes."

"You're not fucking with me, right?"

"Of course not. No way there's a god or heaven, but our spirits linger, Bones. They're still with us. I'm sure of it." Frank was unflinching. "It was Frank Bruno that saved me in the basement of FalconClaw. He alerted me that Cameron St. John had arrived. He saved Penny, too."

"Did Penny see the ghosts?"

"I don't think so. She definitely felt Bruno's presence, though."

"Tell me more."

"Cindy Stafford sent me a sign too. I saw her behind the Creative Minds daycare a couple of times," revealed Frank. "I would've been dead a long time ago without them helping me."

"You got me not wanting to go home, man." Bones laughed through his tears. He thought he would lose his mind if he sat in his garage again and saw the porch light flicker. He would be terrified.

"Embrace it, Bonesie. If and when I die, I'll be paying you a visit, brother." Frank laughed instead of crying. "Maybe even help you catch a bad guy or two."

After a few moments of silence and reflection, Frank stood and said, "It's late. I'm gonna get outta here."

Bones joined Frank in standing and said, "Wait a second. We didn't discuss what comes next. Where do we go from here?"

"We wait."

"For what?"

"Those two motherfuckers are gonna call me soon," said Frank. "And when they do, I'm going to invite them up to where it all began...."

"FalconClaw," Bones finished Frank's thought. "If you go there without me, we're not friends anymore. You got that?"

"I'll be sure to send an invite." Frank smiled at his friend.

Before leaving, Frank walked out onto the Riverwalk and looked up and down the Schuylkill. He was looking for a sign. Suddenly he heard a rasping kack-kack-kack-kack overhead, causing him to look skyward. The snowy landscape and its reflective value helped Frank to make out a black silhouette flying high above between him and the moon. Not sure if it was a falcon, he chose to believe that it was. Was it a welcome or a warning? Frank couldn't be sure.

Early the next morning, Frank pulled back into the hotel parking lot and jumped out of his running vehicle to retrieve Doug from the lobby. He'd texted him along the way, but Doug didn't respond. Looking around the lobby and the breakfast area, Doug was nowhere to be found. Alarmed, Frank tried Doug's cell again, and when it went straight to voicemail, he approached the front desk and waited for the morning attendant. After less than thirty seconds, young Penny came out, bringing some relief to Frank.

"Hi, Penny. Can you ring Douglas Cantrell's room for me?"

"I'm sorry, Mr. Collazo, but Mr. Cantrell has already checked out. He grabbed an Uber about fifteen minutes ago. I believe he was heading for the airport because he had his rollaboard and a carry-on bag with him."

"Right." Frank tapped nervously on the desk and turned to leave, thinking he could get to the airport before Cantrell's 8 am flight.

As he walked into the vestibule, young Penny yelled, "I'll see you soon, Frank!"

Now out on the sidewalk, doors closed behind him, Frank turned to look back at young Penny but saw his Penny standing behind the counter instead. Immediately walking back in, he saw young Penny again.

"Can I help you with something else, Mr. Collazo?" she asked.

A confused Frank said, "No. No. That's okay." He shook his head and walked back outside.

Frank called Doug several times along the way to the airport but got no answer. After arriving, he lit up his blue flashers, parked illegally, and ran into the airport. As he tried to get through the security checkpoint, he was stopped and asked for his ticket.

"I'm a Philly Detective, and I need to get through to catch someone before they board a flight."

The TSA security guard waved two fingers and said, "Let's see some I.D."

Frank reached for his shield, closed his eyes, and said Fuck!"

"Let me guess...."

"Listen, my name is Frank Collazo. I need to get through."

"I've never heard the name before. Come back when you have a boarding pass or a badge."

Frank clenched his teeth and growled, angry with himself.

Getting back into his car, he saw a gray-haired man standing on the curb as if waiting for a ride. Looking closer, he saw Cantrell appear in the breaking dawn.

"Doug! Is that you?!"

The older gentleman turned toward Frank, released the handle of his rollaboard, and began walking briskly along the way, setting his laptop bag on the ground, not worried about its contents.

The two men embraced and cried. "I couldn't leave you, Frank. I couldn't go!"

"Doug, I thought you left. I couldn't get through security. I couldn't get to you!" Frank held his friend.

"I want to see it through, Frank. I want to be here when it ends. No matter the outcome." Doug embraced his friend tightly.

After things quieted down with no words from the killers, the call finally came ten days later. Frank was in Michigan, staying at Joanne's house. "Pardon me, guys." Frank excused himself from the kitchen table to take the call. Now in the living room, he answered the call from a private number.

"Hello?"

"Well, hello, Collazo." The raspy voice of a woman brought an end to his peaceful trip.

"So, when are we meeting, Genesis?"

"You die at midnight on Christmas Eve, in the belly of FalconClaw. Just like your pathetic old man," said Genesis Walker. "There's a mechanical room under the skating rink in FalconClaw Park's City Square. You'll need to access the south parking garage first, and from there, go fuck yourself with how to gain access to it. We'll be there, you piece of shit!"

"Well, this is an early Christmas present," said Frank. "And like a Christmas present, I'm going to open your skull and see what kind of disease makes you tick."

FalconClaw would open on December 26 and be ready to host thousands of patrons between then and New Year's Day. Until then, though, it would lay mostly dormant, with workers and contractors finishing their punch lists while city inspectors signed off on building permits.

"Well, I already know what makes you tick.... A dead father."

"Touché, Genesis. I'll be there. Just make sure you and Junior are heavily armed cuz I'm coming for you." Frank heard the song *Take Me to Church* blaring in the background. "And don't forget what I said about getting a shower or a bath first. Maybe you guys can find a puddle of melted snow or something...." Frank looked at his phone and saw that the call had ended. It was December 21, and he still had one more day with his son before returning home.

Entering the kitchen with a smile, Frank said, "Hey, Con Man...."

"Yeah, Dad?"

"Whattaya say we go ice fishing tomorrow? It's my last day, and we've never gone fishing before, ever."

"Frank, it's a little cold for that, don't you think?" asked Joanne, pouring a second cup of coffee.

"That's why they call it ice fishing, Jo. Duh!" Frank winked at Conner.

"Yeah, Mom!" Conner piled on, laughing at his mother.

"So whattaya say, Son? Wanna go?"

"Heck yeah!" said Conner, his voice getting deeper by the day. He would be turning fifteen in February. Frank noted that Conner was a striking young man, and he couldn't help but to think he was fourteen years old, the same age as he was when he lost his father.

The next morning the two sat in an ice shanty on Lake Erie, and Conner said, "This isn't as fun as I thought it would be."

"It will be once we catch some fish. You'll see."

Frank, like Conner, was freezing but making the best of the precious little time he had left with his son. "We gotta bait the hook better. You can't just feed the hook all the way through the worm's body. You have to make sure it can wiggle a little. That's what gets the fish's attention."

Conner looked on as his dad zigzagged the worm onto the hook, ensuring it wouldn't fall off in the water. Frank handed the rod to Conner and said, "Go ahead, drop it in, Son."

Conner lowered the line into the twelve-inch hole, and the two would wait. Less than a minute later, there was a tug on the line, and the two Collazo men began to celebrate.

Struggling to pull the line up through the hole, the two laughed. When they saw the size of the Walleye coming up through the ice, they laughed even harder, nearly peeing their pants. The two Collazo men fished for three hours and returned everything they had caught back to the lake.

Later in the shanty, while drinking hot chocolate, Frank said, "I love you, Conner. I wish things would've worked out differently between your mom and me. I wish you had a normal life. That's all I ever wanted for you."

"It's okay, Dad. I'm almost fifteen now. Before you know it, I'll be driving down to visit you during the summers."

"Yeah, about that, Con Man." Frank paused, knowing that his son would likely remember his next statement until the day he died.

"Conner, listen. Life's about to get hard, Son. Being a man brings new challenges every day. There will be days when you won't want to look forward, only behind. When your days are toughest, I want you to remember days like this one, not those you choose to forget."

Frank looked his son directly in the eyes and said, "You're never really gone until you're forgotten. I hope you never forget me as you grow into manhood, and remember that no matter how far away I seem, I'll always be close by. When you want to see me, look into your heart, and I'll be there. Always."

"You getting all emotional on me, Dad?"

"Yeah, maybe I am a little." Frank had to look away for a moment, not wanting Conner to see the tears welling in his eyes. "It's just that when I leave tomorrow, I want you to know that I'm gonna miss you until we can see each other again."

"I'll miss you, too, Dad."

Frank's mind raced forward to Christmas Eve, and he looked back to Conner and said, "Let's catch one more, Son."

Frank boarded a plane the next day, and the two would never see each other again.

The following day, Thursday, December 23, Frank and Bones met in Frank's tiny apartment to discuss what would happen on Christmas Eve.

"I brought the blueprint of the skating rink, the parking garage below it, and the mechanical room located on the west side of the parking garage." Bones laid out the architectural drawing across Frank's coffee table that had been hastily repaired after being damaged when the two men fought a month earlier. The two men sat on the couch, and Bones opened the drawings.

Frank perused the drawings and said, "Now, where's a good place for them to hide out?"

"You think they're already there, don't you?" asked Bones.

"They're not under that rat-infested church anymore. So they might as well be."

"Yeah, but they wouldn't take that chance after telling you to meet them there." Bones rubbed his chin, thinking about it. "They probably were hiding out there, got the lay of the land, and then got the hell out of there after calling you thinking that you would've called it in."

"Either way, let's look for a crow's nest they can hide in the hours before my arrival."

Bones looked at Frank and said, "You mean *our* arrival, don't you?"

"Yeah, of course." Frank got caught thinking out loud.

"Frank, don't fuck around and go all solo on me. We're either doing this together, or I'm bringing fifty cops with me. You got it?"

"Yes, of course. Calm down, man. I misspoke," Frank lied.

Looking back at the blueprints and pointing, Frank said, "This seems to be the only way in and out of the mechanical room. Am I crazy?"

Bones studied the prints and said, "It looks like that's it." He pondered and added, "Frank, that means it's gonna happen before we ever get to that room. No way they're not giving themselves a way out."

"Bones, those two lunatics want to die." Frank sat back on the couch and added, "They have nothing left to live for. They've killed at least twelve people, are in an incestuous love affair, are homeless, on the run, and have outdone their serial killer father, he said. "Trust me, if we don't kill them, they'll kill each other."

"So that makes our lives even harder, then."

"Yep." Frank nodded. "I'm afraid so, Partner."

"If they have nothing to live for, they won't think rationally. Everything is on the table." Bones sat back, too. "It's gonna be hard to predict what they'll do."

"It's a suicide mission," said Frank. "Kill and be killed." Before thinking of Penny and Bonnie, his mind went to Conner for a fleeting moment. He thought Conner would forgive him because he died while killing those responsible for murdering his family. Then Frank thought of his father. He wondered if his dad ever thought that Vincent Charmaine Walker was a threat to him and his mother. *If he did*, Frank thought, he never mentioned it.

"Okay, so we load up. Three sidearms, flashlights, cuffs, Kevlar, and a shotgun. Each of us," said Frank. "Pretty sure we won't need the cuffs, though."

"It'll play out better when our boys arrive if we do. If we don't have cuffs, it'll look like we went there to kill our suspects."

"I like the way you think, Bones. But I've made it pretty clear that that's exactly what will happen."

"Either way, we should take 'em."

After another hour of planning, the two men agreed on how the night would go. The end result needed to include the bad guys dead and the good guys alive. They both agreed.

"So, what time, then?"

"Eleven o'clock sharp," said Frank. "We park down on Bedford and get to the skating rink by 11:15, suit up, divide and conquer."

Frank and Bones met at the hotel the next day and discretely reviewed their plans again. Before Frank left, he got hugs, *'Good lucks'* and *'Be carefuls'* from Candace and Doug.

"We'll do," said Bones. "Be outside when I pull up."

"I'll be there," said Frank. "This madness ends tonight."

Frank drove to his old house on East Locust Avenue and got out to see if Penny was around. Sitting on the back porch, he remembered the day of the accident. He remembered seeing Penny walking to the car as he cut the grass. He remembered Bonnie's little head lying on her mother's shoulder. Frank remembered it like it was yesterday. He would see them again tonight. He hoped.

A few hours later, Frank pulled up to the old front gates of FalconClaw at 888 Bedford Street and looked out into the darkness. FalconClaw Park hadn't opened yet, so almost none of the common area lights were illuminated.

Looking at his cell phone, it was 10:45 pm, and Bones wouldn't arrive at the Mad River to pick him up for another fifteen minutes. *It'll be done by the time he figures it all out and eventually gets over here.* Frank thought to himself. "I love that guy," he said aloud, smiling. "The second-best partner I ever had."

Sitting in his car, as the snow picked up, Frank closed his eyes again and saw Penny and Bonnie walking through a park. Both looked back and smiled. When Frank opened his eyes again, it was Halloween morning, 1974, and he saw Frank Bruno walk up to the rusted gate. Pushing his way through, Bruno walked over to the gatehouse just inside and to the left of FalconClaw's main gates.

Moments later, Frank was standing on the sidewalk and saw Penny Bryce show up. "I see you found the gatehouse," he heard Penny say to Bruno as she pushed through the fence.

"It's kind of quaint." Frank heard Bruno say to Penny Bryce. "It makes you wonder what it was like when all of this was shiny new."

"Yeah?! Well, wait until you see the inside!" Penny shivered. "This whole place freaks me out. Can you imagine what this place must be like at night?" Frank Collazo sat back and watched the legendary detectives interacting back in the day.

Frank Collazo heard a thunder crack while standing at the gate, followed by a frigid gust of wind as it rolled down off the hill. When it did, it wiped away the ghosts of 1974.

Standing alone again, contemplating entering the grounds of the infamous estate, Frank looked to his right when he heard two men approaching. Looking closely, he saw his father and Diego Ramirez walking up to the gates almost as if to join him.

Frank heard Diego say, "Why'd they go back to the name Heavenly Gates, anyway? There's nothing heavenly about it." Frank watched as Ramirez stared blankly up the hill. "This place gives me the creeps," Frank heard him say.

"Yeah, and what's with the name FalconClaw?" came the words from his father, Salvatore. Feeling yesteryear crashing down on him like an avalanche of snow from high up on the hill, Frank began to cry. Seeing and hearing his father again was unsettling but cathartic. "Birds don't have claws. They have talons," he heard him say.

Frank wanted to reach out and touch his father but feared he would slip away with the next gust of wind as Bryce and Bruno had moments before.

Frank listened as Diego said to his father, "Listen, Sal. I have a bad feeling about this place. Not just the place but this day, this moment. It doesn't feel like we're supposed to be here right now."

"That's cuz we're not supposed to be here," Sal said to his partner. "Whatta you goin' all religious on me? The element of surprise, my friend. That's how you catch the bad guys."

Frank looked on as his father pushed through the rusty gate and walked through, scuffing the top of his new shoes on the bottom of one of the posts. "Dammit!" he heard his father say.

"Easy, Partner. They're just shoes," said Diego.

Frank knew it wasn't the shoes that made his father mad. He knew his father was thinking about him and regretting not going to his baseball game.

Frank tried to stop his father from climbing the hill to the sleeping giant. Just as he reached for him, though, another gust of wind rolled off the hill and blew away the ghosts of 1992.

Frank stood there and wept. Suddenly it was Christmas Eve 1974, and Frank heard a car's engine revving as it turned onto Bedford Street, the sound of *Witchy Woman* by the *Eagles* blaring as it did. Frank jumped out of the way as Frank Bruno crashed his Buick through the gates, trying to save his friend and partner from Old Man Winter. Looking up the hill, he saw Penny Bryce and Garrison Old Man Winter disappear around the southeast corner of the estate.

Frank started to hear a faint ticking in his ear, wincing as a sharp, searing pain ran through the center of his head. All he could hear was a CSX train roaring over the Schuylkill in a blizzard. *To where? Hell*, Frank thought.

Frank rubbed his eyes, blinded by the white visual snow in his head. Opening them again, he saw Frank Bruno and Garrison Winter. The men stood outside the gates looking at him and then up the hill to the mansion. With a lift of Bruno's chin, motioning for Frank to proceed, he knew it was time to meet his destiny.

As Frank righted his mind and body and inventoried his small arsenal, he looked up at the behemoth and took one step onto the estate of the 1992 version of FalconClaw. It was that version of the mansion that had led him here today. It was the one that altered the course of his past, present, and future. FalconClaw had sunk its Talons into Frank back in 1992 and spawned twin killers who took everything from him. It was time for payback, and Frank Collazo would not only kill those who took his family but would kill the memory of the man who killed his father and who would ultimately leave his son, Conner, fatherless.

Chapter 34 – A Deathless Death

At the top of the hill, Frank didn't see the shiny new infrastructure that awaited North Philly's elite, but rather the near decrepit heap as it looked back on Halloween 1992, just four years shy of its permanent shuttering. On this day, however, it was a wintry Christmas Eve, and the wind howled, stirring the ghosts of yesteryear. As Frank studied the faces of Old Man Winter and Frank Bruno, who were standing next to him, he looked up at the massive double doors flanked by twenty-foot-tall marble columns, two on each side, when they suddenly opened. Frank thought the squeal of their rusty hinges was so loud that the dead inside would surely be awakened.

Back in the Dodge, parked haphazardly down on Bedford Street, Frank's cell phone buzzed. Bones was texting him, saying he was downstairs on Main Street, parked in front of the Mad River.

Back up on top of the hill, Frank admired the grand entrance. It was an entryway built to welcome home a king. *More like a ruler presiding over the kingdom of hell,* he thought.

Frank Collazo had the upper hand. Frank Bruno and Garrison Winter had transformed the blueprint he and Bones had studied for hours into a familiar landscape. It was one that Frank had navigated and grown familiar with since first setting foot on the FalconClaw estate back in 2017. While the Cop Killers would see FalconClaw Park, Frank would see the old FalconClaw estate. His upper hand would seek out and attempt to eradicate the evil that now inhabited FalconClaw.

As Frank moved through the unhallowed halls, deeper into the bowels of the giant, he could hear music in the distance. The familiar lyrics of *Take Me to Church* occupied the air, and he breathed it in.

The heavens seemed to be speaking to both Frank and the unholy pair.

Frank crept along slowly through the halls, and it seemed to get younger with each step. Suddenly a light emanated from the end of the now grand foyer, and the sounds of evil lyrics were replaced with holiday cheer. Walking toward the light, Frank heard chatter, lots of it. Turning into the grand dining hall, he saw dozens of people celebrating. *A Christmas party,* he thought. Nothing made sense.

Frank saw dozens of people dressed up for the holiday, all laughing and carrying on. Unable to reconcile what he saw, all the patrons appeared dressed in clothing from several different periods in time. In the crowd, he spotted Garrison Winter standing in the middle of the room with ten other people. From what Frank could see, Winter appeared to be the center of their attention. Before he turned the corner, Garrison Winter abruptly turned his head in his direction, somehow spotting Frank through the large crowd. Tilting his head and surrounded by saints, Winter held up his glass and saluted him with a smile. When he did, the others in the circle, six men and four women, all turned to look at Frank and raised their glasses in recognition of him. The look on Winter's face suddenly made Frank feel comfortable with his surroundings. Without recognizing the people standing near Winter, he felt as if he knew them. Looking closer at one of the females in the group who turned toward him, Frank's breath was taken away. The woman standing to Winter's right appeared to Frank to be the legendary Penny Bryce.

As Frank stood in awe, something behind him, further down the hall, got his attention. Suddenly, like an ice pick through his brain, he heard an elevator roar to life and was taken back to April 2017 and his first visit to FalconClaw. Now, like then, something or someone was pulling him down the long hallway. Frank could see a light emanating up from the long-retired elevator shaft.

Frank was no longer comfortable in the old mansion. Turning to look behind him, he saw the light from the dining hall fade along with the chatter of the long-dead. The festive holiday music ground to a halt as the tired gears of a broken elevator screamed back to life and began to raise the elevator from its forgotten depths. Now standing before a conveyor to hell, Frank heard the crack of a baseball followed by the cheers of a crowd. He then heard a man crying, followed by the words, "I'm coming, Son! Don't leave! Wait for me!" the voice cried from the depths.

And just as suddenly as it started, it all stopped. The long hall now had a beacon of light to guide Frank further into his journey.... His destiny. A welcoming presence appeared at the end of the hall; it was Frank's father, Salvatore Collazo. The senior Collazo waved his son on, beckoning him to take the final few steps in his passage. Frank smiled, seeing his father, but his smile, like his father, disappeared into the darkness. His dad was gone, along with Frank's hope.

Tearing up, Frank cried out, "Dad!"

Holstering his gun, he hastily walked toward the doorway. As he got closer, he heard his father say, "Come on, Son! Hurry! They're down there!"

Frank cried again for his father, and as he rounded the bend into and through the doorway, he saw his father standing next to an unlocked door. Terrified but determined, Frank moved closer to his father. When he did, his father's voice got shallower until he heard his dad's final whisper. "They're down there, Son."

Frank reached for the empty void occupied by his father just moments before and then fell to his knees and cried. "Dad!" he screamed. "Dad!"

Frank was suddenly cold again. A sobering gust of wintry air reminded him of where he was. Another told him why.

After traversing rickety basement stairs into the depths of FalconClaw, Frank sensed that he was in the parking garage beneath the ice-skating rink. Pipes clanking overhead and the faint whisper of the storm blowing above rivaled the evil lyrics that served as an anthem for two desperate lovers.

The parking garage had become the Cop Killers' new shrine, and they were there to worship their twisted union. Like the song lyrics that echoed, the two were born sick. They were born monsters, and they loved it.

The song emanating from two different cell phones grew louder. Frank knew the killers would not be found at the source of the music, which came from two cell phones placed in separate locations. Undistracted by the song set to repeat, Frank detected something that would help him locate his killers.

Bones began calling Frank's cell phone after receiving no response to his texts. At 10:50 pm, after several calls went to voicemail, Bones stepped out onto a frigid snow-blown Main Street and pounded on the street-level door that led up to Frank's third-floor apartment.

After his attempts to get in failed, Bones made his way to the back of the building, walking down the Shurs' Lane entrance of the back parking lot of the Mad River bar. When Bones turned the corner and failed to see Frank's Dodge, he panicked. He knew that Frank wanted to go it alone from the beginning and knew he was outnumbered two to one and that he wouldn't be there to have his partner's back.

Bones raced to his Ford Interceptor and threw it down into drive, his spinning tires kicking up snow, salt, and slag. Normally a ten-minute drive, Bones knew it would still take at least six to seven minutes due to the snow and now icy conditions. Breaking his pact with Frank, Bones called the front desk of the 39th and instructed them to have every unit in the fleet turn north to Old Germantown and the parking garage beneath the ice-skating rink in the middle of FalconClaw Park's City Square.

The music blared.... Another sacrifice was demanded, and Talon would do his lover's bidding. If he wasn't up for the task, Genesis would attempt to complete the hungry work.

While the music was meant to distract him and inspire the killers, Frank had an ace up his sleeve. In the pristine, untarnished conditions of the new structure, he detected a familiar stench, one he'd smelled two weeks earlier in the basement of St. Peter's Claver. It was the fetid odor of two repugnant killers, and it would give them away.

As Frank looked around, his Smith & Wesson leading the way, the pernicious ticking in his ear was back. Wincing at the pain, his vision went white, and his familiar surroundings disappeared into the visual snow that now hindered his sight. Stopping in his tracks and trying to shake the crippling sights and sounds disabling his senses, he shook off the blizzard in his head and saw the unfamiliar parking garage beneath the skating rink.

Regaining his sight, Frank saw that FalconClaw of 1992 had turned back into FalconClaw Park. Through the darkness of the poorly lit garage, Frank saw a door labeled *Mechanical Room*.

Frank would now have to rely solely on his memory of the blueprints and his sense of smell. He knew the twins were close. To his right, Frank saw one of two cellphones lying on the ground next to one of the many two-foot by two-foot cement pillars that ran north to south through the garage. Getting closer, he looked in all directions as the music echoed through the empty garage.

The words of Hozier screamed until Frank, now standing over the phone, crushed it beneath his boot as a gunshot rang out, the bullet ricocheting off the cement walls and floor nearby. Ducking behind a pillar, Frank looked out and saw a shadow dip into the Mechanical Room and would follow.

Now at the door, its handle broken, Frank looked for his guardian angels, but they were nowhere to be found. Pushing the steel door open, he entered the dimly lit room that got darker the further back it went. The echoing music was muffled by the room's many generators and IT systems, all hard at work. When turning the light switch to the on position, Frank only heard a muted click, but no light came on.

Looking around the room, he saw many places to hide. There were desks, small crates, IT racks, and vertical pipes, one foot wide, in clusters of four, that ran down the center of the room, which had ten-foot ceilings and was roughly half the size of a basketball court.

Inside the room, another shot rang out, and Frank ducked behind an IT rack in the northwest corner and now detected the foul stench of his destiny getting closer. Outside the room, in the parking garage, Frank heard the squealing tires of Bones' Interceptor as it navigated the down ramp of the garage. Seconds later, he heard the car skid to a stop. With the Ford's engine off, so Bones could better listen for his partner and suspects, Frank heard distant sirens muted by the heavy snowfall up on ground level.

Frank had to work quickly. These were his kills, and only he would avenge the death of his family. He would not let Bones steal his moment. Feeling immortal, Frank stepped from behind the IT rack and, without fear, walked down the middle of the room, gun pointed into the governing darkness.

As the music grew louder, the situation became more tense. Out of the dark and smiling in the distance, bad teeth serving as a backdrop to a stolen Glock, Talon Grayson Walker got off a shot, just as Frank did. Hearing the two explosions, Bones rushed through the door, flashlight and gun leading the charge, just in time to see Talon Walker hit the floor, his brain matter painting the wall behind where he stood. Looking at Frank, the blood ran from Bones' face.

The music screamed through the darkness, followed by a shadow. The flashlight reflected the killer's weapon of choice. The shadow, Genesis Harper Walker, would attempt to complete the circle in a ritualist fashion that she felt was her birthright.

Frank, turning toward his partner, smiled. His face warmed by his coming destiny; he was at peace. When he did, a shadow lurched forward, out of the pitch, and ran toward him. Her steely blade raised high overhead. Frank didn't see Genesis bearing down on him from his right side and was vulnerable to her attack.

In the fog of war, death, murder, and desperation, everything went into slow motion for Bones. Lunging toward her muse, just before Genesis plunged her knife into Frank's exposed neck, Bones struck her down midflight with a single bullet.

Bones ran frantically toward his partner.

Frank, again happy to see Bones, wiped blood from his mouth and nose, thinking that Genesis had sprayed him with her blood as she fell in a heap onto the floor.

Frank suddenly felt happy, his smile bringing little comfort to his partner. Suddenly the image of Bones running toward him was replaced. Frank looked around and saw his backyard. As his hand ran along the scars in the fence, he noticed that his sense of touch, sight, and smell seemed keen and vivid, and the wind on his face was divine. He heard the door to the back of his house open and turned to see Penny standing there, her head tilted, with her usual smile, hands tucked submissively into her back pockets. Frank's smile grew at the sight of her and grew bigger when out of the door stepped little Bonnie. Starting to run toward her father, she was stopped by her mother, who, without words, waved her finger at Bonnie as if to say, *Not yet.*

Frank, staring lovingly at his family, was confused when he saw someone standing in the shadow of the dark kitchen and stepping out onto the back porch. Looking closer, he saw it was his father, Salvatore, behind him, a small boy. Frank saw little Isak and smiled through his confusion, no longer trying to understand.

Looking to his right, Old Man Winter and Frank Bruno stood in front of the garage. Someone else was with them this time. Stepping out from behind Frank Bruno was a woman wearing a brand-new gray trench coat. Frank's eyes went to a small rust-colored stain on her lapel, strangely causing him to smile.

Looking back to his family, he tried taking one step toward them, but something was obstructing his path. Looking down, he was terrified when he saw Bones cradling his head as he bled from the mouth and nose, the front of his jacket soaked with blood, with a tiny hole at its center.

Startled, Frank looked back up to his family and saw Penny release little Bonnie, and that little girl ran. She ran to her father, and Frank ran to his little girl.

"Daddy! Daddy!" Bonnie yelled as she ran.

Catching his little Bonnie, he lifted her high over his head and twirled her around, dropping her into his waiting arms, and they hugged. As they hugged, Frank looked at Penny and saw her waving, telling him to come home.

Letting Bonnie down, Frank looked beside him, and his heart bled. He saw Bones holding onto his best friend, screaming his name through unbearable sorrow and pain. Before joining his family on the porch, Frank looked at the others near the garage and nodded his gratitude.

Frank Bruno, like usual, tipped his fedora in Frank's direction as if to say, *You did good, Son.* Frank nodded as if to say, *Thanks.* Frank's eyes then went to Garrison Winter, and the old man just nodded his approval. As they walked away, Penny Bryce, in frustration, scratching away at the rust stain on her jacket, looked over to Frank, and mouthed the words, *"See you around, Detective."*

Looking back to the porch, Frank saw Isak extend his hand to Bonnie, and the two ran back inside while Penny whispered something to his father. Frank saw his father nod in the affirmative and joined the others inside. Penny then turned toward Frank and, with her eyes, told him to come home.

Back in the bowels of FalconClaw Park, Bones held his friend as a sinister, smiling shadow rose from her hell, plunged her dagger through his Kevlar vest, and deep into Bones' back as the lyrics continued to ring overhead.

Placing Frank's head gently onto the ground, the knife still in his back, Bones rose to his feet as the joy on Genesis' face turned to one of dread. Looking up at a growling giant standing over her, she cowered as Bones took her by the neck, raised her over his head, and slammed her to the cement floor. There, he straddled her waist, clutched her throat with both hands, and strangled what little soul she had left out of her body.

As Frank stepped up onto the porch, he was almost afraid to touch Penny, fearing she would disappear.

"Hey, Frankie," she said, smiling at her man.

"Hey, Penny." Frank was terrified that none of it was real.

"I was wondering if you wanted to come inside. My mom's in there and would love to see you again."

"Do you mean it, Penny? Are you sure?"

"I'm sure," said Penny, reaching out and taking Frank's hand.

As the two walked in, Penny first, Frank grabbed the door handle and went to pull it closed. Before closing it, Frank Collazo looked out at the scarred fence and smiled. Pressing his lips firmly together and nodding, he saw the fence was mended and no longer scarred. Nodding and smiling, Frank walked through the back door of the house, and for the first time since May 14, Frank Collazo was home.

Epilogue – For Sale

On a Sunday, just a month and a day since Frank died in the bowels of FalconClaw Park, my friend Bones Sullivan and I sat in Frank's old apartment above the Mad River Bar up in Manayunk. I watched as he quietly wrote in his journal. I know what you're thinking; Bones isn't the type to write his feelings down on paper. But that's precisely what he's done every day since Frank left us. It's been over four weeks, but it feels like years. We all feel a bit lost these days, but our memories of Frank and his family help us to cope.

Bones has been staying here at Frank's old place since being released from the hospital five days after Christmas and having two surgeries. As for me, I'm still over at the hotel at night, but during the day, I'm here with good old Bones. Somebody has to look after the young man. He's still hurting, as we all are.

The knife that Genesis Walker plunged into Bones' back was eight inches long, and doctors have told me that roughly five inches of that knife penetrated Bones' body. The knife entered his back between his spinal column and his scapula, whatever that is, and wedged itself between two ribs, not allowing Genesis to pull it out and strike again. The blade was driven deep enough to break two ribs and puncture Bones' right lung. Doctors said that the average person would have bowled over in pain and been unable to move their right arm due to nerve damage. Bones, however, was able to restrain his attacker and, with both hands, end the threat.

I've been up here with him most days since he decided to move in. Gaye and Candace have become pretty good friends, spending their days hanging around the hotel lobby, wondering when the two of us would make an appearance. Due to her extensive vocabulary, Gaye thought Candace would be good at Scrabble and offered to play with her to help pass the time and to remind her of her dear departed friend, Penny. Understandably though, Candace declined. I'm not sure I'll ever play the game again, either.

Looks like Gaye will be heading back up to New Hampshire tomorrow, and I'm sure I'll join her there soon, but like Bones, I just can't bring myself to leave my friend. Frank's spirit is so alive. I can feel his presence from time to time. I guess I'm hoping that if I stay, maybe, just maybe, he'll show himself to me. I'm terrified to leave. I'm scared I might miss my only chance to say goodbye to him, just one last time.

As for Candace? I'm not really sure what her plans are. The Philadelphia P.D. has offered her a full-time job as a *Special Consultant*, my old job. I laugh. Like FalconClaw from back in the day, judging everything around it for getting younger, newer, and more modern, the Philly P.D. may think I've passed my point of usefulness. I hope she takes the job, but I'd bet against it. This case took its toll on her as it did on all of us.

As for me, well, I'm just an old man now with not much left to offer. I still have my memories, though. I tell Gaye that if I ever start to forget my good friend.... well, she can take me out back and put an end to me. She gets mad when I say such things, and I tell her I'm just joking, but honestly, if I did lose my memories of Frank and all of his mountains and valleys, times of trouble, and times of triumph, I wouldn't want to be around. Like he loved Penny, I love that man more than life.

Thinking of Candace again, she seems a little lost. She wants to be there for Bones, but he's emotionally unavailable these days. He doesn't say too much to anyone. I'm sure she'll head back up to Montreal soon since the city of Philadelphia is no longer footing the bill for her hotel stay. That place isn't cheap, and it's just a matter of time before she leaves. I hope Bones will meet with her before she goes back, though. She really seems to like him, and he could use a friend right now, especially after I leave for New Hampshire.

I guess that Bones feels the same way about her. Those two have a real connection.... Even if they don't know it yet. Thinking of them reminds me of another couple I once knew, a couple that I won't soon forget.

I took him over to the hotel last Tuesday. It was only the second time I was able to drag him out of this shabby apartment. When I get him there, though, he just sits in the lobby staring into the flames.

Hanging out with him there last week, sitting where Frank and I used to sit, I turned to look out the atrium windows, and for a second, I could swear I saw Frank standing out on the Riverwalk. He was just standing there looking up at the Pencoyd Bridge and then out over The Schuylkill.... That damn river is evil. I'm sure of it. But it somehow connects me to him. God, I miss my friend! Every second of every day! His void is cold, and boy, does it make me shiver.

Bones just looked over and caught me crying again. I can see that he's crying a little, too, writing in that journal over there on the couch. I bet he's writing down every memory he has of Frank. Lest we forget, Frank always said you're never really dead until you're forgotten. If that's true, then my old friend isn't really gone because I think about him every waking moment. And I will think about him every day I have left in this life.

I miss the man, the father, and the person, but I don't miss the cop. I miss my friend, and I wish he had stayed retired, both times he walked away, once after The Schuylkiller and again after the Isak Cameron case. It's not his fault, though. It was destiny that wouldn't let the poor man rest. Evil kept finding him time and time again, and he felt responsible and obligated to protect his family from it. Sometimes I even think he felt he could protect his son Conner by no longer being around. Without him in the world, maybe the evil would finally stop trying to hurt the Collazo men and those Frank loved the most. I keep telling myself that, anyway. Call me a fool.

I remember back to the day of the funeral. Whew! That was a rough one. Seeing Frank's ashes laid next to Penny's and Bonnie's.... Man, that was the second worst day of my life. It was made even worse by the unbearable grief Conner expressed through his tears. It was heart wrenching. Seeing him brought to his knees reminded me of Frank's pain at the loss of his father and all the years he suffered and all the years in which Conner would, too. No one there could avoid the parallel. The finality of Frank's death cut deep. It was like the unforgiving talon of a falcon. It left a scar that I will wear until I'm long dead and gone.

The local news reported that evening that hundreds of cars, carrying thousands of mourners, tried to get to his burial. They say they were lined up on Ridge, from Laurel Hill, south to Strawberry Mansion, and north to Wissahickon. How I got to and from the cemetery, that's all a fog, but seeing Frank's name gracing a headstone.... it was something that I'd wished I'd never seen.

The city called for a day of mourning and decided to bury Frank's ashes on New Year's Day in an effort to signal hope. The hope of a new year and the healing and rebirth that comes along with it. A new chapter and a new beginning. The mayor wanted people to remember Frank's life, not his death, and for our friend and his passing to be remembered as a new beginning, not a bitter end. They had asked me to speak, to say a few words. But I declined. Like an author struggling to write the blurb on the back of their book, how do you summarize a man's entire life in just a few paragraphs?

I'd read just yesterday that the ashes of the Walker twins were buried in Potter's Field Cemetery, about fifteen miles west of the city. The place was known as the 'Stranger's Burial Ground.' The city used to bury unclaimed remains of the homeless, the forgotten, and the murdered remains unclaimed and unremembered. The Boy in the Box was once buried there before they moved him up to Ivy Hill Cemetery. As it turns out, the elder Walker was buried out there twenty years ago, or so I'd heard.

Philadelphia is a safer place, for now, at least. All because of Frank Collazo and Bones Sullivan and what they did. I guess that's something. It's no consolation to me, though. Call me selfish, but I want my friend back.

All told, including Frank and those dastardly twins, sixteen souls were wiped away. I hear they're looking into the murders of a retired couple over in Camden. It seems there's a possible connection between the victims and the fraternal menace. Steinecker was their last name, I think. There's probably more, though.

As I look over at Bones, my heart bleeds for him. You see, Frank was his cheat sheet in life. A mentor, a friend, and a guide. Bones never had to guess what to do next; he just followed Frank around like a little boy looking up to his big brother. I promised Bones I'd be there for him and help him however I could. But I'm seventy-seven years old now. Not sure how much longer I'll be around. It kind of makes my heart smile, though. Knowing that I'll die and get to see Frank in a year or two. Gosh. I hope he was telling me the truth when he said he could see those who had passed on. I pray. How empty the afterlife would be without Frank Collazo in it.

"Hey, Bonesie! Let's go for a ride."

Bones looked up from his journal. "I'm not really feeling too good, Doug. I'll pass."

"Trust me. You'll want to go where we're going."

"Where is it?"

"It's a surprise. Come on, Bones. Whattaya say?"

"All right. But you're driving, though. It's cold out there, and I'm not having a good day."

I watched as Bones stood up and tried stretching his right arm. That poor guy's in a lot of pain, and not just the physical kind.

In the car, about halfway up to Old Germantown, Bones realized where we were going, but neither of us said a word. We were heading up to Frank and Penny's old house on Locust Avenue. And I, rather Frank, had a surprise for him.

Minutes later, as we pulled into the driveway, Bones and I avoided eye contact as we stared at the For Sale sign sitting benignly in the front yard. Then, halfway down the driveway, I threw the car into park and surprised Bones when I got out, plucked the For Sale sign, and threw it into my trunk.

You see, Frank had left a note on his bedside table. It was addressed to me. He asked that I sell the house, leave half of the proceeds for Conner's education, and donate the other half to the Fraternal Order of Police. And I'll do just that. I'll pay for Conner's education and match the donation to the F.O.P. But as for this house, here.... no way it's leaving the family.

"Doug, what are you doing?" Bones looked confused, almost panicked.

"Bones, get out and walk with me, would you?"

Bones followed me to the back of the house. When passing by the garage, I looked in through the garage windows and saw it was empty. I was sad, as I'd grown used to seeing Penny's Accord parked there. It always told me that she was home. Of course, it had been totaled after the accident. Looking closer, my heart dropped as I saw a large black garbage bag on the ground in the middle of the garage, its contents spilled and strewn about as if rummaged through. A brand new Scrabble game and a box of *Little Bite* crumb cakes were sticking out of a distinctive white Walmart bag, along with several other items. A tear came to my eye, thinking that Penny must have purchased each in preparation for Gaye's and my visit. I guess the wrecker service had returned the car's contents to Frank before finally junking the totaled Accord.

Minutes later, Bones and I sat down on the back steps. I turned and looked at my friend and said, "Frank told me that you didn't like staying at the house your mother left to you. Is that right?"

"Yeah?" Bones cocked his head, looking at me just as the wind picked up.

"Well, he wished you had a home that brought you good memories, not bad ones," I said to Bones. "Your brother in blue, your best friend loved you, and I think he would want you to have this home."

I watched as Bones choked up and began to cry. When he did, the snow began falling as if Frank was raining down confetti over us. I hugged my friend, and we cried together.

Bones and I sat on those back porch steps, and there, we talked, laughed, and cried for what seemed like hours. The cold be damned.

Then, right before we got up to leave, we both looked out at the picket fence, and I swear to you, I saw a little boy standing there with his father. As I cried for him, that little boy looked back at me and smiled. Through my tears, I smiled back at him. I smiled for a little boy who, before he became a broken man, was just a boy. A boy that loved his father and a father that loved his son. And they were at home. Together. Again. Finally.

The End

The Twins

Genesis Harper Walker & Talon Grayson Walker

Images courtesy of Dunca Daniel Dreamstime.com/royalty-free

(Real Life Inspiration for Genesis & Talon – Meet Sarah & Trevor)

The Cope House at Awbury Autumn

Back of the house (What Detective Calvin Murphy saw before meeting the twins)

Images courtesy of Google Maps

Remains Found!

Life is stranger than fiction. Remains found at the Cope House in 2019. The story was discovered after this book was written.

Laurel Hill Cemetery

Ridge Avenue in East Falls

West Laurel Hill Cemetery

Money Jefferson Crime Scene

Frank & Penny's House
East Locust Ave. Germantown

Frank's Apartment – Mad River Bar

FalconClaw - Fraternal

Billy Murphy's Irish Saloon
3335 Conrad Street

Blue Bell Park

Abandoned baseball field where Genesis met up with Detective Jamie Baumgartner

Jamie Baumgartner's House on Naomi St.

Bones Sullivan's House on Markel St.

The Steinecker's House in Camden, NJ

St. Peter Claver Roman Catholic Church
Corner of 12th & Lombard

Michael Cook

Ice Fishing on Lake Erie December 21, 2021

Conner Collazo – Age: 14
Frank Collazo – Age: 43

Other titles by this author:

Old Man Winter – Heavenly Gates

FalconClaw – The Sleep Room & FalconClaw – Säters

www.FalconClawSeries.com

Black Earth – How We Got Here

What truths lie in the black void between the stars?

Back to Black Earth

What truths will be revealed?

www.BlackEarthSaga.com